Mor 11-04

Blackpool Council

Please return/renew this item
by the last date shown.
Books may also be renewed by
phone or the Internet.

Tel: 01253 478070
www.blackpool.gov.uk

D1419758

3 4114 00733 4443

THE GUN RUNNER'S DAUGHTER

Neil Gordon is the author of four novels: *Sacrifice of Isaac*, *The Gun Runner's Daughter*, *The Company You Keep*, and *You're a Big Girl Now*. He holds a Ph.D. in French Literature from Yale University and is a literary editor at the *Boston Review* as well as Professor of Writing at The New School and Professor of Comparative Literature and Dean of The American University of Paris.

Also by Neil Gordon

THE
GUN RUNNER'S
DAUGHTER

Neil Gordon

PICADOR

First published 1998 by Random House, Inc., New York,
and simultaneously by Random House, Inc., Canada

First published in paperback 2000 by Bantam Books,
a division of Random House, Inc., New York

First published in the United Kingdom 2012 by Picador

First published in paperback 2014 by Picador
an imprint of Pan Macmillan, a division of Macmillan Publishers Limited
Pan Macmillan, 20 New Wharf Road, London N1 9RR
Basingstoke and Oxford
Associated companies throughout the world
www.panmacmillan.com

ISBN 978-1-4472-2785-4

Copyright © Neil Gordon 1998

The right of Neil Gordon to be identified as the
author of this work has been asserted by him in accordance
with the Copyright, Designs and Patents Act 1988.

Grateful acknowledgment is made to Black Sparrow Press for
permission to reprint "Some Brilliant Sky." Copyright © 1988 by
Diane Wakoski. Reprinted from *Emerald Ice: Selected Poems 1962–1987*
with the permission of Black Sparrow Press.

1 3 5 7 9 8 6 4 2

A CIP catalogue record for this book is available from the British Library.

Printed and bound by CPI Group (UK) Ltd, Croydon, CR0 4YY

Visit **www.picador.com** to read more about all our books
and to buy them. You will also find features, author interviews and
news of any author events, and you can sign up for e-newsletters
so that you're always first to hear about our new releases.

This book is dedicated to the memory of Ghassan Kanafani, murdered in Beirut on July 8, 1973.

The fact is that our Constitution was written in a spirit of cynicism, suspicion and distrust, and every clause reflects those attitudes, every clause reflects the attitudes that humans in authority and power cannot be trusted to become angels by virtue of their office; cannot be trusted at all, as a matter of fact, and need to be set watching each other.

Daniel Ellsberg,
addressing Senate Hearings,
May 17, 1973

January 1995.
Florence.

1.

Nobody ever uses my first name—nobody except my business partner, who is pleased to address me occasionally, and in private, as "The American Formerly Known as Peter." The American. No one knows I am American either.

That is why when I finally met Rosenthal's daughter it surprised me that she called me by my first name. She could not have known that no one ever uses it. And yet, she said it with something like a smile, not on her mouth but in the green of her eyes.

As I had thought I would, I liked her immensely.

We met early in the winter of 1995. By then I had talked to her on two occasions, both long-distance. The first was in October of 1994; the second a week previous to our meeting.

Between the first and the second conversation, then, some two and a half months had passed. During this time I had come to know a great deal about her. I was not alone in this: she had been, by then, on the front page of every newspaper in the States, a major figure in the Ronaldgate Affair, as some pundits had named it after her father. There was, however, a big difference between myself and the millions who had read about her with that salacious mixture of envy and blame her Puritan country reserves for those in the public eye. I was the only one to offer her a job.

You see, criminality is no disqualification to me. And as I'd watched her government, that fall of 1994, shudder through a series of scandals that resulted in the resignation of both a senator and attorney general, I had begun to suspect that the investigative prowess of the American media was not even close to understanding her role.

And that made me think: this is a person I have got to meet.

She was twenty-seven, five-six or -seven, slim and strong, very well made. That did not surprise me: beauty is a prerequisite for what she had done—or what I thought she had done. Coming down the corridor from the plane, she wore a short tan dress and stockings, a brown tortured-leather jacket. Her hair was up, her long neck backed by an upturned collar. Her step, on heels, was balanced, confident, athletic. That disturbed me suddenly, and as she came closer, I understood why. It was the walk of a teenager.

Then I saw her eyes, which were green, and I was entirely reassured.

Her eyes are hard to describe. Very interesting indeed.

It was a day of thin sun and ice-dry air. I took her straight to lunch at Le Quattro Stagioni, where she ordered and consumed a plate of pasta, a *bistecca fiorentina* with roast potatoes, and a salad. I did not talk to her while she ate, nor did my silent observation disturb her appetite: she was ravenous. Later I learned that she was then, and would be for some time afterward, always so.

Only when she was drinking coffee did I speak.

"Well, Ms. Rosenthal, let me get you settled. You have a suite at my house in the hills. It is very private, quite separate. This evening there is a cocktail at the Accademia, and then I have dinner reservations. Do you know Florence?"

She wiped cream from her upper lip, and answered directly in her oddly soft voice. "I'm already booked at a hotel, thank you. And I'll be happy for a drink this evening. As for Florence, I know it fine. Shall we skip the tour and get to work?"

"Usually we rest during the afternoons in Italy, Ms. Rosenthal."

That was when I saw the smile come into her eyes, as all the while her mouth sat still, lips slightly open, savoring my reaction.

"Then that must account for your success here, Peter. The tireless American, working while the city sleeps."

2.

While the rest of Florence napped, or read, or had sex, or lay staring out the window at the far blue of winter sky, across the river at my office I explained to her what the job was. She would be building a network of incorporations in Paris, Switzerland, Germany, and London. For some of them, front-end operations were required. We had made a preliminary identification of some targets: an antiques store, an importer with branches in the former Soviet Union, a small shipping company with Liberian registry. The final purchases would be at her discretion.

She listened, asked no questions, and when I had finished, spoke with decision. "Okay. I'd suggest staggering incorporations in small towns and over borders. You could indemnify locally also. You'd want to find brokers who keep paper records: E.C. filings are sure to be electronic. I'll need a Paris lawyer to front for me. That won't be hard. Now I'd like to go to my hotel. I need to shower and change before cocktails."

Natalie volunteered to accompany her. And as they went out the door, for all the world like two girls going to a party, I spoke.

"Ms. Rosenthal. Now that you know all about us, when do I get to hear about you?"

She answered without turning around. "When I have decided whether I want your job."

3.

At the cocktail she stayed close to me, greeting newcomers with an easy smile. When she was drawn away, as happened often, she disengaged herself and returned to my side as quickly as possible. At first I was not sure what to make of that. Then I saw that she was using the party as a chance to observe me in action.

She had changed to a black dress, Versace I thought, very tight over her small breasts and thin waist. Over her shoulders was a red mohair cardigan, smelling faintly of wood smoke and matching her lipstick, which was the only makeup she wore. Her hair was up, and at the base of her long neck was a gold Georg Jensen chain, which lowered a heavy Star of David just into her breasts. That made the colors she exhibited four: black, red, gold, and the gemlike brilliance of her eyes.

Over dinner, our conversation was all interrogative: she questioning as she finished each of her courses, me answering as I ignored mine. Her skin luminous, her raised blond eyebrows, her thin lips moving, pursing, then moving again, the sleek weight of her hair: she was leonine in her personality and avian in her physicality, a strange and powerful combination. I concentrated on her eyes, alive by the near candlelight, and by the last course was able to read her precise emotion by them, at least until she caught on and put the candle out. Those eyes, she clearly knew, were a liability to her.

I told her more than I meant to, that night. I like to think it was a manipulation, bringing me to the moment when I could ask and she would have to answer.

That was a point for which I was growing increasingly anxious.

4.

After dinner I drove her up to my place in Fiesole. In my living room, from the other side of a coal fire, she watched me from a pool of lamplight, her glassine Tiffany eyes like two jewels set in shadow. Then she asked yet another question.

"How well do you know my father?"

"Well enough. We've done business for about ten years."

"And how well do you know his business?"

"I know he represents the Falcon Corporation in the States. I know he's a joint Israeli-American citizen, and that he has ties to the Israeli Labor and American Republican parties. I know that last summer he was arrested for arms export violations."

That made her nod, once. "What did you think when he was arrested?"

This was tiring me. But I answered, as she wanted me to. "Ms. Rosenthal, it's always hard for us, in Europe, to understand when one part of your government acts against another. Our lawmakers do not do that here. It strikes us as very inefficient."

"I see." Her gaze abstracted for a moment, like a switch turning off her eye. Then she was back. "This may take some time."

"And why is that?"

"You've been away too long, Chevejon. You don't know how it works over there anymore."

I considered this for a while, watching her, wondering what it would be like to be her lover. At the same time, I knew I would not be, no more than with the other young women who work for me. The thought made me feel old: nearly twenty years senior to her twenty-seven. Perhaps it is time that I marry: it seems that I have become the confessor of children. Don't laugh: that happens to criminals, as well as to teachers.

It is just a different kind of child that comes to us.

Finally, I said: "Allison. I admit that. I don't understand what happened. I just know that neither did anyone else."

She nodded. "That's right."

"Will you tell me?"

She leaned forward in her chair, hands resting on crossed knees. This brought her face into the light, bisected by one strand of glimmering hair. Like this she held me in the light of her depthless emerald eyes.

And then Allison Rosenthal, née Esther, that is, the courtesan who during the Babylonian exile sacrificed herself to save the Jews, began to talk.

And when she did, I knew that I had been right to help this woman come to Europe, then bring her south and offer her a job. I knew I had been right to humor her, to offer her a virtual tour of my private business. And I knew I would be wise to do everything and anything I could to convince her to stay in my little world. For when Allison Rosenthal began to speak, I knew I was listening to the story of a very brilliant person, in fact, a peer.

PART ONE

After these things did king Ahasuerus promote Haman . . . and advanced him, and set his seat above all the princes that were with him. And all the king's servants, that were in the king's gate, bowed, and reverenced Haman: for the king had so commanded concerning him. But Mordecai bowed not, nor did him reverence. . . .

And when Haman saw that Mordecai bowed not, nor did him reverence, then was Haman full of wrath.

And he thought scorn to lay hands on Mordecai alone; for they had shewed him the people of Mordecai: wherefore Haman sought to destroy all the Jews that were throughout the whole kingdom of Ahasuerus, even the people of Mordecai.

ESTHER 3:1-2, 5-6

CHAPTER 1

July 1, 1994.
New York City.

1.

Only the innocent wake unafraid.

Six months earlier, she had woken when the telephone rang, muted and frantic beyond the bedroom door, and fear expanded in her like a spill of cold water on ice.

A bitter wind on her face.

A distant thunder outside.

In a fluid movement she was up, her body moving of its own volition, turning on the lamp. She was in her bedroom on Jane Street, in New York City. The cold was the air conditioner next to her bed; the thunder fireworks booming through the Village streets. It was night, or rather morning, July the first, and she was leaving in a few hours for Martha's Vineyard, where she was to meet her father at their summer house for the holiday weekend.

Under a sleeveless T-shirt her breathing eased and from her face, tanned and lightly covered with freckles on fair skin, the fear lifted, leaving no trace. Her eyes were a muted green in the dark, wide awake now, perfectly aware. Her hair, blond and heavy, untangling from the pillow, fell shoulder length.

And the telephone was ringing.

But only the innocent wake unafraid. Only the innocent close their eyes in movies, turn from danger, hesitate in fright. Allison Rosenthal went directly through the bedroom door into the living room, stepping smoothly through the trapezoids of light cast by streetlamps through the windows, and without hesitation approached the source of her fear.

Bob Stein, her father's lawyer.

"Allison. Now listen to me, doll. Your dad was arrested yesterday in Arizona. I'm on my way out. He said you could pick up a couple things for him at his place."

"Arrested for what?"

Stein's voice changed pitch. "A screwup, darling. We'll have it straightened out by dinnertime. Can you pop up to your dad's place and then down to my office? I'm on my way in. Then I got to catch a plane, so you need to step on it, honey."

His confidence was clearly forced. She hung up and returned to the bedroom. From her hips she slid the white gym shorts, from her torso the sleeveless T-shirt. Around her neck, falling to the top of her breasts, hung a heavy golden Star of David, and it swung free of her skin as she turned to the clock. It was four A.M.

Her father, she knew, would need fresh clothes, toiletries, and money—a lot of money. He would need a passport, preferably an Israeli one. All of these could be found at his apartment at 454 Park. Shifting her attention, she put on jeans, a black cotton shirt, sandals. Comfortable clothes she had expected to wear that day on the drive up to Woods Hole. Instead, she wore them into the liquid heat of the street and found a cab.

On the way she stopped at a Korean for the *Times*,

where Ronald Rosenthal's arrest was already front-page news.

2.

His business in Phoenix had concluded the morning before. His assistants were dispatched back to the New York office, his security returned to the embassy. That afternoon he was to fly out: a Falcon Gulfstream was at the airport, and it would land him nonstop in Martha's Vineyard. There was no hurry. His daughter would not be there until the following day.

He had a leisurely lunch in the restaurant of the Grand Hyatt. A squat, handsome man, filled with the ease of wealth, eating expensive food with huge, vital appetite. After lunch he packed and stepped into the shower: Ronald Rosenthal spent a good portion of his life in planes and he knew that hot water immediately before and after a flight obviated most of its bad effects. It was while he was wet that he heard noises in his room. For a time, perfectly still, he listened. Then understanding dawned and he opened the glass door.

There were seven federal agents in the bathroom, weapons drawn. They cuffed him and took him naked into the bedroom. In the hallway, a team was staged: they didn't know he had returned his bodyguards. There were a lot—a lot—of nerves in the room.

Dripping with water, he had a strange dignity as he tried to calm his frightened captors.

"Listen to me. I'm unarmed, I'm unguarded. For God's sake, I'm naked."

An agent placed him formally under arrest. The charge was arms export control violations. Rosenthal was profoundly surprised.

"Do you know who you're talking to?"

When the agent answered in the affirmative, he shrugged and held out his wrists.

"Then undo these so that I can get dressed."

In the summer dawn, Allison read the story in the taxi to her father's apartment at 454 Park. So much for the weekend. So much for the Fourth of July weekend, her first chance to go to the island all summer, the first chance to see her father in months. A bitter moment of resentment crossed her stomach. Then, as if in compensation, she suddenly saw what her father had seen when he stepped out of his shower. Some of the federal agents arresting him were women, impassively watching a naked Jew.

3.

"Now Allison, you're not to be scared. Ron'll be out tonight. If he's not, it's utterly out of the question they won't let us post bail on a holiday weekend. So above all, don't you worry."

Once again, Bob Stein's orotund voice carried no conviction. He wore a crisp shirt with colored collar, dark blue tie hanging carelessly open. His hair, silk-thin and white, lay groomed across his pink scalp, his fingernails as he poured and drank a cup of coffee were buffed and trim at the end of his soft, long-fingered hands, one thin wrist adorned with a Mercier. His grooming, somehow, reassured her. When, however, she raised her eyes to his face, in the gray of his smooth-shaved cheeks, she saw exhaustion, then anxiety, and for the first time she began to feel seriously concerned. Bob was speaking.

"What do you know about this business, honey?"

"As little as possible."

"Is that right?" Stein regarded her appraisingly: a blond woman of twenty-seven in jeans and a black shirt. No one had ever believed that her short, dark father had provided the world with two such beautiful children: Pauly too had been blond, tall, and heartrendingly handsome. And no one had ever believed that either of them was Jewish, nor their regal blond mother, but they were. Ronald Rosenthal might have a fluid definition of legality, but he was not about to marry a shiksa.

"How's school?" Stein asked, as though the subject had not changed.

Disarmed by the non sequitur, she shrugged, and perhaps now he saw more a girl than a woman. "How's law school ever?"

"You're in first year?"

"Just finished second."

"Yeah." Stein's voice, suddenly, shifted, and Allison saw that the non sequitur had been deliberate. "Well honey, a third-year law student at NYU. Cum laude from Yale, am I right? Phi Beta Kappa? You know something about your dad's affairs, I'm guessing."

In a neutral voice, she answered with some respect: Bob knew how to be blunt.

"Daddy represents the Falcon Corporation in America. The Falcon Corporation is an Israeli defense manufacturer and dealer. The New York office brokers deals for the Israeli defense technologies, works codevelopment deals with American companies, and handles fulfillment of U.S. sales, grants, and other transfers to Israel."

And yet while she recited, she heard another account, Pauly's account, as he had once delivered it, drunk, at a Yale party when someone had asked him what his father's company did. "Falcon Corporation? Why, Falcon sells Wide Area Penetration Tools for use in Soft-Target-Rich Environments, of course, as well as Very Large Potentially Disruptive Reentry Vehicles and Violence Processing Equipment. All of it is in the interest of something called National Security, which is a term that seems to make the most sense to the people making large profits by it."

Bob brought her back to the present, speaking conversationally.

"Alley, honey, your dad's charged with illegally selling military supplies to the Bosnian Muslims in contravention of the U.N. embargo."

She listened, watching out the sun-flooded window, her green eyes, catching the morning light, nearly on fire. Even she, who tried not to know about such things, knew this was untrue. Clinton was known to oppose the embargo, in fact, had recently sent Warren Christopher to try to overturn it.

"Bob. I don't care what my father was arrested for, so I certainly don't need to be lied to."

"I'm not lying." Stein spoke very slowly now, and carefully. "There's either something we don't understand, or the arrest was a mistake. Either way, we'll have him out tonight. It's the Fourth of July weekend, for Christ sake."

Standing again, she opened her bag and unpacked her father's things under Bob's suddenly attentive eye. "You do that, Bob. Now, there's my dad's stuff, okay? Can I go now?"

"Go where?"

"To the island. I got a four o'clock ferry at Woods Hole."

4.

She did not need to be lied to. She had always known about it. Once, for a month, the entire building staff of their apartment block in Borough Park had been replaced by Secret Service agents; once the Hebrew day school on Forty-ninth Street where she was in fifth grade and Pauly in third had been ringed for a full week by the NYPD. Years later, Leslie Cockburn reported that each occurrence had been to protect against a death threat, the first against her father by the Tupac Amaru when the Falcon Corporation had been selling helicopters to the Peruvian military at Carter's behest; the second against her and Pauly by a business competitor based in Lebanon.

In those days, she had a kind of respect for him. Her classmates' fathers were chemists, shopkeepers, small businessmen. Hers was a romantic, elusive figure, in and out of the country day to day. But that was long ago. When Reagan came, there was no longer any need for that kind of person; the industry in which her father had made his fortune came entirely above ground, and slowly her respect for him waned.

That was the difference between Allison and her younger brother: she knew him before Reagan, he only after. To Pauly he was just a businessman who dealt in instruments of death. Once she had tried to tell him, but he'd shrugged it off with the insolence of the young.

"Don't give me that, Alley. Death dealing isn't Zionism."

"You don't get it. Ben-Gurion built an arms industry when no one else in the world would arm them. The '48 war, right after the Holocaust: Pauly, it was life or death, you know that. And because they had to arm themselves once, they think they have to be able to do it again. No matter what it costs."

"No matter what it costs other countries, you mean. It's bullshit, Alley. It's 1990, not 1948: Israel's about as likely to be annihilated as New Jersey. They sold to the Shah, to Mobuto, to South Africa. Now they can't give arms exports up for the same reason Bush can't: they need the fucking money."

Pauly, after all, had been able to forget Borough Park, the neighborhood of her own childhood where Yiddish, Hebrew, and Russian are spoken more than English and which harbors more camp survivors per capita than anywhere else in the world—a population that included Ronald Rosenthal's parents, survivors of Dachau. He had shed the past as quickly as he'd removed his *kipah* and abandoned David—a king's name—for Paul the first day of school in their new neighborhood, Brooklyn Heights, where Rosenthal had moved his children in 1980. God, how she'd hated to see him do that, or rather, hated to see the ease with which he'd done it. Still, she too had introduced herself in the new neighborhood, and ever since, as Allison rather than her given name, Esther. Pauly was too hard on his father. They'd both adapted to the new surroundings, and so had he.

He had had to. Those who could not change to Reagan's way of doing business were replaced by people who could: people from the department of defense, or lawyers, or MBAs. Her father's Yale law degree was more important, now, than his army service: more lucrative, too. And under Clinton there was no longer any need for cloak-and-dagger because nothing, virtually, was illegal anymore. In the interest of the balance of trade and keeping the vast Cold War arms industry healthy—a vital constituency for Democrats and Republicans alike—Clinton's State and Commerce departments were there to facilitate any little problems with end-user licensing and Arms Export Control Act limitations people like Ronald Rosenthal might encounter. That was when her father completed his trajectory from Borough Park by moving to Park Avenue.

Riding home from Bob Stein's office in a cab, she reflected that that would be what so surprised Bob about the arrest. Her father had made a fortune by his fine knowledge of what the government could be induced to allow: his entire expertise was in identifying market niches in unacknowledged government operations. And Clinton's tacit support of the Bosnian Muslims had been a campaign promise, for God's sake. He had accepted the embargo only to placate the allies in the NATO peacekeeping force, all the while tacitly approving the many pipelines supplying the Bosnian Muslim militias, to the great profit of the many Turkish, Croatian, and former-

Soviet dealers involved. The Israelis, she had no doubt—America's traditional representatives in such matters—resented being left out of that extremely lucrative proxy position. Her father, she had no doubt, had confidently expected to be cut in.

Allison remembered a winter's night in their Brooklyn Heights townhouse at Grace Court, when she was in high school. She'd woken up thirsty and come down the back stairs to get a bottle of seltzer. Through the swinging door in the kitchen, she had seen him sitting in front of a rocks glass and a bottle of Absolut vodka at the dining room table. He had, it was clear to her, just come in, for his overcoat was still on, his tired face with its thinning hair emerging, used and lined, from the bulk of the black cashmere.

"Hello, my Essie. Congratulate me, doll." He was too drunk to attempt to dissimulate his loneliness: with the move from Borough Park had come the departure of his wife, who had gone one step further than her husband in their flight from their roots by moving to California and marrying a goyish art dealer.

"Hello, Daddy." She sat down across the big oak table from him. "What for?"

"Becoming a billionaire."

"Congratulations. Ready for bed now?"

"Yeah." He drained his drink and stood, unsteadily, while Alley rounded the table and took his arm. She smelled Yves Saint Laurent on his cashmere coat, tobacco and booze on his breath. Supporting him gently up the stairs, she breathed deep his smells.

"So are we really billionaires?"

And now her father laughed, happily. "With seven figures to spare, doll. It'll be in tomorrow's papers."

But in his bedroom he stopped, staring out the window over Grace Court for such a long time that Allison began to grow alarmed.

"What's the matter, Daddy?"

And in a soft voice, no longer drunk, he whispered: "Nothing. I just wish Abba'd lived to see it."

Abba. His father. Later, upstairs in her attic room, her father safely asleep, she had allowed herself to feel what Pauly had both understood and misunderstood: the simplicity of her father's ambition, the extent to which money mattered.

The next day the *New York Times* reported the sale of twenty-four rebuilt Mirages to Honduras. The sale, since the Israeli rebuilds used a U.S.-manufactured engine, had been signed off by Ronald Reagan, three weeks into his presidency. And the commission to Ronald Rosenthal, U.S. representative of the Falcon Corporation, was estimated in the hundreds of millions of dollars.

5.

That afternoon, in Arizona, the grand jury indicted her father on three counts: one violation of Arms Export Control Act, two violations of Arms Export Administration Act. Her father was arraigned, and bail hearings were held, at which Bob Stein presented the court's bailiff with three million dollars of Falcon Corporation money in six suitcases. Thereupon her father was charged and released. The national news reported it that night.

Allison watched it from her apartment on Jane Street—despite what she had told Bob Stein, she had no intention of facing the summer community on Martha's Vineyard while her father was in the national spotlight. She had a fairly good idea of what was next.

And indeed, the next morning the papers reported that Ronald Rosenthal had left Phoenix on a chartered helicopter, and that his whereabouts were now unknown. The helicopter, she thought, would have taken him to the Texas coast, from where a private boat probably took him to Havana. From there he would travel to Europe, then to Tel Aviv, where he was not terrifically worried about extradition: he was a citizen, he owned both influence and property, and there was a Labor Knesset seat available to him for the asking. The only mistake, she thought, was that he had already been arraigned. That meant, if she remembered correctly, that he could be tried in absentia.

July 4th. The summer day liquid. The summer night alive with explosions. The phone ringing endlessly, unanswered. Outside the window a television camera set up, filmed her window, did a spot, left. She waited out the day reading by the throbbing of the air conditioner as if it were nothing more than a dream from which she had been awoken by the phone, at night. When she'd finished her assigned reading—Bill Dykeman at the law firm where she was interning believed in continuing education—bored, she booted her computer, logged into Dykeman's Lexis account, and read some Arms Export Control Act law. That confirmed her apathy. Her father would never come to trial: pleas would be bargained, assets exchanged. This was business as usual.

That she thought this was because she did not yet know how deeply her father was in trouble, and how dearly he was going to be made to pay.

Nor could she. The percolation of events that would, by Thanksgiving, erupt again on the front pages of every major newspaper in America was, for the moment, so removed, so secret, that even Bob Stein had no inkling of it.

Which was, in many ways, fortunate.

For as the summer of 1994 crept across New York in a suite of indistinguishable days of ferocious heat, an epic dry spell that was breaking all previous drought records, days of high cerulean skies at noon and brilliantly clear starlit nights, it was, for Allison Rosenthal, the end of a kind of innocence she wasn't aware she possessed but which she would miss for a long time to come.

6.

Michael Levi, her father's second in command and life-long friend, was arrested in mid-July. The press missed the importance of it and Levi's problems were relegated to section B, city news.

Allison didn't get it either. She read the item in the morning over coffee and juice at Brigitte's on Greenwich, the morning sun splashing through the high windows onto the newsprint. She was tired of how long they were taking to settle her father's messy, embarrassing problems. And for the first time the prospect of sitting in the offices of Dykeman, Goldfarb & Barney struck her as attractive: it would stop her thinking about her father.

When, a week later, Levi turned State's evidence in return for limited use immunity, the papers missed that too.

That evening—as every evening—Allison met Martha Ohlinger at a table in the Corner Bistro. At the *New York Observer*, Martha reported on Wall Street and Washington, and had often told Allison things she didn't want to know about her father. In doing so, of course, Martha was immeasurably helped by the fact that her own father was no less than the national security adviser and a close confidant of Clinton, as he had once been of Carter. Pushing back to Allison through the crowded room in jeans, sandals, and a black silk blouse, Martha sat and threw a copy of the *Observer* onto the table.

"You seen this, Alley girl?"

Allison watched her friend shaking her black curls free from under a baseball cap, letting them fall in a frame around her dark, complex, sharply delineated face. Her eyes, black and alive, were showing excitement, and not for the first time Alley thought that what made Martha attractive was intellect more than any of her more obvious assets. Just now, she was very attractive indeed.

"Martha? If you're going to tell me about my father, I don't want to know."

"You're going to want to know this, Alley."

The paper carried the story that the U.S. attorney for the Southern District of New York had announced her intention to pursue a conviction of Ronald Rosenthal, in absentia, using Michael Levi's immunized State's evidence.

And still, Allison Rosenthal did not understand.

"Big deal. My dad's sitting in a million-dollar house in Jerusalem. They'll never convict him, Marty. Peres'll come over and whisper a word to your dad, Falcon'll pay a fine. It's just making rain for Bob Stein."

Martha shook her head emphatically. The two had known each other since Alley's first day, eleven years old, at St. Ann's, and since then they had shared not only every emotional experience, but almost every intellectual one, arguing their way through to joint American studies B.A.s at Yale before their paths diverged, Alley to Paris, Martha to the London School of Economics.

"I don't think so, Alley, and unlike you I know what I'm talking about. The case has been given to Shauna McCarthy. U.S. Attorney, Southern District."

"And McCarthy'll make a deal. It's not about foreign policy, Marty. It's about an exchange of assets."

"That's just it. It *is* about foreign policy. And it *worries* me that you don't understand."

"Marty." Alley lowered her voice, as if explaining something embarrassingly simple. "Foreign policy is conducted by the Executive. Criminal prosecutions are the business of the Justice Department. Come off it."

"That's exactly my point." Calm and methodical, like a doctor administering unwelcome medicine, Martha counted off on her fingers. "McCarthyism. The destruction of the Black Panther Party. Watergate. The Iran-contra pardons. Paula Jones's tax audit. I got an example for every decade since the war of an administration abrogating to itself the tools of the Justice Department, Alley girl. Now, what exactly do you have to prove this administration's different?"

For a moment, Alley thought. Then: "Have they appointed a prosecutor?"

Martha nodded. That, to someone trying to gauge the seriousness of the government's intentions, was exactly the right question. "Not yet."

"Then don't worry about it. Okay?"

"Alley, I heard that Dee Dennis is under consideration."

She didn't answer that, but raised her eyebrows at her friend, who went on nearly unwillingly, her voice lowered.

"Christ sake, Alley girl. Ed Dennis is White House counsel. And his son is just looking for a job after five years on the Walsh prosecutions. Dee's probably as well qualified as anybody in the country to argue this. And he's a damn sight better connected."

For a moment, the two stared at each other, and the expression between them was one that had first been there over fifteen years before. Then Alley wiped her hands over her eyes.

"Let me alone, Marty, okay? I'm already like a goddamn pariah. You know what it's gonna be like going to DG&B tomorrow? I can't help what they're doing to my father."

But Martha was not calmed. "I don't give a fuck about your father, Alley. I'm worrying about what they're going to do to you."

7.

Still, she simply did not see. Nothing was happening to her: a couple reporters, so what. Nor could she see that her father risked much. A very great portion of his business took place in Israel and Europe, and those things left in America had earned their keep long ago. All through the month since his arrest, his checks had continued to arrive from his secretaries at his offices abroad, checks in bizarre amounts—$4,562.17; $12,603.50; $2,998.89— yielded by that day's exchange from deutsche marks, shekels, pounds sterling, checks drawn on Bank Leumi, Barclay's, Crédit Lyonnais.

By day, she went to work at Dykeman, Goldfarb & Barney; by night she went out with Martha, or read, or slept. True, it surprised her how increasingly many people, at work, now avoided her as the extent of the government's determination to prosecute her father came clear. Surprised her, but did not otherwise affect her. She had always been solitary. And she knew that soon the story would fade.

But as July passed into August, it became clearer and clearer that her father's affairs were far from disappearing from the media. She could judge the story's prominence by the treatment she received at work. And Martha, over drinks each night at the Corner Bistro, continued to feed her the most important points, like medicine to an unwilling child.

Allison was grateful, in her way. Sidney Ohlinger had told Martha to stay away from Allison after her father's arrest, and Martha had told him to take his regular chair in the Oval Office and shove it. Watching her friend one such evening at the bistro, Allison smiled at the memory, with gratitude, with affection. When Martha had woken one morning a few years back to see a front-page picture of Ronald Rosenthal testifying in front of the joint committee on Iran-contra, all she had said was: "You see? It's like I always told you, we both got crooks for old men."

Then the smile faded. Martha was the dearest thing in the world to her, but even Martha didn't really understand. Most American Jews didn't quite get it. You had to think of her father not as a boy from Brooklyn made good in a WASP world—like the perfectly American, perfectly liberal Ohlingers—but as an Israeli: he'd spent half of his life there since running away to join Tsahal, the Israel Defense Forces, at seventeen. Understanding that, for Alley, was key.

Once, after a dinner, Pauly had said: "Daddy, for Christ sake. How can you deal with these people?"

It was an evening not at Grace Court but at 454 Park, so she must have been in college. Her father had just ushered important dinner guests out: Amiram Nir, Richard Secord, and a young man with a South American accent who was somebody's son.

"How?" He answered absently, jotting down figures at the living room escritoire while she watched. Then he turned directly to him and spoke in the dimmed lights of the room. "Now you listen to me. Who do you want to have the profits? Portugal? Sweden? Germany? Or the country that has millions of Soviet Jews to absorb? David Ben-Gurion himself said that all military embargoes are embargoes against Israel. You decide, boychik."

That was the end of the conversation. The next day the man with the South American accent who was somebody's son called to invite her out, and she found out his name. It was Stroessner.

Thinking all this, watching Martha across the table at the Corner Bistro. But how could she tell her this? And Martha was speaking.

"I *know* what happened, Alley. Britain and France both got wind of your dad's sales. They know he works with our government all the time, they know he wouldn't do a thing like this without a directive from our government. Only thing is, Britain and France don't give a fuck about the Bosnian Muslims, and they don't want them armed and shooting on their peace-keeping forces, which our damn president forced them to send in the first place. So they filed diplomatic démarches."

Eyes narrowed, Allison was listening now. "Go on."

"So, what the fuck, Alley. If you're the president, that's why you *use* covert programs in the first place. He got his guns to Bosnia, now he has your dad prosecuted to prove he was uninvolved. That's called plausible deniability."

Alley shook her head emphatically. "Christ sake. Clinton's too smart to establish plausible deniability through the Justice Department."

"Oh? Who's the smart guy ordered Paula Jones audited by Treasury?' The voices of both women were rising in pitch now.

"I don't know. A lackey probably. Not the damn president."

"That's right, Alley girl. A lackey. Like my father. Or like Ed Dennis."

Deeply annoyed now, Allison stood suddenly. "Hey Marty? You have any word on who the U.S. Attorney hired to do the prosecution?"

Lips grim, Martha shook her head.

"Then stop telling me about it, okay? I know they're scapegoating my father. I also know nothing's going to stop them, and so does my dad. So let's stop wasting our time over what we can't help."

8.

Her father, his profession, it meant nothing to her: just another of the unsavory things adults did to one another at work. That she was in law school led people to think she was more concerned with her father's affairs—particularly reporters, one or two of whom she came to expect to find waiting in Washington Square as she came out of classes whenever her father was in the news, hoping for a comment. But law school had nothing to do with what she wanted in life: she had never wanted to go. When her father had started pressuring her to study law rather than go to graduate school, she'd obeyed only because she could not, or would not, fight back. That was less fear of him, she vaguely knew, than concern: her empire over her father's fragile emotions—his fear for her, his ambitions—since his divorce was so enormous that she didn't have the heart. She hadn't really needed to fight, anyway: Pauly, as always, had done it for her.

"You want her in the family business, Dad? Another Rosenthal gonif?"

It was at the Shabbos dinner table, and her father had paused in incomprehension, then suspicion.

"What's that supposed to mean, David?"

Her heart was pounding as she watched, but Pauly seemed as calm as usual when he answered.

"For God's sake. I know what you do for a living. You think I've forgotten meeting Oliver North in this very house? Or Amiram Nir? Let's go ask Amiram Nir. Oh, wait, he's dead, right? That's what you want Alley to go to law school for? Or what, you going to introduce her to Greg Eastbrook in the NSC, and she's going to carry on the family business? 'Rosenthal and Daughter.' Sounds like the smoked-fish store on Houston Street. Except you don't sell fish, do you, Dad?"

Her father had listened to Pauly's speech, his jaw falling lower and lower with each name: not even his only son had ever talked to him like this before. Perhaps no one had. When his son had finished, he'd been too surprised to respond for long seconds. Then he'd asked the maid to leave the room, and addressed Pauly with restrained fury.

"What do you know about my work, David?"

He was nearly shouting, his face flushed, his body tensed against the table edge.

"I can *read*, Dad. You'd have to be *blind* not to see your name in these damn books, the library catalog *indexes*, the footnote references. I've seen *enough* of you in the papers."

Her father nodded, as if, despite his anger, Pauly was

merely confirming what he had long suspected about his son.

"Calm down. I know you can read. Now tell me what you know about Greg Eastbrook."

It clearly surprised Pauly that her father had picked that name out of others. He calmed somewhat with his answer.

"I don't know what's your particular business with that scumbag, Dad, but by your response I'd infer that it's particularly insalubrious."

Her father answered now, decisively, and in the language of his business. "Infer, would you? Who made you the jury? And didn't the judge instruct you that if you see fit to 'infer' from ambiguous evidence, the law requires you to favor the exculpatory inference?"

For a few moments, silence reigned in the ornate, high-ceilinged dining room while her father considered his son. And then he turned to his daughter.

"Now you listen to me, Essie, not to this child, okay? You want to talk about my business, then you'd better be ready to be a big girl. First off, the law isn't about truth, it's about appearances. David wants to judge me, fine, but let him learn what he's talking about first. Then I'll debate the issues, not the emotions. You go read Thomas Jefferson, you go read Madison, then read *Curtiss-Wright*, and you'll see that what I do is the same as WASP businessmen in Washington do every day, okay? I work every day with the Pentagon, the State Department, the CIA. I change my name to Gladstone and no one's going to pay any attention to me. Only, I'm Rosenthal, get it? You ever read about the mail Bill Cohen and Arthur Liman got during Iran-contra? You see even the Hawaiian or Italians on the committees getting mail like that? And Cohen only sounds Jewish, he's a WASP himself."

He paused now, thinking so deeply that Alley was afraid to interrupt.

"Secondly, this isn't about me, and it's not about David. It's about you. Men have a lot more latitude. You be whatever kind of lady poetess you want to be, but you're going to do it with a law degree, okay? You do what your daddy says now, Esther. You get a law degree. I don't care if Farrakhan joins forces with the Michigan Militia, you're gonna be protected as sure as you got a gun. You follow me? This is *America*. The country's *made* for the people who know how to use the law. Okay?"

There was no arguing with her father. No one could. Even trying to screw up the LSATs hadn't helped, just committed her to going to NYU instead of back to New Haven. The best she'd been able to do was convince him that a year of finishing in Paris was what every girl needed after graduation, and then she'd managed to extend that to two.

But at the end of the second year, while she had been relaxing into a hot Paris summer, her brother had called her home. And even after he died, the deal had stood. Without either of them questioning it, she'd started law school at NYU in the fall after Pauly's death.

And although her father had never mentioned his business to her again—never directly—he had, after Pauly's death, come to treat her confidence as assumed, which was strange, as if Pauly's suicide had made her an accomplice.

Nothing, then, changed for Allison Rosenthal. As the dry August of 1994 swelled toward fall, by day she went to the offices of DG&B, a meditative, rote exercise in which she had no stake; by night she sat in the Corner Bistro, alone or with Martha, where the bartenders protected her from all comers. Or read. Or padded around her little apartment in her underwear, watching the saturated summer night reflecting from the surface of Eighth Avenue.

In mid-August, in a dinner during a Group of Seven

trip to Europe, Clinton was reported to have referred to the Rosenthal trial as categorical proof of America's commitment to uphold the European Union's embargo of the Bosnian Muslims. Allison stayed away from work that day, and so was at home midmorning to receive, by messenger, a letter from Bill Dykeman asking her, in light of her father's approaching prosecution, to take the rest of her internship off with full pay. When the smart of the affront had subsided, it occurred to her that now she could spend the rest of the summer at Ocean View Farm, her childhood home, and for the first time since her father's arrest the chill lifted.

But not for long. While she was packing that day, to go up to the island, Bob Stein called to tell her he had received a federal notice of seizure on her father's property, including his business, his Park Avenue home, and his summer estate, Ocean View Farm.

She listened to Bob with incredulity. Did they not know that Ocean View had been Pauly's last home? Did they not know that everything else, for her, was gone? Briefly, it occurred to her that one by one the doors of her life were closing, and with each closing door she lost one of the small rosary of people she loved: her grandparents at Borough Park; her mother in Brooklyn Heights; and her brother, her dear, dead brother, from Ocean View. Now her father was exiled and they were taking Ocean View from her too. Then she interrupted.

"Wait a minute, Bob. You're saying my dad's going to be convicted."

Silence. Then: "I'm saying the seizure's going to take place in the fall. You knew they were using RICO, honey. We won't be able to stop that."

"Why?"

Stein let dead air sit on the phone.

"Cause he's guilty, right?"

"Allison. Calm down."

"Bob. Do something for me, okay?"

"Yes honey."

"Don't call me again. You hear?"

She must sound to Bob, she thought as she hung up, exactly like her father.

And it was only then that Allison Rosenthal's quiet courage failed and, alone at the desk of her apartment, in sunlight mediated by the leaves on the London plane tree outside her window, she let herself feel the horror of everything that had happened since July 1st, everything that had happened, just as Martha had worried, not to her father, but to her.

CHAPTER 2

August 1, 1994.
Washington, D.C.

1.

The first hint, to the outside world, that Ronald Rosenthal's arrest on Arms Export Control Act violations was not going to go away was extremely understated. So much so that David Treat Dennis, Dee, might have missed it.

It was August 1, and page 15 of the *Washington Post* ran a short account that the State Department had suspended all open export licenses held by the Falcon Corporation pending the outcome of the Rosenthal trial. A second article, from the UPI news wire, reported that the Israeli envoy had protested the move.

Each article was small, as if not even the writers understood the importance of what had just happened. That was because, perhaps, it was important to so few people. And that it was, to those few, so vitally important did not matter yet.

Dee Dennis read the account in a taxi from Dupont Circle to Thirteenth and F, where he worked on the skeleton staff still assisting Independent Prosecutor

Lawrence Walsh in cleaning up from the *Final Report of the Independent Counsel for Iran/Contra Matters.* And as he read he felt regret.

Ronald Rosenthal. Dee had followed the account of his arrest, the month before, with something close to salivation. This, he had thought at the time, was the kind of criminal whose ass you can lock up without fear of a government pardon and unfettered by the nasty *Kastigar* decision that had so complicated his life under Walsh. It was precisely in the hope of this kind of prosecution that he had so far turned down all the offers of jobs as counsel or analyst that had come to him since Walsh finished, whether from powerful New York houses who had flown him up in company jets to talk over lunch at the Harmony or Maidstone, from congressional offices or committees, or from NGOs—nongovernmental organizations—on Mass. Ave. and Beltway Bandits in Arlington. That he had refused them all was because Dee Dennis wished to work on a criminal prosecution for the Justice Department. One like this.

The weekend of Rosenthal's arrest, the month before, his father had mentioned the case as the two flew up to their family home in Martha's Vineyard, where the rest of the Dennises were already waiting to celebrate Independence Day. That he should be au courant with this affair was, to Dee, a surprise: Edward Treat Dennis, counsel to the Democratic National Committee during the election, was now White House counsel. Rosenthal was properly the business of the Justice Department, and between the two there were meant to be fire walls.

"You see we indicted Ron Rosenthal?"

"Yeah. What's it all about?"

His father had shown surprise.

"Deedee, that's the son-of-a-bitch who took Ocean View Farm off of Gerry Saunders."

Now Dee understood his father's interest. It was Rosenthal, the big property owner on Martha's Vineyard, where generations of Dennises had been born, and where Dee had summered his whole life. Rosenthal had bought Ocean View Farm in foreclosure from one of the island's oldest families during hard times in the sixties, and no sooner had he acquired it than he'd started subdividing. So quickly, in fact, that the State Assembly had passed a three-acre wetlands zoning law to stop him. As for his father's emotion, Rosenthal's tenure on the island was only a quarter century old. Many of the original families, environmentalists before there was any such movement, much resented this newcomer gaining control over large tracts of fragile oceanfront.

Still, even if his father's interest in the case was more personal than political, Dee knew that his influence was both. Watching his father turn his attention back to a report he was reading, for a brief moment Dee considered asking a direct favor.

But caution—practiced caution, never taught but intuitively grasped—interceded.

If his father didn't understand by himself, Dee Dennis knew, there was no point in asking.

It was a shame. But after his return from the Fourth of July weekend on the island, Dee Dennis doubted he had thought about Rosenthal even once.

And now, on August 1st, riding a taxi to work through the morning rush, he read the page 15 item on the sealing of Falcon's John Street office with a sudden spike of attention. Then he closed the paper and stared out the window as the taxi turned and a fall of summer sun struck directly in his face, making his sky blue eyes glint, narrow, and then, like a light extinguished, close.

David Treat Dennis, Dee.

The Treat was the maiden name of a distant paternal grandmother, the same as had lent her name to the often-noted Treat Street in Vineyard Haven, where old Alice Treat had lived and died, centuries before. The same

middle name as was inscribed on generations of tomb-
stones, many actually rounded at the edges by the passage
of time, in the little cemetery on Lambert's Cove Road.

As for David and Dennis, they composed a great-
uncle's name, and could be seen still on his tomb, not in
Martha's Vineyard, but in the World War I graveyard
outside of Brest, peering enigmatically across the Channel toward the country where the first David Dennis had
decided to think big in 1653 and washed up, some
months later, half starved, loose-toothed, and syphilitic,
to reinvent himself on an island off the coast of Massachusetts.

Little dreaming that generations later his namesake—
one of his many namesakes—was about to be required to
reinvent himself too.

That namesake didn't yet dream that either.

2.

Dee entered Walsh's office suite through a windowless
conference room—the offices had been built to house
classified material—where five or six suited people stood
over a table holding coffee and doughnuts. The table was
covered with papers, from the *Washington Times* to *Defense News*; from the centrist, establishment *Foreign Affairs* to the far-left, muckraking *North American Review of
Intelligence Affairs*; since the filing of Walsh's final report,
there was no longer any need for the attorneys here to
avoid being tainted by media coverage of the industry
and now could—some, for the first time in years—read
whatever paper they wanted. Without pause—although
he was surprised by the lack of a greeting—Dee hung his
jacket in a closet and was pouring coffee somewhat self-
consciously when his secretary approached. There was,
Dee noticed suddenly, no noise in the room. In as quiet a
voice as she could manage she spoke.

"Mr. Dennis. You got a call."

"Oh yeah?" Intensely conscious of the silence, Dee put down his half-poured coffee, looking at his secretary. "Who?"

"Shauna McCarthy."

Dee absorbed the news, then without any delay turned and walked into his office, past the studied unconcern of his colleagues.

Shauna McCarthy was the U.S. attorney for the Southern District of New York. Her voice was brusque when, after a series of clerks, Dee reached her.

"Mr. Dennis. Nice to talk to you. I'd like to offer you a job."

"Thank you." Standing at his desk, he answered evenly.

"Line prosecutor. Significant oral argument. The title is special counsel to the U.S. attorney. After the trial, we'll see what's available on staff. I suspect there'll be something good."

"Thank you. I can be there in the afternoon."

McCarthy laughed. "Don't do that. I'm on my way down. Tell me, have you ever been to the old Executive Office Building?"

"No ma'am."

"You're going today. We have a one o'clock meeting. Be at the Pennsylvania Avenue entrance by noon. We'll see you there."

"Yes, Ms. McCarthy. Ma'am?"

"Yes?"

"May I ask what the case is?"

"The sweetest arms export violation since Edwin Wilson did business with Qaddafi. The prosecution of Ronald Rosenthal, Mr. Dennis. I understand you're interested in it."

A pause, and gratitude flooded Dee Dennis's stomach.

"I most certainly am, Ms. McCarthy."

"Good. Can you read *U.S. v. Teledyne* before the meeting?"

"I already know it, ma'am."

Dee Dennis hung up, stunned. Slowly, realization was dawning on him, and with it his scalp pricked, his stomach surged. This was a front-page prosecution. No, it was more. If *U.S. v. Teledyne* was the precedent, that meant that Rosenthal was claiming covert government direction for his transaction. He was saying, in fact, that he had illegally sold arms to Bosnia at the behest of the Clinton administration—as had Oliver North said about the Reagan administration. That defense had never actually been tried, and with a spirited defense—and Bob Stein would doubtless be defending—it could be appealed to the Supreme Court. Then, coming suddenly to himself, David Treat Dennis opened his office door to the conference room and announced:

"Girls and boys, meet the special counsel to the U.S. attorney. New York, Southern District, under Lady McCarthy herself."

And still, as his colleagues, taking notice at last, came to offer congratulations, Dee did not understand.

3.

From then on, for the rest of that day, things happened very quickly to Dee Dennis.

When his taxi dropped him at the gateway to the White House compound, he stepped, somewhat self-consciously, into the stream of traffic moving up through the gate, guarded by white-gloved marines, to the old Executive Office Building. On the way through the gates he recognized Robert Reich, who, coming out, saw him, looked away, and then back, suddenly, with some curiosity.

Inside a set of glass doors his name was checked on a

computer by a young woman. With a nod, he was passed through a metal detector into a second room. Shauna McCarthy and two colleagues were here, flanked by a man and a woman, both in black.

"Mr. Dennis. Nice to see you. These are deputy U.S. attorneys Daniel Edelson and Beth Callahan. They will be with you before the bench."

Dee had just the time to shake the hands of his new colleagues before a young man, no older than Dee and much smaller, approached, shook Shauna McCarthy's hand, nodded to the others, and then Dee was following them, as if in formation, down a hallway.

They continued straight, left, straight again, passing through an octagonal room from which three corridors parted in three directions. Then they turned left, went down a corridor, through a single oak door into a carpeted lounge.

Here, Dee saw a long chesterfield occupied, to his surprise, by Sidney Ohlinger and Dee's father. Ohlinger, a very tall, slim man with jet black hair, had remained seated, but Dee's father rose to shake Shauna McCarthy's hand as she seated herself in an armchair, then turned and winked at Dee. The three senior members of the party shifted their attention to an oak door.

As the junior members of the meeting took seats, Dee, who felt his comprehension to have been lagging significantly behind his perceptions, was able to bring himself partially up to the present. He was in a conference room with the National Security adviser, the president's counsel, and a U.S. attorney. And that was as far as he got before the door opened and Alexander Nelson, a White House aide whom he knew only from the newspaper, carrying a sheaf of papers, entered and began to talk.

"Ed, I have to tell you that the charge has been made that your prosecution represents a cabal."

Dee had not heard the question in the statement, but his father answered immediately.

"Alex, whoever said that should use a dictionary. A cabal cannot represent a sizable plurality of a democratically constituted political party. May I add that it's a plurality that was very important in the '92 elections."

"Nonetheless, why shouldn't the press see it that way?"

"Our defendant's public image was established during Iran-contra, and it was uniformly negative. There is no sympathy for him in the press, either. This is not only the right thing to do, Alex, it's good media."

His father was speaking, Dee realized, in sound bites: punchy concise statements. Moving on, Nelson asked, "What about Congress?"

The answer continued fluently, and Dee noticed that the name of the defendant was not mentioned. "Alex, that's precisely what makes this prosecution so incredibly apt: our defendant has no friends in Congress. Democrats remember his role in the October surprise. Republicans note that the Bosnian Muslim arms supply—alleged supply—is a Democratic initiative. This is bipartisanship at its most compelling, Alex. Both sides have axes to grind."

Sidney Ohlinger picked up the argument smoothly, in his lightly accented Bostonian speech.

"It's not only good for Congress, it's good for the executive. We all knew as far back as '91 we'd be needing a way to show good, strong support for the embargo on Bosnia. We are going to have very, very happy alliances in the G7, come fall. Without that, we bring this to trial, the press is going to be all about the defense's claim that the White House was directing him. With it, this is a president in control of his house, and nothing London or Paris has to say'll make the news."

Nelson nodded and moved swiftly on. "What about the Turks, the Saudis? It's their Moslem brothers who are under fire. We already have blowback from the mujahideen over Bosnia."

Ohlinger spoke again. "That is the reason for which State is to be kept out: there is no official position on this. Meanwhile the president is free to use covert agencies to placate those allies."

"Feasibility?"

The attention turned now to the U.S. attorney, who, in a much lower voice than previously, spoke. To Dee, she seemed the perfect ammunition to pull out now. "Mr. Nelson, this is a case that cannot be lost. Defendant's second in command has turned State's evidence in return for limited immunity. It will be very, very difficult to overturn this evidence: it is eyewitness, memorialized, irrefutable."

"What have the courts done on this kind of prosecution?"

"The text of this trial was practically written by *U.S. v. Teledyne*. Covert direction by an administration—or a portion of an administration—was ruled inadmissible by Shelby Highsmith. We will be delighted to argue this issue before the Supreme Court."

"How prepared are you?"

"We have our witness in protective custody. We are ready to announce as soon as tomorrow."

She paused to let her meaning sink in. Then, softening her tone, she went on.

"What's perhaps more important is that internally, I know of no other occasion where a perfect confluence of values has existed all the way from the White House to, sir, the line prosecutor." She paused, and Dee felt a flash of heat in his head as Nelson's attention turned, for a full second, on him. Then Nelson was speaking again, dryly this time.

"Nepotism, counselor?"

"Sir, David Dennis has worked statutory arms export administration, on which he wrote for Yale Law and which he prosecuted in open argument under Walsh, since leaving law school at Harvard. He is anybody's choice for this job."

"Okay." With a short, humorless nod, Nelson rose now. "Ed, keep me informed."

In the room, as the door closed behind Nelson, there was a sudden lightening of mood, as if these six people had all been instantly released from the same deep anxiety. Slowly, as he stood, it dawned on Dee that for these people, their careers had depended on these slow minutes. For McCarthy, he thought, this was very probably the first time she had ever been to such a meeting. It could be the only time: if this case were to go wrong, it would be, for her, a brutal, unforgiving life turn, as determinant of one's future as a tragic accident—which it could well be. Watching his superiors gather themselves for departure, Dee marveled briefly at the courage with which these people had put their careers on the line.

And only then did it occur to him that, without ever asking him, they had done the same with his career, too.

4.

"Play your cards right, Deedee," Edward Treat Dennis was saying with the slight slur of his second bourbon on the rocks, "and you'll end up on the '96 campaign. *Good* election experience, boy, win or lose."

Dee leaned back in his chair, away from the table, watching his father in the dining room of his childhood home in Georgetown. At the table was also his mother, her face the mirror of his father's pride. For a moment the familiarity of the room, the low globes of the light over the table, the carpet underfoot, passed through him like a swoon.

He watched his father's pleasure with a wide smile.

"How's it good if I lose?"

His father's face shifted, briefly, in incomprehension,

and then cleared. "You can't lose the case. I mean the election. Good experience, whether Clinton wins or loses."

Dee considered that, attentively. So, it didn't matter what happened to the president. That, he thought, was an interesting lesson on the loyalties associated with his new job. It had been a day filled with lessons. His father was still talking.

"It's the fact that Ohlinger is in that makes the case so damn strong. The national security adviser is a cabinet-level position. I was surprised Nelson even showed up, with that kind of credentials. That's what they mean when they call him hands-on."

"Ohlinger seems committed."

"Committed? He was in Tel Aviv a year ago, telling them there was no proxy position in the Balkans, not after Iran-contra. Know what they said?"

Dee shook his head.

"Said Israel could not stand by, like England and France, while ethnic cleansing was being carried out." A short laugh. "Especially not when there're profits to be made. Boy, when those guys turn on their own kind, you see real venom. You know Ohlinger's and Rosenthal's daughters are best friends?"

"Yeah?" Dee showed interest now: he knew Martha Ohlinger. "Who's Rosenthal's daughter?"

"Name's Allison. Didn't you know her brother? Paul? Kid who killed himself? A fag, I heard, right?"

And in a fluid movement the warm, kind dining room turned, for Dee, into a prison.

In a fluid movement the best, most challenging, most exciting day of his life turned into the worst.

Later, he would remember the feeling as a vertiginous drop.

Later, he would remember it. But even at the time, as a realization, a memory, opened in him like a wound, still, in a far part of his mind, Dee observed that this was what it felt like when a life, a whole life, was ruined.

Dee excused himself and went through the living room to the hallway bathroom. By the time he got there, he could feel his shirt damp with sweat. In the wood-framed mirror over a bouquet of dried flowers, he watched himself, his pupils dilated, his sky blue eyes wide. Moments passed before he was again master of his expression. Then he turned out again abruptly and went back to the table.

Edward Treat Dennis was sitting back over an empty plate now, observing his son appraisingly as he sat down. "You want my opinion, Deedee? You wanted to, you could think big. You could think very big indeed."

After such a day of facing the unprecedented, nothing any longer seemed too hard to say. And obscurely, he knew that there was only going to be one chance to say what he was about to. The next time his mother left the room for the kitchen, he took a deep breath, and spoke.

"Dad. Am I qualified to do this case?"

His father switched to scrutiny in a second, and Dee regretted squandering his rare moment of approval. "What's that mean?"

"I mean, with you and Rosenthal both owning property on the island. Isn't that a conflict?"

His father answered with a short laugh. "Why, you do his daughter?"

It took Dee a moment to realize his father was joking, and it was a moment of real fright. By then Edward Dennis was talking again.

"Boy, if every lawyer recused himself on the grounds of real estate investments, there'd be no one to prosecute that shyster."

Slowly Dee realized his father didn't have any idea about him and Alley.

This meant, he realized, that his father did not know how much danger he was in.

And then, as quickly as the moment had come, it was, inevitably and irreparably, too late.

5.

Never in life would he have connected that sixteen-year-old girl with Ronald Rosenthal.

Dee flew that night after dinner to New York and took a cab to the Yale Club, where his father kept a room.

Never in his life would he have connected that sixteen-year-old girl with Ronald Rosenthal: he'd had no consciousness of who her father was when he knew her, no curiosity, no possible interest.

In those days the world was a given: winters at school, summers on the island; in those days the three months a year on Hancock Beach, sailing in Vineyard Haven, riding at Sarah Wright's stables—they were far more immediate interests than the professions or social standing of his friends' parents.

Dee dropped his bags in his room, then at the stand-up bar in the club ordered a scotch and a thin Dunhill Panatela. In Washington Dee would have recognized about everyone around him. Here he was anonymous. Not, Dee thought, gazing around him with a kind of wonder, for long. With the thought, he felt his heart beat.

What was it his father had said? *You wanted to, you could think big. You could think very big indeed.* Well, he was doing that, wasn't he? Turning to the bar Dee smiled to himself, ruefully. He was thinking damn big, but the celebrity he was considering was rather different from that of his father's aspiration. The celebrity he was considering was one that would start if, the very next day, he announced to Shauna McCarthy that Ronald Rosenthal's daughter had been for two adolescent summers his lover, his first lover, and that remaining on the case, the best case any young lawyer could hope to have, could be considered as a serious enough breach of ethics to result in his removal from the bar.

Then, not for the first time, but stronger than ever before, a sense of disbelief swept over him, sudden amazement at the swift, absolute fatality of what had happened.

What was so astounding was the logic of the thing. Each step in its occurrence had, at the time, seemed so opportune, so immensely lucky. So used was Dee Dennis to opportunity, to success, that he hadn't thought for a moment to question it. Now he saw himself as not only blind, but also complacent. Now he saw that each step of the way had had a dual meaning, one in appearance, one in truth, and never in life would it have been possible to know how radically the two would diverge.

The offer from the U.S. attorney? He had been taught the legal territory of arms export control and administration by Lawrence Walsh himself. For a nuts-and-bolts understanding of Rosenthal's crime by statute and paragraph, through years of congressional wrangling and presidential meddling in the relevant acts of Congress, few lawyers in the country were up to Dee. His father's involvement? Yes, he knew that neither his father nor Sid Ohlinger should be directing the Justice Department from the White House. He also knew that Watergate—with its many political innovations—was twenty years old. Who could doubt that this was business as usual? Who on earth could doubt that this was the chance to think very, very big indeed?

And who could have foreseen that at the same time, these unimpeachably deserved, so long anticipated opportunities could carry the germ of their own utter explosion?

For no matter how well he might have known the law, no matter who was his father and how big he might think, that David Treat Dennis, deputy U.S. attorney, had once been the childhood lover of Allison Rosenthal, daughter of the defendant in the federal trial he would argue in open court, was hard to reconcile with opportunity.

As was it hard, very hard, to reconcile that fact with the sudden anonymity that had cloaked him in its protection since he'd entered this bar.

To the contrary. Standing before the high wooden bar in the Yale Club, his back to the room and face toward a mirror, hidden behind rows of bottles, a vivid cascade of realization came across Dee. To the contrary. Anonymity was the antithesis of the attention that would be paid him when this fact became known, attention not just by the New York tabloids, but by the national press, which already had reporters permanently assigned to the trial.

It was an attention that would raise the interest of many, many people indeed. And, in the middle of this delicate prosecution, which was being directed, no matter how quietly, *illegally* by a presidential administration, it would not be a welcome interest—not at all. Dee Dennis knew exactly how unwelcome that attention would be.

The U.S. attorney would take perhaps ten minutes to replace Dee and remove his name from her Rolodex.

The White House, in its turn, would listen to the dim noise of these events in New York just long enough to order someone to order someone to make sure that the name of David Treat Dennis had nowhere been written down, only whispered, and then softly close its doors.

And as for Edward Treat Dennis, on whom those White House doors—noiseless, well-oiled hinges on carpeted floors, with the cream of the U.S. military standing white-gloved, armed guard outside—would also close, his interest would be long-lived indeed.

Dee Dennis endured another long, bitter moment. And only with real mental effort was he able to force it to pass.

When it did, he finished his drink and motioned for another. Immediately as it was put down before him he lifted it and upturned the glass. And while the peaty taste traveled down his throat, his head toward the clouded glass of the light bowls, their dim emanations staining the smoky, swimming air, for the first time in years, he saw her.

Alley at fifteen, climbing from the silver ocean under a lowering moon, the light on her hair, the light on her skin. They had been alone together by the purest chance; the others had gone on a beer run, leaving one person behind so Alley wouldn't be swimming alone. He'd volunteered to stay, without understanding why; he'd settled on a blanket next to the fire and lit a joint, happy to have a few moments alone.

And then she had come from the sea, the light on her skin, and dropped next to him on the blanket, her small chest heaving in her black Speedo, and in a gesture that had gone through to his heart she had taken his wrist in her small cold hand and lifted the joint he held to her shivering lips. And he'd felt something he had only felt before in the abstract, in untutored and clumsy fantasy, and then her hand was on his neck, and his hand was on her small, wet breast. And then he was feeling the sea on his skin as her skin was against his, her whole living, breathing body against him.

And then it was now. Now, and he was prosecuting the sweetest case of illegal, and more importantly politically unpopular, arms dealing since Edwin Wilson. Now, and the prosecution had a State's witness testifying in exchange for immunity from prosecution. And the defendant, the defendant who hadn't a snowball's chance in hell of winning a motion from the most lenient judge in the world, was Ronald Rosenthal.

He couldn't lose. So his father had told him. And yet, in that moment when he should have been listening to his father, Dee's mind had been elsewhere. Dee's mind had been absorbing a different rhetorical emphasis to that phrase. "You can't lose," and appropriately enough, that emphasis came from Alley herself.

Dee was visited again by one of those nights on Hancock Beach, removing the too-young girl's clothes piece by piece on the darkening beach, her emerging body half lit by the little fire. And the deep seriousness of her face. And the profound warmth of her lightly freckled skin. And he remembered that when he had finished and her body was still moving slowly against his she would hold his face against her neck and speak a three-word phrase, "Please don't stop"—inflectionless, ambiguous, and only slowly had the ambiguity come clear to him, making him wonder whether the rhetorical comma went after "please" or after "don't," and she had laughed and pulled his mouth toward hers.

"You can't lose." The phrase had been playing through his mind all night, but never did he surmount the ambiguity of when he first heard it and it had sounded imperative rather than constative; a threat rather than a statement of encouraging fact.

You can't lose.

He was going to play a central role in a very public case. He was going to be in the papers, on TV, on view. If the case was well defended, and successfully appealed, it would probably go, and its lawyer with it, to the Supreme Court.

And as far as anyone in his small world, his only world, was concerned, he couldn't lose.

Watching himself in the bar mirror, standing alone in the room crowded with the kind of silver-haired, cologned men he had believed himself sure one day to be, David Treat Dennis, Dee, lifted a third scotch to his lips and, as his arm rose, felt precise drips of sweat falling under his shirt.

6.

The first weekend of his new job Dee Dennis spent both days in the U.S. attorney's office library, making his first acquaintance with the twelve-hundred-odd pieces of paper that, so far, constituted the indictment of Ronald Rosenthal.

The second week, they had begun deposing Michael Levi, a fascinating and intricate process that knew, essentially, no limits of time: fourteen hours a day was fine; Levi was a federal detainee, required to cooperate.

By the third week of August, therefore, he had worked a consecutive nineteen days, no less than ten hours each, and often more.

Under this pressure, it was easy to subsume the consciousness of his trouble in the formality of his job. Trial was scheduled for the fall; McCarthy was saving the announcement of the prosecution's team until after Labor Day, giving them the time to become sound-bite experts before a news conference. His position on the case still, therefore, was unannounced except to Washington circles. The matter of a recusal, however, had not yet grown absolutely unavoidable.

Or so he told himself.

It would be no harder to do it just before the press conference than now. In some ways, in fact, it would be better to separate the recusal from his acceptance of the job, as if the matter had only just come to him. In any case, his career would be over—in Washington terms, which were the only terms that meant anything. And as far as his father was concerned, he would be finished.

This point Dee did not even need to articulate to himself, so deeply did he understand it. His father, he knew, was a narcissist and, like all narcissists, saw his children only as an extension of himself. When Dee showed himself so stupid as to have compromised himself, ten years earlier, by having a secret childhood affair with Rosenthal's daughter, his father's interest in him would evaporate instantaneously.

And if he did nothing? Well, if he did nothing, then his career would still be over, when the facts came out. Only this time it would be over very, very publicly. It would be over in a way that jeopardized a White House directed prosecution. It would be over in a way that would cause some White House level damage.

But would the facts come out? That was what he could not quite decide, as the days before the press conference evaporated into the summer air. His affair with Alley over those two summers was known, he was sure, to no one but themselves. With adolescent instinct they had kept it secret from the others, detaching themselves from the group of lifelong summer friends only late at night, keeping to beaches and woods, anonymous locales, always outside, always in the dark. Only Alley knew. If he did nothing, then, if he went to work in the morning as if nothing had happened, those ten years ago, would she tell?

There was no way to answer that. But, Dee knew, between the two alternatives facing him—immediate ruin and possible ruin—there was no real choice.

The Friday before Labor Day, Dee was interrupted in his office toward late evening by the U.S. attorney, who came in without knocking and, while he pulled his attention from a videotape of Levi's deposition, stood waiting by the window looking out over the lights of New York Harbor, eighty-five stories below. When Dee had sorted himself out, she directed him a few questions, nodding as he answered.

"Okay, Dee, nice work. We're announcing the day after Labor Day. September six, eight A.M., we'll brief for a press conference at ten. Okay?"

Agreeing, Dee felt suddenly exhausted. Over the

weekend he could call Shauna at home. The press conference would take place without him.

This was his first weekend off. There was only one place to go. At the Yale Club he booked a ticket to the little airport on the Vineyard.

In his room he packed slowly, thoughtfully. Then he lifted his bag and with sudden energy made his way out of the club.

Perhaps he was an optimist. Somewhere, in the furthest frequencies of his mood's spectrum, he felt that if he went up to the island, if he found and talked to Alley, something would change.

It might be, he knew, an illusion. If so, it was a necessary one, because it was his only one, and therefore he simply could not afford to give it up.

CHAPTER 3

Labor Day Weekend, 1994.
Martha's Vineyard.

1.

Beyond the porch of the Up Island General Store, late-summer traffic crawled down-island, Volvos, Cherokees, Land Cruisers, Suburbans, orderly and slow, like a well-rehearsed coastal evacuation under the slow strobe of clouds and sun. The Clintons were on-island this week and the summer traffic, always heavy, now had to negotiate a series of mobile security installations going up at all major intersections. Coming through the store's screen door with her mail, Allison watched the line of traffic go into a cloud shadow, then looked automatically to the parking lot. The short man was there, again, sitting in his rented Jeep.

This was certainly the most cunning of the journalists who'd tried to interview her in the two weeks she'd been on the island: Emily Harden from the *New Yorker*, Charles Sennott from the *Boston Globe*, Douglas Frantz from the *Los Angeles Times*—Stein had informed her each time a paper made a bid to talk to her. How he had known, Alley was not sure: it would not surprise her to learn that Falcon employees were keeping some kind of eye on her. As for the man, he had not yet approached her, but followed her wherever she was going in his little rented Jeep. At first it had amused her. Now it no longer seemed funny. He sat at the wheel of his Jeep in khakis, penny loafers, a white cotton shirt, well shaped, noticeably short. His hair was brown, not recently cut. She had not seen his face.

Squinting as the sun came out again, she watched him while behind her passed the sweep of bare feet on wood, vacationers coming in and out of this social center of this tiny corner of a tiny universe. She heard a woman say that the dry spell was ending, a man drawl something in a Bucks County accent, and then, whispered, the words "Ron Rosenthal's daughter." As if on cue, now, the small man looked up and showed her an even-featured, rather delicate face. For a moment they watched each other. Then she impassively gave him the finger, turning her right hand up from waist level. He smiled suddenly, and she turned away.

In three short steps she was lightly off the porch, swinging a leg over her bicycle seat, clipping a foot into a pedal. In the corner of her eye she saw the Jeep moving, but no car could catch a bike in this traffic. A push and she was coasting while she felt for the other pedal. When it clipped she looked up for a break in the traffic, poised to accelerate.

That was when she saw the other man who had been watching her, across the road, from an open red sports car—nearly liquid red in the blaze of sun.

Only a second passed as she held his eyes before she had passed onto the road.

It felt, however, to Allison a much longer time, as if she were moving in slow motion, her progress checked by the weight of the August sun.

And only after perhaps ten minutes, when she had braked, banked, and in a cloud of dust pumped off onto the dirt road to Ocean View Farm, past a sign announcing to the island a single word, "Private," did she pronounce to herself her emotion, in a long, drawn-out obscenity.

Having some damn journalist follow her around was one thing. But even with all that had happened to her this summer, that she should today, of all days, for the first time in ten years, see Dee Dennis, that was venturing into the realm of the unreal.

2.

How bizarre, how *unheimlich*—the word, from a long-ago class with Paul De Man, surfaced slowly in her memory—it had been, the sight of his face. At the memory of it a sense of comfort, of childhood, swept through her, sweet and familiar. When had she last even thought of him? It had been ten years, easy, since she'd seen him, and that was another life. She'd heard of him a few times: he'd won some prize at Harvard, and turned down a Connecticut clerkship to go work on those doomed prosecutions for Walsh. His family was a big presence on the island, even though only his aunt was actually in residence; the Dennises pronounced *aunt* with an English accent, and had once farmed much of Chilmark. It had been ten years, though, since she and he last spoke, easy.

Alone in the living room of Ocean View, watching a single swan glide across the pond in the falling afternoon light—unnerved by the wind, darting its head sideways at imagined perils—Allison let that feeling of familiarity again pass through her belly.

And in the middle of that feeling, like the cold wind from the ocean that chilled you only out of the sun's heat, a sudden shadow: the knowledge that everything had changed.

In her drying sweaty clothes she shivered, as if in a

chill wind blown through the living room. The wind rattled a window and the house responded with a cavernous silence, echoing, in its very timbers, that sense of change.

God, she had had a happy life. In this room, she felt that very intensely. Then Pauly had died. Briefly, she felt a cold, pitiless resentment against him, as if he were still her annoying, clinging little brother. Then, equally familiar, missing flooded her being.

Heavily, Allison sat at the dining room table, drinking water from a bottle, wiping her mouth against the warm, salty surface of her arm after each sip. Then, with a sigh, she pulled the mail from her saddlebag, and turned her attention to the letters.

Clearly this table had not been used for dining in some time. Central on it was a PowerBook computer; radiating around were neat piles of paper, documents, and correspondence. The books pertaining to Ocean View's finances were here, as Allison had retrieved them from the real estate agent. And finally, visible on the table, the urgent business before her: the ongoing inventory of Ocean View's contents.

At first, when she'd arrived, she'd refused to consider what the end of the summer would bring. The house was as familiar as anything in her life. The familiarity, she found, could not be poisoned by the events that surrounded her presence here; it was too home, too dear. Nor did it frighten her to be alone here. She had always liked being alone at Ocean View.

Bob Stein had followed up on her outburst with a terse, entirely formal letter repeating his legal advice that the house should be inventoried against its inevitable seizure in the fall. This she had thrown away.

Nonetheless, in the days that followed, she quickly found she could not ignore the business of Ocean View. Mail arrived: notices from the government, a mimeographed sheet titled "Preparing Your House for Federal

Escrow," letters from tenants. In time, she'd found herself spending a couple of hours each morning working on it, and at last came to feel that Stein's advice had been correct. Something could change: the house could be seized and, as a result of litigation, or a plea bargain, returned. No matter how unlikely that event, if it happened, she would want to hold the federal government liable for every missing piece of dust. After a few days' thought she wrote a short letter of apology to Bob Stein, and began inventorying the house in an Excel spreadsheet on the PowerBook.

Equally urgent, she had quickly found, was the paperwork generated by Ocean View Farm with its fifteen rentals: outstanding bills, repairs, fees, taxes. All of this work had fallen to her: the real estate agent who had handled Ronald Rosenthal's work for the past twenty-five years had, this summer, declined to be any longer involved with it—but not until, Allison had noticed, the commissions on the current summer's rentals were calculated.

Most of the regular renters had understood without being told that they'd best look elsewhere for their next season's summer rental. To her surprise, however, several tenants seemed not to have heard of her father's arrest and upcoming trial, or if they had, had not realized that it might affect their regular summer rentals, and had sent in their checks for the following season as if nothing in the world were wrong.

And Allison, contemplating those checks, had been surprised by the thought that had come to her.

In today's mail the Newmans, from Michigan, had sent in a deposit of $5,000 pending lease from their landlord. The check was made out to Rosenthal Equities. The Hugheses, with a Chicago address, had enclosed a check for the same amount. The Petersons had decided to pass this year; they would be taking a less expensive, if less spectacular, house in Edgartown, but the Mitchels from Los Angeles enclosed their fully executed lease with their first payment of $18,500, which, with their original deposit of $5,000, constituted half the payment on the full-season rental of one of the most splendid ocean-side properties for rent on the island.

Nearly $30,000 in today's mail alone. She placed the checks neatly in a pile next to the computer. So far, receivables on the 1995 rental season were at $180,000. Real estate, God. She shook her head, momentarily unaware of the absurdity of her emotion. So that was why her father had gotten into land speculation so quickly.

She should, she knew, contact these people. Return their checks, explain that there were no longer any Ocean View rentals.

She should. For if she did not, she would cause them, and the federal government, an enormous amount of trouble when, next summer, these renters demanded their properties.

Which is why, today, she did what she had done for the past two weeks, each afternoon, with the rental checks that arrived in the mail.

From a Chemical Bank envelope, she took out a pile of canceled checks and leafed through them. Then she chose one and placed it before her, facedown, showing her father's endorsement on the back. Finished, she lined up all the rental checks, also facedown, and finally put a blank sheet of paper over them.

When all was ready, staring at her father's signature, on this blank sheet she copied his scrawled name, perhaps twenty times, with the thick Mont Blanc marker he habitually used. Then she raised her writing hand, removed the paper, and, working quickly and neatly, endorsed each check. This finished, she rested for a moment, studying her work. And finally, she filled out a deposit slip, not to Rosenthal Equities from the big business ledger, but to her own account in New York from her little checkbook. Then she tore off the deposit slip, and stuffed everything into an envelope for Chemical Bank.

Let the federal accountants sort that one out when next summer rolled around. Her father would be, at the least, amused to have embezzlement added to the charges he did not intend to face. And by then, she was sure, she'd have found a way to tie up the money so tightly that it would take the government's accountants months to sort it all out.

She stood now and stretched, feeling—as after each of her forgeries—satisfied. That she had no real intention of keeping the money seemed to remove the risk. Five o'-clock on the wall clock. Time enough to shower, dress, and drive down-island to the Oyster Bar. She crossed to the liquor cabinet, under a small, beautiful still life of wine bottles and flowers, poured a bourbon, and carried it onto the porch.

The wind had come up, with a faint hint of cold, per-haps of an approaching storm. She lay on her stomach and, chin in hands, looked out at the surf. On a lone rock in the water cormorants gathered, oily black birds com-ing in to land for the winter; on shore a herd of huddled gulls watched them sleepily. When she was a child, she thought, the gull had been a beautiful bird of flight rather than the ill-mooded, cheeky beast that sidled up to pic-nickers on the beach and settled around garbage cans in town. Perhaps the cormorant would be as common and as little mysterious as the gull had it, too, learned to live on human waste rather than relying on the dwindling in-shore fish population.

And once again not exactly a memory, more a sensa-tion, of Dee Dennis passed across her mind.

As if her consciousness were a cormorant, floating on the surface of the sea before, unexpectedly, plunging un-derwater, out of sight, and emerging with a tiny, strug-gling, wriggling piece of hope.

3.

And while she thought that, Dee Dennis stood at the lead-glass window of the Wright House in Menemsha, staring across the manicured lawn that sloped to the harbor under lowering clouds: the dry spell, it appeared, was coming to its end. Far out, a ketch-rigged yacht, a reef in, heeled heavily in the blow, reaching for harbor. Seen through the window, a vast silence seemed to play over the scene, over the sloping lawn to the water and through the low-ceilinged rooms of Sarah Wright's house in which ticked, tocked, a massive seagoing Breguet, a family heirloom.

He lifted his eyes to the high sky of running clouds and saw Allison draw away again, her moving body flashing chiaroscuro under the absolute shadow of roadside trees. Then his eyes closed, and opened, and again he was watching the parched lawn sloping down to the harbor under lowering clouds.

Alley girl. That was what Martha Ohlinger had always called her. He had never been friends with Martha either; they had just been thrown together within that loose group of kids that gathered on Hancock Beach every summer. Alley girl: wiry thin, tough, quiet. He had never thought even to question her presence, so long had he known her, since his earliest youth: he remembered her in sailing lessons at the harbor, riding lessons at Scrubby Neck, all the way back to day camp at Chilmark Center.

He hadn't really thought of her even as female. Until the day they found themselves alone on Hancock Beach at night and she came walking out of the dark, moving water with the light on her skin, a black Speedo over a golden tan, and she had held his hand to her shivering lips to pull on a joint and a surge had gone through his groin while his heart stopped, stopped, then launched into a tattoo.

But someone was talking. With effort, his heart batting, Dee Dennis brought his attention to the room around him.

The dry spell, it appeared, was coming to an end. Such, at least, was the general feeling in Sarah Wright's living room, where Dee and his aunt Mary had come to dine.

Returning to his seat on the couch, Dee rattled ice in his glass and concurred with this popular opinion as it was proffered by some niece of Sarah's. The niece was wearing riding boots and smelled vaguely of horse, and as he politely directed his gaze at her, he tried desperately to keep himself remembering.

But of course it was gone: beyond a vague lament, a trace of anxiety so deep as to seem permanent, there was nothing left but the voice of the horse-girl, low, accented, filling his ears.

The horse-girl was Scottish, and wanted him to ride with her the next day. He was meant, he thought, to accept: that was why the Wrights had called to invite him as soon as they'd heard that he was on the island. With an effort, he focused his attention on her. She was perhaps twenty-five, he thought, and projected a vague impression of wanting to fuck.

He answered noncommittally, and then everyone was rising for dinner, Aunt Mary waiting for him to help her up. The Wrights' house had been rebuilt in the fifties, entirely with materials and labor donated to Sarah's husband by the Fall River Carpenters' Guild, which he had defended pro bono during a spectacular series of strikes in the late forties. And although the guild had long ago been busted to pieces by Reagan, the Wrights had changed nothing in the house since it was built: they dined on a Wakefield table off Fiesta ware and Bakelite cutlery in front of the sliding doors to the green lawn that sloped down to kiss Menemsha Bay.

Talk was political, in a way Dee was long familiar with from his father's dinner table: it was as if these were people who had emerged from a long hibernation, woken for the first time in many years by the new administration. Washington was alive for them again. Jack Wright, next to Dee at the top of the table, whispered conspiratorially about Dee's coming trial. Farther down the table he heard talk of Haiti, national health care, and affirmative action.

And Dee's mind fighting away from there, fighting for the quiet to piece together what had happened that summer, long ago, and why it now seemed so to matter.

4.

The last summer they had been together had been after his freshman year at Cornell. And then, it was as if she had disappeared. Or rather, not disappeared—three years younger than he, she had gone nowhere. Except from his consciousness, completely. As if, after his sophomore year, he had shed his identity.

It had been a willing metamorphosis, encouraged by fear. In fact, Dee Dennis had nearly failed to go to college at all. Edward Treat Dennis had assumed his son would go to Dartmouth, but Dartmouth had turned Edward Treat Dennis's only son down flat, an affront to the powerful alumnus taken only after very serious debate and, to the admission committee's relief, justified by the same response from every other college in the Ivy League. The problem was, Dee Dennis had not been a good high school student—in fact, he had been a very poor one, devoting his last couple of years at Exeter exclusively to dealing eightballs and ounces of pot, disturbing the peace while under the influence, and being arrested for same at regular intervals, causing his father to scramble in his Rolodex time after time to fish his son out of his legal entanglements. He had been such a poor student, in fact, that for a moment there it had seemed that Dee was not to go to college at all. But at the last minute Dee's uncle, a generous contributor to Cornell and an intimate of its president, had stepped forward, and that institution had decided to accept David Treat Dennis, Dee, on an informal probation.

A wise decision, on a number of levels. Edward Treat Dennis was a fine friend for a university to have, and that friendship would serve Cornell well for years to come. As for Dee, during his sophomore year—by which time he had started having fun—it became evident that the university's faith in him was to bear real fruit.

Four years at Cornell led to a summa cum laude degree and early acceptance to Harvard Law School.

So far, so good.

This shit, he had found over four years in Ithaca, was not as difficult as he might have thought.

He was allowed, for instance, to drink: wine at Lion Hall with the Quill and Dagger; or whiskey at a tailgate party; or anything the hell he wanted, and as much of it, at Rulloff's in College Town. He was allowed to do drugs—everyone else who could afford to did. He was allowed, during all of these activities, to drive the factory-new Fiat with which his father had presented him after his first semester's grades came in, an unimaginable incentive and a very effective bribe indeed. Most of all he was allowed, even encouraged, to have a great deal and a great variety of sex.

Cornell was a moveable feast of body parts, belonging to all kinds of women from all over the world, and all of them, Dee realized to his shock, wanted, these first years out of their parents' houses and out on their own, to have sex. A lot of sex, often and with a minimal involvement of time from their busy and competitive lives. There were tough and accomplished girls from Spence and Brearley and Andover and Rosemary Hall; there were girls from Chicago and San Francisco and Oklahoma City and Galveston, Texas, of whom every one had been among the smartest in their classes, and many also the most beautiful; there were quiet, dark, curious girls from Beirut and Jerusalem, there were practiced and open-eyed girls from Paris and Berlin and Milan. There were graduate students. There were assistant professors.

In the article of seduction, therefore, Dee Dennis found himself gaining valuable experience, far beyond his clumsy encounter with Alley Rosenthal on Hancock Beach, and quickly. It helped that some of the more physical skills he had learned on the streets of Exeter and Portsmouth turned out to have a surprisingly legitimate use on the rugby team, of which he was the captain for his junior and senior years; it helped that his editorial by-line was soon an institution on the campus newspaper; it helped that when Al Gore came to Cornell, or Warren Christopher, or Sidney Ohlinger, they always brought love from Edward Treat Dennis, founding partner of Dennis and McReady and counsel to the Democratic National Committee, and those regards were usually delivered over dinner at the president's house.

All of this visibility, in the article of seduction, helped David Treat Dennis, Dee, and in time this article became naturally ascendant over his more childish and less complicated ways of altering his sensorium which, in the mid eighties, were gradually falling out of vogue anyway.

When he'd come back to the island the summer after sophomore year, he'd been with Dory Kerrigan, and he was never on the beach or at the Ritz, where everyone went at night, because the Kerrigans took him sailing up to North Haven, Maine. And the next summer, and the summer after—perhaps he'd seen Alley once or twice, once walking in town, once at Paul Rosenthal's memorial, but she had no longer seemed quite real but a memory of youth, a mythical experience, and sometimes he wasn't even sure what had happened those nights on the beach. And he assumed that for her, too, he had passed out of memory and into myth. No longer a part of the real present, but of a past, vague, like a memory of a fall of light, or a season.

Until the day he was told that he was to prosecute Ronald Rosenthal for the federal government, a prosecution on which depended his whole future, a prosecution he couldn't lose, and then those nights far in his youth had come back, come crashing back.

And then Dee Dennis saw that what he always had feared was true: nothing was ever forgotten, and no one was ever allowed to change.

He should have known. But Cornell had been offered, and he'd accepted. And that seemingly endless suite of willing women had been offered, and he'd accepted. And Harvard had been offered, and the Walsh prosecutions had been offered, and the U.S. attorney's office had been offered, and in full knowledge that it was an apprenticeship for his own entry into Democratic politics, consulting to the same people he was going to prosecute, he'd accepted, he'd accepted.

And not until he found himself looking at Alley Rosenthal on the porch of the Up Island General Store did Dee Dennis finally admit that it was too late to pretend that it would all go away.

When he could, under the disapproving stare of his aunt, he thanked the Wrights and left their house. For a time he was in the dark of his car. Then he felt a moment of cold rain on his face. And then, at last, he was standing at the open door of the Ritz, disregarding the doorman's request for a one-dollar cover, making out, over the crowd, the figure of Allison Rosenthal, alone at the bar, watching her face, as he had so recently been watching his face, through the shelves of bottles in the mirror.

And what was the right thing to do now? Poised before a decision that could well be irreversible, David Treat Dennis asked himself, what would his father tell him to do? But then, his father wouldn't be in this position, would he? Real frustration was in Dee's stomach now, and beyond it, a big-winged, swooping, real fear.

But what was fear? Everyone he knew, Dee reminded himself, everyone he knew in his little world, was afraid, from his aunt Mary to the Scottish horse-girl he had just left at the Wrights'.

There was no choice, so why be afraid?

That's what Dee thought as he entered the Ritz.

"Life," Joseph Brodsky once said, "is a game with many rules but no referee."

Small wonder, he went on, that so many people cheat.

CHAPTER 4

Labor Day Weekend, 1994.
Oak Bluffs.

1.

At the Oyster Bar, through the picture window, Allison was able to see Martha in black stretch pants and a sleeveless silk shirt, standing with a group of perhaps seven people. Seen in silence from the fogged street, her animation seemed a performance, and as such, Allison could see, it was entirely carrying her audience.

Changing her focus, she checked her translucent reflection in the window of the restaurant. Her sleeveless Donna Karan T-shirt was nearly indistinguishable, in this light, from the tan skin of her neck and shoulders. Her hair was up, a serpentine frame; her lips red, her eyes green.

This was the first evening she had been out in two weeks, and Martha had had to argue hard to get her to do it. But she did not know any of the people Martha was talking to, so she entered the dry warmth of the room, filled with people, loud with conversation, beyond which sounded Tony Bennett and k. d. lang through four large speakers.

Martha introduced her as Alley, no more, no less. Someone gave her a champagne flute, a black guy in Ralph Lauren, who then asked her what she did. For a moment she was unable to answer, unused to the sensations of the restaurant after her solitary weeks. Then she answered that she was in law school at NYU. No need to lie, so far.

The black guy worked for Kennedy, someone else for Knopf. Someone else wrote for Conan O'Brien, someone else was at Miramax. None were paying their own way on the island. Each was intent on establishing that the dry spell was over. Allison drank champagne, ate a plate of oysters, drank more champagne.

The restaurant's tables were filling now, a late-season crowd, homeowners on-island for the last week, cleaning up after renters, closing up summer houses. She kept her back to the room as it filled and Martha, consciously or not, helped shield her, often standing close enough that Allison could feel the heat of her darkly tanned skin on her own. Like that, it was over the curve of Martha's bare shoulder that she saw the short man enter and cross to the bar. And for a moment—far too early, she thought with regret—her evening faltered.

He wore, now, khakis, black shoes, an ironed white shirt, and a jean jacket; perfect island evening wear, Allison noticed—only tourists came out at night in either very casual or very good clothes. And indeed, this man seemed at his ease as he stepped in, a curious and friendly expression on his face. He spoke with the hostess, then followed her in a casual walk to a table for one. Disregarding the seat she proffered, which gave the largest view of the restaurant, he rounded the table and took a chair that allowed him directly to face Allison.

And yet, he wasn't really looking at her, now, but at Martha, who had followed her friend's gaze, turning casually to look over at the man. Allison felt her stiffen as she turned away again, quickly. She stood very close as they regarded each other, Alley raising an eyebrow in question. Martha whispered.

"You seen him before?"

Alley nodded. "He's been following me around."

"You speak to him?"

"I gave him the finger."

Martha nodded, serious. Then without any hesitation she cocked her head toward the door.

And, a dozen oysters and a salad having composed their dinners, the two slipped out onto the street without good-byes.

A deep sea fog was in over the town, a thick, muffling blind through which dripped, dropped, a desultory rain. Circuit Avenue was ghostly, deserted. Only the Ritz was alive, a yellow light leaking into the fog, spilling loud music unabashed into the empty town. Hugging themselves against the moist chill, the two women kept silent until they were away from the line forming at the Oyster Bar's door. Only then did Alley say:

"Okay, let's have it."

Martha did not look at her. "Have what, baby?"

"Who was it?"

A pause. Then, with a deep breath, she replied: "It's not good, Alley girl. That's Nicholson Dymitryck."

"Yeah? Who's that?"

"You're kidding, right?" When Alley didn't answer, Martha glanced at her. Allison was looking down as she walked, shaking her head no. "Christ sakes, Alley. It was Dymitryck who broke the story on your dad for the *North American Review*."

"Very impressive. A reporter. So what?"

"Dymitryck's not just a reporter, Alley girl. No one knows more about the arms trade except, maybe, the buyers and sellers. Dymitryck's the guy who was at Harlanstrasse 14. You with me?"

Alley's stomach was plummeting now. She knew about

Harlanstrasse 14, the address of a brutal bombing in Munich, where a Turkish arms dealer had been killed during an interview, along with a cameraman. Dymitryck, the interviewer, had been the only survivor, and one of the scoops he had brought from the interview—exactly what the bombers, reputed to be Israeli, were supposed to have been trying to prevent—was that Ronald Rosenthal had been doing business in Bosnia. The Turkish dealer had been one of Rosenthal's sources. But Martha was still talking.

"I got a whole file on this guy. I wrote it for the *Financial Times*, and then again for the *Observer*, but neither of them would publish it. Know why? They didn't believe it. Dymitryck's bankrolled by Stan Diamond—you know him? Organic Communications? Old SDS guy turned software magnate? Dymitryck's the one who documented the pipelines to the Haitian attachés and to the mujahideen."

Diamond. For a second, the name was familiar. But she was too busy being scared, suddenly, to pursue it. "Okay, okay. So what's it mean that he's here?"

"It means that he thinks there's something to learn from you, Alley. That's all it can mean."

"Well then, he's wasting his time, isn't he?"

"I guess so." Martha, to her friend's dismay, sounded doubtful.

"What?"

"It's just that this guy doesn't waste a whole lot of his time."

And Alley, thinking about this, forgot to tell her friend about Dee.

They were at the Ritz now. Just inside the door, Martha put her arm around the bouncer's shoulders, and spoke in his ear. Allison knew what she was saying: there was a little bastard in a jacket bothering her, would he keep the guy out? Smiling, the bouncer nodded and took a twenty-dollar bill from her. Then someone put his arms around Martha, and, with a worried look to Alley, she let herself be manhandled onto the dance floor.

Alone, Allison shouldered her way to the bar and ordered a beer. Here, Ronald Rosenthal, who had poured millions of dollars into the island's economy via the construction industry, was something of a popular hero. Someone made room at the bar—in fact, quite a few people, all men, made room at the bar—and beer in hand, she let herself concentrate on Dymitryck. Emily Harden, with her precisely phrased *New Yorker* questions, she could handle. This guy, however, scared her, and it took effort to stop thinking about him as, sipping her beer, she watched the band.

Which was why she did not see Dee until he had pushed his way through the crowd at the bar, shyly, smiling uneasily, and leaned next to her.

2.

She did not seem surprised to see him, Dee perceived in the high awareness of his fright. Perhaps she seemed slightly disturbed. What did that mean?

The answer came to him at once. It meant that she did not know he was the government's attorney. It was so open a secret in Dee's circles that it came as a shock to realize that to Allison it might not yet be known.

Allison, however, was next to him, and there was no time to think of anything else. Leaning to draw the bartender toward him, Dee ordered drinks, for himself, for Alley. Then, the music too loud to talk, he waited, looking down at Alley, smiling slightly to mask his anxiety. What was he going to say? He had no idea. But when the song ended, he found himself talking.

"Looks like the dry spell's about over."

Her eyes on him, she licked her lips with the point of her tongue. His gaze moved up, onto her tanned forehead, very lightly freckled, down her cheekbone, and then to her red, red lips. With relief, he saw that they were smiling.

"So I'm told."

He smiled too, now, broadly.

"How's your summer been?"

"Good enough."

The band was introducing a new song with a long, loud acoustic lead. Now, in tiny increments, his nerve was returning. He leaned down and nearly shouted toward her ear, above which her blond hair was tightly pulled.

"So I hear you're in law school down in New York."

She answered, in turn, toward his ear, and he felt her breath as heat against his cheek.

"Uh-huh."

"That means we live in the same city."

"Does it?"

For a time the song, Chrissie Hynde's "Revolution," was too loud to talk. When it faded, the band took a break and he spoke again at something closer to a normal conversational distance.

"What year you in?"

"Huh?"

"School."

"Oh. Last." That surprised him. She would be, what, twenty-seven? Dee had passed the bar at twenty-five. He started to calculate this, then stopped when she added: "I spent two years abroad before starting law school."

Ah. That made sense. "Really? Where?"

"Paris, mostly."

"What'd you do?"

She shrugged. "Hung. Took classes. Tried to get out of going to law school."

He nodded. This, the longest sentence she had spoken, sounded for the first time like the girl he had known.

He wished he could get her to speak at length. He reminded himself that he had to go. "Any plans?"

"Not to practice law."

And now, without any warning, she asked the question he had not yet decided how he would answer.

"So where do you work?"

She was facing him directly now, her face composed, her attention full on him. On instinct he answered with equal directness.

"U.S. attorney's office. Southern District."

A pause, an observant moment on his part, watching with satisfaction the surprise on her face.

Good.

3.

For a moment she had been feeling okay. The very fact that he was speaking to her had assured her that he must have been passed over for the job on her father's prosecution. Now she suddenly felt betrayed. Before she could talk, he had leaned toward her and was, as much as the bar's noise allowed it, speaking softly, his lips toward her ear.

"I was offered a job that interested me awfully. The constitutional issues were important. And it was clean: only an exchange of assets was at stake. The defendant had already departed the country; his financial loss was irrelevant to him. And then, it was a pretty good deal for him because he's guilty."

She said nothing, and he went on, speaking carefully, and avoiding, she noticed, saying the one or two words that would put him outside the law. "I think, however, that personal considerations are probably going to make me less than entirely appropriate as the line prosecutor. I was foolish not to realize that when I took the job."

That was all. He fell silent, expectantly so. As if waiting for her to make a decision.

He was right, she thought, to put his cards on the table. Masked by the loud music, watching out the window as she fumbled for purchase in her understanding. In a way she was flattered by his bluntness, by the assumption of her preference to hear the truth.

So Dee Dennis was prosecuting her father after all. She pronounced the words voicelessly, with wry wonder. So Dee Dennis was the line attorney on the federal prosecution of her father. Jesus fucking *God* almighty, what was going to happen next?

Then, as her initial shock passed, she thought, why not? He was, what, three years older than she? He was qualified, she had no doubt: he had been in grooming for this job since the day he was born.

Then what exactly did he want? It was extraordinarily dangerous for Dee to be talking to her. She had only to turn to him and say, "Falcon Corporation," and he was compromised. Already what he had done was probably unethical.

Her heart was beating hard now, very hard in the cage of her chest under her sleeveless T-shirt. She turned her face to him for the first time in minutes, but still she did not speak.

He was much heavier than the thin child she had known, and to all appearances the weight was muscle. His hair was blond, like Allison's, but very light where hers was wheaten, straight, shaved close at the sides and left full at the top. The greatest change, however, was in his face, which seemed to slip in and out of familiarity as she watched: now familiar, wry and inquisitive, blue eyes shining, mouth curving sardonically at the corners; now a stranger, the settled expression of an adult, unafraid and, seemingly, in judgment of what it was watching. His hands, she was surprised to see, were long, with knuckly fingers and surprisingly thin wrists, more than a little graceful.

He was a beautiful man, as beautiful, in his way, as Pauly, who had been the handsomest man she had known. She wondered, for a moment, if Pauly would have developed this sense of adulthood that Dee showed, this ease of authority. They were, after all, both males, no matter how different in kind. But of course Dee was not Jewish, and Dee was not gay.

Finally, she answered, speaking calmly, as if making a neutral observation.

"It is unethical for you to speak to me."

He nodded, but said nothing, and she went on.

"I think you're being foolish."

He smiled now, as if enjoying the danger of this meeting. "Maybe. I want to talk to you."

She did not answer that but instead asked herself again, what did he want?

He was still looking down at her, still waiting for her answer, apparently unafraid. His light eyes smiling. His face so open, so cleanly shaven, the lines from his mouth to his chin so defined, like a vision of hope. Perhaps she watched him a second too long: she felt a blush rising to her face, and his expression was shifting. And now he was precisely the person she remembered, little Dee Dennis, reckless and charming, never doing what he should, always just on the outside, and now desire was rising in her. She spoke very carefully.

"Why?"

He answered immediately. "I can't tell you here. Please. Meet me tomorrow."

She turned away, feeling the heat spread through her face and over her chest, her thighs tighten and her legs, just the slightest bit, grow tired. She drank from her beer, composing herself.

But she could not focus her thoughts on Dee. She could only think: if only she were someone else! If only she could make it appear! Appear like her father wasn't a crook who was about to lose his house to federal seizure. Appear like he was not the man the whole nation had watched testify before the Iran-contra committee. If only she could make the truth inadmissible, not to *evidence* but to *reality*. To make love to Dee, right now, tonight, would eradicate everything: the empty house, the dying summer, everything, for the minutes it lasted; it would be like being sixteen again in the days before her brother died and her father was arrested; it would be like being perfectly whole again, entirely at home. She looked at him now and on his face was an unambiguously tender expression, too clear to pretend not to see, and she watched him openly.

"Where?" The music was growing louder, and the word sounded like a shout.

"Anywhere."

Watching him still, watching him, her mind traversing a wordless fantasy in which she did not have to fake and nothing separated her from him.

And then, with an interior sense of factitiousness that was only too familiar, she leaned toward him and raised her voice through the mounting volume of the band, speaking with decision at which she could not remember arriving; at which she could not remember ever not having arrived.

"I'll pick you up at the parking lot at Wasque at noon tomorrow."

When she stepped back again, it was in time to see relief visibly relax his frame, his eyes losing focus as a hint of tears filmed over the so blue irises, and he nodded, and left some money on the bar, and without showing her his face again, pushed through the crowd and out into the street. And Allison, alone, stood in total disbelief at herself, staring at herself in the back-bar mirror until, behind her, she felt the warmth of a soft body, and then arms around her neck, and then saw Martha's face reflected beside hers, cheek to cheek, while Martha's voice spoke in her ear, filled with surprise: "Alley girl, Alley girl, what the fucking hell do you think you're up to?"

4.

"Stop worrying. Who's gonna tell? *I'm* not."

Saturday morning, Martha lay on the living room floor in light moving from the rain on the windows, smiling ruefully as she talked: Allison had taken her to task, until far into the morning, for omitting to tell her that Dee had after all been tapped for her father's prosecution. Now that the fact was known, however, Martha saw not only practical but erotic possibility in it.

It had not surprised Allison that Martha should hide this information from her. Martha, who came from somewhere very similar to Borough Park, had protected Allison since the first day they met, eleven years old, at St. Ann's School. This was because Martha, like Allison, had been subject to a profound deculturation.

The very first day after school Martha had taken her—Allison's first time on the subway—to Greenwich Village to equip herself with the rudimentary requirements: jeans, oversized plaid shirts, a pea coat. Then, together, they'd taken care of Pauly.

Not moving her eyes from her friend, Allison answered.

"Who? Anyone. Anyone at all is going to tell."

"Bullshit, Alley girl. Stay away from old Goodwoman Dennis and you'll be fine. There wasn't a soul there last night that knew Dee."

Allison turned now. "What about your pal from Kennedy's office?"

"Yeah, don't worry about him. I know what he saw last night, and it wasn't your lover."

There was a wide, slightly crooked smile on Martha's

face. Allison savored it for a moment, its familiarity, its pure, brute beauty. But Martha, Allison thought, was babying her: she knew how important this was.

"Martha?"

"Yeah, baby."

"Stop fooling around. Why is Dee Dennis talking to me?"

Martha looked up now, curious. " 'Cause you're beautiful, baby."

"Fuck you."

"Okay then. 'Cause he wants to know whether you're going to speak to the press about your childhood love affair. 'Cause if you do that, it's going to make a lot of people, like, very nervous."

"Who?"

She hesitated. Then, less jocularly, "My father. Ed Dennis. At least. I don't know for sure."

Allison gazed at her friend, blankness on her face masking her thoughts. "Your dad's cabinet. Dennis is White House staff. What do they have to do with it?"

"That's just the point, Alley girl. Nothing legal. Drawing media attention to what will, at the very least, be a serious embarrassment to the prosecution, that's going to make them very, very nervous. You know what'd make them even more nervous? If you met him out on the beach at Wasque. You're gonna fuck him, I presume?"

"Martha."

"Aw, Alley, come on. *Someone's* got to pay for *something* sometime. Tell you what: you fuck him, then I'll publish an article in the *Observer*. That'll take care of Dee's worries, 'cause he'll be off the case. Okay?"

And when Allison didn't answer, but rose to keep her appointment with Dee, Martha leaned up on one elbow and spoke, to Allison's surprise, with a wide smile.

"Alley girl? You know, you can take out the clown. But it won't stop the circus."

Moving toward the door, Alley snapped at her friend. "I know that, Martha. I'm not an idiot."

5.

Dymitryck's rented Jeep appeared behind Allison just before the airport road. That made her heart quicken. Still, she had already decided what she was going to do. She slowed down and was able to see, in her rearview mirror, that he wore sunglasses and was smoking as he drove.

She cruised slowly toward Edgartown, then, at Whippoorwill Farm, picked up speed, passing one, two, three cars before the traffic slowed to town speed. Like this she entered Edgartown proper with a number of cars between them. In town, she turned left, then right, pulled into the Chappy ferry, and by the time the short man was entering town, the ferry was already unmoored, leaving him stranded at the dock. She sighed, relaxing, in the cab of the Cherokee. And that was when she saw, just in front of her, Dee, leaning lightly against his little Fiat, unprotected in the light rain.

Their eyes met through Alley's windshield. He looked away toward a man in a disheveled Barbour who was stepping out of his car, and Alley recognized Ronald Dworkin. At the Chappy-side dock he climbed into his car without looking back, and watched her through the rearview as she followed him through the dirty roads of Chappaquiddick and past Dyke Bridge to the parking lot at Wasque Point.

A strange lightness was in Dee's stomach now, a strange inability to focus on the gravity of what was occurring. Dimly, he felt that the difficult part of his business with Alley had already been completed: in their conversation the night before something had made him sure that this cool, quiet woman was not going to compromise him. This, he knew, could turn out to be more of a hope than a valid intuition. Still, it was all he had, and he could not afford to let go.

At the Wasque parking lot two men in wet suits were loading sea kayaks onto the top of a Range Rover. Alley circled the lot, parked facing him, and while they waited for the men to finish they watched each other through their windshields at a distance of some ten lightly fogged yards.

Or, Dee thought to himself, ten years.

When the sea kayakers left, Dee climbed out of his Fiat, crossed the small parking lot, and got into her Jeep.

Within the car, the gray light did not flatter him as had the soft lights of the Ritz. But it did bring out the pallor of his cleanly shaven cheek and light the light blue of his eyes and so, to Alley's eye, did something more than flatter. She watched him for a moment, smelling shaving cream and the warm, humid rain.

A Suburban drew into the parking lot, carrying two deep-sea fishing rigs on its roof. She shifted into first and went out onto the beach, fishtailing slightly on the low dune, gathering speed along the water's edge. As they breached the point, the fog cleared, a warm, wet sea wind carrying it north. She stopped and they opened their doors, then sat sheltered in the cab of the car, steamy rain dripping on sand.

There was a long silence that she did not try to break. He watched out his door to the water, eyes at quarter profile to her, focused out to the enormity of the sky. When he turned, his face was perfectly flat.

"This is a hard place to lose."

That statement, she thought, contained two separate meanings.

One was undeniable: the fact that he, like Martha, like herself, had been formed in this landscape. It was a sentiment impossible to explain to city people, this lifelong rapport with a natural place. It was a sentiment, she knew, that they shared.

She reacted, however, to the other meaning. "Oh? Are you losing it too? I thought you were taking it."

Now he turned toward her, and she had the chance, once again, to appreciate the power this man had assumed. He spoke, as he had in the bar, entirely directly. "Very funny. Look. I didn't commit any crime. I didn't do anything but play by the rules. You see me being invited back here a lot after my dad finds out about me and you?"

She kept expression out of her voice. "How's he going to find out?"

"Shauna McCarthy's going to tell him."

"And she?"

He paused. "She what?"

"How's she going to find out?"

"From me, of course, Alley. I'm telling her about it on Tuesday morning."

The aggrieved tone in his voice was not lost on her. She just wasn't sure she believed it. "You could have told her when she offered you the job."

His answer came readily. "I didn't know it was your father when I came on. And even when I knew who it was, I still didn't connect him with you."

Was that so? She squinted away out the window, as if truth existed at a distance in the warm rain. Yes, she thought, regretting the implied meaning of what he had just said—the little importance her memory held to him—it was probably so. Then she looked back.

"I believe you. Now, what is it you want from me?"

He answered, she noticed, immediately.

"I want you to know I'm going to withdraw from the case."

She shrugged.

"That's up to you."

❧

For a long moment there was silence, each turned away watching the dripping vista of sea. Finally, as if on cue, she looked at him as he turned to her and spoke in a tone new to their conversation.

"I was so sorry about Paul."

She shrugged, and he watched her face softening. Encouraged, he went on.

"I remember him well."

"Yeah." A small smile from her.

He said, carefully: "I should have spoken to you there."

"Oh . . . I don't even remember the memorial." Now she gathered herself into the car seat, pulling up her legs and wrapping them in her thin, strong, sunburnt arms. At least, he thought, she wasn't being actively hostile now. Although when she spoke again, not looking at him, she was still cold.

"Look. I was a child ten years ago. So were you. I understand your father's . . . interest in this case. I understand your family dilemma. But let's keep in mind, it doesn't really have any standing with me. There's some other Beltway insider with a dot-gov address waiting to take your place in a minute flat."

He answered, this time quickly. "Good. Then you're all set."

"I didn't ask your father to get involved in a Justice Department prosecution."

"And I didn't ask your father to break the law."

Alley turned at this. "But someone else did ask him. You know that for a fact. The Clinton administration wanted those arms sold. Exactly like Reagan wanted to arm the contras."

"If he was directed, then he can prove it in court."

"No, Dee. He can't prove it in court. You know damn well that he can't prove it in court. That's what makes your trial such a charade."

He shrugged. "Your father's a businessman, Alley. If he

can't prove the legality of a transaction, he shouldn't be involved."

"Wrong. You know who authorized him, and you know it can't be proved. A lot of people do what my father does. Most of them were once in the fucking Defense Department."

Now Dee watched her seriously. So that's what she thought, was it? That he was a pawn of an agenda? That was an impression that had to be corrected. He spoke coolly.

"That a lot of people do it is why it's so important we try these cases. I just spent five years fighting constitutional issues. This is a case with as serious, long-term consequences as the Walsh prosecutions. Oliver North was sanctioned by an administration. That doesn't make what he did legal. An acquittal of Rosenthal declares open season on the Third World: arms sales wherever any political interest wants them. I'm sorry about your father. But this is a case that has to be made."

She watched him, wordless, for a moment. Then she nodded. "I hear you. But you know what I hear? Another turf battle over arms and money. You fight, my dad pays."

"Democracy is a turf fight. And I don't work for the president."

She didn't answer, and for a time, in the cab, the rain falling harder against the window, he watched her. He didn't want to argue law with her. He didn't want her like this. He wanted her the way she was when he spoke about her brother. He said:

"I wanted you to know that I was leaving the case. That's all. Now I'll go if you want me to."

6.

And suddenly, bitterly, she did not want him to go.

This witness from the time when Ocean View was the

house next to the sea on the magic island, sheltered by scrub pine, always under the sun. In the intimate interior of the car under dripping rain, she did not want him to go. She wanted him to stay.

She could smell him, the fresh of the rain and a clean, slightly scented soap. It scared her, how healing it felt to be with this man, this man with whom she had been naked when she was a child. But it did not surprise her.

And he? Appraisingly, she watched him before his open door, ready to enter the rain. The papers were desperate for copy about the trial. Not a soul would resist the story of his withdrawal from a Federal case due to a childhood romance with sexy Allison Rosenthal. The publicity could ruin his career. What would he do? What did lawyers like that do? Take up probate and divorce law? Not the future as a brilliant jurist Ed Dennis had in mind for his son. Grudgingly, she admitted that he, too, was losing everything.

For a long fugue of moments she listened to the patter of the rain on the car top, watched the vista of sodden beach. Then she slammed her door and started the car. "Dee. Just sit down."

Now he hefted his weight back into the seat, and looked at her. She spoke immediately.

"Look, I'm sorry. I'm sorry this happened to you. Let's go have a drink."

"Where?" He did not sound surprised.

"My house."

He thought for a moment. Then said, as if in conclusion: "Drop me off round the point. I'll walk back to my car and take the next ferry after you."

This slim, slight girl who had sat next to him in the car, with her hair loose around her face, her body hidden under a loose T-shirt and jeans. In the intimacy of the car, her need had been palpable to him. She was losing everything.

Driving fifteen minutes behind Allison along the Edgartown-West Tisbury Road, Dee Dennis hung poised perfectly in understanding of her, as if she were an image in a mirror before him.

She was waiting for him at the top of Ocean View Road. Then he saw her Cherokee take off again as he approached, skidding in the sandy road. They passed no one on the chase down, and at the small carport outside her house they parked side by side. By the time he had opened his door, she was running through the rain down a flagstone path into the house.

Inside, the rain was fat drops blowing across the burnt grass to slap against the windowpanes. Beyond her frame of vision, he saw from his tallness the lawn pulsing in the ominous darkening of the day; the vista of cattails and hay field nodding in the gusts of wind. For a time, together, they watched. Then she spoke without turning. "Do you know that a year ago Clinton was considering staying here?"

"I'm sorry."

"Forget it."

He found himself, suddenly, unwilling to look at her, afraid—from the tone of her voice, from the need in her voice—what he might see.

"May I have a drink?"

She answered by motioning with her head. He followed her gesture, and saw a small canvas, a still life hanging over a hutch containing bottles and flowers. With a slight shock, he recognized the painting: this was Rosenthal's famous Soutine. He stepped over to pour two scotches in small crystal glasses. Then he carried Alley's to her and looked full at her.

The soft storm light on her skin. The corners of her mouth red at the edges, her expression alive with invitation. Her hand trembled slightly at the end of her bare arm as she took the drink. Then, sipping thirstily, she looked up at him, her green eyes so alive as to make shimmer the light in them. And a decision was made for Dee. When she removed the glass he leaned down to kiss her, tasted scotch and felt cold in the skin of her lips, a damp cold he had felt years before, years before. He straightened and directly, she turned away, hugging herself tightly.

7.

She hugged herself tighter, looking away over the land, at the cattails nodding in the ocean wind, at the hay field stretching pure gold under the long, threatening light. Then she felt his hands on her shoulders, the warmth of his body, chest, stomach, and groin, against her back.

Could this be happening? she asked herself again, her back to him, her face to the storm, interrogating the wave of cattails, the rising ocean swell. Could this be happening? His hands came farther down her arms, whose skin she felt hardening against the warmth of his fingers. Still hugging herself, she turned and lifted her face, decided on nothing.

But a longing so pure was through her. Through and through her, like an ache, from her ears to her eyes to the full surface of her skin: all the parts of her body that perceived, suddenly, felt; and then all the parts that permitted to live too—her heart, her lungs—were pierced.

Against the roar of the surf. She pushed him away, watched him for a moment, then took him by the hand and led him through the living room. The shade of the falling light. The wooden stairway into the heart of the empty house with all its old, familial smell. Gone was the silence, gone was the desertion, and she looked into Pauly's room as if he were there, on his bed, lying with his head between his Boston Acoustics and listening to David Byrne. When she turned to Dee, in her room, that look was on his face, the look of fathomless tenderness, and a flush went clean through her. And then she was in the dry scent of his body, in the airiness of his clean hair, in the beat of his heart and the heat of his skin.

It was like coming home. It was like filling the aching emptiness she had felt from her earliest youth, for her mother, for her father, for her brother. She had tried before, plugging men into the hollow heart of that longing. One or two had fit, for a while, if she worked hard enough at it. And now that hollow heart filled, not with family but in solitude, one person, this person, it filled and in those moments Allison Rosenthal, Esther, felt herself whole.

CHAPTER 5

September 4, 1994.
Ocean View Farm.

1.

There is an unspeakable pathos to a summer house, and it is hardest to avoid by dawn.

It lay across Ocean View Farm, when Allison awoke in her childhood bed, like a spell.

In the sodden light leaking into the little room where Pauly had played with his ancient set of wooden trains, still packed in their wicker basket in the closet.

In the still air of her father's study, where a fine layer of dust lay on the surface of the Stickley desk.

Every window, holding a vista of horse pasture and wind-stunted field, filled with the drizzling dawn of receding storm.

A framed composition, saturated with meaning, illustrating loss.

Allison woke to the neurotic clucking of guinea fowl greeting the dawn. For a moment her body tried to find its way back into sleep. Then Dee shifted beside her, and sleep fled. Like this she rested for a while, eyes wide.

Then, gingerly, she climbed over him, naked, briefly straddling his big sleeping form, and picked up her nightdress as she left the room.

Downstairs, through the big picture windows, the rain had all but stopped and the high sky was filled with fleeing clouds beyond which showed, every now and again, a glimpse of high, anonymous blue. A big, wet wind filled the air, rocking the trees, blowing the hammock on the porch, and for an eerie second, a flash, she saw Pauly lying there, swinging away a long dappled afternoon of shade, beside their swimsuited mother.

For a long time she sat, arms around knees, in the living room, watching over the lawn, to the sky still swimming with the spectacular business of the storm's lull.

Then, with a quickening heart, she heard Dee's foot on the floor above.

He came down barefoot, in his jeans, his white shirttails hanging out. His blond hair was messy with sleep, and when he approached she smelled on him, faintly, the rain from the day before. Wordless, she let him fold her against his chest, against the rough of his shirt. And for a moment, in the still morning, the pathos of the scene receded. Then she felt him tense, and reluctantly she stepped back.

"Alley. I got to be home before my aunt wakes."

"Okay."

He stood, at a loss. And she said:

"I understand. Go now."

"May I come back later?"

"I'll be home after lunch."

"I'll be here after lunch."

Then he was gone.

2.

Dee drove the wet, sandy road up to the highway carefully, afraid suddenly of getting stuck: this was not a place he wanted to have to call for a tow. In Vineyard Haven, only the breakfast joints on Main Street were open, fishermen coming out in boots, smoking, heading for their cars: after the storm, the seas would be far too high to go out today. Billy Poole saw him passing and waved, grinning in reference to the Sunday morning dawn run home. At home, he idled the car into the garage, then slipped in the screen door, careful not to let it bang.

But he needn't have bothered. As he entered, the telephone began to ring, and when he answered it the familiar voice of Shauna's secretary came to him, uncannily, as if from another life. The prosecution team had been leaked, she told him, to Stephen Labaton at the *Times*. McCarthy had talked him into holding his scoop until the following afternoon, but that meant the press conference had been moved up: ten o'clock, Monday morning. He had to be in for makeup—he would be announcing on-camera—at seven.

"She says you got to be here if you have to swim, Mr. Dennis."

"I might have to." No sooner had Dee hung up than his father called. Senator Kennedy's office had secured him an emergency reservation on the first ferry after the seas calmed, which would probably be that evening.

Dee hung up again, calculating.

An early-evening ferry would allow him to get to New York by midnight.

He'd call Shauna from the road and ask her if he could come to her house that night.

By the morning, he thought as his heart quickened, it would all be over.

At Ocean View, Allison Rosenthal, dressed now in her bicycle clothes and sitting with a cup of coffee at the big dining room table, had just dialed her father's lawyer's home on Long Island. There was a pause, which she spent fingering the keys on her PowerBook.

"Bob? Alley Rosenthal here."

Stein's booming voice was so loud that it could be heard in the room. Bob was, Allison thought, trying to smooth over their fight, and her apology, with his loud friendliness.

"Alley girl! How are you, honey?"

"I'm fine, Bob. You?"

"Fine, doll. Margey was just talking about you. You in the city?"

"No, I'm on island still."

"Well, when you get back down we want to see you. What's up?"

"Bob, who's Nicholson Dymitryck?"

His reaction was immediate.

"Dymitryck? What's up with him?"

After the briefest of pauses, Alley answered: "Uh, Sally at Dole Realty told me he was poking around, asking questions. She handles—used to handle—the rentals."

"He spoken to you?"

"No, not at all."

"Tried?"

"No."

"Okay." But Stein still sounded nervous. "Look, honey, keep away from him. Okay?"

"Okay, but what's he want?"

"Oh, God, who knows? Come on, doll, it's hardly the first time a reporter's been after you. I promise you, we'll get rid of him."

Grimacing, she spoke. "Please do, Bob. He scares me."

She listened to Stein's assurances and, the moment he was done talking, hung up.

Standing, stretching, she thought: that should do for
Nicholson Dymitryck. Bob was probably speaking to her
father already, and her father would have Falcon security
kick Dymitryck off-island by lunch.

She could not afford him seeing Dee.

She bent over the desk and wrote a quick note in case
Martha came over. She stepped out of the house, locked
the door, and put the key under a flagstone. Then she
walked to her bicycle, donning her helmet as she went.
When was the earliest Dee could be back? Not, she
thought, before eleven. She could go up to Menemsha
for breakfast, then take the ferry, loop up through Gay
Head, and be back home by then. She taped the note to
the shingled wall of the carport, and in moments was
pumping up the road, in the still slightly dripping air,
leaving Ocean View Farm in peace.

It's no surprise, perhaps, that on this unusually fast-
paced Sunday morning, it was not a peace that lasted
long.

Nor should it be a surprise that the man who broke it,
approaching the house over the dunes from the beach, in
a gray raincoat, walking carefully, then stooping to reach
the key out from under the flagstone, opening the door
and replacing the key, was Nicholson Dymitryck of the
North American Review.

3.

Inside the house, the temperature fell several degrees,
but smells of occupation—a wood fire, perfume—lin-
gered faintly in the chill air. Dymitryck entered and
crossed the room silently, seeming to put his weight on
the balls of his feet, ear cocked to the cavernous silence
under the high ceilings. To his left was the liquor cabinet,
above which hung a still life of flowers and wine on a
white-clothed table. This he examined with some atten-

tion; particularly the lower right-hand corner of the small canvas, holding the signature. Soutine. The painting that Rosenthal had bought for some astronomical sum at Christie's right after Iran-contra, boasting to the press that he'd paid for it with a check drawn on the Bank of Teheran. Satisfied with his identification, he turned, and slowly regarded the room in a long arc.

The kilim was, of course, authentic, its dyes rich and weave nearly saturnine with age. On such walls as this open room possessed, there were bookshelves, save the wall that held a white-brick chimney and a massive open fireplace. The furniture was low, leather and chrome Eames and Saarinen, and the dining room table was clearly a Greene and Greene.

With a low whistle the man inspected the table, circling it entirely, bending slightly to look at the legs. He wore a gray Burberry raincoat with a checkered lining and, emerging from its bottom, khakis and L. L. Bean rubber shoes. His hair was thick, brushed back dramatically across his head, and though he was only five-six, at close quarters a nearly graceful energy animated his movements, one that made his smallness seem rather an asset.

It was with this grace that, now, he set to work.

Sitting at the table, he turned on the small computer. While it booted he leafed, quickly and with a light touch, through the papers before him. One, a ledger for Rosenthal Equities, particularly attracted his attention: he opened it carefully, then withdrew an envelope of deposit slips and leafed through them. By the end of the small pile, his lips were pursed. For a time, looking up, he calculated. Then, as if having reached a conclusion, he laid the last five deposit slips in a row and withdrew from his raincoat pocket a small automatic camera, in whose flash he took three shots of the slips. He replaced them in the envelope and closed the register.

Much of this process was repeated again, moments later, when he came across the small pile of summer leases, each signed only by the tenant. Then again when he reached, in turn, the bank statements and the correspondence regarding the impending federal escrow seizure. When this was finished, he pocketed the camera and turned to the computer.

Here, with practiced movements, he went through the folders on the hard drive, but did not launch any of the documents, which would have changed their date registries. Instead, from his jacket pocket he withdrew two floppy disks in a small plastic case. He chose one, apparently formatted for a Macintosh, for it booted immediately, and copied onto it a number of files. Then he pocketed the disk, closed the box, shut down the computer, and closed its cover.

He stepped away from the desk now, and checked again out the wide glass front doors.

Satisfied, apparently, that he was still unobserved—searching this glass-walled house was rather like searching a fishbowl in a crowded room—he crossed the living room again, then climbed up the stairs, gingerly, as if aware that he was, now, more deeply invading Allison's privacy. Upstairs, he peeked first into the master bedroom, then the three smaller ones, the beds stripped to the mattresses. Only one, facing northward, had a made bed, or rather unmade, the sheets and blankets spilled to the floor. This room, like a strange Goldilocks, he entered.

There was a small desk, a bed, and a wicker chair. The desk drawers were filled with papers, limp, yellowed, clearly old. The closet held clothes of which the contemporaneity was indicated not only by their labels, but by the degree to which they were scattered around the floor; the desk housed a brush, a can of deodorant, a tampon. Finished searching, in the middle of the room he paused. Then he crossed to the bookcase and genuflected.

The books were exclusively poetry, mostly by women, though laced with classics. One was the paperbound *Norton Anthology*, and from its top he could see the edge of a piece of paper. He withdrew the volume and unfolded the clipping, a front page from the *Martha's Vineyard Gazette* with the headline "Suicide at Gay Head." While he read it a car engine sounded, distantly, outside.

Unhurried, he crouched in the little room and watched out the window at the moving gray clouds in the sky. Like this, he remained for a long time, bathing his unusually regular features in the dim light while he considered the approaching noise of a car engine. Then he looked back to the book. There was, with the newspaper clipping, another sheet of paper. He refolded both, and put them carefully into the inside of his shirt. He reshelved the *Norton Anthology*. Still crouching, he took three photographs of the room. Then he rose and, through the window, watched a Fiat pull into the carport. In an unhurried movement he backed away from the window.

Moving very lightly now the man stepped down the stairs, two at a time, across the living room, and through the kitchen. From here, he quickly photographed the living room, three times. Then he turned to a door that gave onto a wooden deck; it opened easily and he slipped out, vaulted the deck railing, landing lightly on the grass, and began to jog, down the beach again, west.

4.

Hope had risen in Dee's stomach with something like an ache when he'd seen Alley's Cherokee parked in the carport. Then it died when he saw the note taped to the wall: "Marty, out riding, don't wait, repeat don't wait, will call."

The strength of his disappointment, in fact, surprised

him. He was early, true. But he had not known when he left Ocean View that morning that he had only hours, not days, before he had to return to the city. The Steamship Authority was confident the ferries would be running by evening, and he had a State Police reservation on the six P.M. from Oak Bluffs. Six P.M. It was nearly nine-thirty in the morning now.

Frustration hot in his stomach, he approached the farmhouse's vast sliding doors, just in time to see three quick flashes light the living room and then, clean through the big windows, a man running away from the house at an angle toward the sea.

Dee was stopped by a jet of adrenaline that seemed to start at his feet and spread iciness to the top of his skull. Without thinking, he stepped through the living room, into the kitchen, through the back door, and vaulted the little wooden fence from the deck to the lawn.

From the top of the dune he saw, perhaps a hundred yards ahead, the man, still moving fast, and, again without thinking, Dee began to run through the wet sand after him.

In perhaps ten minutes or so the man, clearly out of breath, slowed to a walk along the waterline. Dee slowed too, unsure of what to do if he turned around. But, he thought, why would he turn around? There was only one house on the water between Long Point and Ocean View: this man had no reason not to assume that the beach behind him was deserted. Dee wiped the rain from his face, then trudged ahead on the harder sand by the waterline.

After a time the man reached into his raincoat pocket for a small camera, which he unloaded as he shifted direction, cutting now at an angle up the beach. Slowly Dee realized that the man was heading toward the Long Point parking lot, and then he understood: this man had parked there and walked down the beach, putting himself in a position to spy on Ocean View. That's how he'd known it was empty: he would have seen Allison leave.

But what time did he get there? Had he seen Dee? Had he photographed him? A great, debilitating anxiety seemed to overcome him at the thought, and he slowed. At the entrance to the Long Point Beach parking lot, the man shifted direction abruptly and crossed the beach to the little wooden walkway to the parking lot.

Dee hesitated again, watching the figure recede up the path to the parking lot. Then he followed. When he had crossed the wooden walkway, the figure came back in view, and apparently he had been running, for now he was far up the mossy path toward the parking lot.

Still undecided about what he was doing, Dee started up the path at a jog. There were two cars in the parking lot: one a rental Jeep of the sort that filled the island during the summer, parked at the far end of the lot by the entrance, the other a black Land Cruiser, probably a fisherman's, parked at the closer end, by the walkway to the beach. The short man looked behind him, saw Dee, then continued passing the Land Cruiser toward the Jeep.

And then, Dee saw something very strange indeed.

As the short man passed by the Land Cruiser, its two front doors opened and not fishermen, but two men in black suits stepped out. Both were fairly tall, but where one was also large, with a head of close-cropped, curly black hair, the other was slim and wore glasses, looking something like a university professor. Both were perhaps in their forties. Without thinking, Dee stepped sideways and crouched next to a shrub, not too obscured to see the scene taking place.

A short exchange ensued among the three. The thin man stood easily on the balls of his feet, hands in his pocket; the bigger man, meanwhile, moved to the short man's right. As for the short man, his left hand, Dee noticed, seemed to be doing something in its coat pocket. In time, it slowly emerged, and took advantage of its owner's shortness to drop two small objects behind his leg into the sand. One seemed to Dee to be a film canister, the other a computer disk, but Dee had no time to be sure, for the man then stepped back a half step onto the objects, pushing them into the sand under his foot. Dimly, in the muting rain, Dee heard his voice rise.

No sooner had he spoken when, in what seemed from Dee's vantage a casual movement, all the more shocking in its violence, the larger man hit him very hard in the belly. The short man doubled over, and as his head came down the large man kicked his cheek with his knee, a short movement that sent him over onto his shoulder in the fetal position. Then, stepping around, the large man kicked him once again, with his foot, in the stomach, and had lifted his foot again when Dee, without thinking, shouted.

Later, Dee would guess that he had saved the short man from being beaten to death. The thin one looked around, alarmed, while the other searched the short man's pockets, turning him with one hand to get to the other side of the coat. He withdrew and pocketed a small camera. Then he searched his inside pockets, dropping his wallet and car keys into the sand. When that was done he turned and walked back to the Land Cruiser, where his comrade had already started the engine. The Land Cruiser drew up the sand road.

For a long time, perhaps ten minutes, Dee watched the small man lying in the sand under the dull gray sky. A wind had come up, carrying the noise of the surf, blowing before it the thin rain. He waited, crouched by the bush, heart pounding. Then the small man stirred, groaned, and rolled onto his back.

Another period of time passed without the small man moving again, but Dee found he had lost track of time and could not tell whether it had been a minute or ten.

The sun had come out somewhat, he suddenly noticed: the gray clouds parting to show a slash of distant blue, somehow autumnal in its depth. Without thinking, Dee stepped hesitantly out toward the man. But he halted abruptly when the man stood, gingerly, his back to Dee, and then sank again to his knees to throw up while Dee retreated. When he'd finished, he did not rise again, nor did he sit down. Instead, he crawled forward a few feet, then a few more, apparently searching through the sand. Finally, from where he had been standing before being hit, he found and pocketed what Dee could now clearly see to be a roll of film and a blue floppy disk. Then he stood, slowly, turned a half circle to find his wallet and car keys, and made his way unsteadily to his Jeep.

5.

Allison arrived back at Ocean View early, her morning ride curtailed by the rain, and found Dee's Fiat in the carport. She pulled up next to it, dropped her bike into the sand, and ran up the path into the house, unbuckling her helmet.

Inside, it was empty, but through the living room windows she could see Dee approaching, at a run, over the beach. She watched for a moment, then took a towel from the downstairs bathroom and, drying her face, met him at the kitchen door.

Ignoring the towel, out of breath, he told her quickly what he had seen. His face, pale from the cold, dripped with rain. She listened, then dried his face and drew him inside.

"Okay. I understand. Take it easy."

"Alley, your father's a fucking thug."

"Yeah, unlike yours. Sit down."

She spoke with a kind of command, new to Dee, and

calmed, he sat and began taking off wet clothes. Allison, meanwhile, walked to the living room and poured two scotches at the liquor cabinet under the Soutine.

Dymitryck. A reporter waiting at the top of the road to follow her, that was one thing. One who came all the way down to spy on the house? With a camera? That was, she said to herself, something else altogether. The attack couldn't possibly be the result of her call, hours before, to Stein—her father must have had Falcon security watching Dymitryck already. Or were they there to protect her? Anyhow, she thought—with a detachment that surprised her—the important thing was to calm Dee. Later, she would wonder how she had known that. Now, she returned to the kitchen with the drinks.

"Dee. He's just another reporter. I'm telling you, every damn paper in the country's been to the island this summer. If this guy was at the house, it must have driven my father crazy."

But Dee was not placated.

"Crazy? Alley, that was a *criminal* action I witnessed."

"Oh, don't be a baby. My dad isn't some street criminal. His security's provided by the Israeli embassy, for God's sake. They're armed and they're legal. This guy was here, at my house."

"What I saw wasn't legal."

"Maybe not. Go to the police."

For a moment they regarded each other in silence. Then Allison spoke in another tone.

"I told you: I'll speak to my dad. I'll make sure that's the last time."

"That's not all." Calming, somewhat, with his drink, Dee—now in his underwear—crossed his legs. "They've called me back to New York. I have to be on the six o'clock ferry."

"Why New York?"

"Press conference, tomorrow. Announcing the prosecution's team."

"What are you going to do?"

"I told you. I'm going to quit."

For a long silence, they gazed at each other again, but this time, instead of hostility, with anxiety.

And as they did so, suddenly, unexpectedly—more shocking than any of the events these past forty-eight hours—a movement of enormous force went through Allison's stomach.

She turned away from him and struggled to come to terms with the feeling.

Turning back, she regarded him gravely.

"Would you have left the case if we hadn't . . . met again?"

Dee answered in a soft voice:

"I don't know. It doesn't matter."

"Why not?"

"Because that was then. Everything's different now."

"And what then? After you withdraw?"

Dee stared back. When he answered, it was simply.

"I want to see you."

She approached him now, crouching at his knees, her hands on his bare waist. "You don't have to do it for me."

He nodded. "Thank you. I hear you. I'll be off the case by the time you get back to town."

Alley watched him for a long moment. So he was determined. And if that was so, whatever doubts she had, they were her own. She exhaled a huge sigh. Then she rose, taking his hands, pulling him after her, relief flooding her, her words coming in whole breaths, like the big wind from the ocean. Soon he would be off the case. That was that. But what was it she felt, with the relief? Whatever it was, it was hard to distinguish in the rise of her longing. "Okay. Come upstairs now. Dee. Before you go. Come upstairs."

CHAPTER 6

September 4, 1994.
Ocean View Farm.

1.

After he left that evening, she lay watching grayness creep across the ceiling, the evening falling outside so starkly she could nearly hear it, a faint exhalation, like a sigh of defeat.

He had dressed, standing next to the bed, his eyes on her body. Watching him watching her, she had wondered if anything ever happened in one focus, not two; if anything was ever single, not double. She did not wish to hold him, she wished to *cleave* to him, her face buried in the crook of his neck, her breast against the muscle of his chest.

When at last he was ready, she sat up and swung her legs out of bed, wrapped the sheet across her waist and legs. They did not kiss, but watched each other, silent, serious. At last he leaned, ran the back of his fingers against the inside curve of her breast.

And then he was gone. He was gone. By the morning, he would have spoken to Shauna McCarthy and she would have scheduled a hearing with the trial's judge to have Dee replaced on the prosecution team.

There might be some media attention to her following that. She needed, she knew, to be ready for it. But more important, at the moment, seemed to her that Dee was gone, with the deserting summer crowd, leaving the island to its winter, empty, isolate, at the edge of the killing sea. From now until spring the Atlantic snows would drift over the duotone countryside, the ocean churning cold and alien, the occasional ferries the single lifeline to the mainland. And when she, too, left this place to its bad season, it would be for the last time.

She rose and dressed, went downstairs and out to the car, moving slowly, deliberately, as if in mourning. By the time she reached Oak Bluffs Dee's ferry would be gone, the Ritz beginning to take on its winter desolation. She hit the main road and turned right, not even looking for Dymitryck, no longer caring if he was there.

The evening, against the windshield, falling, sighing, in defeat.

Inside the door of the Ritz the familiar noises of the bar swirled: the clink of glass, running water, the murmur of conversation. As she entered, Allison felt entirely, irremediably, alone; so alone that as the door swung shut behind her she felt her mouth, entirely out of control, turning down at the corners. A few seats were available at the bar, and without thought, she took one and slowly sipped a beer, looking over its rim to the bar mirror. In its frame she watched, behind her, a couple of men in Timberland boots shooting pool. They wore plaid shirts and jean jackets. The few other people in the bar were also islanders. And the man who had just walked into the bar was Nicholson Dymitryck.

Even in the mirror she could see the bruise that spread from his right eye on to his cheekbone. He was carrying two bags, one for clothes, one a briefcase. That made her think that he had not followed her here, but was waiting for a ferry—the six o'clock, clearly, had been full.

And he was approaching her. Without thinking she turned, holding him in her green gaze.

He noticed her now and stared back, his face grave.

For a moment, everything paused.

Then he altered his direction to sit next to her at the bar.

2.

Even with his bruised cheek, she could make out the extreme regularity of his features. His eyes, large and brown, his hair thick enough and well enough cut not to need combing. Unshaven, his lower face was a perfectly even shadow of black, and his expression—curious, interested—held, as far as she could see, not the slightest aggression. She judged him to be in his mid-thirties.

After a time he broke their gaze to gesture to the bartender and hold up two fingers. Felice approached with two beers and one shot of bourbon, asking Allison protectively: "You want this, doll?" Alley nodded, and after Felice had gone the man extended the silence long enough to drain his shot and light, from a pack on the bar, a Marlboro Light.

When he spoke, it was in a low, hoarse voice, flat with a Californian accent, and a conversational tone, as if resuming a long-standing discussion between old friends.

"So, thanks for everything. Wanna do me a favor?"

He sounded, she thought, exhausted. She nodded, and for a moment he paused, as if noticing, with unknown perspicacity, something about her. Then he went on in a slightly less aggressive pitch.

"Tell your old man I'm under subpoena to the House Intelligence Committee, and I got to be in Washington tomorrow. I don't want him to think he chased me away."

Alley nodded okay, and there was a silence, during which she drank a single sip of beer. Then she spoke again:

"I'm afraid your trip's been a waste of time, Mr. Dymitryck."

"Nicky."

"Pardon me?"

"Call me Nicky. And not at all. I've had a very interesting time."

Now Alley allowed herself a smile. It was, she thought, her first in a long time.

"Well, Mr. Dymitryck, you have an interesting idea of what's interesting."

"Um-hmm." He seemed to say this to himself. Then he returned his attention to her.

"Hey, Allison?"

"Yes, Nicky."

Still speaking pleasantly, the man went on. "You think I'm one of your little pals from the *New Yorker*, right? You think I'm looking for a quote from you to dump in my chatty little fact piece? Well, let me tell you something. I don't give a fuck about you. So, think what you want to, okay? But don't kid yourself that you know the first thing about what I'm looking for, or what I found."

Absorbing the change in pace immediately, she found herself, suddenly, glad. She smiled now, widely, and as she spoke, in a new tone also, she watched this man coming to attention.

"Excuse me, you're quite right. I thought you were a knee-jerk liberal from a paranoid rag come out here looking to confirm, somehow, what you already believe. Now I see you're in fact a deeply mysterious character with a black eye who can use the word *fuck*."

He smiled back, as if happily, but she noticed his eyes squinting.

"Oh, my dear. My worst enemy wouldn't call me a liberal. A liberal's someone like your buddy Martha's father. Or his good friends John Kerry or Ted Kennedy, who so support your father's business activities. You can say whatever you want about me. But you can't call me a liberal."

Allison felt her smile fade. That both Democratic senators from Massachusetts were friends of her father's had to do with the high importance of munitions manufacture on the East Coast: no one could be elected here without the support of the enormous high-tech defense industry, with the thousands of jobs it guaranteed to the state. But was this guy really inviting her to debate the politics of the arms trade? That, she thought, for sure was a change from what most people wanted from her. She licked her lips and then answered precisely.

"I follow you exactly. The difference between you and someone like Kennedy or Kerry is that they got themselves elected. That's called a constituency, Nicky dear, and their constituency, like it or not, works for Raytheon and Electric Boat. Please don't interrupt me."

This last statement was in response to his indraw of breath, ready to answer, and in turn he exhaled and watched her go on.

"Their constituency built this country's defense during the Cold War. Now that the war's over, they're supposed to be fired, right? They did their job, and they've got families, and pensions, and mortgages, but sorry: we don't need them any more. Well, Mr. Dymitryck from the *North American Review*, you know, and I know, that every piece of equipment we build and sell can be just as easily bought from France, or Germany, or Russia, or England, and those bastards'll equip them for nuclear payloads in the bargain. And you know, and I know, that if *we* don't sell them, *they* will. So don't give me your moralizing, tired, liberal—repeat, liberal—bullshit, okay?"

Far from silenced, Nicky answered the moment she stopped.

"You know, that answer's always depressing. But it's the worst when you hear it from someone your age. Listen, the same company that builds F-16s in America sells separately packaged nuclear conversion kits, so so much for your precious moral high ground. And as for your heroic blue-collar constituency who needs arms exports to survive, open your eyes. They're being pink-slipped from Lynn to Salem while their employers conduct a massive industry downsizing and hold up shareholder profits by exporting *our* jobs and *our* technology in offset deals, and no one in this country, in this whole fucking country, gives a good goddamn. You take what the CEO of Defense Dynamics makes in one year, it could pay two hundred people fifty-thousand-dollar salaries and still leave him seven figures to keep up his house on South Beach. Don't kid yourself: Kennedy's constituency, and Kerry's, and Clinton's, aren't blue collar, but they *are* your father: CEOs drawing multimillion-dollar salaries and feeding them into election coffers while they're downsizing workforces and laying off *thousands* of workers. You know that."

"No, I don't. I know that there's an industry in trouble, and millions of people depend on it."

"Bullshit. There were larger military drawdowns after Korea, after Vietnam. We survived those. The Pentagon Defense Conversion Committee just last winter said the national impact's smaller now than after those."

"Yeah. It's arms exports that's keeping it smaller. It's people like my father who are giving us the breathing space to convert technology."

They were both speaking very quickly now, and without smiling.

"No way. It's people like your father keep us from retooling. See Japan have a problem with conversion after the Second World War? See Korea struggling to convert to auto production? How come they can do it and we can't?"

"Oh, write the president. My father doesn't make these damn things. He just fulfills orders *your* elected government originates."

His face showed contempt, seeming to age with the expression. "I'm surprised to hear the daughter of the great Zionist using that kind of defense. And in any case, it's wrong and you know it. Your father originates deals all over the world. It's the backbone of Clintonian democracy that anything can be sold, anywhere, and he'll throw in the State and Commerce Departments as salesmen. Do you know you can get an export license for cattle prods under the Export Administration Act? Who exactly do you think's defending democratic sovereignty with cattle prods? And if, in the unlikely event that the administration won't sign off, then what the fuck, your daddy just ships to Taiwan and diverts. Or uses Israeli stockpile. Or does whatever he wants: an end-user certificate means nothing anymore. If I had a Falcon jet at my disposal, I could be back here with a Thai EUC for two dozen AMRAAM missiles before this bar fucking closes."

"Well, that's likely, given that last call here's at four. So tell me this, Mr. Dymitryck from the *NAR*. What did my father get his ass arrested for, if it's the goddamned Wild West out there in the arms market?"

And at the question Nicky, suddenly, stopped and slowly smiled.

"You see, you haven't been listening to me. I told you, I'm not writing an article for the *New York Review of Books*. I know all about the sleazy politics behind your dad's arrest. I don't give a fuck about that."

3.

Allison hid her shock in a draw from her beer. This was, she thought, a very, very smart person, as smart as Dee, as smart as Martha.

He was, even with the black eye, an oddly attractive person. She watched him now, for a moment, watching her while he ordered another drink with an authoritative nod down the bar. When he turned his face to her again, she noticed the thickness of his lips around the cigarette they held, and again, the diffuse bruise from his eye onto his cheek. Her dad's people had hit him, she thought, very hard indeed. Would they have killed him had Dee not shouted?

"Jesus, Mr. Dymitryck, I don't know what. You were interested enough to get him arrested in the first place. I'm sorry you didn't hit the end of your attention span a little earlier."

He laughed outright now, his face transforming with the smile, and Allison had a feeling that, under other circumstances, this was a person who laughed easily. When he stopped and spoke again in his funny, raspy voice with its flat Californian accent, it was with a different expression. Appreciation, or very nearly, Allison thought.

"I'm gonna tell you something, Allison, and you can take it to the bank and deposit it with one of your daddy's checks from Bank Leumi. You ready? When I'm done with your dad, he's going to be truly sorry he didn't have me killed this afternoon."

Quickly, something tightened in Allison's stomach. But without taking the time to understand what, she answered.

"You're living in a fantasy, Mr. Dymitryck. My father doesn't have people killed. Or beaten up."

Nicky answered only with a withering look.

But there was something else bothering her, and now,

with a small shock, she defined what it was: how had he known her father sent her checks from Bank Leumi?

She thought about that for a moment, feeling her cheeks suddenly hot, before she turned back.

"Now let me tell you something. In fact, let me tell you two things. Firstly, I don't know what you're talking about. Secondly, if you're looking for some secret about my father, don't even bother asking."

"Thanks. Thanks for your advice. Now, I got to go check my boat."

"Your boat?" During their conversation, she had forgotten that he meant to leave the island tonight. Suddenly it seemed extremely important that he not leave. Not until she knew what he meant by that Bank Leumi reference. She spoke quickly.

"Good luck. I'll keep your seat warm. There's no way on earth you're getting a seat on that boat."

He stood. "I agree. But I do believe I can get a ticket on the freighter at eight. Watch my bags?"

Looking down, she saw at the foot of his stool a small leather garment bag and a matching briefcase. Her heart quickening, she looked up, and nodded. Then the small man was walking, slightly unsteadily, out of the bar, and she was alone.

4.

The clearest thought she could bring to mind was that this man was going to disappear in a minute, as Dee had just done, and like Dee—her stomach plummeted at the thought—he could be hard to get back. For a moment she was torn between getting rid of him and keeping him here. While he was here, this little man could get sloppy drunk and tell all. She could confront him with a direct question about his interest in Ocean View. She could seduce him. That thought, as crazy as it was, sent a movement of excitement through her.

Then she turned to Nicky's briefcase at her feet, and her heart, already quickened, began to pound.

What had he meant by that Bank Leumi comment? This was, perhaps, her only chance ever to find out. Casually, she picked it up and carried it down the length of the bar to the women's room. It was occupied, and for a couple of endless minutes she experienced severe anxiety. Then, from within, the toilet flushed and the door pushed open.

Inside, the door locked, she sat on the closed toilet and opened the case on her knees. There was an empty pint bottle of Jim Beam, a couple of floppy disks in a plastic case, a roll of film, and a number of green files pertaining to various subjects: Greg Eastbrook, Jennifer Harbury, a union dispute in southern California. Under this, there was a single manila file marked "Diamond."

The name was familiar. She opened the thin file and found, inside a Xeroxed map of South Beach from Long Point to Ocean View. Under this was another, broader map, and under that two pictures: one from a newspaper in the '80s, showing herself, her father, and Pauly on the steps of the Capitol Building coming from the Iran-contra hearings; the other a grainy print showing herself sitting on the porch of the Up Island General Store.

She paused now, breathing through an open mouth. Next in the file were some newspaper clippings about her father, both then and now; then a document that proved to be a lease for one of the Ocean View Estate rentals signed by a Stanley Diamond. Briefly, dizziness passed over her mind, and she closed the file.

She remembered Diamond now. His had been one of the checks she'd deposited when she had first arrived on-island, in mid August.

But there was no time to panic: Nicky could be back

any time. She replaced the file, then quickly completed her search of the briefcase: underneath was a book, *The Wild Colonial Boy*, a novel. She lifted it out, and a piece of Corrasable typing paper, folded in four, fluttered to the floor. She retrieved it, unfolded it, and received her second shock.

"Mother." The word escaped her mouth before she could stop it. It was a poem, her own, written after Pauly died and typed on the old Olivetti at Ocean View.

That was how he knew about the Bank Leumi checks.

This man had not just photographed Ocean View, he had been in her house. And searched it.

In the brief instant before she became scared, looking up, she wondered what he had been looking for.

Whatever it was, however, she knew that he would not have searched her house without good reason to believe she had it.

Which was one of the things that now made fear come.

Hands shaking, she repacked the briefcase and closed it, wondering with a feeling of horror if this was the only copy of her poem. She opened the bathroom door, looked out to see that he had not yet returned, then hurried back to her bar seat and dropped the briefcase again on the floor.

Mother. She said the word again, to herself, and added this time the qualification: "Fucker."

And then Nicky was back.

5.

Funny, she managed to think, as she watched him coming in, how well dressed this guy was for a self-proclaimed radical. He wore, over jeans, a splendid gabardine jacket, and a silk shirt that must have cost, alone, more than most journalists made in a week—and alternative media writers, like himself, in a year. Something about that reassured her.

Taking his seat at the bar, he told her he was on the eight o'clock ferry, and she nodded with something like pleasure. Then there was a silence, which he filled by downing his shot of bourbon, and then she spoke.

"Want to dance?"

"Pardon me?"

"I asked you if you want to dance. I mean, you don't care about my father's crime. And I'm not going to tell you anything. But you're not going away. So you want to dance?"

He watched her without answering, and she spoke again.

"Oh all right. Listen, the truth is, Clinton authorized the shipment during a Whitewater shredding party with my dad, during which he groped me. Now let me ask you a question."

"Shoot."

"You've been chasing my father, or people like my father, your whole career. Now you've closed him down. Why don't you take a break?"

"Oh, I haven't gotten what I want from your father yet." He was not watching her now, as if the conversation had degenerated into real animosity.

"Why? What are you, the self-appointed protector of the Constitution?"

"Nah, the Constitution's a crock."

Surprised, Alley laughed, and Nicky looked up. Then he leaned back, and laughed too.

"I mean, what a malign, mistrustful little document. Talk about lowest common denominator, man."

Both laughed now, for a long time, and Allison registered that she, too, was drunk. Certainly she couldn't remember the last time she had laughed so much. When she could speak, she repeated her question.

"So? What is it then?"

He turned, watching himself in the bar mirror while he thought for a moment. Then he turned back.

"You see, arms are like roaches in a restaurant. Everyone has them, but most restaurants, they stay hidden till the customers are gone and the lights are off. If you see them during business, you'll never see just one, and that's because you don't see them at all unless there's a serious infestation. You with me?"

"Um-hmm."

"Good." For a moment, he marshaled his thoughts. Then he went on.

"Now, a guy like your father, if you're smart, you don't just whack him with a newspaper the second you see him on the counter. What you do is, you try to let him lead you back to the nest."

"Very funny. That still doesn't answer my question."

"Which is?"

"Why you care?"

"I'll tell you. Then you let me ask you a question. Deal?"

"Deal."

He paused now, thinking. Then he answered her, speaking carefully and holding his eyes, wide open, on hers.

"There's nothing surprising about me caring, Ms. Rosenthal. What's surprising is that you even ask. You think you come from some rarefied world of insider knowledge. Bullshit. Your cynicism, your worldliness, that's nothing new. If you had some historical perspective, you'd know that you're a product of the seventies' commercialization of the counterculture—you're co-opted; and of eighties Reaganism—you're cynical. That's how they got Watergate and Iran-contra by you, for one thing. I care because I didn't let them do that to me."

As if having taken a blow to her body, Allison pulled together a counterpunch.

"I'm cynical? You mean you're an idealist."

"Not at all. I accept entirely your father's profession. I'm interested in the people who tell him what to do. That's all."

Allison had recovered herself now. "Is that all? Thanks for the mission statement. Now, let me tell you one thing I know about you, Mr. Dymitryck."

"Go ahead."

"You're doing what you're doing because of your father."

That surprised him. "What do you know about my father?"

"Oh, I don't need to know anything about him. Either he's on the right and you're rebelling, or he's on the left and you're following. My point is that you're a product of your environment just as much as I am."

He nodded, and perhaps his answer was all the more aggressive for how deeply she had hit him where it hurt. "I follow you. And it's not just that you're wrong. It's that the way you're wrong is so revealing."

She shrugged. "Prove it."

"Oh, I can prove it. But I'd have to tell you my life's story. And I have a boat to catch."

"I see." Allison was not too drunk to know that it was time to end the conversation, and that she had best be the one to do it. "Well, maybe another time, Mr. Dymitryck."

"Nicky. I hope so, Allison. Now my turn?"

"Go ahead."

"The guy I'm interested in, you know who that is?"

"No. I don't care, either."

"His name's Greg Eastbrook. He's the Republican candidate for the Senate in California this November. He's also a guy who's worked with your dad since they met in Vientiane in, like, the Summer of Love. I'll bet you know him."

She did not respond, and for a moment they watched

each other. Then he smiled and spoke with the intonation of a kindergarten teacher.

"And that's really what this is all about, Allison. It's that you know a bunch about Greg Eastbrook. In fact, I believe that you know a very great deal about Eastbrook indeed. And that's why I want to offer you a deal."

"No thanks."

But his face, hardening suddenly, showed he was not to be stopped.

"No, please, it's my pleasure. All you have to do is agree to talk to me about Greg Eastbrook. And if you do, I'll consider not letting the Massachusetts state attorney's office know that you just made nearly two hundred thousand dollars' worth of fraudulent deposits from renting property soon to be under federal seizure to unsuspecting tenants. And I'll also not tell my very strong suspicions that the endorsements on those deposits were forged by you."

Wordless, now, she watched him stand, shrug on his jacket, and then suddenly face her and smile, a wide smile that was as much in his eyes as in the wry pose of his lips.

"See, Ms. Rosenthal. I told you I wasn't like one of your little friends."

6.

Ever after, those two late-summer days, September 4th and 5th, 1994, would be, in Allison's memory, one long day.

After Nicky had left, she stayed in the bar for a long time, until closing.

She sat and drank, alone, as the boozy jukebox played through smoky air to an audience of five islanders, one asleep with his head on the bar. And as she drank, she marveled at how quickly, how efficiently, the world had closed around her. First her father. Then Dee. Now this.

When the bar closed she drove, dead drunk, through the empty night to the terror of home.

Unwilling even to process what she now faced.

September 5th, she woke supine on the living room couch under a throw, unable to remember falling asleep. Against the windows, a windy rain pounded the glass; through the water running on its surface she saw a leaden sky leaking a slight, ominous light. After a moment she raised her wrist to her eyes and saw, dreamily, that the time was nearly twelve. Then, with a small shock, she realized that it was day. That meant it was not midnight but noon.

Surprised, she sat up, and as she did so from her chest a plastic orange medicine bottle, open, rolled onto the floor. She lifted it, feeling her head pound, and made out on the label the word *diazepam*. That scared her, suddenly, and she rose.

As she made coffee, her fright subsided. She had slept through the morning on Valium and booze, but she had survived, and strangely, it had been therapeutic. What had she been doing before? The memory of the night, dim, stayed at bay, and then her mind turned to remembering that she had missed the press conference that morning. By now, Dee had recused himself from her father's prosecution. That should have been a relief. Only now, she knew without detailing them, she had a new set of problems to face.

But she didn't care. A deep relaxation was through her, a sense not that anything was all right, but that everything was so entirely wrong that she no longer really cared. And she was hungry: that was a good sign. In the cupboard was a can of soup, which she heated and ate, hungrily, watching the now quiescent ocean from the kitchen window. Finished, she went back to the living room and booted her computer. She launched Netscape, then logged in to the on-line *New York Times*. While the front page loaded she sipped coffee, watching the headline come clear: "U.S. Attorney Announces Rosenthal Prosecution Team."

There was no headline reference to Dee, she saw. Was that good? Impatient, she clicked through to the article and, heart sinking, saw a straight reporting of the press conference, conducted by Dee, announcing the prosecution's team. There could be no confusion: Dee was quoted directly, and he referred to himself as the third member of a team of three.

Finished, she hit the *back* button and returned to the front page. There was a short analytic piece about the trial by Labaton, but that was all. What could that mean?

For a long time she stared at the screen, unable to understand. Then, as if a voice calling insistently from far away, another headline caught her eye. It read: "Reporter Victim of Stabbing." She clicked through to this article, and read about a crime at Logan Airport the night before. Some guy had been beaten, then stabbed in a bathroom and left for dead. The airport was practically deserted—the victim was booked on the first flight the next morning to Washington—and even though he'd managed to crawl along the floor, and out onto the concourse, he had bled to death by the time he'd been found.

Only then did Allison Rosenthal, all hint of relaxation fleeing every corner, every interstice of her body, her mind suddenly acute, again, to the world of pain that had been waiting while she slept, absorb why the murder warranted such a big headline.

The dead man was the chief investigative reporter and associate editor of *North American Review* in Los Angeles.

Nicholson Jefferson Dymitryck.

PART TWO

Then Esther bade them return Mordecai this answer, Go, gather together all the Jews that are present in Shushan, and fast ye for me, and neither eat nor drink three days, night or day: I also and my maidens will fast likewise; and so will I go in unto the king, which is not according to the law: and if I perish, I perish.

ESTHER 4:15-16

CHAPTER 7

September 4, 1994.
New York City.

1.

Woods Hole. Buzzards Bay. Fall River, Mystic, Groton, New London. The night before, still blissfully unaware of Dymitryck's death, Dee had taken the I-91 connector through New Haven and accelerated down the Merritt to New York, speeding. The road humming under the light tires of the little car, engine revving at eighty, he took the unlighted Merritt in smooth sweeps of his arms on the wheel. His mind drained of any thought beyond the speed. Only the foolish, Dee knew, reflect at night.

Perhaps he did not reflect. But some mental process was spinning itself on nonetheless, and north of Larchmont he pulled off the road and into a little restaurant parking lot, still wondering what he was about to do.

Inside, he ate dinner, slowly, thinking. After perhaps an hour he rose hesitantly and, at a bank of telephones, punched Shauna's home number from his pocket diary, then his credit card number. A man answered, obviously just woken. Without saying who it was, Dee asked for

Ms. McCarthy. Waiting, Dee felt fear and courage, intermixed. The courage surprised him.

Then, in an aural refocus, he became aware that a radio was playing the news. A man had been attacked and stabbed at Logan Airport. Police suspected an attempted robbery. But the case was complicated by the fact that the man was a reporter on his way to testify in Washington before the House Intelligence Committee. The newscast announced the reporter's name just as Shauna's sleepy voice came on the other end of the line.

Without a word, acting purely from instinct, Dee hung up.

In the city, at the Yale Club, he got the details on CNN. Dymitryck was on his way to Washington to testify to House Intelligence on the bombing at Harlanstrasse 14, which was under investigation by Bob Torricelli from New Jersey. Now, Dee heard the details of the familiar story. Nicky had been interviewing a Turkish arms dealer, Mehmet Hourani, who claimed to have proof of American involvement in a Chilean cluster bomb factory that was supplying Saddam Hussein up until the Gulf War.

The interview had taken place in Hourani's apartment on the outskirts of Munich, and about halfway through, a bomb had gone off, killing Sargonalian and Nicky's cameraman. Dymitryck himself had been badly injured, but not too badly to come out, days later, with the original article detailing Rosenthal's role in the Bosnian sales. Hourani had been killed before giving Dymitryck the Iraqi story he had come for. He had, however, given him the Rosenthal story.

Nonetheless, CNN reported, the murder was being called a robbery gone awry by the Boston police, although on what evidence, Dee could not see.

And now, step by step, Dee began to understand how correct had been his instinct in hanging up before

Shauna came to the phone. Stomach sinking, he began, in minutes, to understand what his instinct had seen in a fraction of a second.

For no matter what fantasy the Boston police were feeding the media about a murder gone awry, the FBI was certainly, right this minute, covering every step of Dymitryck's movements prior to his death. The most cursory investigation, he knew immediately, would reveal that this man had just come from the island. And the most idiotic of investigators would be able to connect his presence on Martha's Vineyard with his interest in Ronald Rosenthal.

Then, suddenly, an image of the roll of film the man had dropped on the ground came to him and Dee felt sweat rolling down his sides.

And that was it. Had he been photographed going into the Ocean View farmhouse? And was the FBI going to find those photographs in the effects of the dead reporter?

If so, his explanation to his boss, that he had simply not connected his onetime sweetheart to his current defendant, would look very thin indeed. If Dee were connected—not in the past but in the present—both to his defendant's daughter and, by extension, to a brutal assassination, then his recusal was practically irrelevant.

And that Dee understood made it crucial that he do nothing.

For if, by some chance, he had not been photographed, then the connection between Dymitryck's death and Allison Rosenthal, no matter how big a media sensation it may be, would not affect him.

And, if there were any chance at all that he had not been photographed, then the last thing in the world he wanted to do was, by his public withdrawal from the case, connect himself with Dymitryck's murder during a trip to Martha's Vineyard to investigate notorious gun runner

Ronald Rosenthal, a story that would, Dee had no doubt, be on the front page of every newspaper in the country the next morning.

The only thing that could eclipse such a story would be the revelation of his secret love affair with that notorious gun runner's daughter.

What Dee's instinct had seen the moment he heard the news of Dymitryck's death was that he could not do that to himself, and, even more important, he could not do it to Alley.

At three o'clock CNN reported that the FBI had determined that Dymitryck was at Logan Airport en route to Washington from Martha's Vineyard. Following this report, Dee went out to a pay phone and called Ocean View. But the telephone rang and rang until a machine answered with a curt command to leave a message, and he hung up.

A process that he repeated, and with the same results, every hour until seven A.M.

By seven, CNN had not reported anything new since three.

A last call to Alley had produced nothing.

With a glacial dread in his blood, Dee showered and dressed for the office.

With no idea at all what he was going to do.

2.

At first, he thought that the murder would not be mentioned until he spoke to McCarthy. But when he did, she said nothing about it. As he let himself be carried through the preparations for the press conference, Dee Dennis realized that the connection had either not been made, or was for some reason not being discussed.

After all, as Steve Post had said that morning on the

radio during Dee's taxi ride downtown, Nicholson Dymitryck, in his writing for the *NAR*, had moved from virulent denunciation of what the magazine called the "Reagan-Bush Junta" to a steady, bitter critique of the "Clinton Compromise" without missing a beat.

And now, watching his fellows in the U.S. attorney's office, Dee realized that no one in his little world had connected the murder with what they were doing. The realization made a sense of unreality pass clean through him.

That was growing to be a familiar sensation, and it only heightened as time accelerated—so it seemed—to the conference. In truth, it was already impossible, but he did not want to admit that. An hour before the press conference the team watched CNN's preconference coverage of the Rosenthal trial, only to find it following the story of Dymitryck's murder. Now the FBI had concluded that the murder was definitely a robbery: Dymitryck's wallet and briefcase were missing, and witnesses had identified the perpetrators as two young black men. The report pushed the sense of unreality to some sort of an apogee, for Dee. No one—least of all the FBI—could believe this nonsense. What did it mean? As if physically crippled, Dee watched the report helplessly, feeling the moments pass.

A powerful dread was now in him. Only a schizophrenic, he thought with a feeling close to tears, could avoid feeling the impossible ambivalence, the pure duality of his position. Nothing meant what it seemed to mean, nothing.

This thought, without warning, loosened the clutch of his dilemma, and in a practiced mental maneuver, Dee seized the chance to turn his mind to the challenge ahead.

It was a challenge for which, he thought wryly, he had been bred.

≈

The David Treat Dennis who presented himself to the cameras was a composed, articulate, handsome young man, inspired by a sense of righteousness, of moral probity, and manifesting a winning level of nervousness. Behind him, as he spoke, a slide projector showed images culled from Bosnia, Rwanda, Nicaragua, Guatemala—all unattributed—showing the various effects of antipersonnel land mines, cluster bombs, and combat weapons, largely on young children. Showing these images had been Ed Dennis's idea, and that they were entirely irrelevant to the prosecution of Ronald Rosenthal bothered no one, least of all Dee: this was not a courtroom. His voice, when the audience finally hushed and he began talking, was only helped by the raspiness of his night awake.

"Ladies and gentlemen, we talk about the arms trade, and the way we talk about it obscures the reality of what people like Ronald Rosenthal do for a living. Yes, they wear suits; yes, they work in offices; yes, they pay taxes. But the reality of their work is selling death and profiting from war, and our prosecution of Ronald Rosenthal sends one message, pure and simple: munitions sales are governed by the law of the land. They are a matter of foreign policy that only our executive branch can alter; a matter of legislation that only our Congress can rule on; and when they are illegally undertaken they become a matter that our courts cannot ignore."

Coming from this earnest, handsome, articulate young man, the speech got the benefit of the network cameramen's kindest attention: this was prime-time material, straight into the can. Only one lone reporter, a young woman in the back of the room, sounded a note of discord when she asked in a precise, confident voice, "You don't mean to say, Mr. Dennis, that there aren't more arms being exported under the Clinton administration than any other previous government? And a follow-up: how is your prosecution being affected by the reports of a secret arms pipeline between the Falcon Corporation and the Bosnian Muslims being blessed by the White House?"

With a showman's instinct, Dee answered only the follow-up.

"The Justice Department has, to my knowledge, found those reports groundless, Ms. . . ."

"Laura Isenberg, Pacifica Network."

A name, clearly, the handsome young lawyer found easy to disregard, as he turned his attention to a man from ABC.

The conference was aired live on C-SPAN, and when Dee arrived back in the office his father was waiting on hold.

"Deedee. Tremendous. The way you handled that girl was word-perfect. Who briefed you on that?"

Hollow with fear, Dee had hung up the phone, and after receiving the rest of his congratulations, made his way to his office.

Shauna was taking the staff to a champagne lunch at Delmonico.

Watching the harbor water glinting, steely, dispassionate, Dee lit a thin Dunhill Panatela, pulling the smoke deep toward the aching anxiety in his stomach.

It was like a wound.

3.

Once, during her time in Paris between college and law school, Alley had surprised her father by picking him up at the airport on one of his business trips.

Her father had emerged from customs in the escort of four black-suited men. Outside, two BMWs had been waiting: one for her father, one for the men, and they'd driven straight to the Israeli embassy, where, while her father conferred behind closed doors with the ambassador, the four men had drawn handguns—big, automatic nine-millimeters—to fit the holsters they wore under their suit jackets.

What business required this security—unusual even for her father—Alley had known better than to ask, and she'd managed to forget that the four men were even there, most of the time. But one night at the Flore, while her father was in the bathroom, a very drunken man tried to pick her up while she sat alone, upstairs, at a small table. She ignored him, he got mad and lurched toward her, and before she could raise a hand to stop him he was lying on the ground with a knee on his chest while one of the bodyguards searched him with violent efficiency, then dragged him out of the café. She watched, horrified—he had been harmless. But she had been too surprised to intervene.

When her father returned, enraged, she told him never to allow that to happen again, and hushing her, aware of the attention they were getting, he'd agreed. But she'd suspected that all he'd done was ask the guards to change their clothes, and whenever her father or his work were in the news, she'd noticed that casually dressed Israeli-looking men in jeans and sports jackets happened to be discernible around her.

A drunk getting taken out of a bar, that was one thing.

But what kind of a threat did Nicky Dymitryck pose to be the victim of a murder?

During the afternoon the clouds raced from the sky, replaced by a backdrop of pastel blue high above the gusty wind. A thin luminescence was over the sea, dappling the water with diamondine glints of light. The end of the season, Alley knew, and recognizing it, she turned from the window.

Of course Dee had announced. Of course he had not recused himself. Dee would have heard the news of

Nicky's death by the time he arrived in New York. He would not have known what to do. He could not risk associating himself, and by extension her, with the media firestorm that was sure to erupt. With dread, she felt what he must have felt. Then he had announced. Of course. And now, if he were to try to leave the trial, it would draw enormous attention, enormous. And as she thought that, time—the summer, the strange feeling of early autumn—seemed to halt.

When she could, she trained her mind again on the murder. Nicky had said he was not interested in her father's arrest—not beyond knowing why he was lying down for it. What had he wanted? Something about Greg Eastbrook. Dimly, she brought her mind to the night before as best as she could. Then the memory came clean.

He had actually tried to blackmail her. He had actually searched her house, found out about her deposit of the Ocean View rental checks, and tried to use that knowledge to make her tell him something about Greg Eastbrook.

Now, pacing the living room, she thought with greater clarity than she had found all day. Colonel Eastbrook was running in the November midterm elections for a Senate seat in California. Like most people she knew, she had followed the campaign with interest. Eastbrook had been in the NSC during Iran-contra, and his campaign was modeled closely on North's in Virginia.

But what did Nicky think—what had Nicky thought—she could tell him about Eastbrook? Pauly, maybe: Pauly had been the political one, and he had known a lot about their father's business. The thought stirred a memory in her, too vague to catch, and after a time she turned back to the computer screen and logged in to Bobcat, the NYU card catalog. The *NAR* was collected there, she saw: when she got back to New York she could go and look at it. Perhaps that would tell her something. Again, the memory, distant, tugged at her mind, and perhaps she might have found it had not the sound of a car skidding to a sandy halt in the carport caught the focus of her dizzied mind.

It was Martha, come to spend the night. She'd closed her father's house for the season and was delaying her return to New York to help Allison finish the Ocean View inventory and close the house. Then they'd go together down to the city, Martha to the *Observer* and Allison, a day late, for the beginning of her last year of law school. Theoretically.

Watching Martha jump out of the car and hurry toward the house, her face a picture of worry, Allison doubted that would be happening.

And it was only as she opened the door for Martha that she realized one last fact.

Nicky had threatened her with prosecution for her embezzlement of the Ocean View rental money.

God, what had she been thinking? So much had she enjoyed the pure bloody-mindedness of complicating life for the federal accountants, she had never even considered that someone might take it seriously as a crime.

But of course they could. Nicky had seen it as a crime, and a prosecutable one.

Did his death, now, save her from that?

4.

Coming inside like a burst of wind, dropping her bag on the couch, Martha was talking immediately, calmly but intensely, like a doctor during an emergency.

"Alley girl, now, answer me a couple questions, then we'll figure out what to do. Did you have any contact with Dymitryck?"

"None."

Her friend peered at her through squinting eyes, but

Alley, feeling her face grow as blank as an adolescent's, held her ground. Relenting slightly then, but only slightly, Martha went on.

"What happened with Dee?"

Now a small shock pierced Allison as she realized that the revolutionary, cataclysmic events of the past few days were unknown to her friend. Quickly, before she could think, she answered:

"Nothing, Marty."

This, however, Martha was unwilling, or unable, to swallow.

"What? Didn't you meet him after the Ritz?"

"I saw him the next day. Out at Wasque. No one saw us."

"And?"

Alley turned to the window, as if moved. "And I guess he had been drunk at the Ritz. He was sober enough not to say anything. Christ, Martha. What's there to say?"

"Well, how about your father's name, doll? That's enough to get him off the case, isn't it?"

Her back to her friend, she shrugged. "Marty, let's be big girls, okay? My dad's guilty."

"Yeah, right. Unlike about six dozen of his colleagues." Deeply worried, biting her lip, Martha sat on the couch and Alley, turning, watched her friend as she thought.

And in the pause, incongruously, she remembered how as children they'd sat for hours next to each other with their legs linked, swinging them in unison, thigh to thigh and calf to calf, utterly unconscious of their intimacy.

Now there was a dark, full, complex woman before her, as beautiful as she could be in the intensity of her calculation. Her boyfriends, when she had them, were either casual or much older: few men of their age and circle interested her or, for that matter, could handle her. Allison thought of her sometimes as an olive: dark, foreign, too salty to keep eating but too irresistible to stop. Martha had been nearly estranged from her father since she'd told Clinton at a White House dinner that the only person in America fit to be president was Gore Vidal. Clinton, the way Martha told the story, had seemed rather to agree with her, but Ohlinger had turned beet-red—not a pretty sight—and later, in the privacy of their government car home, had more or less banished her from Washington, a family exile from which, she suspected, only a Republican victory in '96 would rehabilitate her.

But could she tell Martha about Dee? And could she tell her about Nicky?

Before she could decide, Martha went on.

"Everyone in Washington knows the FBI's lying about the murder being a robbery. But this is the thing, Alley girl. Everyone thinks the killing was to stop him from testifying to House intelligence. They think it was probably the same people as set the bomb in Harlanstrasse. That means no one has connected him to you."

Alley nodded. "That's good."

"Damn right it's good, Alley. Otherwise you'd have six dozen reporters trampling what's left of your damn lawn out there. Do you understand what's at risk here?"

"Yes."

"Good. Now look. They know he was on the island, big deal. His interest in your dad is public record. You didn't have any contact with him. He was about to testify to the U.S. House of Representatives on the killing of an American citizen at Harlanstrasse 14. There's the story. Fuck Martha's Vineyard."

For a long moment, Alley thought. If Martha thought that's why Nicky was killed, she was not going to argue.

"If you say so."

Martha nodded. "I tell you what, though. I'm not leaving you for a second till this house of yours is closed and you're back in the city. Something changes, you'll need

Governor Weld to get the national guard to protect you from the press out here. In New York, you can hide. Know who taught me that? Kathy Boudin. So let's hop to it, doll. This fucking island's starting to feel like Auschwitz to me, and we got *arbeit* that'll *macht* us the fuck *frei*."

5.

Five o'clock. They had returned from Delmonico at three, the federal prosecution team tipsy, high with the success of their announcement conference. Back at the office, Shauna had given them the afternoon off, advising them to be at the breakfast conference the next morning sober, serious, and ready for the hardest work of their lives. Edelson and Callahan had taken off immediately, McCarthy a half hour later. But Dee had stayed in his office, standing by the window, smoking, staring out. It was time, Dee thought, to do some thinking.

This he knew. Ronald Rosenthal had been arrested for papering a sale of post-Soviet weapons through Falcon subsidiaries in Europe. There were automatic machine guns, mines, grenades, and some small artillery. He'd transshipped through Turkey, joining the established Bosnian corridor there, shipped to Croatia, paid his percentage there, and trucked on to the Muslims.

The sale was directly prosecutable in the United States. Justice had therefore caught up with him in Phoenix and kicked in the door of his hotel room to arrest and arraign him in federal court.

So far so good.

Now, Rosenthal had not been much intimidated by his arrest, to judge from Bob Stein's attitude. He had grown up, Dee knew, in Brooklyn when Brooklyn was a scary place; put himself through Brooklyn College and then Yale Law on scholarships and his own work, and that was

132 *Neil Gordon*

after running away at seventeen to join the Israeli army. To Rosenthal, his arrest was business as usual, and Dee's experience tended to agree: white-collar prosecution was 99 percent selective, and the arms trade, after all, was the ultimate business of suits. Dee had seen it over and over again while he worked for Walsh: businessmen push the envelope, every now and again the Justice Department decides to set an example, lawyers make rain, assets are exchanged, and maybe, if the government's feeling vindictive, the businessman serves a little minimum-security time in a salad-bar jail. That these particular businessmen brokered lethal armaments rather than, say, commodity futures or real estate did not alter the legal principle.

So what was wrong? Murders had occurred in other investigations of this sort. Amiram Nir, John Tower, Robert Maxwell, Gerald Bull: suspicious accidental deaths and outright assassinations, Dee knew, were frequent backstories to this kind of investigation. That Israel was involved made it only more believable: "Nothing is implausible," Dee remembered the CEO of an American military contractor saying to him, "for the Israelis." Nor were only players killed: Danny Casolaro, Jonathan Moyle, Linda Frazier, all journalists, all dead. The murder itself was not the issue.

The problem was that no one in government knew what Dee and Allison knew: that Dymitryck's bruises did not come from his murder, but from his beating on the island by Rosenthal's minions. And, therefore, no one knew that in fact his murder was much more likely to do with the Rosenthal affair than with Harlanstrasse 14.

And that changed everything. It changed the issue not only of the murder, but of the entire Rosenthal prosecution.

It put the whole thing into the arena of, say, the Inslaw affair, in which many respectable people claimed that Danny Casolaro, an investigative journalist, had been murdered while looking into the Justice Department's role in the intelligence usage of the Promis computer databasing program. Israelis, Dee reminded himself, were involved in that, too.

Shifting to the window again, Dee shook off the thought. Inslaw was that vast area of parapolitics, conspiracy theory, the Octopus: no one knew if—or rather, how much of—that stuff was true. What he had before him, however, were facts.

First: Nicky Dymitryck had searched Rosenthal's house, and had the shit kicked out of him for his efforts.

Second: that had not stopped him from saving, as Dee had witnessed, both pictures and computer files taken from the house.

What were they? There was no way to know. All he could know was, third, that in Ronald Rosenthal's house, Dymitryck had found something that seriously upped the ante. Seriously enough to have him beaten up. Seriously enough, no matter what the papers reported or the Congress believed, to have him killed.

For a long time, David Dennis's mind skated over this terrain, unable to find purchase for the feeling of suspicion that animated it.

Then, like a bolt shooting into its housing, he found what he was looking for.

It was subtle, but it was true, and it could be expressed in two sentences.

One: that in this trial being prosecuted in open courts, with full disclosure by the government to the press of their motives and evidence, Nicky Dymitryck had still seen fit to come snooping for material.

Two: this short man from an obscure publication in Los Angeles, however, represented a threat worthy of Ronald Rosenthal's having him killed.

Conclusion? That there was something involved in this case that Dee Dennis was not being told.

The waters of New York Harbor, far below, went out of focus in Dee Dennis's eyes. And it was not until many minutes later that his eyes focused again.

Alley had said she lived on Jane Street, above a bar called the Corner Bistro. With the first feeling of resolution he had felt since the night before, he decided that he must go there tomorrow night when—very late, he had no doubt—he got away from the office.

6.

Tuesday morning, in one marathon session, Allison and Martha finished the inventory: the living room furniture, the contents of the garage and carport. They packed Allison's clothes and loaded the car, then went through the house one last time, Martha making sure never to leave Allison alone. Then, following Martha's Land Cruiser, Alley piloted her father's Cherokee for the last time up the road from Ocean View.

Waiting for the ferry, they ate lobster at the Black Dog with two bottles of an '82 Mouton Rothschild from Allison's father's cellar: even though she'd removed and buried next to the pond some of the finest brandies and ports, a fantastic cellar was being sacrificed to the federal government. Then they went, somewhat unsteadily, to load their cars.

On the ferry Martha went off in search of beer while Allison, on deck, watched the houses of Vineyard Haven draw surely away into the nascent September light, heavy, saturated not only with color but with the annual pathos of leave-taking, of the end of the kind season.

It was the twenty-seventh time she had taken part in this ceremony of loss.

Only this time, she watched with none of the assurance that the cold lurking in the depth of the wind was transient, that the benign season would come again.

And then she began, suddenly, to cry: alone on the cold metal of the ferry's deck, just softly, just slightly, and just for a second. A child's grief, at separation, at loss, at the steady, slow, and remorseless way that the water was carrying her away.

Like Pauly had cried, a child, when, on the first day of their new school at St. Ann's, Allison and he had been forced to separate into their separate crowd of sneakered and T-shirted strangers, Pauly bewildered and scared in his long, untucked white shirt and *kipah*, Allison curious and ashamed in her long woolen skirt ending above black pumps. Then, too, it had been an authority, implacable and undeniable, that was separating them. She cried only briefly, but in those two or three brief tears, everything was: Pauly, Ocean View, her mother, her grandparents—dogs and cats and toys and vistas and afternoons long gone, things and times that had not been visitable for years. Rarely were these things present to her so vividly; rarely was the great divide between her present and the time when Pauly was alive so vividly breached. But now, watching Vineyard Haven disappear into the blind of harbor light with all the broken promise of summer, was such a time, and she let the cold wind snatch one, two, three hot tears from under her eyes before, inhaling a great sniff, turning away.

Late the night before, she had been woken by the telephone and, lifting it, heard the distant hum of long distance.

Dee? Dee should know not to call her here, she had thought. Nonetheless, her hopes soaring, Allison listened, and after a series of clicks a voice came through, not Dee's, she perceived slowly, but her father's.

"Esther, *ma shlomech*? I've been calling you every day in New York. What are you doing on-island? Hasn't school started?"

Heart sinking, she forced herself to answer. "Tomorrow, Daddy. I needed to clean up. How are you?"

"I'm okay, my darling. I'm okay. Are you okay?"

"I'm okay."

"The checks getting to you?"

"Yes, Daddy."

"Good. This stupid charade of theirs. You taking heat, doll?"

"No. A couple reporters. Bill Dykeman asked me not to come in."

"I'm not guilty of anything, my doll. Remember that."

Listening, she stared into the fire. Then she spoke without thinking.

"Is that right? Then tell me something."

"Of course, my doll. What's up?"

She imagined him at Falcon's Hamalekh Shaul office in Tel Aviv.

"What's up with this Nicky Dymitryck?"

There was a long pause. Then he said, softly, "Who's that, sweetheart."

It was a statement, not a question, and its message was to be quiet on the telephone. For a moment she struggled, trying to find a way to communicate around the possibility of a phone tap. Then, suddenly, she didn't care.

"Daddy, damn it, don't be coy with me."

But the speed with which Rosenthal changed courses was typical.

"Oh, him? He's that little shithead works for that anti-Semitic rag out West."

"Daddy, the *North American Review*'s editor is a Jew."

"Yeah, right." Her father's voice was careful now, filled with warning. "Doesn't make him any less anti-Semitic or anti-Zionist, Essie."

She struggled for a moment with her reply, and then blurted out: "Well, maybe we can have them stabbed in an airport bathroom too."

"Darling, I don't know what in God's name you're

talking about. Next time I call, try to be a little less hysterical."

And then the line went dead, leaving her, once again, enraged.

Now, hugging herself against the chill wind on the ferry, sniffing, she thought: my father. My father. Like a singsong, the word went through her head. Their conversation, she thought, was a tiny blemish on her father's day. Right now he was probably talking to three members of Knesset, entirely disregarding the fact that he was about to be convicted of federal charges. Her father would probably react to this conversation by telling Bob Stein to tell his secretary to send her some money, and in a few days another one of his checks for $4,345.16 would arrive in the mail.

Anxiety was flooding her body again, as if the wind were chilling her blood. What had Nicky been looking for? What could he possibly have found that was important enough to have him killed? What was her father hiding? What was the role of Greg Eastbrook in this?

And then Martha was back from the commissary, carrying two tall cans of Heineken, her voice, her warm, familiar voice, as if taking the chill from the remorseless, oracular wind.

Midnight. The Corner Bistro. Allison, at the bar, drinking a second bourbon, the liquor dulling the dullness in her mind, the hourless memory of road passing under her wheels. She had parked at the hydrant in front of the house, rung her next-door neighbor Chris's bell; he and his boyfriend had helped her unload her Canondale and Pauly's Bianchi, the things from Ocean View. Chris had invited her in, she had declined, climbed again into the cab of the Cherokee and gone around the corner to the parking garage on Eighth. Then, her sandy sneakers incongruous against the concrete pavement, she'd gone to the bar to let bourbon dull the dullness that was in her mind.

Perhaps it was a mistake. The small bar crowded, lousy with men, loud with the good jukebox. Both the men on either side of her had felt they had license to talk to her. One was okay, a calm, Jewish guy with a shock of white in his full head of hair. She knew him slightly from the neighborhood, he did not offer her a drink, and she was happy to talk, a little. The other did offer her a drink, was frankly hitting on her, and she had to keep him at bay by talking to the first. But then a woman came to meet the first man; they moved to a table, and she was forced, finally, to acknowledge the second with a direct look.

"Listen. I'm sorry. I'm very tired, and I'd rather be left alone." She kept her voice down, which the man seemed to appreciate. Still, his face showed bitterly wounded pride. And then she was alone, wondering how deep an injury it had been for that man, her unwillingness to be hit on. She thought, what a strange fragile kind of pride men carried. Everyone had to present a face to reality, she thought, but men had it hardest: they were allowed so few of the buffers that women used, and what was understandable reserve in a woman was touchiness and mood in a man. That they had, she thought, such a shallow well of rage, so immediate to erupt, made sense.

And then Dee walked in, swinging the door open hard in a breeze of cold air, and against the lamplit night she saw his form develop like a photo in a tray of chemicals.

His hands under her jacket, along the small of her back, her warm sweater against his palms. Before him the promise of her breasts, rounding against the jacket; the rise of her neck under her chin, her face, her wondering face framed by a fall of blond hair. He noticed her eyes, dark and large in the dimness of the bar. Her lips, open, the tip of her tongue visible between her teeth, her lips widening with wonder, into a smile. He stepped back, his face telling her without telling her that they must be circumspect. Smiling, she lifted her drink, and for the first time he felt the illicit nature of his attraction, the secrecy of their union, and it ran electric through his limbs, to his hands. And she, as if the eyes were indeed the window to the soul, seemed to absorb all that he was thinking, and moved away from him in the noise of the bar, turned to her drink and, in profile now, downed it in two careful sips, then replaced her shot glass and downed the chaser.

He felt the distance between the bar and her apartment as a brief instant of chill, then climbed the stairs in something like a trance: far were the trial and his bosses, far were her father and his companies. Inside her apartment she turned at the door, slamming it behind him with a shove that made the windows shake in their housing, and he saw her bags and boxes and two bicycles on the small expanse of floor in front of a desk; he saw a bedroom on the left, a kitchen behind her. And then he saw that she was removing, one by one, her jacket, then her sweater, then her bra; her sneakers, then her pants, then her underwear. Perfectly aware, perfectly naked, and perfectly exposed; a naked being, a spirit, and then she was warm, warm and round, through the cold sheen of his clothes, holding him hard while everything in his body leant to her, trying to touch.

CHAPTER 8

September 1994.
New York City.

1.

It was not an Indian summer, exactly. More an elaborately staged descent into fall, each remaining day of September like another wine in a series of increasingly rare vintages, each complecting, elaborating, the one that came before.

That first night she told him what she had devised. He was to arrive at the Corner Bistro around nine. If she was not there, he was to leave. If she was, he was to wait until, after she left, Bobby—the bartender and Allison's close friend—ushered him through the kitchen to the interior staircase, which led up to Allison's third-floor apartment.

Like that, they spent nearly every evening, and every night, of that slowly evolving autumn, in her apartment, together.

That was good, because New York City had become a very isolated place for Allison.

She hadn't expected so many people to be interested in her father's trial. Certainly she hadn't expected so many to care. And the degree to which it mattered surprised her. At school, the rare occasions she went, people avoided her; professors looked uncomfortable when she seated herself for class.

For herself, she hadn't really minded. Martha's job at the *Observer* was not one that required any particular moral rectitude, and they met often: afternoons at downtown bars, evenings when Dee was busy, weekends at Martha's mother's place in Amagansett.

For Dee, however, that attention was the central experience of his autumn, and would probably continue to be for some time.

When, after a few weeks, not only had no mention been made of Dymitryck's death but the FBI had failed, day after day, to approach Dee on the subject of why he had been photographed by Dymitryck visiting the summer house of the man he had been prosecuting, Dee began to relax. Clearly, Dymitryck had either not photographed him, or the film was lost, or both.

Of course this meant, it occurred to him, that he could have left the case after all. That was regrettable. And yet, Dee was honest enough to ask himself, how regrettable was that, really? He was prepared to give up the case in order to keep Allison, but what if he could, after all, keep Allison without giving up what was shaping up to be the opening to the greatest possibilities his chosen profession had to offer?

Allison couldn't really blame him. The attention he was receiving was immense. Already his lunches were booked weeks ahead: the Century Club, the Harvard Club, the Knickerbocker. It was instructive, Allison felt, to witness the way Dee rose, as he had been taught, to the challenge: he worked through dinner nearly every night, showing up at the Corner Bistro only at nine, and even at her apartment, after making love, he sometimes worked till dawn. Sleep or no, each day he left immaculately tailored and groomed: friendly, handsome, and on the surface, relaxed.

Allison couldn't really blame him. And had she, that blame would have been tempered by the evolution of Dee's mood, as the autumn progressed.

Because slowly, she came to see, he was turning into something further and further from the confident, easy, handsome young man who went each day to be groomed at work, and lunch, and dinner.

Slowly, as that September progressed toward the trial's opening day, she saw him losing his certainty about the trial that everyone was sure he couldn't lose.

There was no smoking gun. There was no scandalous fact that suddenly cast everything in a different light.

There was just a slow process of demoralization, of ever-growing doubt.

That was not a good thing, for Dee to be losing confidence in a trial that he would be arguing on the front pages of every newspaper in the States. A trial that had every chance of going to the Supreme Court.

It was, in fact, a very destructive thing.

For that, Allison knew without quite admitting it to herself, she was responsible.

Or rather, Nicky Dymitryck was.

It started in the single discussion they had concerning Dee's withdrawal from the trial.

Nicky's death, of course had rendered any such way out impossible. Recusal now would put them in every publication in the country, from the *Wall Street Journal* to *People:* young lovers in the liberal elite, no editor could refuse that. Early on she had understood that Nicky's death had made Dee's planned recusal impossible, and now it was too late.

When, therefore, the first night they spent together in New York, Dee suggested leaving the trial whatever the cost, Alley listened, calmly, gravely, lying next to him in the dark. When he finished, she rose, naked, and left the room.

He followed her to where she was sitting, knees to

breasts, at the little Formica table in her kitchen. And when he sat, opposite her, she spoke immediately, her green eyes focused intently.

"Now you listen to me, Dee. You recuse yourself over this now, you ruin your career, you ruin my life, and the one thing you make sure is that you and I will never, in our whole lives, be able to sit together in a restaurant. Meanwhile, your boss replaces you. Right quick, too. And they still convict my father."

"All right." It was as if she were the fast-track lawyer and he were the student who wished, rather than studying the law, to be writing poetry. "And if I don't recuse myself? Then what, Alley? First I put your father in jail. Then, that's all done, we go celebrate at the Bowery Bar. I don't think so."

But Alley had thought far beyond this. "First off, you're not putting my dad in jail. You said yourself, the trial's an exchange of assets. My dad isn't ever coming back to the States."

He interrupted her. "They'll take everything he owns in this country. They'll take Ocean View."

Now her green eyes were full on him, her face grave. "Then we'll just have to go to your aunt Mary's house when we want to go to the island."

"Alley. How the fuck we going to do that?"

"Like this. A week after the trial's over, you and I are going to meet at 120 Wooster. I am going to be with Martha. You are going to walk up to the table and tell me how sorry you were to be instrumental in my father's prosecution. I am going to tell you that I understand you were doing your job. You are going to sit down. And Martha is going to put it in the *Observer* : 'Federal Prosecutor Woos Gun Runner's Daughter.' You with me?"

Staring at her eyes, Dee nodded.

"Three days later we are going to meet at a party and talk to each other at length. Then we are going to go to dinner. Then you are going to come here and take my virginity. And I will give you dimes to dollars that by next summer you can take me up to Aunt Mary's and I'll cook you a ham dinner after church. 'Cause by next summer, no one is going to give a fuck about my dad. You will have closed him down. You with me?"

But Dee was more than with her. "No. I mean yes. But no. You know what's better? Six weeks later I resign my position with the U.S. attorney. And why do I resign it? 'Cause I can't possibly be associated with the office that once prosecuted the father of the woman I now love. It would be unethical. And we're out of here before the ink's dried on the papers."

She was smiling appreciatively. "Deal."

"And what if we fall out of love?"

She shook her head resolutely. "Then it's a handshake and a secret kept between people who remember loving each other as one of the finest moments of their lives. Or some such shit. I'm not going down that road, Dee. I've known you way too long not to trust you."

"Okay."

"Good. Then we're all set if you win. Now tell me this. What if you lose?"

That stopped him for a second. "Lose? Alley, I can't lose."

"No?" There was something nearly cruel, she thought, having made him agree that he could not withdraw from the case, in now bringing up the possibility of losing. But it was a real possibility, after Nicky's death. And it had to be faced. She explained it to him in icy precision.

"Imagine this, Dee: what about when some smart reporter decides to look into what Dymitryck was doing before he was murdered?"

"Alley, that's why I stayed on the damn case."

"Right. But imagine that this particular reporter isn't an idiot. In fact, imagine it's someone pretty smart. Smart enough to see through this bullshit about Dymitryck's death being connected with the Harlanstrasse bombing. Smart enough to wonder what it was Dymitryck found out on the island, about my father, that made him worth killing. And then they start wondering why the U.S. attorney's office hasn't done the same investigation, and asked the same question?"

"No one in my office has even *mentioned* Dymitryck's name in connection with your father."

"Isn't that interesting." She stood now and turned her back to him for an instant while she crossed to the sink, then leaned against it, her naked form unprotected, her green eyes alive. "Isn't that interesting. What do you think it means?"

"I don't know."

"No? I do. Dymitryck had no friends in Washington. As far as anyone's concerned—anyone who counts— Dymitryck's death is a godsend, and they don't care who did it. That's why they haven't investigated."

"Yeah." Dee was following her, she saw, but still, she drove the point home.

"Maybe it'll never happen, Dee. But it could, and if it did, it'd be very bad press. Very bad for a jury, too."

She watched him understanding that. Finally, he spoke. "Okay. What's your point?"

"That there's no such thing as a lock, Deedee. Especially not with the kind of people you're working for. Between their cheating, their idealism, and their incompetence, you say you can't lose, you're kidding yourself."

2.

Even more destructive than undermining his confidence in his case, however, was the degree to which Dee's intimacy with Alley had undermined his assumptions about the person he was prosecuting.

Dee's experience of his work had been so much from the inside that he had not yet had the time to learn who these people he prosecuted actually were. He had not been prepared to learn that the devilish Ronald Rosenthal was also a father, a husband, a person who existed for his daughter with the same ambiguity that he felt toward his own powerful, domineering, ambitious father. Now, as the weeks of that September went by, under Allison's tutelage, he could not ignore that the same complex emotions through which he viewed his father were not so different from those she held toward hers.

Night after night, in her kitchen on Jane Street, pacing between the stove and table, they talked. And as the days mounted closer and closer to the trial, the tenor of their discussions mounted too.

Perhaps more important to the gradual dissolving of Dee's confidence in his prosecution was the fact that Dee, like most people who have been raised in privilege, had been around Jews his whole life and yet had managed not to know very much about them.

"That's bullshit, Dee," Allison was saying now. "The trial's not about the Arms Export Control Act, for God's sake. You go in there talking about that, they'll crucify you. No one's going to deny that my father's prosecutable, that's a given. They're going to make the case from the jump—and they're going to make it not in court, but in the press—that this is a witch hunt. They're going to call it 'business terrorism.' They're going to say my father's being prosecuted to keep a government program deniable. That's going to make him sound human, and a lot of people are sympathetic to that kind of talk."

"Juries follow the law, Alley."

"Oh nonsense. White-collar prosecution is overwhelmingly selective, you know that. How the hell are you going to justify the government going after my father when the damned administration's taking every arms export limitation they can off the books to facilitate foreign trade?"

"I don't need to justify it. I just need to show he broke the law. I show that, Stein loses their sympathy, no matter what heartrending stories he has to tell."

"Do you?" And now Alley stopped pacing, paused by the kitchen window and stood staring out. Then, crossing to the table and sitting in front of him, she began to talk, as if simply unable to stop herself.

"I *see* him, Dee. His name's Yossi Nehanyu. I see him so *clearly*. He's got a factory outside Tel Aviv, makes bomb casings, the motherfucker. He led my father into Iran-contra like a cow with a ring in its nose. Made him believe it was patriotic, for God's sake. You have no idea how innocent people can be when it comes to Israel. You come with me to Brooklyn, I'll show you God-fearing, Orthodox Jews who've torched their own factories and broken unions to save a few dollars, but you mention Jerusalem and their eyes mist over. Nothing could have happened without Nehanyu, and I swear to you, Dee, nothing Nehanyu did could have happened without high-level, U.S. permission—nothing. Every one of his orders came straight out of the NSC staff during Iran-contra, and every one of them came out of the White House for Bosnia: one after the other after the other."

"So what?" Dee asked curiously, a real request for information.

"So imagine Bob Stein telling a jury that. Imagine Bob Stein asking a jury what the fuck is the government of the United States doing now? It's a vendetta. Your Walsh put one person in minimum-security prison for a few months. But my father's going to lose everything he owns. What for? You know, I know, that someone sanctioned Falcon. Fucking Greg Eastbrook sanctioned cocaine traffic into this country to pay for contra arms. But in two months, dimes'll get you dollars, he goes to the

U.S. Senate. You say what you want, but the fact of the matter remains that Greg Eastbrook's spending the next six years of Sundays in an Episcopalian church while Ronald Aaron Rosenthal is exiled from the country."

"Your father's a criminal, Alley. This isn't about being Jewish. It's about a crime."

"Oh yeah? You prepared to ask your father that?"

Dee's answer to this was silence.

And in that silence was a reflection that, for Dee, was very hard to make: that Ronald Rosenthal, seen through Alley's eyes, was not all that different from Dee's own father. Dee's father, too, did harsh and duplicitous things in his job; Dee's father, too, thought these things were in the service of something other than himself. The fundraising, the virtual marketing of access to the president in return for soft, unregulated dollars: it was a necessary evil, given the pioneering work in this field the GOP had done with Reagan and Bush. The cold, harsh calculations on health-care and welfare reform, Dee knew, the petty retreats on everything from Haiti to gay rights in the military, it all went against everything his father believed. "You have to keep your eye on the prize, Deedee," his father liked to say. "People like us, it's our job to focus on the greater good."

The greater good. Night after night in her bed, staring into the blackness above their faces, Alley made him understand that her father, too, thought that he worked for a greater good. His own father, Alley's grandfather, had spent five years in Dachau, from the age of thirteen to eighteen. Ronald Rosenthal had been born in a refugee camp in Italy, while his parents, the only two survivors from a little town in Lithuania, had grown up under the shadow of the Holocaust in a neighborhood of Brooklyn that held legions of battered, scarred people, passing their lives without any doubt as to what people were willing, and able, to do to one another. When, at thirteen or fourteen, Rosenthal had met his first Israeli, the experience was, to the street-smart, embattled Brooklyn boy, revolutionary.

Whispering into the dark of her bedroom, naked beside him, Alley told Dee about it. "You have to understand. My grandfather, he didn't set foot out of Borough Park for the first ten years he was in the States. Then he ventured as far as downtown Brooklyn, because he opened a store on Jay Street."

"But why?" Staring up, trying to imagine this world that he had never even dreamed existed, Dee whispered too. "He was safe here. Christ sake, Alley, it was U.S. soldiers that rescued him."

"I know. It's not that. I mean, it's not the people. It's the government. God, Dee, you know that denazification was a farce. Those bastards were putting Nazis right back in power from Bonn to Buenos Aires. They were rearming Germany! People like my granddad, they couldn't believe it. But it was also other people. This country's always had a vicious strain of anti-Semitism. My dad got his first broken bone at ten: he and his friends were jumped by an Irish gang on their way out of yeshiva. By thirteen, he was in gang fights every weekend."

But Dee still didn't see it. "Alley, my grandfather used to have lunch with Felix Warburg once a week. There were Jews in every firm on Wall Street, every bank in the country, and every department of the government. I've had Jewish friends and girlfriends from Exeter to Cornell to Harvard, and colleagues as long as I've been working."

"Right. In the schools. And at the jobs. But not in the clubs. Not at the Nisi Prius luncheons. You've been around Jews your whole life, right? Forgive me, but can you tell me when Rosh Hashanah is? Not the month even: just the season. Can you? You see, there's a difference between tolerated and accepted, Dee. Borough Park was a long way from Wall Street. You don't understand that, then you don't know a thing about people."

But Dee did know a thing about people. Dee knew more than a thing about what people were prepared to do to each other. During the war, his grandfather had worked for John J. McCloy on the internment of Japanese-Americans, one hundred thousand of them, forced into primitive camps for the duration. And lying there, Alley's quiet voice traveling from her lips to his ear, the air around them not a separation but a conduit, skin to skin, he knew she was right.

3.

That he knew made him all the more ready to listen when she asked him, suddenly, the most important question that lay between them:

"Dee. Why are they after my father?"

For a time, there was silence. Then Dee:

"I don't know. Do you?"

She shook her head against the pillow.

"No."

He licked his lips before he spoke again. "I mean, it's a valid process, Alley, setting the parameters of a law's interpretation."

Watching him. "Okay, it's valid. It's a shame they chose my dad. But that's not it, is it?"

He admitted it. "No."

Now she raised herself on her elbows to look him in the face. "Dee?"

He changed his focus to her now, as if unwillingly. "Yes?"

"Why don't you know?"

Another silence. Then he spoke hesitantly. "Alley, you said it yourself. These guys don't care that Dymitryck was killed."

"So?"

"So think about it. We've got a prosecution of a man who was clearly sanctioned in his crime. I mean, I accept that it's a valid legal process to try your father, but let's be honest: if Dymitryck hadn't brought the Bosnian sales to public attention, your dad would have been doing his business with tacit government approval. Right?"

Nodding slowly, she agreed. "So what?"

"Now, not only is that all true, but now the guy responsible for the prosecution even starting has been killed, but they don't want to admit there's any connection."

Again, she nodded, waiting.

But Dee was done. "There's something wrong here, Alley. These guys better be damn smart to be sure it doesn't blow up in their faces."

"They're smart."

"Oh yeah? Have you been reading the papers the past two years?"

"Of course."

"Then what the hell makes you think they're so smart?" His voice was rising now, and Alley recognized that she was hearing something that had been thought out clearly, but never before articulated.

"There's something wrong. The prosecution of your father—it's too vindictive, for one thing. And it's too aggressive. People who are . . . sure of themselves, they're not this aggressive. You know? It's like they're trying to rush the thing through while they can."

"Is it midterm?"

"The elections? That's what my father says. They need good press on this before the elections. They're afraid of losing Congress."

"You don't believe it?"

He shook his head. "I don't think so. I mean, I'm sure Clinton wants to come off like he's the Bosnian embargo's biggest champion, and all that crap. And I'm sure these guys are scared as hell at the prospect of a Republican Congress. But that's not enough to justify this charade. Can I ask you something?"

"Um-hmm." Their faces were inches apart.

"What do you think that guy from the *NAR* was looking for?"

That was not what she had been expecting. She turned away, showing him her neck.

"I don't know."

But then, as if honesty demanded it, she spoke again. "I took a look at the *NAR* last week at the NYU library. You know their biggest concern?"

"Uh-uh."

"Iraq. The arming of Iraq, before the Gulf War. They say there were extensive CIA-supported operations to sell arms and technology to Hussein. They say the Iraqi tilt was coordinated out of the NSC by Greg Eastbrook. You believe that?"

This interested him, clearly. She watched him think, and then answer in a considered voice. The voice, she thought, of his profession.

"Yes. I mean, sales to Hussein were commonplace. Everyone was doing it: Germany, Switzerland, Belgium. Dozens of American companies. *U.S. v. Teledyne* is a big precedent, so I've looked at it. But the relevant issues are pretty straightforward."

"What was it about?"

"Well, Teledyne was an American company, indicted on charges of supplying zirconium for the manufacture of cluster bombs to a Chilean company. Carlos Cardoen. He then sold the bombs, as well as a considerable array of armaments—helicopters to chemical warfare components—to Iraq. The U.S. indicted him, too, but he was abroad."

Alley watched with considerable interest now. "Sounds pretty familiar, doesn't it?"

"Oh yeah. It's a very relevant precedent. Teledyne's prosecution was a real surprise too. It was a real surprise that Teledyne or Cardoen was targeted. And then, theirs was the first time your father's defense was attempted."

"Meaning?"

"Meaning the defense that an illegal arms sale was part of a covert U.S. government program. Teledyne—and Cardoen—documented CIA and embassy knowledge of the entire operation. And they had valid end-user documents—nearly valid, anyway. So the defense was that they were unprosecutable in that they had received a nod from the administration."

"Did it come to trial?"

Dee shook his head. "No. Teledyne settled. They paid out nearly twenty million on that charge alone. I would have wanted to see it come to trial. Shelby Highsmith was on the bench, and pretrial rulings said pretty clearly that tacit government approval did not excuse illegal activity. There was considerable plausible deniability on the part of Commerce, anyway, who approved the export licenses. It would have gone to the Supreme Court, no question. I would have wanted to see it tried. In fact, I'd go further: if the government had really wanted to see the constitutional issues addressed, it would never have accepted the plea."

She was silent for a while. Then she said, carefully, avoiding using Nicky Dymitryck's name: "If the *NAR* was interested in Greg Eastbrook, why would they come after my dad?"

"I don't know. Think your dad was involved with Iraq?"

"I don't know." She paused. Then: "You ever hear of the Doctrine of the Periphery?"

"Uh-uh."

"It was Ben-Gurion's. It says Israel has to arm a periphery of allies surrounding its enemies. Iran, Turkey. Maybe it includes Iraq."

Dee shook his head. "Not after Iran-contra. Don't forget where I've been working the past five years, Alley. I know all about this stuff. Israel was a historic supplier of the Shah, and they went on arming Iran covertly after the revolution, partly to help them in the war against Iraq. Hussein dumped Scuds on Tel Aviv in the Gulf War. He'd have had the nerve to put chemicals in those warheads, he'd have slaughtered thousands of Jews, just like he slaughtered thousands of Kurds—only, someone would have given a damn about Jews getting killed. They say Cardoen was supplying him with FAE technology. Fuel air explosive. Bombs that spread a cloud of gaseous fuel, then ignite. One blast can be miles wide—cover a city like Tel Aviv."

"Yeah, and then they have a nuclear response on their hands. No question, Dee."

"Right, right. Nonetheless. I don't see Israel turning a blind eye to sales to Iraq."

"Um-hmm. The Doctrine of the Periphery's always been pretty profitable, though. I wouldn't think ideology would get in the way of money. I mean, the governing principle of that kind of commerce is arm them, then bomb them before they can use the weapons, but after they've paid. It's win-win: you make money arming them, you make money bombing them, then you make money arming them again. Right?"

"Uh-huh," Dee agreed. Then: "You know, there was a journalist killed in that one, too. Jonathan Moyle, a Brit, investigating Cardoen's helicopter production. Sedated, then hung by the neck in a Chilean hotel."

Silence again, as they thought, each alone. When Alley spoke again, it was hesitantly.

"Dee. If there's no trial precedent for my dad's technique, then he might win?"

He turned away, and when he spoke, it was with a different kind of passion.

"No. Not if the prosecution's handled right."

She heard doubt in his voice. "Will it be?"

"But that's my point. That's what I'm scared about. It's that"—he turned away, as if unwilling to go on and unable to stop—"that they've screwed up so much. Vince Foster. Whitewater. The health-care bill. It's as if they're willing to . . . stick their necks out too damn far. For a principle. Like some kind of damn social activists. And they don't understand. They aren't masters of their own party, never mind ready to go out and fight. We've just had a twelve-year administration move out. They're fucking beginners."

She was quiet, thinking, for a long time, so long that he asked her what it was. And she answered, hesitantly: "They *were* beginners, you mean. Two years ago, when they hatched this thing. The problem is, if they really don't have the will for this prosecution, they're not going to come out and say that. They're going to let you say it for them. By losing."

Before her eyes, he turned his face to the ceiling, then shook his head.

"I don't believe it. They're still the government of the United States. It's my own father, Alley."

But even as he said it, Alley was hearing something else.

She was hearing doubt that had come from her, and that was not going away but, to the contrary, was growing with each night of talk.

It was, she thought guiltily, unfair, what she was doing to Dee.

To the man she loved.

Comparisons, Allison knew, should never be made between people.

Especially between a living person trying to find his best way through real quandaries and a dead one, frozen forever in his idealism.

Dee was taller, stronger, handsomer, and in every way more successful than the man she had met at the Ritz.

And still, watching Dee, that fall, trying to find a middle ground through the manifold and, often, contradictory demands of the people around him, Allison could not help wondering what Nicky would have done.

4.

The evening after this last conversation with Allison, Dee Dennis had finished work early, at 7:30. Finished his assigned work, at least. But he did not go to Alley. Instead, he left his office in his shirtsleeves, and went down the interior stairs to the library.

So deeply, in fact, had Dee Dennis come to doubt the government's case against Ronald Rosenthal that he had decided to ask some questions.

Tonight, Dee Dennis had decided, he was going to do a little research.

The U.S. attorney's library, which also served as a conference room, was about the only room in the office suite that could rival a corporate law firm: lushly carpeted chambers lined with oak shelves and containing a fold-out wet bar. A few workstations running Nexis were available here, and one long table filled the center of the main room, while a suite of smaller rooms to the side housed the bulk of the library in metal stacks.

Dee, at 7:30, found the library deserted. He started by consulting the small card catalog, then made his way to the stacks and emerged with the past five years of the quarterly *North American Review* in his hands.

Immediately he saw that the arms trade was one of the foci of the journal: each issue included, in what Dee's magazine friends called the front-of-book, a column called "Arms Watch," written by none other than Dymitryck. The hook, he saw quickly, was that much of the column contained material that no major newspaper would cover: innuendo, rumor, unsourced reports. Clearly the *NAR* was daring one of the column's subjects to sue; clearly—most of the names mentioned in the column, in and out of the government, were familiar to Dee—none was going to, for the information, Dee could see, was very good.

Alley had spoken about Greg Eastbrook, and his name, indeed, was frequently present. Dee knew all about Eastbrook, the one major Iran-contra player Walsh had declined to prosecute: his role was far too murky. Most people didn't even know about his involvement, very behind-the-scenes support for his boss and fellow marine, Colonel North. But the *NAR*, clearly, had committed itself to documenting that role: article after article, all Dymitryck's, were devoted to him.

Dee considered this for a long time. And then, as if on cue, a recollection of last night's conversation with Allison came to mind. Turning back to the stack of journals, drink in one hand and cigar in his teeth, he saw immediately that, indeed, by far most of the recent issues were largely devoted to an examination of the U.S. role in arming Hussein prior to the invasion of Kuwait.

With a sigh, Dee turned away. That explained nothing: no one had ever accused the Israelis of arming Iraq. And Rosenthal's rise to fame, to the contrary, had been for his role in the arming of Hussein's mortal enemies in Iran.

Fine. Dee rose and returned to the window, standing with his drink, staring down at the harbor as if over a puzzle.

It made no sense. Dymitryck was interested in Greg Eastbrook, particularly in Eastbrook's role in the U.S. tilt toward Iraq. Rosenthal was involved in exactly the other side of that fight. Yet Dymitryck had come to search for something about Eastbrook in Rosenthal's house. It made no sense.

He said as much to Alley, that night, lying in the darkness of her bedroom on Jane Street. He said as much, and she listened, and quietly they talked it over until, after midnight passed, Dee fell into sleep.

This night, however, Alley stayed awake, listening to her lover breathe, thinking.

Iraq. Eastbrook. What did this have to do with her father?

Lying in bed, for a long time she let her mind play over the question. Her father had done business with Greg Eastbrook, she knew that: she had even met him. And his was the name that had so infuriated her father the one time Pauly had used it.

Pauly had known a lot more about her father's business than she had. It was as if, after her mother left, she had been tied to her father by their shared loss. But Pauly had been his mother's son, and he had taken every chance he could to learn about the things that the Falcon Corporation and Rosenthal Equities did, inside and outside the law. Pauly would have known. She wished she could ask him.

Nicky would have known, also. And not for the first time, bitterly, she regretted his death.

When she calmed, somewhat, she turned her mind to the fact that there was one other way to learn, and as she thought that, her heart quickened to the point where she knew she would not be sleeping for many hours yet, that night.

She rose, slipped on gym shorts and a T-shirt, and, quietly shutting the door to the living room, took her Canondale racing bike from the closet and began carefully to clean and oil it.

She was going, she knew without admitting it to herself, to take a bike ride the next day to Borough Park.

CHAPTER 9

September 30, 1994.
Brooklyn.

1.

Cristo ama te. So said the bumper sticker on a gypsy cab, fishtailing from the right lane of Court Street in Cobble Hill through blaring cars, then in front of her skidding bicycle and left around the corner onto Union, radio blaring: *Cristo ama te.*

Alley followed it in a tight turn and then for a time down the street as it bounced on its springs along Union, musing on the sentiment. On balance, she thought it unlikely. When the cab slowed at the Gowanus drawbridge, she coasted easily past it to the gate, then circled slowly while she waited for a tug to pass on the filthy water.

Now, before her eyes, the vista dizzied: the opened bridge, the canal stretching into Brooklyn's industrial graveyard, the pastel blue of the autumn sky, the street of low industrial plants, then the sky again, a silver airplane in descent toward Kennedy glinting in the sun. And for the first time since leaving the island, for the briefest moment, perhaps a full revolution of her wheels, she felt happy. Then she lowered her eyes in time to see the taxi driver leering at her, his mouth open, his red tongue lifted to touch his top teeth.

The drawbridge descended, and she wheeled across.

It was a trip no one else in the world would have thought of taking. No one else in the world, after all—not even Bob Stein—knew that Ron Rosenthal still kept his parents' apartment on Forty-ninth Street and Thirteenth Avenue in Borough Park. No one else knew that he kept a set of filing cabinets there, as well as a safe.

Allison knew. She knew because her father had directed her there, years before when he was in some other trouble, to fetch an Israeli passport from one of the filing cabinets. That was the single time she had entered her grandparents' apartment since their deaths.

As for the combination to the safe, not even her father knew that she had that. Not even her father knew of an afternoon she had spent in her grandfather's watch-repair and lock store on what had once been the shopping district on Jay Street, thirteen years old, watching her grandfather while the old man, peering through magnifying glasses, set the combination as the letters of her Hebrew nickname.

And because Allison knew all that, she knew that whatever Nicky was searching for when he broke into the Ocean View farmhouse, he had gone to the wrong place.

If he wanted to know about her father's business, she knew, he should have come here.

2.

The Noor School, Arabic writing, one entrance labeled Boys; another, Girls. Fourth Avenue, Sunset Park, the Pentecostal Meetinghouse, the Iglesia Pentecostal de Jesu Cristo, Inc. Greenwood Cemetery, its turning trees imparting a soft yellow light over the bordering avenue.

She turned left somewhere in the Forties, her breath coming fast and easy, took the long uphill out of Sunset Park in a measured acceleration. As she crested the hill, a commercially zoned district appeared. She passed signs for Tallis and Tefillin Beitlach, then Bobov Meats, then Yitzchak's Fish Store, two large Hasids in bloody aprons behind the window. Borough Park. Passing the open door of a used-furniture store, she was assailed by the atmosphere of its interior: the precise smell of her grandparents' apartment, when they were living.

She dismounted on Thirteenth Avenue and walked her bicycle on the sidewalk. Black-garbed men in wide hats and *payess*, wigged women staring with frank appraisal at her skin-tight bicycle pants. Three girls in calf-length plaid skirts and black down jackets came out of the Sara Shenhler Teachers' School, happy and confident. She had ridden nearly ten miles from her apartment now without strain, but at this sudden vision of her onetime self she was, at last, breathless.

Her grandparents had lived here, had insisted on dying here in a tiny apartment on one of the long blocks off the avenue: her grandfather had spent his entire life traveling between this neighborhood and downtown Brooklyn, where he had come to own a watch-repair store. Her father had offered them houses from Long Island to Florida; offered them rooms in his own later homes. Nothing would do for her grandfather but this, the neighborhood they had come to after the war: the soldiers who'd liberated him from Dachau had been eighteen-year-old Italian-Americans from Bay Ridge, and old Mr. Rosenthal had never again considered living anywhere but Brooklyn.

There were two of them, and they had been the old man's only non-Jewish friends in his life, the annual Christmas Day visit to them the only day of his calendar not governed by Torah. She had gone with him when she was young, with her father and Pauly: a long table laden with stuffed artichokes and manicotti, the massive family reclined around it, the children gazing in wonder at the visitors from another world, the parents with bemused pride. These neighborhoods had provided the ground force of the D-Day invasion, and the older men had witnessed horrible atrocity, horrible murder and privation in the European theater that had culminated in their utter stupefaction—eighteen-year-old Brooklyn boys, away for the first time in their lives—before the just-deserted camps, the guards hastily decamped, the phantasmagoric inmates unearthly. Joe Grasso and Peter Corsi, childhood pals from Bay Ridge, had taken Allison's grandfather—one of the few prisoners who could muster the strength to walk—straight to the barbed-wire square where huddled a few miserable captured guards and offered him a gun. Allison's grandfather had held the gun in complete confusion, unable to understand what they wanted him to do. So they did it for him, hard boys, used to death, and from then on, they made it their business to take care of the half-dead Jew.

To Allison, it made sense. The rescue of her grandfather had redeemed the war for the two boys, redeemed the atrocious experience to which they'd been subjected. They'd nursed him back to health, coddling him with food, buying his immigration with cigarettes and favors. They'd gotten him into an Italian refugee camp, which was where he found his wife, one of the other five survivors from the Lithuanian shtetl where he had briefly been a child. Almost immediately, she had become pregnant, and they'd been interned there long enough for her to deliver her baby, Ronald, named after Corsi's recently deceased father. Then the two Italian-Americans succeeded in sponsoring his entry into America. Together, the two had found the couple an apartment, and later Grasso's uncle had provided the down payment for the Jay Street storefront where old Mr. Rosenthal spent the rest of his working life.

Nothing at the Christmas Day dinner could be eaten by the visitors. When her grandfather had died, Allison had stopped seeing the Italian families. The Jay Street storefront was razed for the Metrotech Building, and her father, who had inherited the property, had made a fortune from its sale to the monolithic corporate development.

Only much later, Allison had learned that her father had put both Grasso and Igneri's sons through college at Haverford, paid for each year of tuition, each dorm bill, each book, and each date with a Bryn Mawr girl, then law school in Michigan for one and medical school at Notre Dame for the other, the first professionals the two families from Bari had ever produced, as Rosenthal himself was the first lawyer from his family of tradesmen and shopkeepers.

Near the apartment building, Allison locked her bike to a parking meter with two Kryptonite locks and entered a store on the avenue, the Menashem Bakery. She ordered a spinach knish and a cup of coffee; while waiting for the microwave to heat the knish she read the Xeroxed signs on the wall offering, in Hebrew, Yiddish, and Polish, the guaranteed services of an immigration lawyer, six-week yeshiva-sponsored English lessons, computer courses, and tours to Israel.

While she waited she listened to the Yiddish of two women standing in line for challah—this evening was Erev Shabbat, or Erov Shabbos to these women—discussing the World Trade Center bomber.

"You know why it is? It's because we let anybody into the country."

"We should cut off his fingers! Do like they do!"

With her food and coffee, Alley wandered out onto the sidewalk to eat, but at the first bite her throat closed so effectively that she had to step to a curb garbage can, spit the mouthful out into her napkin, and throw it, with the knish, into the garbage. On reflection, she threw out the watery coffee, too. Then she walked down Forty-ninth Street and entered her grandparents' building.

3.

Everything was the same: the elevator's wood paneling gleaming with lemon-scented polish, the worn red plush velvet with gilt edges along the door. Everything was the same: the corridor with its dim Deco lighting, the muted sound of Chopin from behind a closed door. In the hallway she understood why she had not been able to eat: her throat seemed to have closed, and for a moment she felt suffocation. Only then did she realize how frightened she was. She hurried down the hallway, opened the apartment door with a key, then, as her hand automatically lifted first to her lips, then to the mezuzah, she experienced a moment of real fear.

But everything was different: the dark parquet floors empty, the green papered walls showing the unbleached places where pictures had once hung. Most of the furniture had been removed from this room, and in its place were four walls of legal filing cabinets, the center of the room occupied only by the massive oak dining table that had once been this home's heart.

In this room, she felt slightly calmer: it was too changed to be frightening. But to find the safe meant a full search of the house, and at the thought her heart began to thump. She paused there in the dining room, trying to even her breath. After a time, using real physical strength, she was able to walk across to the sliding doors that closed off the living room, and hesitantly opened one.

Here, muffled light from the shaded windows showed the furniture covered in white fabric, the tables with their lamps, the framed watercolors of long-gone villages and landscapes that her grandmother had liked to buy from a store, owned by a Lithuanian survivor, that specialized in remembering these shtetls, rich and happy places from the time before the war. Oddly, it was a fall of light through the shaded windows that most vividly struck her: the sensation of timelessness in the muffled light, the silent room. Her grandmother would sit just there, at the end of the couch, her brunette wig above her half glasses, her short body curved to the couch's angle. Alley felt her stomach clench at the memory, as if half expecting to see her there. But then the room came back into focus, the covered chairs, the empty couch, and she stepped hesitantly into the sunny silence.

She turned to the sideboard, her eyes finding exactly the little painting of the Jaffa Gate, the framed *ketubah*— marriage license—witnessed by Joe Grasso and Peter Corsi, hanging in the musty, foreign smell, as if suspended in time. She retreated into the dining room again and rested, as if from an exertion. Finally, slowly, she closed the sliding doors. Nothing, she thought, could be worse than that. And as if liberated by the thought, she went down the hallway, the remembrance of the apartment returning to her with a reminiscence of queasiness in her stomach. The bathroom with its light blue ceramic tile, a phantom smell of soap. The bedroom, a heavy oak bedstead, mattress covered in plastic. At the end, in shadow from the hallway light, was the linen closet. When she opened the door, it let forth the faintest suspicion of her grandmother's perfume, the lightest hint, but enough to bring a swoon through her. She crouched on the floor, eyes shut tight, balancing herself with one hand on the doorknob. No. She was wrong. Nothing could be harder than this.

When she opened her eyes she found herself staring at the squat black safe. And without a pause, she put forth a hand to turn its combination.

❧

Before her eyes now was the day, so long ago, she had learned it. She'd been visiting her grandfather at lunch hour from St. Ann's in his downtown watch shop, and he had made her memorize it against the possibility of his memory failing. It had been easy to retain: the old man had customized the lock and set it himself, the consonants of her Hebrew name, Tziporah: he never had mastered English well, but he was fluent in Hebrew, Yiddish, Russian, and Lithuanian. Later, when her father had started using the safe, her grandfather had been too far gone to remember that she also had the combination, and then he died. She remembered him now, his capacious linguist's mind, his dry hand, callused with age and work, caressing her face that day as he watched her with swimming eyes, saying, as he always did, in the Hebrew or Yiddish in which he spoke to her: "Esther. Hadassah. The girl who saved the Jews."

The last tumbler fell on the "hay" of Tziporah and, hesitantly, she swung the door open, then reached a hand inside. It was surprisingly full: a large amount of various currencies in stacks tied by rubber bands. Next she felt something hard, and removed an object that, with a shock, she found to be a large nickel-plated handgun with two extra magazines held against it by a rubber band. Now she leaned down to the floor to peek in, and saw that the remaining contents were manila files. These she removed and put on the hallway floor.

Still crouching, she paused for breath. Looking up, and down the hallway. She was very frightened, she knew. But, she thought, only a fool would expect to be calm.

The thought was some comfort. She began to look at the first page of each manila file as she leafed clumsily through them. There were letters of incorporation for each entity in the sprawling Rosenthal Equities. There were letters of reference, some bearing the letterhead of U.S. government agencies, some military, and many Israeli. There were personal letters, on the stationery of figures like John Singlaub, Amiram Nir, Ahmed Omshei, Robert Gates, David Kimche, Earl Brian—many, many such names. There were six end-user certificates from six countries, some filled out for a wide variety of matériel, some simply signed, and some blank. And then there were documents with no letterhead at all, some in files containing photographs and accompanied by notes from her father, others containing notarized and witnessed documents.

Another pause for breath. She concentrated her attention on these last documents. Most of them detailed small weapons sales, largely to substate entities, which she assumed made them illegal. Some of them included the use to which the weapons had been put. Each was referenced by departments of governments, U.S. or Israeli. Where possible, her father appeared to have obtained signatures from the participants as well as what lawyers called "memorialization" in the form of photographs. Where this had evidently not been possible, there were his own handwritten accounts.

Allison nodded to herself. If MBAs were ever taught the covert arms business, Alley thought, they would learn to keep such records. Clearly, however, he had not yet had the chance to assemble the paperwork on his Bosnian dealings: nothing in the safe referred to them. That meant that there was no clue as to Nicky's death in there.

The thought, casually come, made a sudden nausea rise in her again. Once she had spent long afternoons playing with her grandparents. Now she was a person looking for a clue to a murder. She breathed deeply, three times, four times. Then she went back again through the documents with a slow, mechanical movement. However it happened, she thought with sudden impatience, this is who I now am.

This time, halfway through, her eye was caught by a Hebrew document.

Reading, she saw it was the transcript of an interview.

The interviewer was Nicholson Dymitryck, the interviewee Dov Peleg.

The subject was her father, and Greg Eastbrook.

Pictures, clearly taken with a surreptitious camera, for they were at floor level, showed the two in a small restaurant.

For a long moment she did nothing. Then, peering closely at the photographs, she saw that Nicky was no younger than he had appeared to her in person. If she could trust the photographs.

What had Nicky been talking to Dov Peleg about Greg Eastbrook for? Scared now, she leafed through the transcript. It ended, and she reached for the next pile of documents, held separate by a rubber band.

Behind it was another transcript, this one in English, and other photographs.

And then the memory came.

Martha had tickets to Patti Smith at the Beacon, they had come home late, seventeen-year-old girls crossing the Brooklyn Bridge in a taxi, stoned. She had left Martha on Monroe Place and wandered down the Heights among the lights of the brownstones. The brief glimpses of ornate interiors, many housing her classmates. Her heels echoing loud and long in the deserted, late-winter streets.

Rounding the corner from Hicks Street to Grace Court, she'd seen that outside her house was a limousine, engine running, parked illegally. There were two men on the street, and one spoke into a radio as she approached. Then, having received a response in an earpiece, he wished her good night. The front door was opened for her by a third man in a dark blue suit, and in the hallway her father was emerging from the living room, shutting the massive door behind him.

"Essie, *manishma? Aich haiya ha concert? Tov meaod.*

Listen"—leaning down to her—"business tonight, doll, I know it's late. Straight up to bed now, okay? No noise, no nonsense. Keep Pauly up there. We'll talk tomorrow." And with a kiss he was gone and she was climbing the stairs, nearly wincing, in her stoned state, under the scrutiny of the blue-suited man, the presence of all these strangers in her house, each bringing on his coat the cold air of winter.

She'd climbed up the steps to the second floor, her father's bedroom and his office; the third floor, her room and Pauly's room; and then to the attic, where, she knew, was Bennie Friedman, and he was, with Dov Peleg, young Israeli men she had known for years, hunched around a reel-to-reel tape recorder and a video monitor, on which the living room played in black and white. None of this was strange: business as usual in her father's house. Nor was she interested in what they were doing: during these taping sessions, she often sat chatting with Dov, on whom she'd had a schoolgirl crush for years.

Tonight, however, was different. Dov, whispering, ushered her in with a smile: "How are you, love? Shh, big business tonight. Come see your dad tell the White House to go to hell."

On the monitor, filmed from an angle above, she saw her father, Michael Levi, and another man at quarter profile from their scalps. The other man was in uniform. Next to each sat a crystal rocks glass and a cigar. And her father was speaking.

"Greg, you're backing me into a corner. You know that."

The uniformed man looked slowly around the room before answering, and Allison glimpsed his face: outsized, handsome, confident. When he spoke, it was with a light Western drawl.

"Ron, the president sees Iraq as our best bet in the region. You know that. Saddam's no idiot. He's not going to use American supplies against Israel."

"He's used chemicals on the Kurds."

A shrug. "Kurds aren't Jews. Halabja isn't Tel Aviv."

Her father drew on his drink. When he spoke again, his tone was still pleasant, conversational, his syllables agreeably clipped with his faint tinge of a Brooklyn accent. "I don't think you'd like this to be exposed, Greg. I don't think you'd like the *New York Times* to publish that a senior naval officer assigned to the NSC staff is facilitating the sale of chemical-ready warheads to Iraq."

The other answered in the same conversational tone. "Ron, forgive me, no one's going to listen to accusations from you."

Her father nodded now, as if Eastbrook had just confirmed something he'd long suspected. It was, Allison thought, like a tennis game, the three of them in the taping room turning their heads in unison to follow serve and volley. "If we can't stop you, we'll have to stop the suppliers."

And now the other laughed. "Why? There's plenty to go around here. You know what'll happen if Hussein gets out of hand? My president will bomb him into the Middle Ages. Then fortunes'll be made resupplying him. Christ sake, Ron, you're killing the golden goose."

But her father wasn't amused.

"You're making a serious mistake, Greg. This isn't about money."

"Oh, come off it. Don't get all Zionist on me, okay?"

With a nod, her father stood up.

"Colonel Eastbrook, I'm speaking now as the direct representative of Prime Minister Shamir. And I am telling you that Mr. Shamir will not stand by while Jews are gassed by Iraqi chemicals. If the United States will not interdict the supply of Iraq, Israel will, and we will do it by any means necessary. Have I made myself clear?"

"Yes, Mr. Rosenthal. You have." As if tiredly, Eastbrook unfolded himself from his chair and turned to the door. Then he turned, and only now, for the first time, did his tone change. "You tell Shamir to do what he has to. But be damn sure that it stays away from me. You hear?"

That was all she remembered, except that when the meeting ended there was soft applause in the little dark room around her, and then Dov pushed her to the door:

"*Yalla*, sleep now. They'll be gone in ten minutes. Your father is a wizard."

Then she was in bed, in the dark of her room, as far below doors closed, and the cars drew off, and, after a long time, she heard Pauly pad to her bedroom, always at a run, and then a long time later her father's quiet step mounting the carpeted stair.

Perhaps this precise memory seems implausibly detailed. The only part of it, however, that she'd had to recall had been the parts that occurred to her alone. As for what had happened between her father and Colonel Eastbrook, that was transcribed word for word on the transcript before her, accompanied by more photographic memorializations, which, to Alley, were just another memory aid: a dozen precisely focused black-and-white photographs of Eastbrook in the Grace Court living room, and—in case her memory was still missing details—a videocassette that she could consult later.

Briefly, a movement of regret went through her chest. This is what Nicky had been looking for. He was looking for a videotape that Dov Peleg had told him about in a café, weeks before Dov died.

Dov had been disavowed, completely, during Iran-contra: she knew that because it had been in the Israeli papers.

So, embittered, he had given an interview to a reporter.

Telling him about a video he had made, years before, of a meeting between Ronald Rosenthal, Michael Levi, and Greg Eastbrook.

Then Dov had been killed. Quickly, she leafed back through Dov's interview with Nicky. And her eye caught on her name.

"There was me, Bennie Friedman. Ron's daughter, Esther, came in for a minute. She saw the whole thing."

And so Nicky Dymitryck had come to Martha's Vineyard to find the only other witness of the meeting. Hoping to find a way to make her tell.

Wonder was passing through her. How gratified Nicky must have been to discover her forgery and embezzlement. Now he had found a way to force her to help him. It was, in fact, the only chance he'd ever have to get the tape Dov had told him about, and he knew it. A coincidence? Not quite: he'd hoped for a crime of some sort when he'd had Stan Diamond send in his rental check. That was the only coincidence: that Diamond should have been a tenant.

It was a good plan Nicky had had, to capitalize on that coincidence. So good that only his death, probably, could have stopped it.

Allison's breath was coming in sharp gasps now, her hands trembling. Without looking any further through these papers, she bundled them back into their plastic holder and put them aside. Then, with a big effort, she forced herself to leaf through the rest of the safe's papers, trying to read the minimum possible, nearly wincing with disgust. She caught the words *Iran, Promis, Honeywell, Casey, Kashani,* and many other words and names familiar to her from the papers. But she did not read them and when, by the bottom of the pile, she had not encountered anything else relating to Iraq, she replaced all the papers, save those in the Iraq file she had put aside, in the safe with the gun and the currency, swung the door closed, and spun the lock.

She should not, she knew, be surprised. She knew more than enough of her father's business not to be surprised by the grim reality of the proofs before her. Yet this was different than the clueless half-truths of newspapers. Many of these documents she had just seen had been direct copies of classified intelligence reports, Israeli and American. Many of these documents would never again be seen outside of the highest security apparatuses in those governments. And seeing the black, blurred type of the photocopies had breached the wall of doubt she had so long held in place.

Carrying the Iraqi file, she walked slowly back to the dining room, and fumbled the file into her backpack. Her movements, she found, were hurried, clumsy, and for a moment she felt a new kind of fear, as if she were being chased, a fear reminiscent of childhood. Perhaps, she thought suddenly, all fears were reminiscent of childhood, fairy-tale terrors. That thought made this fear easier to handle.

But how brilliant Nicky was! In the dining room she stopped, suddenly appreciating the enormity of his intelligence. Someone like Eastbrook, she knew, was virtually impossible to pursue, for whatever his crimes may be, any government—Republican or Democratic—preferred ignoring those crimes to the national security risks of their revelation. What she had, now, in her backpack was probably the only thing in the world that could stop Eastbrook's senatorial campaign, and there was not now, nor had there ever been, another way for Nicky to get it except from her.

With that realization came another. A slower and much more shocking one.

Crouching on the floor by her backpack, she slowly examined it.

And slowly, step by step, she saw that what she had just found in her father's safe could, used properly, not only stop Eastbrook. It could also assure her father's conviction.

Had Nicky known that, too?

But that was not all. For now, more slowly, came the third realization, and it was the most shocking of all.

Nothing ever means one thing, Allison knew that. Every meaning is always double, and only the slightest shift in perspective is required to go from a simple truth to its opposite.

These documents, in one context, ruined Eastbrook and convicted her father.

But in another context, they meant something else altogether, something so astounding that for minutes, squatting on the dining room floor, she did not even know where she was.

Minutes during which she suddenly understood what else could be done with those documents. Minutes in which she suddenly understood, perfectly, as if it had been whispered into her ear, not now but every day since her father had been arrested, what else could be done with these documents.

It was impossible. And yet, she knew, it was also perfect. Meeting Dee again, after ten years, and falling in love. As if they had never parted, but always been secretly, surreptitiously together. Nicky arriving, looking not for anything about her father, but for something— this thing—about Eastbrook's role in the covert arming of Iraq. And then the embezzlement of her father's property. If she had planned it, she could not have thought it out better. Briefly, she wondered if this is what they taught in the CIA: to take advantage of chance, to string chance events into an unexpected meaning, and so alter the course of politics. It was perfect.

Or could have been. Slowly, still thinking, she rose. It could have been perfect, but only if Nicky had not died. As it was, Nicky's death ruined everything.

And even if he had not died, would she have the courage? The . . . the courage, yes, but also the total unscrupulousness required to use these documents in that other context.

Did she? Grimly, looking at nothing, she asked herself. Once before she had done something terrible to save her father, something so unspeakable that even now she only approached its memory barely, not even acknowledging it to herself. But then, she had only sacrificed herself to hide an unspeakable truth from him. For what she was envisaging now, she would have to sacrifice not only herself, although that sacrifice would be enormous, but others too.

In return, however, she would save the most important thing in the world.

She shook her head, as if to free herself of the thought. Really, it didn't matter. Nicky was dead, and without him, she could do nothing. And with that comforting realization, she slipped her arms into the backpack, picked up her helmet, and, turning off the lights, went quickly out the door.

4.

In the street again, in the thick October light, she unlocked her bicycle with clumsy movements, still trembling, mounted, and kicked into motion onto the street in front of a van, the outraged face of its driver, a Hasid, flashing out of his window. Allison didn't notice. On the avenue she entered the line of traffic and accelerated, then banked tightly down Fifty-fourth Street, gathering speed, standing straight-legged on the pedals, dropping her hands on the handlebars and lowering her helmeted head against the wind, the wind that grew with her speed, and then, more suddenly, fell as she braked to a stop in front of a small storefront, which a faded sign advertised in Hebrew and Yiddish as housing "Klavan's Religious Articles."

Jesus. In shock she stared at the storefront. She would not have believed that it could still exist, never mind be open for business. In disbelief, she hesitated. Then in doubt. Both were brief, and she dismounted and walked her bike into the dusty interior of the store.

Again, the pervasive smell of old fabrics and cooked food. She paused as her eyes adjusted from the bright sunlight, then gradually the view of a man in shirtsleeves, *payess*, a yarmulke, and a sparse, untrimmed beard came into focus. Somehow she had the impression that he had been watching her through the window. To his back, she spoke.

"What are you doing here, Drew?"

The man answered without turning. "The name is Peretz, and you fucking know it." His accent, strangely nasal, was flat and clipped.

That made her stop. But what, she thought, had she expected? "I'm sorry. I forgot."

"Remember it, okay?"

Silence. Then, relenting, he turned and stepped into the dim sunlight that the store's dirty front permitted, revealing a thin face with a massive nose, complexly and unusually crooked. His eyes were slightly squinted, as if their degree zero was somewhat searching.

"How are you, Esther?"

Esther. She could not remember when last she had heard her real name used but by her father. In wonder, she watched the man before her. "And you?"

"*Baruch ha shem.*" He shrugged, watching her carefully, his black eyes squinting over his nose, which, she now noticed, was badly scarred.

"Don't tell me you've broken that nose of yours again."

"No, but they had to operate for a deviated septum, from that prick cop at the Russian embassy." Drew had, during his time in the now defunct Brooklyn Jewish Defense League, held some kind of a record for breaking his nose in street fights. That was before he joined the JDL's more religious, more militant, more right-wing successor, Kahane Chai, and changed his name.

"Lemme see." She stepped forward, reaching a hand up, familiarly and with affection.

"No. Don't touch me. Come on, Esther. Show some fucking respect."

She let her hand fall, unaccountably hurt. They had been children together, best friends before Rosenthal had moved her and Pauly to Brooklyn Heights. He had kissed her once.

Drew spoke again. "Sorry. I'm sorry, Essie."

She nodded, not looking, still aching. But her answer did not show it. "So, what are you doing in Brooklyn? Aren't there Arabs to shoot in Hebron? Or wait: you all do peacenik Jews now too, don't you?"

He ignored the comment and answered, instead, in the rising tone of frustration. "There's no one to take care of this fucking store. Since Dad died, and my brother's out in L.A."

"Sell it."

"Yeah, right. You got anything for my mom to live on?" Quickly, he seemed to regret the question. "Don't answer that. How's your dad?"

For a moment she registered, curiously, how completely the expectation of shame disappeared here. Answering was a luxury. "Trial starts in a few days."

"I heard when this is over he's going to stand for Knesset."

"Buy himself an election, sure."

Drew paused, then spoke with a kind of hesitant argument. "Well, he's not going to get any justice here."

He was surprised by the response, as was she. "Oh, fuck him, Drew. Peretz. This isn't about justice."

She was looking down now, fingering an object on a display, and her cheeks were red. Perhaps in all the world, she thought, only Drew knew what she thought about her father.

He answered softly. Nearly beseechingly. "Don't say that, Essie. It's a crime and you know it. Anyone's earned a Knesset seat, then why not him? You know what he's done over there? Shuls, yeshivot, hospital care. Myself, I'd have done six to ten in Dannemora without your dad, and believe me it's hard to keep kosher while you're being shtupped by the Nation of Islam. Don't let the goyim turn him into a criminal to his own daughter. It's not true."

But in Allison's mind, she heard her father's voice: "Truth? What the fuck is truth, okay?" Outside the window, a woman passed in a gold wig and a flowered dress. In her mind's eye was Drew, a long-haired high school boy in an oversized plaid shirt, dirty blue jeans, a tiny knit *kipah* bobby-pinned to his head, balancing a basketball in his lap while they listened to Mott the Hoople at a diner jukebox. After she'd left Borough Park he'd been arrested for possession of a handgun; his father had called Rosenthal for help, and Rosenthal had called D'Amato. Then Drew had had his nose broken by a cop during a protest in front of the Soviet embassy, and his father had called Rosenthal again, this time in panic because the cop had been hospitalized from a blow to the ear with Drew's heavy boot, repeated three times. Stein had avoided trial with a plea that put Drew at Wiltwick for nine months, a harsh and punishing experience, immediately after which he'd joined the Israeli army.

Even after they'd left for the Heights, she'd still see Drew sometimes. She'd bike out and they'd sit at a diner; he'd meet her on the promenade. Then she'd gone to college and he'd gone to jail, then Israel, ultimately putting his reform school experience to use in the Bekáa Valley, and she hadn't spoken to him but twice since then. Once he'd called, after Pauly died. Then again when her father was arrested. She turned, longing to touch that boy with the long hair in the oversized plaid shirt.

But how could she explain to him this other world? The world of her new life for which he had such contempt? The world of her father's business: Switzerland,

London, Marbella, Madrid; would Drew even understand her indignation at her father's activities? And how could she tell him of falling in love with Dee, and then meeting that idealistic man on the day of his murder? She felt pressure against her lungs and she drew in a big breath, as if about to speak. Then she let it out again.

"Is there anything I can do? Tzippy?" Her heart warmed at the Hebrew nickname, but at the same time she knew that for all his pleasure at seeing her, she was the past and he wished she hadn't come. She shook her head.

"You could leave all this behind. You could come to Israel."

She shook her head again, and forced a smile. "Yeah, right. Quite a catch I'd be. They'd marry me to the town fool."

"You underestimate us. You underestimate yourself too."

"Yeah, right." She laughed briefly. "Allison Rosenthal. A jewel of Orthodox femininity."

"Esther. Esther Rosenthal." Drew was speaking very seriously now. "That's not a name you can run away from. What did your zaideh call you? 'The girl who saved the Jews,' right? You're brilliant, perfectly educated, and soon you'll be a lawyer. You could be a central, productive, important person for us."

"Oh God, Drew, Peretz, don't give me that old garbage. I'm the daughter of a criminal, living like a goy, not virgin. I have nothing to offer you or your damn community."

But Drew just shook his head, gravely, patiently. "It's not old, and it's not garbage. Essie, your father's no criminal—not in Israel. Not to the Jews. You don't understand: the story is biblical: your father is Mordecai, Sid Ohlinger is Haman, Clinton's the king, and you're Esther. Don't you see?"

"No. No, I don't see." Allison stepped closer now,

smelling the stale sweat on her childhood friend's white shirt, feeling like crying. "All that proves is that politics are ageless and the one constant of history is how horrible people can be to each other."

Drew was whispering now, urgently, across the small distance between them. "No. You're not listening. You think this is a story about politics. It's not even a loyalty."

Rather than answering, she watched him, and after a long moment, he stepped back and spoke sadly.

"Essie, you need me, all you have to do is pick up the phone. You understand? One call, whenever you want, and I'm there."

She nodded.

"And one more thing. You tell your father the same thing. Any time he needs me, I'm ready, and so's Menacham Abramowitz and Ben Gordon and Yankel Shapiro. You with me? Any time, any place, anything. All you gotta do is tell me."

Allison frowned, nodded again. Then she spoke in a normal voice.

"I'll tell him. Hey, Drewski? I'll see you later."

And before he could stop her, she had darted over and planted a kiss on her old friend, her dear friend's cheek, and then, steering her bicycle, was out the door.

5.

Prospect Park, at the head of Coney Island Avenue. Alley pedaled hard along the drive, pushing herself, her breath coming fast in the cold air, her body sweating steadily under its tight clothes. At Grand Army Plaza she exited the park, shot out really, through the changing light and full into the stream of traffic around the monument, disregarding the blare of a horn.

How odd it was that across the gulf—the abyss, really—between them, Drew's loyalty remained intact. He could have done a lot for her, she thought. He could have added so much to the field of possibilities. Thinking that, she became aware of the weight of her father's documents she carried on her back. Then she shrugged off the thought. Nicky's death ruined everything.

Four o'clock. An hour or two of daylight left. Before the bridge she found herself somehow unwilling to return to Manhattan, and she detoured west into Brooklyn Heights, and against the traffic down Pierrepont Street. Outside her high school, of its own volition her body paused the bicycle and her eye turned to the low wall next to the art room.

Two girls, tight T-shirts showing their small-breasted, slim-shouldered bodies, sat smoking, talking to the small group of boys gathered around. That was where she would have been, with Martha, her own blond hair shoulder length and parted at the middle, Martha's black and curly and tied back with a band so it exploded around the nape of her neck. Across the street, in the big sycamore whose lower branches you could reach with a boost from a friend, Pauly would be climbing with Michael Numeroff and Richard Robbins, waiting for her to take him home. She looked to the right, expecting to see other children climbing the tree. But the lower branches were now twelve or fourteen feet high, and no one was climbing the tree.

A car approached, so she pushed off and down the street, then turned left and coasted against traffic on Hicks Street to Grace Court. Midway on the small street was the ornate brownstone mansion in which she had grown up, and here she paused again.

Not for the first time, she wondered why her father had moved here. Perhaps, she thought, when he had decided to withdraw his daughter and son from yeshiva and move the family out of Borough Park, perhaps he'd been too scared to go out of Brooklyn, and settled on this enclave next to Grace Church as a compromise. A class of children from the church school passed behind her, crayons and papers in hand, and settled to copy a street sign, and her eye traveled up the facade of the house to the windows of her third-floor bedroom. They rested briefly there, then dropped as she mounted her bicycle and rode slowly off.

Still, she could not quite bring herself to leave, and paused at the end of the street, watching Manhattan rising in an aura of smog. Funny that she should feel so at home here now, she thought. Moving had been the trauma of her life, the first trauma: eleven years old, an odd-shaped creature with long legs, showing up the first day of school dressed in the ankle-length skirt and starched white shirt of her yeshiva. Only Martha, who had also been subject to a deculturation—although much earlier in life when Ohlinger had pulled himself out of the Bronx and headed, a brilliant young yeshiva *bucher*, to Harvard Law—had befriended Allison. Then together, they'd taken care of Pauly.

Which was funny, because it had ultimately been Pauly who'd taught her everything she knew about living here. Those two years had made all the difference: his memories of yeshiva disappeared the moment he took his *kipah* off, the first day in school when he realized no one else was wearing one. Now, watching the river just beyond her childhood house, Allison thought that Pauly had always been more indigenous to the Heights than she.

Later on the divorce came, her sophomore year of high school, the winter—she thought now—after she had made love with Dee on Hancock Beach. Her mother had quietly, with no preparation and no explanation, disappeared from their lives, leaving their father to explain. Two summers later, while they were on the island, her father had quietly sold off the Grace Court house and bought a prewar apartment on Park Avenue. Without ever returning to the house, she had gone off to Yale,

Pauly had moved uptown with her father, and started at Dalton. And now the roles were reversed. Now it was Allison, escaped from her family just when her family had fallen apart, who was at home in this new world in New Haven with Martha and a quarter of their graduating class from St. Ann's, and Pauly, torn apart by the divorce, who had to master a new place alone.

God, he had had a bad time that year. First the divorce, then her departure, then the move, all within a couple of years. Her father had had her bedroom moved intact to the new apartment, and she had come home every weekend, and every weekend night little Pauly would huddle his tight, sullen body next to her, sleeping a tragic child's sleep in which he tossed and talked and cried out all night long.

And now a terrible ache was in her stomach as, step by step, starting from those nights in this house, the logic of her brother's death came back to her. She didn't say it, even to herself, but she knew it. It all started here, in this house: this was where Pauly learned everything about love, and everything about hate, and it would be that hate that would lead him to be killed on the cliffs of Gay Head.

Nobody knew that. It had nothing to do with suicide, Pauly's death, and it had nothing to do with being gay. Being gay for Pauly meant having fallen in love only once, and that had been with a man. That man had been like him in so many ways: so quick to laugh, so strong and beautiful, so in touch with that strain of yiddishkeit black humor and yet so at home in a world of WASPs. But it wasn't about being gay, it was about the fact that Johnny Eisenberg could have been his brother.

Or his sister.

No one else knew that. Not her father, not their neighbors, not the newspapers. They saw a traumatized child, sick with homosexuality, and when the day came that he stole his father's gun and on the red clay cliffs at

Gay Head turned its muzzle into his chest, his beautiful strong chest, they saw an inevitability.

Only once had she had the chance to tell her father the truth, at the unveiling of Pauly's gravestone, a year after his funeral. Only she and her father had been there, Acacia Cemetery in Queens. Afterward, they'd gone to see her grandparents' tombs, and stooping to put a pebble on his mother's gravestone, his father had said, not looking at her but into the green depths of the cemetery, "When did Davey take my gun, Esther?"

She knew he was referring to the night her brother shot himself. "Why, Daddy?"

His voice carried on under the vault of summer sky.

"I was thinking about it this morning. It was in my bedside drawer when I went to sleep. That night. I know because I checked it."

"So?"

"So, Davey went out before I went to bed. According to the police report, he never came back."

Watching her father crouching by his mother's tombstone, she wondered what story, what other story, he was telling himself, and how close it came to the truth. That was when she had a chance to tell him. But what she said was wooden, factual:

"He came back. During the night. I heard him. He came upstairs, then he went out again. I thought he was in the bathroom, but he must have come to take the gun while you were asleep. I thought he was going back out to party. I let him go. I—I could have stopped him, Daddy."

And now her father was standing, approaching her across the small distance of his mother's grave, and then she was in his arms and as her tears came she knew he had, once again, believed her.

With a start, she came back to herself. What was happening? All the implacable discipline of the years past, years where she had never once revisited this time in the past, was falling apart, falling apart. Tears in her eyes—the second time she had cried since that day at the cemetery—she mounted, turned, and accelerated, hard, toward the bridge.

6.

Eight P.M., on Jane Street. Allison, drying her hair by the mirror, dressing after her shower.

She had met Martha for a drink, downtown at the Ear Inn, on her return to the city. Martha ordered dinner, Allison, waiting to eat later with Dee, had a couple of beers. Afterward, she'd cycled home, somewhat drunk after not having eaten all day. Encouraged by the mixture of exercise and beer, a great lassitude had gone through her, and she had rested for a long time on her bed before, noticing the time, rising. First she'd unpacked her knapsack, hiding the documents she'd taken from Borough Park in her desk drawer. Then she'd gone to shower.

Standing in front of the mirror in her bedroom, brushing her wet hair, she considered her eyes dispassionately. It was time to go downstairs to the bar, to show herself so that Dee would know to follow her up, but she found her mind resting not on that meeting she had awaited all day but on Drew. Drew, his pale face framed by black hair, his bent nose, his strong body hidden beneath a crumpled white shirt above drab black pants, the fringe of his prayer shawl hanging loose above his pants pockets.

And suddenly she was consumed by a sensation of hatred for her old friend, a heat that swept through her, hatred for his right-wing politics, his disregard for freedom, his righteousness; hatred for the pure unaestheticism of his life, the dreary clothes, the sun-starved skin.

God, the audacity of his sanctimonious nonsense. Bitterly, she thought, not for the first time, of the hypocrisy of the religious, thinking themselves holy for their willingness to sacrifice everything to their belief. But how holy was that? Everyone, Allison knew, thinks they are making some holy sacrifice. Her father was prepared to sacrifice the lives of people and the freedom of countries to protect Israel's ability to defend itself. Dee was prepared to sacrifice her father to bring legal questions into court. Dee's father was prepared to sacrifice justice to satisfy the overarching demands of foreign policy. And even Nicky had been prepared to sacrifice her—her very freedom—to stop Greg Eastbrook from being elected. So how different was Drew, thinking he had given so much to the pursuit of sanctity?

And then, as that anger faded, she just as suddenly felt something other, and as it grew she acknowledged that it had always been there, and it had always been guilt. Guilt for her goyish good looks, guilt for the changed name, guilt for the happiness she had had, guilt for the degree to which she had escaped the thorny obligations and questions of these people's lives.

And as she felt guilt she felt a longing, shocking in its depth, for the pure simplicity of Drew's beliefs, the conviction that God has 613 rules, no more, no less, and all we—Republicans, Democrats, gun runners, or rabbis—have to do is follow them. How quickly, how easily, she could turn right around from her entire life and go back! Slip clearly into the religious belief, the xenophobia, the racism, Zionism, faith. The zealotry. As if all her life, to this moment, all her cherished beliefs, faded as easily as an ex-smoker gives in to the seductiveness of tobacco and suddenly, from a militant antismoker, becomes again a profound addict.

Longing. That longing flowing through her, alive and hot. She carried it across the room, out the door, and down into the night to find Dee. Carried it downstairs, carried it around the corner, carried it to the bar and to Dee—cradling it, cherishing it, nursing it until she could masquerade it as that other longing—until she could end this terrible day with Dee's body in hers.

And still, that long, long day had another surprise coming.

Or, to be exact, two.

A large crowd was in the bar, and she had to maneuver for position before she could see that Dee was not in yet.

Nervously, impatiently, she waited while Bobby brought her a beer and a letter, a messenger delivery, which he had received for her during the day. It was from Bob Stein, and idly, expecting more in the endless stream of court-related documents, she opened the envelope and leafed through its contents.

And then the first thing happened. Inside, a letter with a handwritten note on top from Bob:

Alley honey—tried to call you all day. What is this about?

Dear Mr. Stein,

I am writing to advise you that I have in my possession evidence of Allison Rosenthal's fraudulent rental of her father's Martha's Vineyard property known as Ocean View Farmhouse to my client, Stanley Diamond.

I am able to prove that Ms. Rosenthal knowingly rented this property to my client although it was under a federal seizure order, and furthermore that in so doing she committed forgery. It is therefore in Ms. Rosenthal's best interest to contact my office to discuss the terms under which she may make restitution to my client.

Failing this, I will be bringing my evidence to the Massachusetts State Attorney's office, which will cer-

tainly produce a criminal action, following which
Mr. Diamond will be filing for civil damages.

Your sincerely,
Gillian Morreale
Partner
Stockard, Dyson & Struck

That made her, nearly, smile. Stein would be shocked
indeed, she thought, to find out what this matter was
about, and that it was certainly not going to be resolved
in any timely manner.

She put the package down and turned to her beer.
What would Stein find out? That in addition to her father's other problems, now she—not her father, but
she—was going to be pursued for wire and mail fraud.

Later, she knew, she would be scared. Later, when she
came to think seriously about what had happened to her,
she would be even panicked.

For now, however, in the familiarity of the bar's noises
and smells around her, she smiled, not just at the thought of
Stein's surprise, but also at how perfect it could have been.

For it was perfect. What had Drew called her? A mod-
ern-day Esther? Drew didn't know how perfect the anal-
ogy was. After all, hadn't Esther—in the king's
harem—slept with the enemy in order to save her own father? Hadn't Esther sacrificed her very virginity, and
then, from her conjugal bed, ordered her people saved
and her enemies destroyed?

The only thing lacking was that Nicky was dead. If
Nicky were alive, she thought, she would have the perfect
plan. If Nicky were alive she could, just like her namesake, save the Jews.

And then she shook her head, as if to wake from a
dream. Of course, nothing was the same. Nothing. Esther was taken into the harem with no control over the
choice, but she, Allison, had loved Dee from her childhood on, adored him. And deep within herself, she ad-

mitted that she would love him still, just as much, had she not met Nicky.

But far in her mind a voice was saying to her, so what? Her precious love for Dee, was that worth allowing her father to be convicted a criminal before the world? Her father was innocent, innocent. Everyone knew he had been authorized to sell arms to the Bosnians; everyone knew he was being scapegoated for a foreign policy agenda, and that were he not a Jew, it would not be happening.

And Dee, the instrument of a vicious king, was carrying out this scapegoating, this terrible injustice. So what did it matter what happened to Dee? And what was she prepared to sacrifice, not for some religious myth, or for some political aim, but for her father, a real person, and even more, for the truth?

Then the second thing happened.

With a sigh, she turned to the second letter, a FedEx envelope sent to her care of Stein from California. It had left California, she noted idly, the day before. Something, no doubt, to do with the Diamond prosecution. For a moment she considered leaving it unopened. Then she tore the perforated tab and pulled out the contents: legal documents relating to the filing of a criminal action against her, motion for discovery in Massachusetts court, a filing for interstate warrant.

Slowly, she realized that these were letters from the inside of the Diamond prosecution. Now, at last curious, she turned to the cover letter accompanying the documents, her eye falling on the signature.

Nicholson Jefferson Dymitryck

She read the letter, or better, devoured it in a glance.

Dear Allison Rosenthal,

I would like to advise you that, per the enclosed documents, Stanley Diamond is about to inform the

Massachusetts State Court about a number of crimes committed by you, ranging from forgery to embezzlement to interstate wire fraud.

You will be well advised to review the enclosed documents carefully, and then do nothing until I am in touch with you personally.

Although it will no doubt come as a shock to you to find that I am alive, please be assured that it is a fact easily explained.

Although you may believe that this letter is not bona fide, please be assured that I am able to recount what you drank the evening we spent together on Martha's Vineyard—and, nearly word for word, what we talked about—from your father to the Constitution—and a host of other details.

And although you have already expressed your lack of interest in my researches into your father's affairs, you will do well to consider these researches a subject of the greatest and most personal importance to you possible, as I can and will put you in jail.

Yours sincerely,
Nicholson Jefferson Dymitryck

He was alive.

It did not matter how. It did not matter how, it did not matter why.

As Allison sat on the bar stool, the Corner Bistro disappeared, and in her ears a roaring silence seemed to obliterate her surroundings.

Nicky Dymitryck was alive.

And if Nicky Dymitryck was alive, then she knew precisely—precisely, although she could not remember ever having thought it out—what to do.

Grimly, she pushed Nicky's letter back into its envelope. Thinking: so. So I do have to make the choice.

What would she sacrifice?

Dee? She would deal him a terrible blow, she knew.

But it would be a lesser one than the one he was delivering to her father, and it would be far less, far less, than what she would do to herself.

Could she do it? she asked herself; but once again, at the end of the long fugue of thought, she came back to the one indisputable fact: her father might be guilty, but he was not guilty of the crime for which they were scapegoating him.

And if she lost her father, the last remnant left to her of her childhood, she had lost everything.

And then the bar came back with its noise of glasses clinking and people talking and, in amazement at herself, Allison Rosenthal, Esther, knew that she was going to do a terrible, terrible thing.

PART THREE

So Esther arose, and stood before the king, and said, If it please the king, and if I have found favour in his sight . . . let it be written to reverse the letters devised . . . to destroy the Jews which are in all the king's provinces: For how can I endure to see the evil that shall come unto my people? or how can I endure to see the destruction of my kindred?

ESTHER 8:4-6

CHAPTER 10

Spring 1992.
New Haven, Connecticut.

1.

To understand the death and resurrection of Nicky Dymitryck, it is not enough to look at the suspicious circumstances of his visit to Martha's Vineyard late in the summer of 1994. The course of events that resulted in his murder in a bathroom of Boston's Logan Airport—and, incidentally, in the arrest of Allison's father—had started two years earlier, in the spring of 1992. And indeed: that he had been reported to the press as dead instead of, as was really the case, only very nearly dead was because, since the spring of 1992, Nicky's life had been continuously at risk. So much so that declaring him dead, for public purposes, had come to seem the only way out.

The incident that launched this series of events happened to Nicky in a fairly dramatic fashion. In this it was unusual: all appearances to the contrary notwithstanding, most of Nicky's best work came from research into arcane government documents, multiple source comparisons of Freedom of Information Act requests, and double reads of policy analysis, rather than being approached by mysterious strangers in hotel bars.

This one, however, came exactly that way, although the hotel bar in question was in neither Vientiane nor Beirut, but rather downtown New Haven, and Nicky was neither covering a war nor tracking a gun runner but rather delivering the Porter Fellowship Lecture in Journalism.

The Porter is of course a great honor for a journalist, but the kind of journalists whom Nicky tended to know viewed it rather as the opportunity for some serious seduction of people younger and much better looking than themselves. When he won the Porter, unfortunately, that wasn't a big concern. For one thing, in 1992 he was about to be married, and the trip east was, for someone who traveled as much as he, a sad waste of precious time with his fiancée. For another, he had been to college at that same institution. He hadn't liked it then, and he didn't like it now. There was something pathetic, he had felt then, in the scared run for the status quo that by far the vast majority of his peers had been making. And there was something tragic, he felt now, watching the audience at his five-lecture series, "Lawyers, Guns, and Money: Post-Cold War Arms Export Policy," in the fact that by far the vast majority of them seemed still to be doing the same.

That was why, his last night in town, instead of listening to undergraduate girls sing for drinks at Mory's with the group of deans and professors who had awarded him the fellowship, he was drinking alone at his hotel bar when he was approached by a tall, disarmingly handsome young man.

"Mr. Dymitryck?"

"Nicky," he said automatically—even then, at thirty-three, he disliked being called "Mister"—as he looked up into the boy's startlingly green eyes, so green that they seemed to glow behind a fringe of blond hair. "Yes?"

"I wonder if I might talk with you a moment."

"About?"

"Something private."

An aura of booze hung around him like a cloud. He was dressed in Paul Stuart and wore a Rolex. And, while it was more a matter of intuition than vision, to Nicky it was as clear as day that this boy had sought Nicky out to tell him something that the boy should not even have known.

"Then I advise you to wait."

This surprised the boy. "For what?"

"Not for. Until. Until you're sober. Otherwise, you're going to regret telling me."

The boy laughed, briefly.

"I doubt that. You know who's going to regret my talking to you? Greg Eastbrook is going to regret my talking to you. Now, you just order me a drink and I'll tell you a good story. Okay?"

Half an hour later, the boy was gone, and Nicky was alone in his hotel room speaking on the phone, long-distance.

"Jay? Listen, you remember Mehmet Hourani? Turkish broker for Hussein, working out of Munich? Brokered chemical warhead sales to Iraq out of a Munich holding company until the Gulf War?"

The person on the other end of the line seemed to remember, and to be commenting on it at length. At least, until Nicky went on.

"Jay, shut up a second, okay? I just met a kid who says that the sales were coordinated out of the NSC staff by Greg Eastbrook."

Now, on the other end of the line, there was silence, and Nicky allowed his wide mouth to smile. Then, responding to a question, he said:

"I'll tell you why I believe him. You know who I think he is? I think he's the son of someone in the trade. He was drunk as a sailor, and as gay as a box of birds. I think I just got a scoop from a kid who hates his daddy."

A short silence while he listened. Then:

"No way. I'm going to Munich. Tomorrow, before someone tries to assassinate Hourani. Yeah, I met him at the Dubai air show. And I want to get this on camera. So get someone to meet me, okay?"

Then he hung up, and called Lufthansa.

2.

Nicky Dymitryck never really got his interview with Mehmet Hourani—at least, not the part he was looking for.

He got to Munich, and he found Hourani's house at Harlanstrasse 14. And Hourani, surprisingly, let him in: he was, it turned out, somewhat in fear for his life, just then, and that made him eager to go on record. He didn't, however, want to talk about Eastbrook. He wanted to talk about Ronald Rosenthal, which he did, and dutifully, Nicky took down the rather prosaic details of the Bosnian sales that would, two years later, put Allison's father in jail. Only when that was done, and Nicky had turned the conversation back in time to Colonel Eastbrook and the Iraqi tilt, did Nicky's cameraman begin to run tape. Which was fortunate, for Nicky's memory of what happened over the next few minutes was wiped, instantly, clean and never returned again.

The surviving film shows three establishing shots: the living room in low spring daylight; a close-up of Hourani, sweating in a dark suit, and a medium-zoom to include Nicky, in jeans and a black shirt, holding papers. Then there is a flash and a sudden electric zip, and the video dies while the audio—which was on a separate and, luckily, digital deck—after a silence comes back to the sound of moans.

It is not hard to imagine what had happened. The blast that spiked the DAT was loud enough to shatter windows on the street side of the house. It came from behind Hourani, nonnegotiable, absolutely without preamble. The couch—Biedermeier, very likely—splintered in the middle, throwing clouds of stuffing into the air. The man in jeans, protected by the interviewee, who was in the process of coming, literally, apart, was tossed over the low back of his armchair into a set of glass bric-a-brac on oak shelves.

As for the cameraman, the newspapers reported it plainly. The shoulder-mount video camera shattered into the side of his face, which disintegrated while his right ribs and hip caved inward. His right leg was severed in a jagged line running from his gluteus inferioris to his kneecap, half of which was left exposed.

The screen, showing darkness, plays his moans for perhaps three minutes. Then there is silence. It seems to last a long time. But it is only a few moments until there sounds the tinkling of glass and a groan, and then the dialing of a phone and a voice saying, over and over again, too loud and with an American accent: "Police. Emergency. Harlanstrasse 14. Police. Emergency. Harlanstrasse 14. Police."

As the commentator on *Nightline* explained when they aired the tape, the blast would have temporarily deafened Nicky, and he was repeating himself on the telephone in the hope that someone would hear.

3.

It was neither the violence nor the death: there had been far too much of both in his life since, at twenty-one, Nicky had turned down graduate school fellowships from the three best American Studies departments in the country and gone to answer telephones and fetch coffee for the furthest-left-wing editor in the country, submitting to years of Jay's infamously cruel clerical abuse before winning his first chance to proofread, then, after years of Jay's famously niggling editorial demands, finally being allowed, at last, to report. Oddly, once he had let Nicky loose, Jay supported his every venture, and so Nicky had gone from a life of Blackwing number two pencils and editorial markings to a tour of the most shocking violence and death the world had, really, to offer. In Rwanda he had been the first to enter a barn where three hundred Hutu women and children had been massacred by machete and machine gun. In Islamabad he had seen sixteen adult men hanged, one after the other after the other, during four hours on a sunny afternoon. As for more direct experience, Nicky's small body had borne interrogations in cities as diverse as Kinshasa and San José, and a close inspection of his back showed that one of these interrogations had involved something that most people only hear about: a horsewhip.

It was, rather, the futility. This was the closest he had ever gotten to Eastbrook, and by 1992 it had been nearly ten years that Nicky had been following this singular man's tracks through the major hot spots of the world. In fact, it was the hunt for Greg Eastbrook that had led Nicky to writing for the *NAR* instead of, like his classmates James Dix, Ellen Dyson, and Thomas Barrett, writing for, respectively, the *New York Times*, the *Wall Street Journal*, and the Honorable Gentleman from Connecticut. No one but Jay Cohen—a La Penca survivor and one of the plaintiffs in the Christic Institute suit— thought it was possible to convict anyone from Eastbrook's little underworld, and no one but Stan Diamond, Jay's SDS comrade who had since made one of the country's biggest fortunes in telecommunications, was willing to pay to try.

That the *NAR* had allowed Nicky to pursue Greg Eastbrook for the ten years since the joint committee on

Iran-contra had first granted him immunity from prosecution was because, precisely, the magazine was generally considered—by the kinds of people who had been Nicky's classmates—the "alternative media." They were not quite right about that.

True, the *NAR*'s longtime emphasis on tracking the movement of American armaments, legally and illegally, to their various uses around the world was hardly calculated to develop a viable advertising rate base, especially since this field led the *NAR* less to high-profile scoops in war zones than to detailed reviews of often highly arcane U.S.-Israeli transactions, foreign military grants, and defense contracts.

But it was also true that its subscribers included nearly every current employee of the U.S. intelligence services and the Foreign Service, much of the Council on Foreign Relations, and many members of the U.S. Congress. As it was true that the *NAR* had long been supplied to the Kremlin as intelligence, translated by supposed KGB analysts in Washington, until Gorbachev's staff reformed the practice by buying an airmail subscription, as Castro had done since the first issue. As had Noam Chomsky, as had Jesse Helms, as had Daniel Ortega and Theodore Shackley.

It was, in short, the perfect place for a person who had fallen victim to a political obsession.

Especially when that person was entirely unconcerned with his salary because he was the son of Johnny Dymitryck, who, up until his blacklisting, was among the highest paid screenwriters in the studio system and who, from the blacklisting on, invested his earnings wisely enough to allow his son to become, in Jay Cohen's often repeated description, the "best dressed lefty in the country."

If the people who'd blacklisted, investigated, and harassed his father had still been around, Nicky's field of expertise would have been different. As it was, he had to focus his journalistic sights on the longer-lasting Cold War institutions, and this he did with what can only be called obsession. His area of expertise was the small group of ex-army and intelligence officers who run through the history of covert military actions of postwar America, from the Bay of Pigs, through Laos and Cambodia, to the Mossadeq overthrow in Iran and the coup against Arbenz in Guatemala, and to their highest moment in the public eye, known as the Iran-contra affairs, and then, the placidity of their profitable enterprises barely rippled by the exposure, onward.

Theodore Shackley, Felix Rodriguez, John Singlaub, Richard Secord, Thomas Clines: Nicky was not the only writer to have fallen victim to the temptation of figuring out what these men did, and how they did it. But in that small community of journalists who gave—more often lost—their careers to the conspiracy theories that united these kinds of people across the history of postwar America, Nicky Dymitryck was perhaps the most tenacious. That was fitting, because so was his chosen quarry, Greg Eastbrook, who had, since his closed-door congressional testimony on his work for Oliver North in South America, so convincingly succeeded in his government work that in 1992 he retired his naval commission and announced his intention to represent California in the United States Senate in 1994. A political ambition about which, in 1993—when Eastbrook won a bitterly contested Republican primary for the candidacy—Nicky stopped laughing.

He recuperated from the Harlanstrasse bombing, that April of 1992, in, of all places, Jerusalem, where he wrote his article on Allison's father from his hospital bed. The research was easiest here, on the spot. In addition, the hospital was first-rate, and not even that much-criticized country's severest critic had ever denied the high degree of journalistic freedom that was available there. His story to bed and largely recuperated from his injuries, Nicky flew out for brief visits to sources in Istanbul and Beirut, and had returned home to Los Angeles by the time his Rosenthal story was published, in May.

It was not a good time. Nearly immediately upon his return, his engagement fell apart, and by the end of the month he found himself spending more nights on the couch in his office than at home. And that was why he was at the office when, on an evening in early June, the *NAR* received a call.

"Mr. Dymitryck, please."

"This is Nicky." Half reading a newspaper, he answered automatically.

"Ah. Hello." The voice at the other end was a man's, and it was young. "I'm sorry about what happened with Hourani. I felt responsible."

Recognizing the voice of the green-eyed young man from the bar at New Haven, Nicky let the newspaper fall. "Did you set the bomb?"

"Of course not."

"Then you're not responsible. Listen. I'd like to talk with you."

There was a short silence, and Nicky began to worry that he had gone too fast. But then the boy was speaking again.

"Why?"

"I'd like to know who you are. How you knew about Hourani. Listen, there's no one in the world who mistrusts my discretion. It can all be perfectly confidential."

Again, a pause. Then the boy spoke carefully.

"Who do you think I am?"

"Somebody's son. Somebody in the industry."

The boy sighed. "Mr. Dymitryck. You don't want to speak to me. I'm just a kid. What you want is to speak to a man called Dov Peleg. Do you hear me?"

"Yes." Scribbling, the phone between shoulder and ear. "Who is that?"

"Someone interesting. He worked for Israeli intelligence in the eighties. I believe he'd like to speak to you, too. He's in Paris, and I've got the number. But you want to catch him as quick as you can, 'cause I believe he's in trouble. Can you write down the number?"

"Yes." While he wrote, Nicky thought. This boy was going to tell him nothing else, he knew. But was there one thing he could get before the boy hung up? When he had taken down the number, he said:

"What should I ask Peleg?"

It worked. Without pause, the boy said: "Ask him to show you a video he made of Greg Eastbrook and Ronald Rosenthal in Brooklyn."

"Okay. Will you call me again?"

A slight, humorless laugh. "I doubt it."

And then the line went dead, but only for the second it took for Nicky to dial Air France.

4.

Dov Peleg met him at a restaurant on the Place Balard toward three on a Sunday morning. That was a good choice, Nicky thought, as he crossed the deserted intersection toward the restaurant: there was not another soul in this obscure southwestern corner of the city, and had there been, he or she would have been clearly visible. The restaurant was equally deserted: it was open only for the truckers who would soon arrive for the greenmarket on the square, but it was still too early for them. Nicky waited for a few moments over a drink. Then Peleg came in.

He was scared, bitter, and drunk. He stood a few inches taller than Nicky in old jeans and a wrinkled, ill-smelling polyester shirt. The hair over his nearly spherical head was thin and greasy in a way that bespoke not only a lack of cleanliness, but also ill health. But he was also clearly a practiced agent of some intelligence arm. He searched Nicky, quickly and cleanly, in the bathroom, then examined his tape recorder. Satisfied, he led him back to the bar and they began to talk.

Peleg was a former Israeli intelligence technician. He had been ousted in the fallout surrounding Iran-contra. He could not return to his country. He hated Paris. If he was to help Nicky, Nicky would have to pay, very handsomely, and help him leave the country. Nicky explained that his resources were very large. But he needed something very difficult. At last, Peleg turned his yellowing, bloodshot eyes to his interlocutor.

"What do you need, friend?"

"I'm told you worked for Israeli intelligence in the eighties."

With no acknowledgment, the other waited.

"I'm told you videotaped a meeting between Rosenthal and Greg Eastbrook in Brooklyn."

Again, no response.

"I want that videotape."

Now the other nodded. He didn't have the tape. But he could tell Nicky where to get it. His price was a ticket to Australia and ten thousand dollars. For a time they haggled, while the restaurant began to fill with the drivers of the trucks slowly filling the square, outside, in the dim morning light. In time they agreed that Peleg would tell him what was on the tape for the ticket and two thousand dollars. On the spot, Nicky paid him cash—a portion of the funds that had been wired from Diamond's Organic Communications account to Paris that morning: he was not allowing the time for any assassinations. And then Peleg began to talk, leaning close, whispering.

"There was me, Bennie Friedman. Ron's daughter, Esther, came in for a moment. She saw the whole thing. Ach, that girl. I used to think I'd marry her when she grew up. Beautiful, these eyes like nothing I've ever seen." Peleg's eyes unfocused, and he fell into silence.

"So I have to find Rosenthal's daughter?"

"Hey?" For a moment, the other looked lost. Then: "Oh no. She won't help you. She's Daddy's girl. No, what you want is to find the son."

And now he leaned across the table, breathing his breath of sour wine into Nicky's face, and lowered his voice. "Listen to this, okay? No one knows this but me. The son was there too."

"What do you mean?"

"I mean, Eastbrook's security checked the doors, the street, and scanned for bugs. But they never checked for a fourteen-year-old boy coming in through the maid's door from the kitchen. Why should they? The meeting was as dangerous for Ron as it was for their boss. They assumed he had secured the rest of the house. Remember, no one ever gave Greg Eastbrook high marks for competence, right? And in the middle of the fucking meeting, this kid in pajamas walks in, half asleep."

"What'd they do?"

"Oh, well. They laughed. Ron took the boy out, and they went on. But I was watching, and I know that boy. He is sly, just like his father. He knew what he had seen."

"Why should he tell me?"

A pause. "You're not Jewish, are you?"

"No."

"Then you won't understand. Trust me. You find him, you play him, you can make him do anything you want, so long as it hurts his father."

"Why does he want to hurt his father?"

"To avoid going to the army."

"The army? People like the Rosenthals don't go to the army, Mr. Peleg."

"Not in America. I mean Israel." At Nicky's silence, he went on. "I told you you wouldn't understand. Just find the boy. If he can't get the tape, he can testify about what he saw. No one'll believe an alcoholic Israeli spy. But they'll believe him."

"Where do I find him?"

"What month is this? June? Go to Martha's Vineyard. Ocean View Farm. Go soon."

At the door, Nicky asked suddenly:

"This kid, Rosenthal's son. He has what color eyes?"

"Like his sister. Green as a field in spring."

"Mr. Peleg. He was the one who sent me to you."

"Was he?" The Israeli was clearly anxious to leave. Had he, Nicky wondered, recognized someone in the now crowded restaurant? "That doesn't surprise me. The kid's fighting for his life. His father has his way, he'll spend three years on the Golan. He's a lefty, he's queer, and he hates his father. When you see him, tell him I did my best. But if he really wants to help, he's going to have to do it himself."

It turned out the Place Balard wasn't as good a choice as one might have thought. Nicky returned to America safely. But Peleg, that same afternoon, died in a car accident on the way to Charles de Gaulle Airport to catch a plane to Australia.

And, it turned out, Nicky had not been fast enough. Two days later, in late June of 1992, Nicky Dymitryck arrived on the little island-hopper to Martha's Vineyard only to read, in a copy of the *Martha's Vineyard Gazette* that he found at the airport, the headline "Suicide at Gay Head" and the story that Paul Rosenthal, son of one of the island's wealthiest residents, depressed at his recent diagnosis as HIV-positive, had shot himself in the chest and fallen from the cliffs at Gay Head to die, as Allison would later write in a poem, under some brilliant sky, in the sea moving like eels.

Summer 1992. Nicky left Martha's Vineyard without trying to contact the Rosenthals. He knew there was no point. Back in Los Angeles, he locked the Peleg interview in the office safe, with another copy at his father's Malibu house, where he'd lived since the dissolution of his engagement. Nothing in the interview could be substantiated, and without substantiation, it was only color. Besides, Eastbrook had just announced his bid for the Senate in a joint conference with Oliver North, and there was, for the *NAR*, serious work to do.

So it was not until two years later, in the summer of 1994, when Stan Diamond rented a summer house on South Beach in Martha's Vineyard, that Nicky thought about Allison Rosenthal again.

5.

At first, the coincidence seemed too much. Stan had just come back from Martha's Vineyard, where he'd rented, for the following summer, a magnificent property on the southern coast of the island, paying a $5,000 deposit on a total of $47,000 for a three-month rental. He'd received a lease, which was due back in mid August. Stan had signed the lease and written a check. And only after mailing them back had he connected his landlord with the man in the newspapers.

Sitting in Jay Cohen's office, holding Stan Diamond's lease and canceled deposit check, Nicky considered. The property was under notice of a federal seizure, to be executed in a matter of weeks. Renting the property was clearly illegal, but more than that, it was impossible: Ronald Rosenthal was known to have absconded to Israel. Clearly, the signature on the lease was a forgery. Clearly, the intention of completing the rental was embezzlement.

His first question to Stan had been whether he was willing to execute the lease and send in, as required, the balance of one-half of the rental amount. It was a long shot, Nicky explained, but he might be providing a valuable lever against Ron Rosenthal, whom Nicky knew to be in possession of damning evidence about Greg Eastbrook. That he conveniently left out the fact that the only person the leverage could in fact be against was Rosenthal's daughter, who was capable of testifying to Rosenthal's interaction with Eastbrook—if not actually providing a video of it—was because he doubted Stan would have the stomach for that. In any case, Stan agreed. The signed lease and check were sent, overnight mail.

Nicky waited as long as he could, until just before Labor Day weekend. That allowed whoever had forged the signature on the lease two weeks to deposit the check. Then he left: he was under subpoena to testify in Washington about the Harlanstrasse bombing, which, two years after the fact, the House Intelligence Committee was finally looking into. That left him only a few days on the island.

More important, Eastbrook was, by that August, three points ahead in the polls, and the election was only two months away.

This was, Nicky knew, a pretty long shot. But it was more than likely his last shot, so he could not afford to let it go.

And he was right. On Martha's Vineyard, his suspicions were confirmed, three times. First when he found proof of the forged endorsement of rental checks. Second when he was beaten up.

Things became more complex when he met Rosenthal's daughter, a strange and impressive woman, graceful and courageous as the world around her came tumbling down. He liked her immediately—as much, he thought, as he had ever liked anyone. Adding to her misery was not an easy thing. But he reminded himself that at stake was an imperative: nothing was sacred if it might help keep Greg Eastbrook out of office, and he made his pitch.

The third proof was the most categorical: that at last, after all these years of work, he had gotten close enough to Eastbrook to scare him.

That was when, in a bathroom at Logan Airport, en route to Washington during Labor Day weekend, a thin, tall man slipped behind him at the urinal and spun him around by the hips, as if they were dancing. And as he turned he felt a sensation that could only be a blade cutting flesh, and then he was being pulled off his feet, his whole body weight on the blade moving cruelly upward through his abdomen, and his arms were around the man's neck, and the smell of the man's evil breath was in his nose, and then he was falling, falling, while the blood of his body drained onto the tiled floor, and his consciousness fled without even the chance to appreciate how right, how perfectly right he had been all along.

6.

That night, the night before Labor Day, at Massachusetts General Hospital in Boston, at one in the morning, Harry Essex was putting on his coat.

It was the first time he had done so in over thirty hours: during the Labor Day weekend festivities he had performed emergency operations on no fewer that five gunshot victims. When a bleeder had been announced by EMS, he had just finished changing out of scrubs for the first time in two days, and was about to head back to his home in Newton. The bleeder, he told himself as he listened to the EMS radio, hadn't a prayer anyway: his intern could call the code and look into organ donation.

Still, before leaving, he hesitated. It was a moment during which a choice was made as to whether Nicky would live or die: no one else in the hospital, this night, could have saved him. Perhaps Dr. Essex knew that. And perhaps it was why, when he emerged from his fugue of thought, he removed his jacket and called for scrubs again.

⁓

Before the bleeder arrived Dr. Essex was already in the operating room, having his gloves put on while the rest of the team assembled. As the nurse worked on his gloves, he began to speak in the calm and certain tone of a professor addressing a classroom.

"Ladies and gentlemen, we are waiting on a thirty-five-year-old white male stabbing victim, one hundred and thirty pounds. He was stabbed in the lower left quadrant with an unknown blade. The EMS team reports a definite arterial bleed, and a very grave degree of blood loss. Dr. Armstrong, what will we be looking for?"

A young black woman spoke, gloved hands held up as her facial mask was tied. "Besides the bleed, sir, we'll want to look straight to the spleen, the lungs, and the other hollow viscera, depending on the nature and shape of the wound."

"Good. Dr. Thomas, what will we be preparing for?"

"We'll be ready to crack the chest cavity and clamp the aorta, while transfusing aggressively. Additionally, we'll scrub for an emergent splenectomy. Given the EMS report, sir, we've already notified organ donation of a likely candidate, and they are contacting his next of kin."

"Okay." Clearly, Dr. Essex's control over his operating theater was entire, and clearly this control was very much one offered by his respectful staff, rather than demanded by his authority. But before he could go on, the door was opening as the patient was brought in, the EMS technician squatting on the gurney while still keeping his hand, deep within Nicky's stomach, pinching off the arterial bleed.

As for Nicky, he appeared to be, rather than dead, in the grip of exhaustion—hopeless, painful—old far beyond his years, his eyes clenched in a frown, his face tightened as if in concentration. He was, of course, perfectly unconscious, probably already comatose. Still, when they transferred him to the operating table, it seemed as if the many machines and monitors connected to him were, rather than sustaining him, only remaining on-line by his massive effort, so massive that in his gray face the skin at the end of his lips, around his nose, and at his temples was strangely, entirely, bloodless.

Before Dr. Essex's eyes, now, Nicky was moved to the operating table. Some of the team connected him to a variety of machines, drips, and transfusions; others, monitoring the machines, began to call out vital signs; and still others began cutting away his shirt, spongy with scarlet blood. For a long moment, the doctor stood, his gloved hands held fingers-up before him, apparently lost in thought. Then, from the table, a voice called:

"Sir, I think we should notify organ donor stat. This patient will not survive a chest crack."

"By all means." Nearly absently, Dr. Essex spoke as he approached the table. "By all means. Now, young man"—speaking to the EMS technician—"I want you to keep your fingers on that bleed. Very well done, very well. Dr. Armstrong, I agree with you. We cannot open the chest. But we can try something else. I want a lateral cut from the center of the wound. Be careful of this young man's fingers. Dr. Thomas, I want you to prepare to clamp the mesenteric artery by feel above this young man's hand. Then I'll suture the bleed blind from the abdominal opening. It might work. We'll move from there directly to a splenectomy, I have little doubt. Young man, was your hand sterile? No? Well, let's give cefoxitin, two grams IV stat . . ."

The operation lasted four hours. And then, still not satisfied, Dr. Essex accompanied his bleeder to the recovery room, where he asked for some dinner, and then settled in for the rest of the night. Becoming, by the morning, the man who had saved Nicholson Jefferson Dymitryck's life no fewer than four times.

He would do so again four times before, in early evening, East Coast time, Jay Cohen arrived at the hospital, having taken Stan Diamond's Gulfstream from its berth at LAX.

7.

At five-thirty on the morning of September 9, Nicky awoke again in his hospital bed, hearing his voice, his dull, drugged voice saying things he never would have said to anybody, anybody. The room was dark, and for a long time he lay, saying unutterable things, as if emptying his soul in a vast paroxysm of all that had been secret, had been kept secret, all of his life. Then a nurse was there, inserting a syringe into the tube in his arm, and then she was gone, on a cresting wave of morphine, and once again, before the eyes of Nicky Dymitryck, all was black.

A night. And then a day.

This time, when he awoke, it was slowly.

Consciousness came before vision, a slow dream about darkness.

There were thoughts, but they were preverbal: sensations of time, of memory. As if there were, floating before him, out of reach and entirely without words, an idea of identity that, although he felt it to be assured, would not, could not pronounce itself. For a long time he lay in this weightless space, free of all past, free of future, trying to reassemble his awareness, fractured by massive bodily injury and then by wave after wave of cruelly numbing drugs.

Finally, as if far above, the rouge light of his lids pierced through the channel of his optic nerve into his awareness, and with it a sensation of pain; and then, as if rising from the bottom of a deep canyon of water, his identity returned.

He was in a white room next to a black window, un-lighted save for the red glow of a readout next to his head. For a long time he watched that glow. Then, moving only his eyes, he let his gaze wander over the ceiling, the window, the chair in the corner, and the mass of instruments around him. And only then did his eye fall on the person standing next to the open window, leaning out. It was Jay Cohen.

Slowly the room assembled itself: a space of low fluorescent lights, a monitor beeping, the smell of antiseptic in the air mixing with the smoke from the cigarette Jay was trying to keep out the window. For a long time, he gazed up at Jay, his familiar face with its Coke-bottle glasses under his ring of black hair around a bald scalp, and at the sight, a wave of peace seemed to pour down the IV into his arm. His throat hurt when he spoke:

"Since when you smoke?"

Jay started, flipped his cigarette out the window, and turned. "Since the late fifties."

"Thought you quit."

"Well, I started again, so shut the fuck up."

A pause while Jay shut the window and came to sit next to the bed, and Nicky noticed now a massive peace through his body, a relaxation so thorough, so total, that it seemed all his pain, all his days of pain and fear, had been concentrated into the ache in his throat. He wondered if he had ever felt this way before. Perhaps, he thought, in the womb.

"Jay?"

"Yes, Nicky."

"Tell me what happened."

An immediate response, in a curious tone, as if asking for information. "Don't you remember?"

Looking away to the black window, Nicky considered.

"I do remember. I was stabbed at the airport. I mean after that."

Jay hesitated, then spoke in a neutral voice. "You had

an arterial bleed and a ruptured spleen. A sharp goddamn EMS worker held the artery closed all the way to the hospital, and your doctor improvised a procedure to save you."

Staring at his boss, Nicky asked: "How close was it?"

"You were coded eight times. I was here for the last one."

"Jesus."

"You said it."

For a moment they regarded each other in wonder. Then Jay said:

"How you feel?"

"Like I been stabbed and coded eight times."

"Good, boy. You just relax now."

But Jay, Nicky saw, did not want anyone to relax—Jay wanted to talk. He rose, fetched a pint of scotch from his jacket, drank, and sat again. For a long time there was silence, the weight of Nicky's near death between them. Finally, Jay:

"Does she know?"

"Who?"

"The Rosenthal girl."

"About what?"

"What you're up to."

"To a degree. She knows I know about the embezzlement. She knows I want her to tell me about Greg Eastbrook."

"What's the story, you think?"

"She's scamming money off her father's properties. Did they find my things?"

"Uh-huh. The hospital had put them away, so I got them before the FBI. The film's at a lab, and the computer disk's in my pocket."

"Yeah." For a moment, Nicky struggled to remember, fighting against the somniferous effect of the pain killer. Then: "The film has images of endorsed checks from renters. The disk has an Excel spreadsheet tracking the income from rentals. Oh, yeah: the film also has a sheet of practice signatures, if they came out. I was right. The girl's forging her father's endorsement. When Stan's cancelled check comes back, we can prove the forgery."

Jay nodded. "We got her."

"Uh-hmm."

But Jay was racing ahead.

"Man, it's gonna be fun telling Rosenthal that. Nicky, when you get out of this bed, I'm going to kick your ass, then fire you. You hear me? But until then, I got to admit, this was sweet work."

Nicky paused at the praise, vaguely aware that once it would have meant a lot to him. Much of what he had done in his career, he knew, was designed to win praise from just this source. Now it seemed immaterial, an unnecessary delay in the conversation. "What's the plan?"

"Threaten to inform the State Attorney in Massachusetts. Gillian Morreale'll do it out of Stockyard, Dyson. Let Rosenthal know that we can put his daughter in jail. Then let him know what we're looking for, and how he can make us go away."

"Good. I'm doing it."

Now Jay smiled. "Uh-uh. I haven't told you the whole story. You're dead."

Nicky considered this for a moment, as if it might really be true. Then he spoke with the almost petulant defensiveness of the very ill.

"No I'm not."

"Oh, but you are. Check it out. The FBI thinks this whole thing's about the Harlanstrasse bombing, right? So I tell them, the only way to protect you is to announce to the media that you died under the knife. They say, no way, so I mention that the second you open your eyes we're giving a press conference to say that they wouldn't give you federal marshals although we warned them of the danger. So we announced that you'd died. Your obit was a few days ago. Made you sound kind of like an ass-hole, by the way."

Staring up, Nicky nodded hesitantly, as if still unsure that it wasn't true.

"You're shitting me."

"No, friend. I'm serious. You're a dead man."

"All right." For a moment, he absorbed the news. Then: "Now what?"

"Now we get your ass into a bed out West, thanks to Stan's Gulfstream sitting out at Logan, and then you sit tight while I go find Rosenthal and get this sorted out. You with me? You show your fine self anywhere and sure as the sun's coming up tomorrow, you're a dead man."

"No." Without any hesitation, Nicky emerged from the thought into which he'd descended while Jay spoke. "No way. What happens now is you get Stan to file suit. You need a month for that anyway. When you're ready, I go east and find Allison."

"Nicky . . ."

"Jay, don't fuck with me. It's that or nothing. I swear to you, I'll check myself out of this fucking place the second I can walk and go straight to New York."

"Okay. Okay." Jay rose and crossed back to the open window to light a cigarette. "You want some of this?"

"Yes."

So he crossed back and gave the lighted cigarette to Nicky, who drew hungrily. While his mind swirled with the nicotine, he asked:

"Think it's gonna work?"

"What?"

"Pressuring Rosenthal."

"I don't know." Jay allowed Nicky a last drag on the cigarette, then tossed it out the window. Nicky went on.

"I mean, he's only a criminal to us, right? These guys, this isn't crime to them, it's a religion, right? It looks like illegal arms dealing to us, to them it's Zionism."

Jay considered that.

"I don't believe that. Rosenthal's a businessman, not an idealist. The survival-of-Israel argument hasn't had any merit in years. It meant something once, but it still never covered half of what these guys have done. In fact, I'd go further: in terms of religion, they're on very shaky ground. Judaism's a religion based fundamentally on a story of liberation from slavery, of legitimate national aspiration. Now, Ron Rosenthal comes to me and says I got to help overturn democratically elected governments all over the globe, from Iran to Guatemala, to protect Israeli interests. That puts them in fundamental contradiction of the principles of their religion. Plenty of people in Israel know that. They're the WASPs of their country— White Ashkenazi Sabras with Proteksia, with influence. Powerful, yeah. But they don't define the national agenda alone. Right?"

Nicky nodded in response to Jay's piercing look, and after a suspicious moment of thought, Jay went on.

"These guys, they're just taking advantage of the fact that once upon a time, the country was built on the manufacture of armaments. David Ben-Gurion, you know what'd have happened if instead of concentrating on the Galil combat weapon he'd put his efforts into the internal combustion engine, or the computer chip? Israel'd be Japan, and the West Bank would be the Silicon Valley. Tel Aviv'd be employing Arabs from Jordan to Damascus, and Palestinians'd be beating down the door to get a job and a three-room ranch house with a swimming pool next to the mall in Hebron."

Now Nicky spoke. "That's not fair. Japan was disarmed and reconstructed by America. Israel had to arm itself. After the Holocaust."

"Right, ain't that a weird twist of history." Jay was sounding like himself now, and Nicky knew the lecture was over. "I still don't buy it. You know the numbers: there's been forty million deaths, worldwide, by conventional arms since World War II. What, we don't care about that because they weren't six million Jews? I don't buy it. I don't care why they're prosecuting Rosenthal, and I don't care whether he's guilty or not. I got no sympathy for him. Whatever you found in Martha's Vineyard, we're going to shove it right back up Rosenthal's ass, and when we get up there, you know what I think we're gonna find? I think we're gonna find Greg Eastbrook."

Nicky listened.

But all the while he was listening, Nicky was not thinking about Greg Eastbrook. Nor was he thinking about Israel, Zionism, or Ronald Rosenthal.

He was thinking, rather—and to his surprise—about the woman with green eyes who had been the last person he spoke to before he was stabbed and whom he was going, as soon as he was better, to see.

CHAPTER 11

October 11, 1994.
New York City.

1.

Later, it would seem to her that she had planned it from the very beginning: from the last, high, dry days of summer on the island; when she had met Dee, and when she had met Nicky.

Later, it would seem to her that she had been planning it all along, and each event, each meeting, each thought that seemed so coincidental, so fortuitous, each had its place in an itinerary she had been directing, without ever acknowledging, from the very start.

She wondered if her trip to Borough Park had really been the first time she knew what she was going to do. She wondered if, rather, she hadn't known long before.

Such as when Nicky was killed. Or when he came to Ocean View.

But then, Nicky meant nothing to her until he had discovered her fraudulent rental of the Ocean View properties.

When she began fraudulently renting out Ocean View, then.

But that was impossible—so impossible that the thought made her feel dizzy. Nor was it all. Nicky would have meant nothing to her had Dee not been hired to prosecute her father, and that had been well before.

And then she thought: but nothing would have been possible had she not fallen in love with Dee, ten years earlier on Hancock Beach. Had she not been present at Dov Peleg's taping of her father. Had she not gone that night to see Patti Smith. Had she not met Martha at Saint Ann's.

Then it was no longer clear to her when anything had started.

It was like, she thought, the way conspiracy theorists thought. Only, the conspirators were not operatives working for government agencies, but intentions hidden in covert agencies of her mind.

She remembered a Passover Seder she and Pauly had attended with her father, accompanying him on a trip to South Africa. It was at the home of a wealthy procurement officer on the South African-Israeli nuclear program, a palatial house surrounded by high walls and electronic gates in a suburb of Johannesburg. They had congregated around a heavily laden table for the annual rehearsal of the Jews' escape from Egyptian slavery into nationhood, and then the black servants had brought in the knaidlach and gefilte fish. The host had escaped the Holocaust, traveled, penniless, across the sea to Africa, and here in one generation he had risen to the highest possible wealth and influence. The wine was poured, and without looking up the host held out Elijah's glass to a servant, who carried it to the back door. Then he told a joke about the servant who returned to the Seder table with an empty glass, saying: "Master, Elijah here and he want more wine, Master."

Later, in the guest house with its own staff, Pauly, lying in a deep armchair, had said: "Daddy. How do you take that guy seriously?"

"How do I take him seriously?" Standing by the window, gazing out at the sweep and roll of perfectly green lawn around a swimming pool, her father had answered thoughtfully. "I take a guy who's made a billion dollars and brought nuclear capability to his country seriously very easily."

"Oh for God's sake, Dad, stop being dense."

And her father had laughed.

"Boy, the *shvartzim* get together a P.R. machine like we got, then they can have their own servants."

Watching, Alley had realized her father's success was not a fantasy, not a pretense, but a reality, and the fact that there was another reality—that of a police state and a vast, impoverished, repressed populace underpinning the white power elite with whom he did business—never entered his mind.

Now, considering what she had learned about herself since her visit to Borough Park, she thought: plausible deniability was not really a new political doctrine. It was an old psychic one, first, and long, long before.

She thought these things very early on Tuesday morning, October 11, sitting at her desk by the window on Jane Street, staring out into the chill night. It was 2 A.M.

In front of her, in a brown envelope, were 250 thousand-dollar bills, the entire take from her rentals on Ocean View, which she had withdrawn the day before. She'd tried to take it out on Friday, but the bank had required a day's notice. That had given her pause, but only briefly, for when she had gone to collect the money, in an armored room next to the bank's vault, it had been given to her with no questions.

Next to the money were the transcripts, photographs, and video she had taken from her father's safe in Borough Park.

Now, carefully, she wound each pile separately in Saran Wrap, turning them over and over in front of the box until thickly and tightly wrapped. She rose and carried them to the little, unused half bathroom off the kitchen, where she placed them on the tile floor directly in front of an ancient pedestal sink which had not been in use for years. With an effort of her legs she tilted the sink backward, exposing the hollow interior of the pedestal base, then with a toe gently shifted her jewelry box to the side and pushed the packages under. Next she lowered the sink again, inspected her work, turned off the light, and made her way quietly back to the bedroom.

Here, Dee slept, heavily, on his stomach, his arms wrapped around his head. Instead of joining him, however, she stepped to the closet and pulled off her nightdress. She dressed quickly in silk bicycling tights, a woolen sweater, and a down vest. Back at her desk, she took her wallet, the keys to her grandparents' apartment. Then she crouched in front of her bicycle and oiled it with a can of WD-40: she'd have to ride fast if she wanted to avoid getting robbed, or raped, and she couldn't afford a misshift in the middle of the Brooklyn Bridge. Briefly she stopped to wonder if she should drive. But she concluded, as she had concluded before, that it would be easy to follow her in a car, but virtually impossible on a bike. So she strapped on her helmet and then slipped quietly out of her apartment, carrying her bicycle and bicycle shoes, and into the night street.

The ride was nearly ten miles, and in the dark city, surreally lit and deserted, she sprinted nearly the whole way, high on her pedals over the Brooklyn Bridge, silently gliding through the streets, so fast that the few people she passed nearly didn't notice. On Third Avenue a Camry filled with Puerto Rican kids followed her, but she ran a red light and then banked the wrong way down a side street, leaving them far behind. The dangerous part was the hill into Borough Park, necessarily a slow climb, and once, approaching a group of men on the sidewalk, she wheeled round, sped down the hill again, then took another street back up. That delayed her a bit, but even so she arrived on Thirteenth Avenue in about forty minutes.

This time, she did not go down the hallway to the safe, but turned on the light in the dining room and began to walk the perimeter of the room, head cocked to read the file cabinet labels. Toward the end of her revolution, she found what she wanted. She put her backpack and helmet on the floor, opened a drawer, and began to finger through the files.

She knew it was there, for that was the very reason for the existence of these files: "My self-insurance policy," her father had called them, and he'd documented there, far from his legitimate business files, his private transactions. Such as his art purchases. And in particular, his purchases from a man she remembered him talking about.

Her father had bought a lot of art and antiquities, but only a few pieces came from this man, and not remembering the name, she had to search by the piece. Finally, in the paperwork for the purchase of some coins minted in Jerusalem in the second century before Christ, she found him: Peter Chevejon, with an address in Florence. Leafing through the paperwork, she read the development of the deal, then followed the cross-reference notes to ensuing deals: this, apparently, was an early one, as the coins had a legal provenance and her father had had them appraised, then paid fair market value. In later deals, she learned, as she found her way through the filing cabinets, Rosenthal would come to pay vastly inflated prices, from which Chevejon—in correspondence, her father addressed him by his last name—would exact a hefty cut, then deposit the balance in a numbered account. Still later, it appeared that Chevejon had abandoned all pretense of commercial process, and come to use the same network by which he smuggled illegal antiquities into America to take large amounts of Rosenthal's cash out, heavily discounting the exchange to European currency in return. Finally, there was a typed written report, in Hebrew and apparently the work of an intelligence operative, in which she read that Peter Chevejon was an alias of Peter Luria, an expatriate American living in Florence.

Now, in the shaded silence of her grandparents' apartment, kneeling on the parquet floor, Allison Rosenthal noted the name and Florence address in a little notebook and closed the file cabinet.

Chevejon could help her in a small, but essential portion of what was ahead of her.

Very possibly, she had known as soon as she had received Nicky's letter, she would be wanting to leave the country. And she would need money to keep her safe wherever she went.

As for leaving the country, that, she thought, she would work on. For the money, however, all she had in the world were her father's checks, which she would not touch, and the stolen rental money.

She was fairly sure that Peter Chevejon would know what to do with that.

By four-thirty she was back in her apartment at Jane Street. She undressed again in the bedroom, replacing her clothes while Dee slept. She put on her nightdress, made coffee in the kitchen. What was next? She withdrew her diary from a drawer, and opened it to the last composed page: Wednesday, August 31. She drew a rule under the last entry, dated a new entry Thursday, September 1, and then began to write.

An alarm sounded from the bedroom, and hastily she hid the diary in a locking drawer of her desk. Then Dee emerged from the bedroom, naked, and crossed to the shower, stopping to kiss her on the way. Allison paused at her desk for a moment, then went to shower with him.

This, she did unwillingly: somehow, since her trip to Borough Park, their intimacy had become a bit suffocating to her.

Still, she stepped into the steam with him. She, too, was in a hurry; she, too, had a busy day planned.

2.

As soon as Dee had left, she dressed in jeans, a sweater, and a woolen jacket. At a deli she bought a phone card for fifty dollars. Then, after trying several pay phones, she settled on one down Hudson Street, and made two telephone calls.

The first was to the number she had gone to Borough Park for, an office in Florence, Italy. A woman answered, "*Pronto*," then there was a brief pause before a man's voice spoke.

"Mr. Chevejon?"

"Yes?"

"Sir, my name is Allison Rosenthal. Ronald Rosenthal's daughter. You don't know me."

"Ms. Rosenthal. It's a pleasure to speak with you." Without even the briefest of hesitations, the urbane voice went on in, she was surprised to hear, a perfectly British English. "What can I do for you?"

Encouraged, she explained to him briefly what she needed, and again, as if she were asking the most normal question in the world, he responded without a pause.

"I see. And when can you have the . . . material ready?"

She considered. "Immediately."

Far across the line, Chevejon laughed. "Shall we say Thursday? I'll have to send one of my colleagues from Europe."

"Thursday then."

"Good. Why don't you bring your material to the piano lounge of the Waldorf-Astoria at, say, teatime? Four o'clock?"

"Okay." Allison waited for him to go on, for she felt

that such a transaction could not be this simple, but Chevejon seemed to have finished, and after a few sentences of small talk, they hung up.

Next, after a pause for thought, she called Bob Stein at his offices on Pine Street. Stein was out, and with some frustration, she returned to her apartment to wait for his call back. But evidently his secretary had deemed the message important enough to pass on, for he returned the call from his cellular just before lunch. Allison thought that he must be in court, judging from the sounds behind his voice, but later in the conversation he'd interrupted to ask "Billy" for "another one," and then Allison had pictured him, correctly this time, at the Yale Club stand-up bar, drinking martinis out of their big glasses.

"Alley girl! How you doing?" His booming voice sounded, after Chevejon's precisely British diction, very American.

"Fine, Bob. I wanted—"

But he was speaking again. "We must talk. I got some news about this Ocean View thing."

"Yeah. Could we meet?"

"Of course, honey. Is everything okay?"

"Yes, sure." Allison was not sure how to change the track of the conversation. Sooner or later, she realized, she had no choice but to be rude: not unlike when resisting a pickup at a bar.

"You hear anything new from California?"

"No. Bob, that's not what I wanted to talk about. I wanted to ask you some questions. About the case."

"The case. Of course. Opening arguments are, what, Monday next. I got disclosure last week."

"Right. And?"

"And?" Stein sounded confused now, and Allison went on.

"And you filed for dismissal, I'm sure."

Pause. Then, kindly: "Alley, honey, there won't be any dismissal."

"Of course not. But a motion would have effected a stay of seizure on my father's property."

A long silence now, and then Alley went on. "Or are you planning on losing the case?"

A laugh. "Honey, take it easy now. All I mean is, we're in damage control right now. I tell you what, give me a couple days. Before the trial starts, I'll go over the case with you, that's a promise. Say, let's see—Thursday. That suit you? We can do it at the club. Twelve-thirty?"

"Fine. I'll be at the bar."

The bar was a place traditionally reserved for men, and Stein hesitated audibly. Then, covering the annoyance at the bottom of his big voice, he said: "Lovely, my dear. I'll look forward very much."

3.

The person Bob Stein found himself facing over a lunch table at the Yale Club—he had tactfully strong-armed her away from the stand-up bar—was very different from the girl he had known all her life, and he saw quickly that the avuncular attitude with which he had opened the meeting—pleasantries masking his bafflement about why this girl was making him eat lunch with her—was not going to fit the bill at hand.

Like many big men, when he was nervous he used a kind of patronizing jocularity as friendliness. But he was also, as a good trial lawyer must be, a very sensitive observer, and he quickly saw that something was not striking home in this girl, the daughter of his dear friend and oldest client. When he tried to open a conversation about the letter he had received from Gillian Morreale, she brushed him off. Confused, he tried expressing hope as to the trial's outcome. That made her look annoyed; when he asked how school was going, she didn't answer. They ate in an uncomfortable silence, and when they were finished, and all the tables around them in the dining room had cleared, the girl leaned toward him and spoke in a low, surprisingly deep voice.

"So Bob, let me ask you this: what am I supposed to do now?"

He stammered—just slightly, and purposefully—in his response. "Alley, honey, you know we're doing everything possible."

She stopped him by looking away. Under the white of her blouse, open at the neck, a thick chain hung, ending at a heavy golden Star of David at the V of her bra. The chain gave a straight measure to the contour of her neck and breast: a slim, strong, grown woman. Stein had not realized, perhaps, what an impressive person she had become. She looked back and spoke.

"Who exactly are you working for, Bob?"

He thought it was Ron speaking, so exactly was it her father's intonation. Like that movie, he thought, where the guy turns into a chick, and he had to remind himself that this person in front of him was in fact not Ron, was just a girl, and that he didn't have to answer. And, in fact, he didn't have a chance to answer, because she was continuing, her eyes directly on him and her face calm, to talk.

"How can you possibly say you're doing everything possible? What exactly is it you're doing? You know, and I know, you're just waiting for conviction. You've already tried him."

He started to respond, and then stopped, as something occurred to him. He thought: if this girl speaks so exactly like Ron, then he should probably treat her forthrightness the way he would have treated Ron's more brutal honesty, which, no matter how confrontational, always left you the option of matching it. So he switched strategies and answered her as directly as he would have her father.

"The prosecution has a State's witness testifying that

there was no government directive guiding Ron. I got full disclosure last week. I've got a claim of government direction based on Ron's testimony. There's no paper trail: no presidential finding, no end-user documentation, no Commerce or State records."

"Of course there's not. That doesn't mean he wasn't directed."

Bob nodded impatiently. "Alley, let's cut the crap, okay? I know he was directed. That's not the point. Just because it's in criminal court doesn't mean this is a criminal trial, Allison. You know that. And you know that doesn't only work against us. The political winds might blow our way yet. My job is to make this trial last. It's a waiting game."

She nodded impatiently, and Stein felt suddenly convinced that Ron had no idea that his lawyer was meeting with his daughter.

"So what's your plan?"

"There's no choice. Try to establish that Ron was acting under orders. We can't do it, but we can make the trial last, try to get into a higher court. And then we see what the news brings. Court cases have a way of making the bodies surface."

"Will it work?"

Stein paused now, considering. "There are issues that could go to the Supreme Court on their own merits, but there's a lot of pressure on the court. The Teledyne precedent never went to trial, which is good and bad. I'll of course try to make it good."

Stein hesitated, then went on. "I'll be straight with you, honey: I've never seen a more direct line of pressure, the White House right down to the line prosecutor. I wouldn't have thought it could be done. This isn't Clinton-business-as-usual, doll. Someone's been very, very smart."

"I see." She drank her coffee, watching him over the

rim of the cup with those serious green eyes. Then: "How full has prosecution been on disclosure?"

"Punctilious. It's the government."

"Good." She put the cup down and motioned for the check, adding, nearly incidentally, "I want to see their case. Everything you've got up to now, and daily transcripts."

To this, Bob reacted immediately, without calculation and with real amazement. "Are you crazy? Your own father wouldn't ask me that."

She watched him, affectless. "Is there anything unethical about showing me?"

"No, of course not. Client's family? Of course not. It's not unethical—it's insulting."

"Can I insist that you do?"

"Not unless Ron backs you up. At which point, I'd quit."

She licked her lips, regarding him impassively, looked away, then shrugged, as expressively as any lawyer he knew. The check came, and she reached it from his hand, then signed it without looking and handed it back to the waiter. When he went, she continued in a careful tone that contained less earnestness and more—he felt—challenge.

"Then quit. In fact, I think you better quit."

"Oh, do you? I think I better speak to your daddy."

"I wouldn't do that, Bob. Know why? Because you are two seconds removed from plausible deniability. In two seconds I am going to put you in the position of choosing between colluding in a felony or exposing me for the intention of committing one. How do you like the idea of telling my dad that?"

Bob paused, something close to flabbergasted. "I have no idea what you're talking about."

"And you don't want to. Take it from me."

Was she serious? He stared at her, calculating, aware

that any question right now could well receive an answer he didn't want to hear. He asked, "What is it you want?"

"What I told you. Disclosure and daily transcripts. I'm warning you: don't ask me another question."

"And if I quit?"

She shrugged. "Then you have to deal with my father."

Bob Stein was used to having to make hard decisions. This one, he found, came with unexpected ease, unexpected confidence in this suddenly powerful figure before him. There was nothing more he could do for Ron, he knew that. If she thought she could, well . . . She was on target about plausible deniability: the less he knew about any illegal action she might be contemplating, the better. Was she going to hang herself? That was her decision.

In fact, she left him no choice: not as an officer of the court, and not as her father's friend.

But in the end of that brief pause, the decision was made more on a hunch than on reason.

And, of course, with a threat.

"You put me in a position I can't say no. But I tell you what. The only person here has anything to lose is me. Ron's in Israel. You're, forgive me, just a girl."

He stood now, towering over the seated daughter of his oldest client, a girl he had known all her life, a girl suddenly transformed.

"You keep that in mind, Alley."

4.

From the Yale Club, Allison walked meditatively to Park Avenue, a young woman in business dress, arms crossed against her chest, eyes thoughtfully to the ground. It was educative, she thought, to see Stein in action. She had always suspected his avuncular affection to be a farce. But once, on the drive back from a summer's day at Stein's

Amagansett house, she had mentioned that to her father, and his response had surprised her. Driving, without a pause, he'd shrugged off her concern:

"I don't got to trust Bob. Nor him me. He works better for me that way."

She hadn't understood then, but now she thought she might grasp the utility of being defended by someone you didn't trust. That way, she thought, you didn't owe them anything. That way you could better manipulate them.

She entered the Waldorf hesitantly, feeling as if she were being watched, and found a seat at a table for two by the piano. She ordered tea, watching curiously out over the lobby. What, she wondered, would happen now? And who would it be that approached her? Unconsciously editing all but suited men out of her vision, she tried to make out the choreography of surveillance that was undoubtedly taking place in the lobby, and after an hour of watching was surprised when a blond woman in a black pantsuit approached her and spoke in an accent she recognized as German.

"Allison?"

Disarmed, she stood and automatically shook the woman's hand, trying to place her. She was perhaps thirty-two, and at first Allison thought the woman must be some forgotten college acquaintance. But then she spoke, calmly and fluently.

"I'm from Chevejon. Kiss me on the cheek, now, like we're old friends. *Gut*. My name's Natalie. I take it this bag has your thing for us? *Gut*, just sit now, and put the bag on the floor."

They sat, and as the woman talked she leaned down to transfer Allison's envelope into her small leather attaché case on the floor.

"Very good now. It's the big envelope, I take it. *Voilà*. I don't think anyone's watching, but why not be sure?

Now, when we're done, you'll take your bag and go, and I'll stay here for a bit. Okay?"

Alley answered, trying to mirror the girl's bright, not evidently forced, smile. "Aren't you going to count it?"

She answered without looking up, buckling the case, which, Allison now noticed, was attached to her left wrist by a silver chain. "Chevejon said not to. He also asked me to tell you that he can't be bothered discounting a sum of this size. He will take his expenses, and hopes you will accept his service as that of a friend."

Allison absorbed this, then asked: "Does that mean it's too small, or too large?"

The woman looked up and smiled, a wide, pretty smile showing the pink tip of her tongue between even white teeth, and suddenly Allison found herself liking her. She wondered how someone like that got into such work, and wished she could ask.

"Far too small. He says he'll put it in a numbered account for you. Shall he choose a bank? Good. Mr. Chevejon assumes you'll be coming to Europe before long?"

Allison nodded.

"Do you need any help with that?"

Confused, she shook her head. Then she added as an afterthought:

"Such as what?"

"Ach, I don't know. A passport? Anything like that?"

"Oh. No, thanks. I'm set."

"Set to jet, good to go. Fine. Just contact Chevejon when you arrive, and he'll let you know the bank location and account number. Just one more thing, now."

Sitting, looking up, Allison waited.

"Chevejon would like you to know that he's at your service, now or any other time, for anything at all that you might need. He particularly wished me to tell you that . . ." She hesitated, as if her English were failing her, and then went on: "That this is regardless of your father's wishes. That is . . . that his help is not dependent on your father. I don't know what he meant. Do you understand?"

Allison nodded. The interview seemed to be over now, so she thanked the woman, who offered her right hand for a handshake, accompanied by a curious and, somehow, amused look directly at Allison's face. Then Allison stood and walked off with her empty bag.

As she left the Waldorf, a brief moment of nervousness overcame her. But no one stopped her, and nothing happened. She crossed the street and then, on sudden inspiration, stopped and leaned against a doorfront to watch the entrance to the hotel. After ten minutes or so, the woman in the black pantsuit came out, the silver chain of her attaché case around her wrist hidden under her sleeve, balancing on high heels with the easy confidence of a businesswoman leaving a meeting, but flanked by two large men in well-cut Italian suits.

The three of them climbed into a taxi, the taxi pulled out, but Allison kept standing there for a long time, lost in thought. This amused person, she thought, an out-and-out criminal, was the most sympathetic presence she had been in for months. And when she came to herself again, she found herself humming a tune, the familiar tune of a song, except that in the fugue of thought her mind had mistaken the words:

> *It's like I told you,*
> *Only the guilty can play.*

5.

On Wednesday morning, October 19th, the *New York Observer* ran a picture of Allison Rosenthal and Bob Stein leaving the Yale Club. Later Allison found out from Martha that an acquaintance from college, now an editor at *Vogue*, had seen them lunching, called his girlfriend at the *Observer*, and the *Observer* had sent a photographer over. Martha had delayed them for a week, then been powerless to stop them from running it. At first, she was very worried about that. Then she saw that the publicity suited her perfectly.

That made her realize something important.

It made her realize that events were in conspiracy with her. They had been since the beginning.

She thought about that, Thursday morning after Dee left, for a long time, sitting over coffee in her sunny kitchen. Then she shrugged the thought off. Probably, she thought, anyone with an objective in mind found that pure chance sometimes helped, and sometimes hurt. When it hurt, they didn't notice. When it helped, well then, it was like riding a bicycle downhill, drawing on the well of potential energy, enjoying its effortless transformation into kinetic.

Until you have to start climbing uphill again.

Anyway, she had long known that most people never rely much on chance: they're too frightened to be anything but safe, running scared for a safe spot in the status quo. Only those who try their luck, she knew, ever find out how good it might be.

Luck, however, needed help, and she rose now to dress again in business clothes.

All the while knowing that to explain the processes occurring to her as luck was grossly to evade the question.

That day, she went down to Bob Stein's offices, where a secretary had arranged the complete documentation of her father's trial, including the prosecution's disclosure, in a little office off Bob's. She thanked the secretary, accepted a cup of coffee, and started reading. She was there when Stein arrived in his office at eleven, there when he left at seven. And on Saturday morning, dawn found Allison Rosenthal in her father's lawyer's office, watching through the sealed window down to the river, in a rumpled business suit, drinking cold coffee from the afternoon before.

She couldn't blame Bob for his pessimism, not altogether. He, after all, did not know what she knew: he did not know Dee, did not know of his steadily shrinking confidence in the government's case. From Stein's point of view, she saw, whatever doubts Dee might harbor about the prosecution's chances of success, there were very many reasons to expect it to succeed. The reasons for this were less in the facts than in Stein's handwritten marginal notes.

For where Dee saw a central moral weakness in his prosecution, Stein saw another, possibly more serious one, in his defense. What Stein saw was that no matter how skilled his defense, no matter how careful his jury selection, no matter how thorough his P.R. and spin control, there was a fact that cut through all the complex legal issues of the case.

That fact stemmed from his inability to document the Clinton administration's direction of Rosenthal's Bosnian sale. And without that, when the day was done there was a rich Jew on trial, a very rich Jew, and one who, unlike any of the defendants in the Walsh prosecutions, was absolutely out of the running for any executive pardon. What Stein saw, and was right to see, was that even with the many and varied weaknesses in the U.S. attorney's case, when the jury went out, they would convict a very rich Jew.

As for the weaknesses in the prosecution's case, Alley, with her privileged view of her father's files from Borough Park, found to the contrary that the government knew a very great deal indeed about the Falcon Corporation. Not, of course, the truth, but a sufficiently plausible version of it to convict.

She considered this bleak prospect until, carrying his *Wall Street Journal* and stopping in his tracks with surprise, Bob Stein entered his office and found her there, precisely where he had left her the evening before.

She crossed to the couch and sat, rubbing her eyes with the heel of her hands while he lowered himself into his chair and regarded her curiously.

"You find what you need?"

She yawned, stretching her arms above her. "Um-hmm. They have a good case."

Bob nodded, waiting, while her gaze abstracted, marshaling thought, and then came to focus on him again. "This is what I need you to do. Try to establish a distance between what Michael Levi knows and what the prosecution knows. Every chance you get."

"I don't follow you."

"I mean, look for the limits. Is there a discrepancy? Do they only know what Levi told them as State's witness, or are there corroborating sources? And what's the source of Levi's evidence? Insist on the sources."

Her authority, to judge from Stein's response, had grown—backed up now by the gravity of her exhaustion. They paused while a secretary brought in coffee on a silver tray, and when she had gone, Stein shrugged.

"Why?"

She looked at him for a moment, as if in warning, then continued. "Also, the prosecuting lawyer, he'll have rehearsed Levi's testimony, right?"

"Sure."

"Then badger him. Make the jury think he's leading the witness."

"Alley. I attack their lawyer, the media's going to be on my ass *tout de suite*."

"I know. That's good. Who's their true prosecutor?"

"Some hotshot kid, Ed Dennis's son. They're giving him the exposure on it, seeing they figure he can't lose."

"He any good?"

"Don't know. So far he's just following orders."

Allison nodded. "Well, make him look bad." Now she rose to get her coffee from his desk, then leaned against the window while she drank it, looking out. "One last thing. I need daily transcripts of the trial. Can you do that?"

"Yeah." Bob nodded, as if having abdicated all responsibility for himself. "How do you want it?"

"You have a computer geek here? Good." She crossed the room now to her backpack, and took out a computer disk. "Just tell him this is my PGP key and Net address. Tell him to go via penet-fi, okay? That makes it anonymous. He can send it once a day."

Stein nodded, holding the disk—clearly an unfamiliar object to him—by the edge. Then he rose and stepped around the desk, looking slightly embarrassed. "Is that all?"

Allison nodded, moving toward the door, as if to avoid a handshake, and Bob, uncharacteristically meek, asked:

"Anything else you can tell me?"

She shook her head, once, decidedly, and then she was gone.

Outside, leaving Bob's office and walking uptown through the bright autumn sun rising in the cold morning air, Allison stopped on Broadway. Stopped and stood, in the middle of the sidewalk, for a long, hesitant moment. As if unsure of where to go. As if unsure of what to do next. And for a moment, her confidence wavered.

True, she had come a long way. True, the pieces on this crazy chessboard had so arranged themselves magically.

Still, there was a lot that had to happen—a lot over which she had no control, and for a moment, everything that had seemed so clear, everything that had seemed so magnificently arranged as an itinerary, felt instead a mad series of disconnected events.

Then she shook off the thought. In her heart she

knew, surely and absolutely, that that which had to happen, would happen, and when it did, she would recognize it. She had taken the golden scepter, and now, against the king's highest law, she was going to speak. *And if I perish*, she thought suddenly, with a flush of determination, *I perish*.

Recognizing the quote, she blushed, clear through the light skin under her blond hair.

CHAPTER 12

October 24, 1994.
New York City.

1.

On Monday morning, October 24th—opening day of
U.S. v. Ronald Rosenthal—Nicky Dymitryck arrived in
New York and checked into the room at the Sherry-
Netherland Jay had reserved for him under the name of
Neal Cassady.

Very funny, Nicky thought, after three days of traveling across the country, leaning weakly against the open
doorway while the porter placed his bag on a stand.
Dimly, against the skin of his face, he felt a cold sweat,
and his hand trembled as he gave the porter his tip. The
door closed and he made it to the bathroom just in time
to throw up, painfully, the paroxysms burning the length
of his belly's dual scars: one the slim track of a scalpel
from his splenectomy; one the jagged, evil flare of a knife.
When he could, he staggered into the room, flipped on
the television, and tuned it to NY1, just in time to see the
scene outside the federal courthouse where Ronald
Rosenthal was about to go on trial.

Three TV uplink vans were there, and on the screen

Nicky recognized the Israeli ambassador entering, a small group from the Coalition for a Code of Conduct, a number of government observers, and reporters from every newspaper he knew.

Jesus, he thought to himself as he lay, willing his nausea down, weakness washing over him. Every fucking person in the world wants a piece of Ronald Rosenthal.

His trip had started out well. After a month in bed at his father's house in Malibu, attended by a private nurse and discreetly visited by Stan's doctor, his health, always resilient, had seemed to have returned nearly completely. True, Dr. Bromberg had warned him against getting up: Nicky needed at least another month of recuperation, he said. In another month, however, Colonel Eastbrook would be Senator Eastbrook, and Nicky had convinced Jay to make the arrangements for him to go east.

From Los Angeles he traveled to Mendocino in the back of a van, feeling fine. That night, he slept in Bill Cusimano's Mendocino house, back to the rocky coast and front protected by armed guards not, Nicky suspected, hired specifically for the purpose of protecting him. A suspicion confirmed later that night when Bill took him through a trapdoor under the kitchen sink and showed him, surreally lit under grow lights and bathed in a soft fall of artificial rain, a massive sea of green: shiny fat marijuana plants, glistening with resins and almost ready to harvest.

Here, he knew, was the source of the funds that had kept Mimi Luria on the run for so many years, then paid her legal expenses at Stockard, Dyson in Boston. And here, he realized, was a nearly perfect place for Bill's small organization to find out if anyone was following Nicky: on these narrow, winding Mendocino roads, where nearly every house harbored a plant or two of exquisitely hybridized dope, no stranger passed unnoticed. Lying that night on a futon on the floor of Bill's young son's room, a cold northern sea rain pattering the window, Nicky hoped that tonight was not the night that the little operation was going to be raided.

From Mendocino to Denver, Nicky had driven in two days, high in the cab of a moving van, in the back of which five pounds of Cusimano's bud was hidden in the household items of a San Francisco stockbroker, relocating to Denver. The van drove slowly, followed by two cars: business as usual for Cusimano's well-oiled smoke operation. The driver, a lanky man of perhaps fifty, was unaware that he was carrying upward of two hundred thousand dollars worth of dope. He thought Nicky was a friend of the customer, needing a ride east. In any case, he was glad for the company.

In Denver Nicky climbed down from the van and experienced the first pain in his belly. He checked into a Day's Inn and waited for Jay to call. Here, examining himself in the mirror, he attributed his pallor to tiredness. No sooner, however, had he fallen asleep than Jay called and announced that he was virtually certain that Nicky's departure from Los Angeles had gone unremarked, but that in his opinion Nicky should travel overland to New York.

Nicky wasn't interested in traveling overland; he was far too tired. When he hung up, he caught a cab to the airport and bought a ticket to Newark in the name of Don Hymans on a credit card supplied, along with a number of other pieces of ID, by Cusimano. Twelve hours later—after an evening sitting in the airport and a night in the plastic sanctity of an airplane, Nicky arrived at the Sherry-Netherland, exhausted, nauseous, the scars along his stomach throbbing. And no sooner was he alone in his room than he threw up.

Now, feeling somewhat better, he watched Allison climbing the court steps in a charcoal-black dress suit on TV. Briefly, he considered where he was going to confront her. He knew she would be leaving the court at five, but he also knew where she lived, and that she collected her mail at a bar downstairs from her apartment: Gillian Morreale had gotten a New York process server in place, and he had in turn done the research.

Outside, golden sunlight filled the well of the street, a crisp chill in the air that he could feel through the windowpanes, a chill that brought back in full force an awareness of where he was: on the East Coast in autumn. He slept for a time, waking with an image of Allison in his mind. She had been, in his dream, soundlessly cresting a small hill of grass and then, with a friendly wave, descending the other side, out of sight. Knowing that it was an image of anxiety did not diminish its influence. As he sat up, dizziness crossed his mind, and he had to lie down again. Finally, he managed to stand and light a cigarette.

Smoking, he sat at the room's little desk and unpacked from his briefcase the things he needed to prepare for that meeting. There were the relevant parts of his interview with Dov Peleg, which would show Allison that he knew what he was looking for. There was the legal documentation that, on his word, would be filed in Massachusetts court. This would show Allison that he knew how to get what he was looking for. And finally, there were the pictures he had taken at Ocean View farmhouse, in what seemed like another lifetime.

Still, as Nicky moved himself heavily toward the shower—he seemed to be sweating an unusual amount—he wondered why he had the feeling that what was in front of him, as represented by these documentary tools of blackmail, was not really what he had come for.

2.

Earlier that day, while Nicky's taxi had been pulling up to his hotel, Allison Rosenthal had been sitting at her desk before the window of her apartment.

In front of her eyes was Jane Street, three stories down, deserted but for a lone man in a black knit cap walking a dog. Both dog and master's mouths let puffs of steam out into the morning air, air that later would be warmed by the strong sun to the heat of another Indian summer day but which, this early morning, held far more anticipation of winter than reminiscence of warmth.

Beyond apprehending the winter in the tableau, Allison, at her desk by the window, saw nothing of this.

In her eyes was an image of the last days of summer on the island, the days shown in the set of photographs tacked to the wall above her desk: a wide stretch of yellow sand beach next to the luminous green sea, empty Atlantic coastline under the deep blue sky of summer, a lone gull hovering, about to dive, above a lazily curling wave.

She looked at this last image, on the wall above her desk, for a long time. She looked at it as if in it hung the key to a decision she was weighing, and in this respect, the image was telling. It was as if the picture captured not just Ocean View farmhouse, but also the most abstract of everything that was at stake in the decision before her. A place is never just a place, she thought, but the sum of what had been experienced there. In this place was everything that had ever mattered in her lifetime. To look at a picture of Ocean View farmhouse was to feel a direct sense of her entire identity. Nothing, she thought, is ever only itself. But was the abstraction hidden behind this picture worth what she was about to do? Was even the truth worth what she was about to do?

A half hour passed with the even rise and fall of her breath, the radiator emitting gasps of steam that ended in an abrupt metallic clank. It lasted until 6:27 exactly. Then Allison rose, fetched a cup of coffee from the kitchen, and walked into the bedroom to wake Dee.

While Dee showered, she returned to her desk. The

calmness of meditation had flown. Her heart rate, she felt, was increasing. That was not surprising.

Dee emerged from the shower, dressed in the bedroom, and came out again, his shoe heels sudden on the floor. She rose now, examining him, his hair moussed away from his face, his cheeks close-shaved, and his eyes showing their peculiarly aqueous blue. It struck her, suddenly, as a cold color.

She straightened his tie, the heels of her bare feet lifting from the wooden floor, and then stepped two steps back, toes first. But instead of taking his briefcase and heading for the door, Dee sank onto the living room couch, Alley returned to sit sideways in her desk chair, facing him.

Alley wondered if his heart, too, was pounding. But then, she thought, he had no idea what was about to happen to him.

And that, although Dee perhaps could not see it on her face, was on her mind as she regarded him, expressionless, from her perch at her desk.

And yet Dee, too, was experiencing fear: perhaps most justifiably of the three scared people. His was, after all, the largest stage on which to play—for the moment, in any case. And he was arguably the least prepared for this exposure of the three. Nicky and Alley, fighting for their lives, were only too sure of what they were doing. He, on the other hand, was about to commit himself publicly, irrevocably, and, incidentally, illegally. That he felt badly frightened was no surprise.

It was funny, she thought—not for the first time—the degree to which Dee had become another person. He had started so sure of himself, so confident in his position as Ed Dennis's brilliant son, being happily groomed to assume his position in the Beltway hierarchy. Now, after peering at the world through her eyes, nothing any longer felt sure to him.

Watching him, she remembered how he had come

back from a weekend at home, not two weeks ago, and told her about a conversation with his father. He had not told his father about Nicky Dymitryck, nor about his researches into the *NAR*'s dual interests in Rosenthal and Eastbrook. He had, however, told his father that he thought Eastbrook had information relevant to the Rosenthal prosecution, and he was considering requesting permission to depose him.

The iciness of his father's smile, to hear Dee tell it, betrayed his concern more than did his voice.

"Dee. You don't want to be looking to Eastbrook."

"Why? Defense is going to."

"No, sir. Defense will not say a word about Eastbrook."

That gave Dee pause. Then, he said: "Dad. Eastbrook and Rosenthal have been involved in the same business since Laos. There's not a serious piece of arms trade analysis that doesn't mention the one within three pages of the other."

"The same's true about a good half dozen other players."

"We've deposed them already."

Against his will he felt a glare of adolescence seeping into the water of his eye, as if he were not a thirty-year-old man but a child again who'd just been caught with a quarter-z of pot. And after watching him awhile, his father spoke, quietly.

"Deedee, it takes security clearances you've never heard of to depose Eastbrook. Discovery of classified materials alone would hold up your trial for a minimum of five years, and you'd still get nothing. And you don't need it. You can convict Rosenthal on what you have."

"That's my point. I can convict, but it's with half the truth."

Now his father stood and, standing, showed his back to his son. "White House counsel feels that this is a misdirection."

"Is he willing to put it in writing?" Dee spoke before he could stop himself.

And indeed, now it was White House counsel who turned to his son.

"You have no authority to pursue any further investigation. You have had a privileged conversation with White House staff. Now go and make your case."

Of course, Dee had said to Alley when he told her about this conversation, Walsh had had to make hard decisions too about which cases could be made in court, and which had to be overlooked. There were no statutory arms violations charges brought in the Walsh prosecutions, even though arms export violations were discussed before Congress and broadcast throughout the world. Walsh didn't even try, going for lesser charges of lying to Congress and even extraneous charges—North's security fence, for example—instead, where the case could be made.

But this, Dee felt, was different. This, Dee felt, as he considered the case before him, was something different indeed. Dymitryck's investigation of Rosenthal, and his death, showed that there were forces swirling behind this trial that were being deliberately kept unacknowledged. And as for the people who were trying to keep them that way, Dee was no longer sure they knew what they were doing.

It was, Allison thought, watching him sitting in her living room, on the morning of the biggest day of his life, a bit heartrending.

She was to blame for the dissolution of all Dee's certainty. As if she had infected her lover with a disease that had long plagued her, as couples used willingly to share incurable cases of syphilis.

Dee remained silent, his face showing excitement, stage fright, as it should, but also a sense of dread, which it should not. She rose now, walked into the kitchen for another cup of coffee, and drank it, half sitting against the kitchen table, watching her lover in the living room through the small arch of the kitchen door. Then, her arms crossed, she spoke matter-of-factly, as if continuing, uninterrupted, the conversation of the night before.

"I think you are making way too much of this."

He didn't reply, and she went on.

"What my grandfather would have called a 'matzoh pudding.' "

Now he spoke, without looking at her.

"Your grandfather ever try a defendant whose guilt he doubted in a case he thought was politically motivated for employers he thought were concealing relevant evidence?"

Nodding, she answered in a neutral tone.

"Why don't you go do your job and see how it pans out."

"You mean, go do what I'm told."

"The people who prepared this case weren't idiots."

"That's not the point, Alley."

"You're overreacting," she observed after a short silence, although she knew he wasn't.

He replied without emotion. "You know I'm not. Alley, everything I know about what's really at stake here, I either found out for myself or learned from you."

She waited now. The moment of commitment was coming. With a distant pang of regret, she wished she could put it off.

She tried again. "No one has shown any proof my father was following orders. They have a State's witness, Dee. They have a crime. He has no standing in this government; the defense has only his word that he was directed by a government source."

"So what? We both know that's just a cover-up. Dymitryck was killed precisely because he was looking underneath that."

"May have been. May have been. We don't know who

killed him. That's not evidence. And besides, Dymitryck is—was—partisan."

"Partisan is exactly what this thing isn't, Alley. I'm about to be sacrificed to a cover-up, and you know it. It's just like Iran-contra—not even the Democrats on the committee wanted to see Reagan impeached. Now they don't want to stir up anything about the Iraqi tilt. They'll let me lose the fucking case before they do that."

That was supposed to be unanswerable, and indeed, Allison paused. Now the decision was directly before her, more baldly stated than ever before. When at length she spoke, it was quietly and with courage. "Then win the case. That'll surprise them."

He answered with a withering look, then an apologetic one, then by putting his head between his hands. For a moment, there was silence, and had Dee looked up, he would have seen Alley watching him with the cool green light of her eyes.

"When's Levi on the stand?"

"First thing after opening statements. Maybe this afternoon." Dee's voice came from inside his hands.

"Start by asking him about Carlos Cardoen."

He didn't look up, but his neck stiffened. Another moment of silence, this time a very long one. Then Alley went on in the same quietly happy voice, and what she was saying came straight out of the safe in Borough Park.

"Ask about my father's trip in 1985 to Chile. Ask what he was doing there?"

"Alley," Dee interrupted. "What in God's name are you talking about?"

"Shut up. Listen. Stein says my father wouldn't have gone ahead with the Bosnian sale without U.S. approval. Stein says my father's a puppet for an administration contravention of the embargo. But you ask Michael Levi, bless his heart, what my father was doing in Chile, and listen to what he tells you."

"I don't know what the fuck you're talking about."

"Yes, you do. Think. Carlos Cardoen was building cluster bombs and chemical weapons for Iraq. We know that because Teledyne was a supplier—zirconium, remember? He was selling them up to the day before the Gulf War. Only, Israel didn't like that. They liked arming Iran, 'cause they'd been doing it since they trained SAVAK for the Shah, and they liked Iran to keep Iraq fighting, and anyway they never had wanted to give up the revenue stream. But they didn't like arming Iraq. That wasn't about money, it was about blood. They thought Hussein could turn his Scuds from Teheran to Tel Aviv, and it turned out they were right. My father went down to Chile as Israel's direct representative to buy Cardoen off, then, when that didn't work, threatened him."

Watching, listening with intense attention, Dee considered. Then he nodded.

"Okay. This has nothing to do with my case."

"Listen to me, Dee. Cardoen was indicted by a grand jury in 1991, along with Teledyne. Pretrial, his lawyers proved U.S. government support for his arming. Proved. No one even denies it. The Iraqi tilt is documented. Right?"

"Right. It didn't have any bearing, though."

"Doesn't matter. What matters is my dad, in Chile as a special envoy of the Israeli prime minister, pursued absolutely the opposite policy. Tried to buy Cardoen, then threatened to shut him down. He did it in direct contradiction of the U.S. government. And he did more."

Beginning to understand, Dee nodded. Alley went on.

"So fuck Bob Stein and his claim that my dad was directed by someone in the administration, 'cause when he doesn't like what the administration does, he goes his own way. And you can prove it."

Now Dee focused on her again. "How can I prove it?"

"You ask Mike Levi, under oath, what I tell you to."

As if simply unable to comprehend what she was saying, Dee stared at her, the processes of his mind, complex, confused, transparent on his face. "That's new evidence."

"So what? It's not exculpatory on the charges you're prosecuting, there's no obligation to disclose. Levi's taking an immunity bath in that court. You bring an illegality up, he'll admit to it. Why not? And he doesn't care if it implicates someone else: he can't, he's afraid of jeopardizing his immunity. You know how State's witnesses are, they have no pride—they're not allowed to. He's not going to perjure himself for my father."

In the face of Dee's amazement, she smiled suddenly.

"Feeling better now?"

3.

Dee nearly blurted his next words. "Why are you telling me this?"

Leaning against the kitchen table, her worn flannel nightdress hanging round on her naked shoulders, she showed him in profile her face, her breasts under her nightdress, her stomach. "I've been thinking about this, Dee, and I don't want a lecture from you. You understand?"

"No. I mean yes. I understand you don't want a lecture. I don't understand what you're talking about."

"Then listen. There are two people on trial here. Whichever loses is exiled from home. One's my dad. Two's you."

Dee nodded comprehension, then shook his head.

"I see. You can't do it. I can't do it. He's your father."

"And you're an asshole."

Silence. And now Alley intensified her tone.

"I told you I don't want a lecture. My father's fine. You think he's in trouble? Look at this." Rising suddenly, she stepped to the desk and pulled out an envelope containing perhaps a dozen of her father's international bank account checks.

"This bullshit means nothing to him. He owns half of Israel. By the time his appeals are finished, he'll be a Knesset member, totally unextraditable. All they want from him, anyway, is a fine. You said so yourself: only an exchange of assets is at stake. You, you have to come out of it in one piece. I need you."

Dee's reply was unexpected. He rose, crossed to where she sat in her wooden desk chair, knelt, and put his face against her stomach. She felt his lips through the nightdress, and let a hand fall to his hair. Like this, they rested for a moment. When he rose, straightening his hair, he said:

"I'm not going to use it."

"Use it."

He crossed back to his briefcase, his expression altered to tenderness. Dee moved, Alley thought, was the person she had fallen in love with. Shrugging on his overcoat, he said:

"What's your source?"

"His personal papers."

"I could never introduce them without provenance."

Feeling slightly desperate, she spoke urgently. "You don't need to introduce them. Just ask Levi about the Israeli Iran-contra chronology Israel prepared for the joint committee. It's printed everywhere in the world, Dee. It showed my dad down there in Chile: they had to give that to prove that he wasn't in a Ghorbanifar meeting, and no one asked any questions about it. *U.S. v. Teledyne* makes Chile directly relevant. Levi'll explain everything. I told you, he's not going to perjure himself for the man he's already turned State's evidence on."

Overcoat on, he stared at her. "I'm not going to use it."

"I want you to use it." It came out with unexpected

force, and he looked up at her, analytically, for a long second. Then he looked at his watch, and swore.

"I'm fucking late."

"You got plenty of time. It's seven A.M."

"No, I don't. I got a FedEx to drop off. And I'm due for breakfast in the office in fifteen minutes. Shit." He opened his case, suddenly, clumsily, and pulled out a FedEx envelope and a letter, then reached into the breast pocket of his jacket and withdrew a pen.

And Alley suddenly felt her heart pound in her chest.

As if she could hear a precise, mechanical click as another piece of the puzzle fell into place.

A feeling, she thought over the pounding in her chest, that was growing oddly familiar.

Before she could think, she said: "Leave it for me. I'll take it across town on my way to court."

"Would you? Thanks. Let me address it."

"No, Dee." She crossed the room in a few quick steps and took the paperwork from him. "Let me address it, you get going. Just sign the slip."

"Okay, thanks. The address is on the letter." He signed quickly, replaced his pen, closed his briefcase, and rose. From his height, in his suit, he regarded the woman before him, in a nightdress. But whatever words were in his mind were clearly too much to say now. He kissed her, then turned to the door. Then he turned again.

A moment later, he emerged onto Jane Street, carrying his case, and stepped away down the street with the briefest of glances up to her window.

Alone in the apartment, Allison's heart slowed gradually. She leaned down for the FedEx slip on the couch, and held it under the light. The return address, preprinted by Federal Express, was from David Treat Dennis at the U.S. attorney's World Trade Center office. His signature sat at the bottom of the form.

It was amazing the speed with which it had come to her. Now, she thought, she could fill in a fresh form at the FedEx office. She'd go at lunch from court, when the trial recessed.

The result? She had a clean, undated FedEx form preprinted with the U.S. attorney's address on it, and with Dee's verifiable signature.

And, should someone need them, his fingerprints.

Smiling, suddenly, in disbelief, her hand still on her forehead, now, in the empty apartment, she spoke out loud: "Jesus."

It had been an exciting morning.

4.

Dee's state of shock carried him through the taxi ride from the West Village right down to his office, like a cheerful companion encouraging him in his hour of nervousness. A welcome companion, he thought, but a very strange one.

The information she had just given him was like a talisman, and the magic energy that it held was the proof of her love. It moved him profoundly, and continued to move him through the breakfast meeting, a last review of the jury makeup by cards held in a polished wooden holder, showing the twelve jurors by seat and the four alternates.

The two senior attorneys, Daniel Edelson and Beth Callahan, with whom he would sit at the prosecution's table, were impeccably groomed and animated by an air of suppressed excitement. After the short meeting the three lawyers, together with the four paralegals who would sit behind them in the benches, crossed town by car. In front of the courthouse, from the window, he counted uplinks from NY1, WPIX, WOR, the three networks, and the BBC. Stage fright surfaced strongly at the sight, and he was grateful to be able to follow his well-groomed elders through the gauntlet of television and still cameras and up the stairs into the federal courthouse.

Inside, the defense team had just arrived. Dee was conscious of shaking Bob Stein's large, soft hand and looking, briefly, directly into his sharp eyes. Then he was in his seat and behind him he could hear the room filling slowly with people.

There were many reporters, but even more observers. A strange entertainment, he thought with nervous detachment. He had a glimpse of Alley entering in a charcoal suit and sitting a row behind Bob's team. Then, in front of him, a stenographer took her place, and fear, unexpected in its intensity, mounted. But there were still neither bailiffs nor a judge, and in the pause that followed the talisman which Alley had given him exerted again its strange power.

What did it mean? To his surprise, he found that without his knowledge a corner of his mind had been following the ramifications of Alley's strange betrayal of her father to its logical end. And that end was twofold.

First, in legal terms, it altered the entire course of the prosecution. It meant that the questioning of Levi had to change dramatically, for one. Did he know how to do it? Like magic, Dee's nighttime researches into the *NAR*'s interest in Rosenthal came fluently to his mind: names, dates, locations. Even in his nervousness, he appreciated the irony that he should be using Dymitryck's work to win this trial. It meant, in fact, that Stein's key defense—the claim that Rosenthal was following government directions—could be dealt with on the very first day of trial. From there, it would be a rout.

Second, in personal terms—and here Dee's heart swelled—it meant that Alley was prepared, literally, to sacrifice her father for him. That was an astounding thought, all the more so in this state of heightened awareness under pressure.

Time was running out. The bailiff entered and called all to rise, then Judge Thomas stepped behind the bench. Now he would instruct the jury. That could take a very variable amount of time. Then Dee would rise for opening statement, then Stein. After that, Levi would come in, and Dee would go to work.

For the next ten minutes, Dee did not hear Judge Thomas.

For the next ten minutes, Dee barely heard his thoughts.

When he came to himself again, he found the judge was looking at him. And then he felt himself rising, as calm as he had ever been in his life.

Head down, a thumb and forefinger pinching his lips, Dee Dennis paused for effect. When he looked up again, he spoke in a low tone. It was sufficient: the room was dead silent.

"Ladies and gentlemen, during this trial, the defense is going to speak to you a lot about a certain portion of our government's business. Specifically, you are going to learn about how our government regulates its contacts with other countries, and even more specifically, you are going to learn about how a certain class of arms transfers are made between our government and other governments. This class of arms transfers is usually referred to as covert, or gray-market. And the defense will claim that now, as in the Iran-contra affairs, the executive branch of our government directed Mr. Rosenthal's activities.

"That's a strong argument, ladies and gentlemen, because it's impossible to prove, and as such it's also impossible to refute. Where we show you proof of guilt, the defense will claim that the proof of Mr. Rosenthal's innocence is classified. Where we show you crime, the defense will talk about plausible deniability.

"Ladies and gentlemen, if I could ask you one thing, it would be to not be fooled by this, this . . . confusion about covert activity. There are two things that I can tell you, from years of experience, are always true in the arms business. The first is that every person who makes an illegal arms deal pretends he has some CIA agent directing him; and the second is that every time an Israeli breaks the law selling arms, you can be sure that it's in defense of the safety of Israel. But when it's time to count the profits, don't kid yourself that any of that money is going either to the U.S. taxpayer or to the Jewish people. It's going into private, secret, numbered Swiss bank accounts, and the only people it's helping are the individuals who broke the law to get it.

"During the course of this trial I will show you in the clearest terms possible that not only has the Falcon Corporation historically operated in the world theater without any U.S. government direction, but that they have, again and again, specifically fought our government's direction and acted precisely contrary to our interests. And I will do so in the perfect confidence that this jury will act on behalf of the citizens of the United States, whose membership in the United Nations specifically forbade the foreign military sales of which Ronald Rosenthal stands today accused. Thank you."

Dee rounded the desk and sat, feeling Edelson's hot breath on his ear, but he did not listen to what his fellow attorney was whispering. Nor did he pay attention to Bob Stein's slightly longer introductory remarks.

What he listened to was in his ear only, and it was Allison's low voice, expressionlessly emerging from the kitchen.

What he saw was her slim form, leaning cross-armed against the kitchen table, her face expressionless as she calmly delivered the verdict of a struggle he had not ever even suspected.

And what he felt, slowly mounting in his breast, was rage: a pure, clean rage that he had not felt since he was a child.

Rage at this process of compromise; rage at his ill use by his father and his cronies.

Rage at the way he had once again, through the years and years of his life, been so surely, so inescapably, cornered.

5.

Looking at him revealed nothing: to Alley, watching his quarter profile from an angle slightly behind him, the drama taking place in Dee was entirely hidden. He sat collected, calm, gazing at Bob speaking, then looking away at the floor in front of his table. Her hands, she suddenly found, were clenched in her lap, and her attention was entirely concentrated on one word: Please. Please.

Stein concluded, Levi was sworn in, and the room paused. For a terrified moment, Allison thought that Dee was not going to remove his fixed gaze from the floor. And indeed he did not, speaking without looking up into the silent room.

"Good morning, Mr. Levi. I'd like to start with a very general question. I'd like to ask you why Mr. Rosenthal undertook to sell military supplies to one side of the civil war in the former Yugoslavia."

He continued to watch the floor while Levi answered, carefully rehearsed in just this introduction to his testimony. And only when Levi had finished did Dee rise, moving slowly around the table, then stopping midstage to look up at the witness.

"Now, in his opening remarks for the defense, Mr. Stein announced his intention to prove that Ronald Rosenthal was following a governmental directive in undertaking this sale. He pointed out that President Clinton himself supported the Bosnian Muslims, and claimed that Mr. Rosenthal acted—in effect patriotically—in accordance with the president's wishes. Is it true that Mr.

Rosenthal, in his business dealings, only acts in accordance with American governmental directives?"

"Objection." Stein, sounding a bit surprised.

"Sustained."

"I'll rephrase. Mr. Levi, are you aware of any endeavor by Mr. Rosenthal that acted against U.S. interests?"

A long pause. "No."

"Really? That seems so surprising. I mean, there are, after all, points in the diplomatic relationship between the U.S. and Israel where the two friends have disagreed, are there not?"

"I wouldn't know."

"Well, what about the Lavi affair?"

"Falcon had no position in that, Mr. Dennis."

"No. But it's nonetheless an example, is it not? Or Gerald Bull. Have you ever heard that Israel was responsible for his death?"

"Those are only rumors."

"I agree. Now, Mr. Levi, Falcon Corporation supplied the joint committee on Iran-contra, per the Israeli prime minister's order, with a chronology of events relating to sales to Iran. And in that chronology, it specified that Mr. Rosenthal was in Chile in 1985. That was important, sir, if you remember, in that it cleared him of participation in a certain meeting with Mr. Ghorbanifar. Mr. Levi, could you confirm for us that Mr. Rosenthal traveled to Chile in 1985?"

A stirring behind him: Edelson trying to attract his attention. While Levi hesitated, Dee kept his back turned on his partners.

"Well, I'll have to check my records. I'm not sure of the exact date."

"But Mr. Rosenthal did travel to Chile around that time, Mr. Levi?"

"Well, yes."

"Thank you, Mr. Levi. What was the purpose of that trip?"

Confused, Levi hesitated. "It had nothing to do with this trial."

"Please answer the question, sir."

Stein was on his feet now. "Objection, your honor. This line of questioning has absolutely no relevance."

Dee answered without hesitation. "Your honor, if you'll allow me, the defense has stated that Mr. Rosenthal's activities are uniformly guided by U.S. interests. In 1985 the U.S. had interests in Chile, ones that were directly relevant to *U.S. v. Teledyne*. I believe it relevant to explore how Mr. Rosenthal acted within those interests."

The judge answered, tonelessly, to Levi: "You may answer the question, Mr. Levi."

Pause. Then Levi answered. "Well, sir, it was a diplomatic mission for the government of Mr. Shamir."

"Was it really? A mission to whom?"

Levi hesitated visibly, as if making a decision. But Alley's prediction held true.

"To a defense manufacturer down there. Industrias Cardoen."

"Thank you, Mr. Levi. If I remember correctly, Mr. Cardoen was supplying weapons to Iraq. Cluster bombs."

Levi spoke more freely now, as if on surer ground. "Yes. Mr. Rosenthal was sent to stop that sale. The government of Israel feared coming under attack from those armaments."

"Thank you. Were other firms in the United States also supplying Iraq?"

"Yes. Mostly with high-tech components of their nuclear program."

"Thank you. And in western Europe?"

"Everyone. Saddam was acquiring the technology to produce chemical warheads, and nuclear warheads, and ballistic missiles capable of delivering them. Everyone was selling to him, everyone. Israel was forced to act unilaterally to knock out the nuclear program, but the chemical went full speed ahead. Saddam dropped gas at

Halabja, Siwsinan, Balakajar, and more. All Kurdish villages. Only Israel opposed the arming of Iraq. The whole world was making money off technology that was gassing Kurds and could gas Israeli towns."

"Thank you. Are you aware that Cardoen was indicted in federal court two years ago for those sales? And that when he was indicted, he offered convincing documentary proof that a branch of the United States government was permitting—even encouraging—those sales?"

"Yes."

"So Mr. Rosenthal was not successful in interdicting Mr. Cardoen's sales?"

"No sir. Cardoen claimed CIA support. There was a limit to how far we could go."

"Thank you. Now, Mr. Levi, let me ask you this. Was Mr. Rosenthal following an American governmental policy in this endeavor?"

Stein was up again, entering an objection in a loud voice, and with restrained fury, Dee addressed the judge.

"Your honor, it is a matter of public record that from the mid-eighties until the Gulf War a presidentially blessed program of covert arms sales to Iraq was in effect. The witness has just told us that Ronald Rosenthal, representing the Israeli government, made every effort to interdict this flow of arms, as a direct representative of the Israeli prime minister. Your honor, this establishes a clear precedent of Rosenthal's willingness to act on the international arms market not only independently of U.S. government directives, but in direct contradiction of them."

"Answer the question, Mr. Levi."

"No."

"No what, Mr. Levi?"

"No, Mr. Rosenthal was not following an American governmental directive, certainly not. He was acting to save Israel. We all were."

"Was Mr. Rosenthal acting against a U.S. government program?"

"Yes, he was acting against one."

And, in the long moment before the judge could call the court again to order, in perfect unison both the prosecution and defense teams' jaws dropped.

While, in Allison Rosenthal's stomach, deep in her stomach, joy was born.

6.

At the end of the day, Allison had no intention of leaving her departure from court to chance. Directly across the street, Martha was waiting in a cab, and she swung the door open as Allison approached. No sooner had she slammed the door closed, than the taxi had pulled out and headed across town. She watched the circus in front of the courthouse draw away into the distance, a couple of photographers chasing the cab with lenses pointed, then turned to look at her friend.

Martha. Her black hair gathered regally behind her head, her smiling wide eyes, her full mouth bright red with lipstick. She wore a tight white T-shirt under a leather jacket, her breasts full. Her neck with its warm skin rose out of the leather jacket's lapels with what seemed to Allison, after the shock of cold air outside the court, an inviting warmth, and for a moment she wanted to bury her face in that skin of her friend's neck. Then, for a moment, she wanted to cry.

Martha was speaking. "Man, what the fuck happened in there? I haven't seen Dee Dennis look so good since he kicked Billy Poole's ass on Menemsha Dock."

Allison shrugged, smiling at her friend. "Who cares?"

"New York One reported the whole fucking day. Dee's crucifying your old man."

"Don't worry about my old man. Let's get a drink."

"Oke. Leave it to me, babe." Martha leaned forward to confer with the driver; he turned the cab west, and

Martha, seeing Allison slump into her seat, a hand over her eyes, continued chatting with the driver.

In the care of her friend, Allison felt the tension of the day flowing out of her in huge breaths. Martha, she thought, had always taken care of her, taken care of her with this rude competence. A deep feeling of gratitude flowed through her, a feeling of something like love, and she wanted to touch her. She sank into the seat, turning her head to the window, her hand over her eyes, listening to Martha, who'd switched to a slangy French, chatting idly with the driver about Haiti.

Now, the sun through the window swimming blood-pink through her closed eyelids, she let her mind picture Dee again, dropping his bombshell in the opening moments of the trial. He had been word-perfect: composed, quiet, not attempting—as Stein did—to win over the jury, but adapting his tone to the gravity of the evidence he was presenting. His superiors, she had noted, had been shocked, more by his demeanor than by his surprise line of questions, but that shock had transmuted gradually into delight as the success of the ploy had come clear. She had wondered if he would be taken to task for the renegade move; but when the trial had reopened for the afternoon, Dee's line of questioning reflected very powerful help from his office. That meant that someone had decided that the references to the Iraqi supply program weren't as dangerous as they'd feared—either that, or they'd decided that the cat was out of the bag, and they had to put the best face on it. He had spent the entire afternoon establishing that Levi and Rosenthal had opposed the U.S. trade with Iraq at every point. That made it doubly impossible to argue that Rosenthal wouldn't have acted on Bosnia without instructions. These guys, she thought, could turn on a dime.

No, she concluded soberly, she doubted that Dee would be in trouble with his office. Not after, in the opening day of the trial, virtually assuring her father's conviction on one of the main points under prosecution. She doubted that his employers would mind finding an effective, powerful prosecutor, where they were expecting a boy following orders: initiative surely had a high place in Ed Dennis's hierarchy of virtues. Briefly she pictured him as she would see him later that night: his body filled with suppressed excitement, the master, again, of his fate. That was how Dee liked to be. That was how she wanted to see him.

And, she thought, when that attitude flagged under Stein's counter-offensive, she would give him something more. She had much more to give. Much more to share with him of the fruits of her short afternoon with the Borough Park files. Really, it was incredible: her father had been in the lap of Israeli and American covert arms transfers for, what, a quarter century? She could turn that whole dark world underside up to the light, and take Dee through it like a tour-bus guide. She could show him things that secretaries of state were not able to see, things that perhaps even presidents didn't know. Yes, she had much more to share with Dee Dennis.

He had no idea how much.

7.

The night was turning very cold, the invasive cold of a New York autumn, a wind from the river carrying the metallic feel of winter. The street was half deserted on a Monday night, and those who were out in it were, Nicky noticed, far younger than he. That intensified, somehow, his feeling of isolation.

He had not been down to this neighborhood—the West Village—in many years, and was not quite sure of his directions in the narrow, winding streets. Guessing which was west, Nicky followed a street through darkness, shivering in his jacket. The street curved into an intersection with a wider street, and as he approached, a red neon sign came into view. The Corner Bistro.

The bar was fairly crowded, but still some seats were empty. No one was playing the jukebox. Taking a seat and ordering a drink, he tried to dispel the feeling of discomfort that weighed in his stomach, sipping his bourbon, staring at his own face in the mirror behind the cash register.

Partly, he knew, it came from having done too much too soon. Now, having slept a feverish sleep the entire day, he admitted to himself that he was not strong enough, nor well enough, for this trip. He should not be here, he knew, and if he were here he should not be smoking, or drinking. Still, that was not the worst of it.

The worst of how he felt, he had to admit to himself, came from not liking what he was about to do. Perhaps the feeling of dread that oppressed him was intensified by feeling sick, but even healthy, he would not like it. Threatening Allison Rosenthal with jail was just not the kind of thing he had anticipated when he had decided to go work for the *NAR*.

Most people thought of his commitment to Jay Cohen's left-wing rag as an idealistic sacrifice of income, but money had never been the issue: his father had been a successful screenwriter for nearly five decades, and Nicky, who was again living in his childhood house in Malibu and driving his father's 1956 Mustang, had never had to work a day in his life. Rather, the *NAR* had offered a protection from the kind of compromises a mainstream job would have entailed. It offered the chance to pursue precisely what he wanted, without having to justify it to an editor's sense of the topical or to tailor it to an owner's politics.

As for the danger, Nicky's fiancée had said, just before she left him, that Nicky no longer knew what he was after: data or danger. That line had popped into his mind years later as a chartered plane circled over Eritrea looking for a place to land near a firefight. It made him admit, for the first time, that the singing of the blood in his ears, the little bursts of nearly sexual excitement in his belly, the superawareness of his every sense, was not fear but joy, and that his fiancée, in many ways, had been right.

What he was planning to do tonight was, however, worse than danger and worse than any of the compromises a reporting job may have required and, as he anticipated it, Nicky could not help wondering what had brought him here. His fiancée had thought that his politics, his idealism, were just an excuse for adventure. What would she say now? And dimly, without fully articulating it, Nicky knew what she would say: that if Nicky were only looking to use Allison to get to Eastbrook, he would have done it through lawyers.

He shook his gaze free from the mirror and turned on his stool, letting his eye travel down the bar. When it reached the end, he found himself looking at a familiar face. Their eyes met, and he looked away. Then he looked back, to find the man still watching him with an expression of shock. It was, he realized, the prosecutor from the Rosenthal trial. David Treat Dennis.

He turned, hoping that he had not shown his recognition, but all the while his thoughts swirled. Was he imagining this? He turned for another quick look, and found Dennis staring at him with an expression of equal astonishment. Of course, he thought dimly, this guy thought he was dead.

And before he had time to absorb this information or, rather, to disregard it, for there was nothing he could do with it, it seemed to act in conspiracy with the heat of the bar and the bourbon he was drinking to cause a swoon of dizziness to pass through him. In its wake, the skin of his face felt both cold and moist with sweat. And as he tried to collect himself, the door swung open into the night and Allison Rosenthal, still in her clothes from the day in court, entered the bar.

Had she already remarked Dennis's presence? Nicky thought so, but he was no longer sure of anything. She saw him immediately, and stopped dead still. Then she crossed the room and stood, wordless, before him.

Her face, he saw, was flushed from the cold, her breath coming quickly, as if she had been hurrying. Nicky, unable to speak, watched her openly and wonderingly, his eyes traveling from the blond hair tied up in a knot, to her eyes, green and alive, to her cheeks, red, to her mouth, slightly open and showing her tongue between her teeth as she caught her breath. Her overcoat—black cashmere—was open, her charcoal-suited body underneath like a warm, plumed bird.

He returned his eyes to her face, and started to speak, then stopped. He licked his lips and turned away for a moment, not feeling master of himself. Then he said, with great difficulty: "That guy, David Dennis. Your father's prosecutor. He's at the bar."

She nodded. "Forget him. Are you okay?"

He answered without thinking. "I don't know. I think I'm going to pass out." Having said that, he returned his eyes to her inspection, as if awaiting a command.

And indeed, after a short inspection of his eyes, a short, piercing look, Allison did in fact issue an order.

"We have to get you upstairs. I can't have you fainting here. Quickly now."

And powerless to stop her, Nicky let this woman put her arm around his waist and, half supporting him, take him out of the bar.

CHAPTER 13

October 24 and 25, 1994.
New York City.

1.

In her apartment, Allison helped Nicky to the couch and, when he was sitting, pushed his head down between his knees with a hand on the back of his neck. For several minutes they rested, Allison squatting on the floor in front of him still in her coat, Nicky doubled over. When, finally, Nicky sat up, she let herself fall backward until she was sitting on the floor, and regarded him. His thick, perfectly even brown hair. His mouth pursed, the thick red lips that much more striking for how pale was his face.

"Better now?"

He nodded. "Thank you."

"How bad were you hurt?"

"Very bad."

"You shouldn't be here. You should be in bed."

Nicky shrugged and reached into his jacket pocket for cigarettes. "That wasn't an option."

"No, that's right." She spoke thoughtfully. "The election's next month. Time's running out."

At Nicky's expression of surprise, she went on in a careless tone.

"Oh, I know the whole story. Stan Diamond's the *NAR*'s patron. He was a tenant of my father's. You found my embezzlement of the Ocean View Estate rentals. Now you are going to threaten me—and my father—with my prosecution."

She paused now, briefly.

"The thing is, you don't care about my embezzlement—not legally or morally. That's just a lever. You care about my father, and more specifically, you care about my father and Colonel Eastbrook. So you're going to threaten me, but you're going to offer me a deal. Messy work, Dymitryck."

He watched, wordless, and she smiled.

"Good. Now, this is what happens next. I've got to go do something. While I'm away, you're going to take a hot shower and then get into my bed."

"And why?"

"Because, Nicky dear, you are very cold, and very weak, and you and I need each other too much for you to die on me."

Downstairs, at the bar, she briefly signaled to Dee that he should go by cutting her throat with her finger. She didn't pause to see his response, but leaned across the bar to speak to Bobby. Bobby gave her a bottle of Jim Beam and, holding it, she flew up the interior staircase.

Nicky was in bed now, smelling of soap, the color much returned to his cheeks. As efficient as a nurse, she put an extra blanket over him, then sat down on the side of the bed with the bottle of bourbon.

"Feeling better?"

He nodded, and she offered him the bottle. She felt, suddenly, physically aware in every pore of her body. When he had drunk from the bottle, she lifted it to her lips while he talked.

"How did you know I had searched your house?"

"Because I searched your briefcase. In the Ritz. While you were checking on the ferry."

He very nearly smiled at that. "I underestimated you."

"Join the crowd."

He nodded. "Why do you and I need each other so much?"

"You need me to give you what you want about Greg Eastbrook."

He thought now. Then, rather than asking her for details, he asked something that surprised her.

"How can you do that without including your father?"

She hesitated, watching him. Then, carefully, she answered: "That's not your problem."

"I see." He nodded, and took the bottle from her hand. "And what do I have that you want?"

She shook her head. "First tell me something."

He nodded.

"Why did you come east?"

"You know that. You just told me."

"No. I told you how you're planning to force me to give you Eastbrook. Your lawyer could have done that. You didn't need to come."

"No." He looked away now for a time, and when he looked back, she was surprised by the expression on his face. She nodded.

"I see."

"What? What do you see?"

"You don't have the stomach for this, do you? I mean, putting my father in jail was one thing. He may not be guilty of this, but he's guilty of so much else it hardly matters. But you don't have the stomach to do it to me."

"Would you?" He had followed her perfectly.

"Yes. But I don't count. I'm different."

"And what makes you different?"

She shrugged, and drank from the bottle. Then, as if changing her mind, she said: "I had too strong an experience of death, too early. That's all. I'm not being dramatic: it's a typical psychological profile. After my brother died I stopped being scared of anything. Anything. It's like anesthesia. I feel fear, but it's . . . depersonalized. I have the stomach for anything."

He nodded. Then he said, as if, in the anomaly of their position, there was nothing that could not be discussed:

"Why did he kill himself?"

"He didn't. He was murdered." Not watching now, she spoke tonelessly, without emotion.

"I read it was a suicide."

"No. He was killed. Now, we're not going to talk about that anymore, okay?"

Looking up at her, sitting, the curve of her thigh pressing through the blanket against his, he felt as if they had known each other forever. Her suit jacket was off now, her white shirt open at the collar, and his eye followed the curve of her skin from where a golden chain fell between her breasts up to where her heavy blond hair fell against the straight of her neck. He lay looking at her. Then without a thought he reached a hand up and placed it against the skin of her neck. Looking away, she leaned into his palm. And now, his voice seeming to come from his belly, he spoke.

"I thought any price was worth keeping Eastbrook out of office. That's all. I thought it was an absolute."

He felt her nod against his hand, but she did not answer, and he went on.

"Stan Diamond's going to give his proof to the Mass. state attorney. They're just waiting on my word to have you arrested."

Again, he felt her nod of comprehension. She answered: "I know."

A small pause, then Nicky said: "It doesn't matter. I can stop them."

"How?"

"Because I searched your house. All their evidence comes from an illegal search."

"Yeah. That would screw them." She spoke meditatively. "If you didn't do that, then how long could you delay him?"

Silence. Nicky found he didn't even wonder how she knew all about this. Or rather, he didn't care.

"A few days. But you don't understand. I don't need to delay him. I can stop him dead."

Again, he sensed her thinking in the dark. When she spoke, it was in a new tone.

"Believe me, I understand. How did they make everyone think you were dead?"

"FBI announced it."

"That was smart."

"Thanks. Jay's idea." He felt her neck pivot under his hand as she turned toward him now, and he pulled his hand away. But she caught it between hers and replaced it, flat against the warmth of her throat, and as she did, he felt his vision begin to spin.

"You ready?"

"What?" Even the one word seemed suddenly difficult to pronounce.

"To negotiate."

He watched her, his eyes traveling from her neck down the planes of her shirt to her small and full breasts and then back up to her somber green eyes.

"No."

This made her smile, more in her eyes than on her mouth. "We can't put it off forever."

"Okay. Just not tonight."

"Okay." Her eyes steady on him, still smiling, she rose now.

"Where are you going?"

"You'll see." She left the bedroom, turning out the light as she went.

❧

Alone, she crossed the living room to the bathroom, her mind blank. She undressed entirely—except for the golden chain and Star of David on her neck—with quick, efficient movements; then showered, dried herself, and brushed her teeth. Finally, the apartment dark but for the faint, orangish light from the street lamps, she opened the bedroom door and stepped in.

He was on his back, his bare shoulders above the quilt, his eyes closed, his chest rising and falling under the covers. While she watched him his eyes opened. Leaning, she carefully pulled back the duvet, exposing his chest and stomach. The scars from his stabbing formed an awkward V, rising from above his groin. Deliberately, she ran her hand over them, feeling the faint bulge of the skin, the warmth of the wound. Then she carefully stepped over him on one knee, into the bed.

2.

Her skin was hot, not warm but hot, and scented with orange soap. Her eyes were steady, serious, and unafraid; her mouth, unsmiling. Her touch, returning his, was firm and unambiguous. But it was also, in a way accentuated rather than lessened by its lack of hesitation, profoundly tender.

There was no romance. Just the unmitigated reality of her nudity, of her exposure, of the heat of her skin. Unthinking, he let his body be drawn toward hers, surprised by how hard she was, surprised by how warm. Breathing hard, she shifted her body until it was under his, as efficient as a prostitute, carefully avoiding hurting his wound, but leaving him no choice but to follow, as if to emphasize that this was not about giving or receiving pleasure, that this was not about sex, and as he complied with the demands of her movements he lowered his lips to her neck, feeling the fast beat of an artery over taut tendon. Then came a suite of minutes in which Nicky neither saw her nor felt her, but rather experienced her, utterly thoughtless. And then, floating on the deep breaths of this woman beneath him, the world returned again.

Recovering her breath, she spoke in a whisper.

"You know the funny thing."

"What, Alley?" He whispered too.

"That when I met you at the Ritz, you know what made me talk to you?"

"What?"

"That you were prepared to hurt me. That you were prepared to do anything for what you thought was justice."

"Um-hmm." He put a hand to her hair. "Now you're disappointed."

"No. And you?"

"Me? I'm not disappointed, if that's what you mean."

"No. I mean, what did you . . . recognize in me? At the Ritz."

"Oh. God." His hand on her forehead, as if taking her temperature, he looked away. Then: "You see, I'm like you in so many ways. My dad's rich, I've had every advantage possible. But I've always had this . . . taste for the gutter? I don't mean sex or suchlike, I mean . . . the moral gutter. Do you know?"

"Yes. You like the ones with dirty hands."

"No. I mean yes. I admire the high ground, you know? I just don't like it. And I don't admire the kind of people I deal with. But I like them."

"Uh-huh. And when you met me, you thought . . ."

He interrupted. "When I met you, I thought that I had met a peer."

A wide smile from her, a happy smile, of understanding, of sympathy. "The funny thing is, I don't agree with you. I think justice is absolute. I think whatever you have to do to stop Eastbrook is justified, no matter what it does to me."

He paused, finding his mind unaccountably clear. Then, at her smile, he smiled too, suddenly. He said:

"Want to do me a favor?"

"Um-hmm. Anything."

"Don't make me talk politics with you anymore."

"Okay, baby. Later."

"No, not later. Never. My whole fucking life is politics. I can't make love with you without it being political."

She laughed now, her mouth open, and turned to the ceiling. "Well, politics are personal."

That made him laugh, too, his chest and stomach moving against hers. This small, warm body. This drunken spirit. She felt desire, with a force that shocked her. Ignoring his injury, she pulled his body full against her and said: "Nicky. I'll tell you everything tomorrow, okay?"

And as if his assent had been a confession of love rather than a commitment to suspend trust, she buried her face in his neck.

3.

In the bar, Dee had waited exactly ten minutes, watching each one pass on the clock. While he waited, he drank four shots of vodka, one after the other after the other. Then he put his briefcase on his stool and crossed to the phone. It was taken: another short guy, this one balding with a beard, and for an instant Dee considered lifting him bodily and throwing him into the crowd. Disgusted, he pushed his way back to his seat, shouldering his neighbor away from his stool and, opening his briefcase, took out his cellular. He had been avoiding using it to call Alley in case the service kept some kind of record, but now he didn't care. In any event, her machine answered, and he hung up, turned in his seat to the window, deeply disappointed.

The bar was packed now. Above the noise of the conversation, he heard music playing from the jukebox, a song too distant to recognize but too insistent to ignore, and without properly being able to understand it, Dee nonetheless absorbed the emotion of the manic falsetto that carried the melody. Even without the words the song's plaintive emotion was clear, and suddenly it seemed to Dee that that song and this night were the sound track of his destiny. There were tears of frustration in his eyes now, making swim the view of the street through the window. Even there was an object lesson in exclusion: a homosexual couple, walking by, cast a look at him in his suit and tie, his lawyer's briefcase balanced on the window seat; they commented something to each other, and looked away.

Who was this fucking little geek? Why wasn't he dead? And why the hell had he made everyone believe he was? Dee wanted to put his fist through the window of the bar; better, to pick up his stool and smash the window with it. He turned now, to the man standing next to him, the one who had been pushing against Dee for the past half hour.

"Stop touching me."

The man looked surprised. "Pardon me?"

"Stop touching me. With your arm. Or I'll break it."

A shocked expression, a shift away from him, and the man turned his back while remorse flooded Dee's stomach. But there was no point in apologizing, and he turned back to the bar.

For the next hour, Dee called again every ten minutes, growing steadily drunker until finally she answered, quietly, "Hello?"

"Alley. Can you talk?"

"Yeah. He's gone to bed."

"What the fuck is up with this midget? They fake his death?"

"Yeah." Surprise in her voice. "Sort of. He almost died. When he didn't, they let it be known that he had, to avoid another attempt while they investigated."

"Yeah. I should have seen that coming. Oh, Alley. I could have dropped the fucking case."

"Dee, take it easy."

Real complaint in his voice. "Couldn't you unload him?"

"Dee, come on. This guy is dangerous. Besides, he's so sick, he nearly passed out in the bar."

"What you been doing?"

"Taking care of him. He shouldn't be out of bed. I was afraid you'd call, so I turned the ringer off."

A pause. Then Dee, as quietly as he could through the noise of the bar: "Shit, Alley, I need you."

"I know." Her voice so soft, his heart actually seemed to swell. "I do too."

"Tomorrow night. He'll be gone, I hope to hell."

"I don't know. I hope so. Dee. I can learn a lot from him. You can go for a directed conviction."

"He make a pass at you?"

She laughed again. "You're kidding, right? A pass, that'd be an infringement on my rights as a woman."

Slightly mollified, Dee: "Some kind of sixties burnout, huh?"

"Worse. A seventies burnout."

Despite himself, Dee almost smiled. Then: "I miss you."

"And I you. Don't worry about Dymitryck, I can handle him. Go home now, baby. Call me before you go to bed."

"I'll wake you."

"I don't care."

Silence.

"I love you, Alley."

"Me too, Dee."

She answered, he noted gratefully, immediately.

Dee hung up, pocketed the phone, and turned back to the bar, finding the bartender, Alley's friend Bobby, standing before him with crossed arms. He leaned forward and asked: "What's up?"

"What's up is you can't hold your liquor. It's time for you to go, pal. I don't care who you're friends with. I'm tired of you pushing my customers around."

Oh, good: immediately, Dee felt this was a good thing. Nothing in the whole world could be better than a fight right now, and this man was big enough to make it fair. He looked to his right, and saw that a small space had cleared around him, the man he had threatened edging away. That made him feel powerful. He'd start, he thought, by breaking that little shit's nose.

And then, through the acceleration of his heart, he thought, he couldn't afford to be shitcanned from this bar; he couldn't afford to be in a brawl. With infinite regret, he took in a vast breath, released it, and moving away, reached his wallet from his back pocket and put some money on the bar.

"Sorry, man."

The bartender nodded, a respectful nod. "Good. We'll see you again, man."

And Dee, feeling as defeated as he'd ever felt in his life, went out into the wet street.

4.

Spent, Nicky had tried to shift his body off of hers. "No, stay," she had whispered, and in a moment his entire body had lost tone, weighing on her like a living blanket as he succumbed to exhaustion and dropped into sleep.

For a long time, she lay under his breathing, absently running her hands down the long muscles of his back and over his buttocks, feeling that profound, almost impossible peace again. Then she slept herself, very briefly, waking after less than an hour into a clean consciousness of what she had to do next, as if having, in her sleep, written a to-do list.

When the phone rang with Dee's call from home, she rolled Nicky gently onto his side, rose, and talked to Dee. Then she showered again. Wrapped in a towel, she sat now at her desk and flipped on her computer. Its clock showed two A.M. With practiced movements, she logged on to her computer account, then downloaded the transcript of her father's first day in court and opened it on the screen. From the locking drawer, she took out her diary. For a time, she read the court transcript, wholly absorbed. Then she turned to her diary, and although she looked up again occasionally for reference, for the next two hours she wrote steadily, in pencil, in a neat, quick script.

Four-fifteen, now. She locked up the computer with a password program and shut down, then locked the diary. Then she joined Nicky, where, in the bedroom, he slept heavily, on his stomach.

Nicky woke in what first appeared to be darkness. Raising the curtain, he found the sky lit, but the bedroom still in an urban, crepuscular shade. Seven o'clock. The bed was empty.

He rose, picked up his jeans from the floor, and pulled them on, then came out of the bedroom. Alley, he found, was fully dressed in court clothes, at her desk, absorbed in the computer screen. She noticed him, however, as he crossed to the smell of coffee in the kitchen, poured a cup, and then came back through the small arch into the living room. She looked up and spoke.

"You okay?"

He put his coffee on the edge of her desk, next to her lit computer screen. "I want . . . I want to say thank you. It sounds wrong though."

"Not at all." She spoke absently as she finished shutting down the computer and putting papers into a drawer. Then she rose, walked around the desk to him with energy and, her face level with his, ran both hands into the back of his jeans. He shifted to feel her breasts move through her silk blouse against his chest. Then she stepped away, leaving his bare chest and stomach feeling cold.

"I can't do this now. Tonight. You stay here, in bed. Okay? You need to rest."

"My things are at the Sherry-Netherland."

"I'll get them. Give me the key."

He smiled, despite himself, as he handed them over. "You going to search my bags?"

She returned the smile. "When I get back here. We can do it together. Now I've got to go to the law library. I have to study mornings before the trial if I'm going to get through this."

"Wish it was televised. The papers got good coverage?"

"They got everything. Front page and two inside." She smiled suddenly. "You mean, you don't know what's going on?"

"Nope."

"Hold on to your hat, then. They are crucifying Mike Levi."

"Oh yeah?" Nicky no longer sounded like he cared.

"I have to do something after court, then I'll get your bags. I should be home by seven." She stepped back. "Can you tell me one thing?"

He nodded, and she went on. "When's Diamond going to go to the state attorney?"

"I told you. Forget Diamond. They can find some other way to play their politics."

"Yeah, right. Jay Cohen's gonna welcome you with open arms after you scuttle the suit."

"Fuck Jay."

She smiled. "That's very sweet, Nicky." Now she stopped smiling. "Promise me you won't do anything about it today."

"Why?"

Alley did not feel she could ignore the question. "For a lot of reasons. I'll explain later, okay?"

Now he turned away, crossing the room to refill his coffee, drink, and put it down again, then showing the puzzle of muscles on his back as he ran his hands through his hair. "Sooner or later, we're going to have to trust each other a little."

"Maybe so. Tonight. We'll discuss it. Just one day."

"All right. Now you tell me one thing."

She nodded, and he went on. "What do you have about Eastbrook? And what do you want from me?"

But instead of answering, she crossed to him, putting her arms around his waist. She felt him tense beneath them.

"That's two things."

Her breath on his face. He watched her. And she said: "Nicky. Just wait until tonight."

5.

Alone in the apartment, Nicky experienced a familiar sensation, the long forgotten feeling of being in the house of a woman just met, just seduced. The college-boy sense of security in knowing you had just gotten laid, and that now a whole world of new intimacy was open to you. That there was no comparison possible between what he was experiencing now and any other experience of his life did not diminish the fleeting familiarity. He wandered for a while, shirtless in his jeans, drinking coffee and smoking, exhaling big breaths of smoke into the light shafting through the windows. He had not remembered, he thought, that morning sun could have this depth. Finally, gratefully, he returned to the still-warm bed and, in the thick autumn sunlight through the window, fell deep into sleep.

At Bobst Library, a couple of hours before court opened for the day, Allison found a carrel high up in the stacks. By the window, she paused now, standing.

A feeling of comfort was through her, so profound, a relaxation of her every muscle. For a moment she let play through her mind the feel of this small, strong body that had slept beside her. She saw the intensity of his eyes under their worried brow, the careful movements of his full lips as he talked. How close had she come, she wondered? How close had she come to him?

As close as he, to her?

At the thought, she turned from the window. It was not time to think, she knew. It was time to feel. And to act. What was happening to her, she knew, was now a matter for intuition, not analysis.

If she thought about it, she knew, she would not be able to do it.

She sat, shrugged off her coat, and withdrew a pen from her bag. But rather than taking a law text out now, she took out her diary and her printed copy of Monday's trial transcript and, again, set carefully to work.

She worked for an hour before tiredness began to swirl her attention. By then she was finished with the entry in her diary, and as she flipped back to the beginning of the entry, it could be seen that the date on which she was working was not October 25, 1994, but rather August 22. Without reading it over she closed the notebook and replaced it in her bag. Then she tore the transcript into very small pieces of paper, which she gathered carefully and put in a side pocket of her leather backpack.

Now. She sat back in the chair at the little carrel desk, and, for perhaps fifteen minutes, her mind was not her own. When she returned to herself, as if following directions dictated elsewhere, she tore a blank page from her diary and wrote a note to Dee. This she folded carefully into an envelope, also from her backpack, then addressed the envelope to David Dennis in the Federal Building, Part 4.

Outside she walked down Thompson Street, all the way to its intersection with the corner of Canal and Sixth, where a small group of bicycle messengers were gathered on the sidewalk, waiting for their dispatcher to assign runs. The messengers shifted to make a path for her, one taking the liberty of saying softly, *"Hola, chiquita, que rica que estás hoy."* To this one, she gave the envelope and a twenty-dollar bill. When she turned east, the sun had shifted, and now lit the sidewalk with what seemed to her a blush of warmth. Suddenly confident, she headed down Canal, hurrying through the crowds toward court.

Dee glanced at her briefly, expressionless, as he seated himself. Then he resolutely ignored her. Her note arrived at about 10:30, and she watched him open it, read it, and lean over to speak to his female colleague, who in turn spoke to the male one. That scared her suddenly. And her fright remained with her as he took up the day's business with Levi, a step-by-step chronology of her father's work in Chile. Now she felt reassured: they'd done their homework since last night after court.

At lunch, she walked into Chinatown, and from a pagoda telephone booth called, first, information for the number of the *New York Observer*, then asked the switchboard there for Martha. She told the assistant who answered who was calling, and Martha picked up the phone after a short pause.

"Alley. You okay?"

"I'm fine. You?"

"Good. Why aren't you in court?"

"Lunchtime. Listen, Marty, I need something."

Pause. Then: "Sure."

"Send a photographer down to the Shark Bar. You know it? Mulberry Street. At five-thirty tonight."

"Why?"

"Don't ask why."

A silence. Then, Martha: "Look, doll. What are you asking me to do?"

"Just your job, Marty. I promise you, you'll get a Pulitzer out of it."

Hanging up on her friend's unasked questions, she suddenly doubted that Dee would be there.

But at five-thirty, just as her note had asked, he entered the Shark Bar on Mulberry Street.

She watched him approach, through the dirty window, from a back table, where she sat alone; then she kept watching the street as he approached through the smoky room, moving briskly, and sat. They talked briefly and intensely, Dee launching the conversation.

"I have five minutes. We're working all evening."

"Okay."

"What the fuck is going on?"

"That guy from the *NAR*. I'm learning a lot from him."

"Shit." That this meant she had to occupy herself with the reporter, Dee did not need explained. "Can't we do it without him?"

"No. It'll be quicker this way. I miss you bad."

"I miss you."

"You're acing this trial."

He looked at her resolutely. "You sure you want me to do it this way?"

She nodded once. "Yes." Now she lowered her voice. "Now listen, Dee. I might not see you for a few days.

When you finish, with Levi, talking about my father's trip to Chile, you want to ask about Gerald Bull."

"Gerald Bull?"

"Yeah. Remember the supergun story?"

"No."

"Okay, read up on it tonight. Bull had invented a gun that could shoot a weapon hundreds of miles, even into orbit. Not a new idea, but Bull's design looked like it could deliver chemical, biological, or atomic payloads. He'd been turned down here, Canada, South Africa, Israel. No one wanted him. Hussein bought."

Listening carefully, Dee nodded. "Okay. I remember now."

"He was assassinated in 1990, in Brussels, at his home. You ask Levi who did that."

"I asked him once already."

"Doesn't matter. You'll get in the news."

"What do I want to know?"

"Why Israel killed him, and who else was on their hit lists. You can ask the first directly, but not the second."

"What's the basis of inquiry on the first?"

"The newspaper. Public record. You run a Nexis, I'll bet you a thousand dollars you'll find someone who speculated that the Israelis killed Bull to keep Iraq from getting supergun technology. More good proof of Israeli determination to oppose the Iraqi tilt."

"Will I find the hit list referred to?"

"I doubt it. Dymitryck tells me there was one, though."

In the pause that followed this lie—she had seen the hit list in Borough Park—she looked across Mulberry Street to see a black-jeaned man lowering a camera as Dee shook his head.

"It's unbelievable." His voice brought her view back inside the bar.

"No it's not. Goddamn it, Dee. Stop thinking like *them*. I keep telling you. Iran-contra wasn't some big scandal. It was just a window that showed a little bit of how these things are done. This stuff is all just business as usual."

Dee shook his head, as if to clear it. Then he stood. "I've got to go."

"Go."

"Listen to me. I got a firm offer from Andy Speigel. The state attorney in San Francisco. Marin County."

She nodded, suddenly dry-mouthed.

"You don't want that job."

"Yes I do. If you'll come with me."

"What about a government appointment?"

"Fuck that. None of this"—he motioned with his arm, in a downtown direction—"has any meaning unless you come."

She nodded. "I know."

"Yes or no?" She was surprised at the sudden tension in his voice, and answered quickly.

"Yes. Yes."

Then he was gone. She sat for a time, weakened. Then, at a phone booth in the back room, she called Martha again.

"Marty?"

Her friend was worried. "What's this all about, Alley?"

"I'll tell you later. Listen now: you hold those photos and I'll give you a story to go with them. But you have to wait."

Noncommittal. "I haven't seen the pictures."

"They're good. But the story is huge. National."

"How long do I have to wait?"

"Couple weeks. I promise you it's worth it."

Pause. Then: "You sure you know what you're doing, Alley?"

"Sure."

Suddenly exhausted, Alley hung up and left the bar. The sun was down, and the chill wind seemed to whip right into her bones. Wrapping her overcoat around her-

self with her hands in the pockets, she walked quickly up
the street. She still had to get Nicky's things from his
hotel before going home.

Even then, she did not suspect how very long this very
long day was still to last.

6.

Nicky woke toward evening, stretching in Alley's bed
with a feeling as luxuriant as any he had ever known.
Naked, he padded around the apartment for a time, feeling the heat of the steam radiators, warm and familiar,
against his skin. Finally he showered and dressed in his
jeans and a T-shirt of Alley's and sat down to call Jay.

"Boy, what the fuck you up to? I called four times
today."

"Sorry, Jay."

"I'm *worried*, Nicky. I want you *out* of there."

"Take it easy. Nothing's happened."

"Of course it hasn't. You'd be dead if it had. That
doesn't mean it's not going to."

"Jay. I'm almost done here."

"What are you doing? You seen the Rosenthal girl?"

He hesitated. Then: "Yes. Jay?"

"Yeah."

"Look. Don't ask me any questions right now, okay?
Let me speak to you when I get back."

This would never have worked in person, but the distance between them rendered Jay powerless. Not for the
first time, Nicky thought to himself that the real reason
he traveled so much was probably that it was the only way
to get away from his crazy boss. Smiling, he hung up the
phone and stepped to the window, smoking.

Later, he would remember what ensued as one long
moment, a single, inexplicably complex and impeccably
choreographed action.

Standing by the window, smoking, he first noticed a man sitting in a small parked car looking up. One rear window was open.

Instinctively, he stepped back, just as a lower corner pane of the window shattered.

For a moment he did not understand. He felt the cold wind through the broken pane, he saw the man in the car say something to someone behind him. Only then did he manage to shout, and drop to the floor.

A second bullet buried itself in the bedroom wall, drilling a little crater into the plaster.

Then there was silence.

Nicky crouched on the floor next to the window, feeling suddenly like a child playing a game of hide-and-seek. A second passed, a second in which panic came and passed clean through him.

Then he forced himself to crawl across the living room floor to the front door, his body as slow and clumsy as if caught in thick syrup. He checked the bolts and pushed closed the police lock that Alley had left open. He crossed back and, sitting on the floor, pulled the telephone off the desk by its cord.

He called the Sherry-Netherland and told the desk that there was a woman either in his room or coming to his room. They must find her and tell her to call home. It was an emergency. Then he hung up and considered.

Of course. Alley had been under surveillance. They'd recognized him when she brought him upstairs the night before. They'd have been waiting all night and all day for a clean shot at him. And by the purest of chance, they'd missed.

But what now? His heart pounding, he tried to think it through. He doubted that they'd risk breaking into the apartment—not, in any case, while the bar was open: there were too many people around. Later, it would be another question. Of course, he could call the police, or the FBI, and receive immediate protection. But then, how would he find out what Alley had in mind? And whatever it was, wouldn't police involvement ruin it? A car started outside, and he moved to peer, kneeling, out the bottom of the window. But then he retreated again, finding he didn't dare. Dimly, he realized that he was scared, more scared than he could ever remember. That was strange: danger usually made his mind clear. Dimly, he realized that it was because Alley was now in danger too.

Then the phone rang: Alley, calling from the hotel. He explained to her what had happened, and she whistled softly.

"Jesus God, Nicky."

"Should I call the police?"

"No. For God's sake, no." A pause while she thought. Then: "Sit tight, I'm coming."

"Alley, they won't let you in."

"They won't see me. I'll come through the bar. They won't dare come in. I'll be there in a half hour."

The phone went dead, then to a dial tone, then to a loud, angry beeping. But Nicky kept holding it, sitting on the floor, as if it were his lifeline to her.

CHAPTER 14

October 25 and 26, 1994.
Manhattan and Borough Park.

1.

For the first time, Allison could not see how to make a virtue out of what had happened. This was nothing, nothing but an impediment, and her heart faltered as she considered it.

Should she have foreseen it? In the taxi, heading downtown from the Sherry-Netherland with Nicky's bags, she berated herself angrily: she should have, she should have. She had been spoiled by the degree to which chance had conspired with her. Of course her father still had her guarded, probably by the exact people who had been after Nicky on the island, the exact people who later caught up with him at Boston's Logan Airport. Of course they recognized him when he showed up. Possibly they had known—through diplomatic connections, through Eastbrook himself—that Nicky's death was a fiction, and had been simply waiting for him to show.

The taxi stopped on Eighth Avenue, a few short steps from the bar's entrance. Were the two men who had shot at Nicky watching the bar? She went in without looking up, as if ignoring them would protect her. Then she went through the little interior door to the staircase while Bobby went out to get Nicky's things from the taxi. Upstairs, Nicky let her in and, crouching, led her by the hand to the couch, the single spot in the living room that could not be seen through a window.

Still holding hands they regarded each other in silence. Was he angry? Fleetingly, she thought: it's too early to see this man angry. And then, to her surprise, he smiled his strange, wide-mouthed, slightly sardonic smile.

"I came here to blackmail you. Instead you have to save my life."

She returned the smile, suddenly and without intending to. There was, she thought, something slightly evil in his expression, something that made her think that, after all, there was hope. And if there was hope, then she had to think. Now, for the first time, she turned her mind toward a practical solution.

They had to leave this apartment. They had to get rid of the two men outside. Nicky had to get back to Los Angeles, where he could hide, and finish the recuperation he had so jeopardized to see her. And before he went, she had to make a deal with him. Those were the problems, and when the solution came to her it was fluidly, without thought. It was, she thought, just like everything else she had done. The solution had always been there, always. She had just forgotten she had it.

"Okay. Hang on."

Sitting on the floor in the darkened room, far from the window, she pulled the telephone to her and punched a number. As she waited for an answer, she walked on her knees to the window and peered out over the sill.

There was no hesitation in what she did, and yet, when it had become so entirely clear to her what had to be done, she could not say.

2.

Sitting on the couch, watching her in amazement, Nicky heard her speak suddenly, unaccountably, in another language.

"Efshar ledaber im Peretz?"

Then, after a pause: *"Peretz. Tzippy. Ani meod tsricha autcha."*

Hebrew. Nicky stopped listening. He lay down on the couch, closing his eyes as if to block out the present. He had to leave, he thought, and so did she. He tried to concentrate on a solution to that problem. But so completely had he come to perceive his role as a patient of Alley's decisions, rather than an agent of his own, so strong was his sense of her as his guide in a new world, and so great was her empire over him in that role, that rather than attempting to plan his immediate future, he simply watched her at work.

And as he did so, the warmth of her body still on his skin, he found himself strangely happy. Who was this strong and brave woman? What was she doing? Far above the many matters that weighed on his mind and stomach, he felt intensely curious about her, as curious as he had ever felt in his life. For Nicky, curiosity had always been a happy experience, an experience that made him feel alive.

He heard her hang up the phone and opened his eyes, finding himself staring up into her face. More to make her respond than because he cared, he said: "We have to leave now."

"Forget it." With a lithe movement, she lifted herself onto the couch.

"I have to get to the airport. You have to get me out of here. You'd better come with me."

"I told you, forget it. Your friends are still outside."

He sat up, and she pushed him down again, half lying against him. "Don't show yourself, idiot."

He acquiesced. "How many?"

"One now. I think the second's around the corner—he keeps looking that way."

"What are we going to do?" He asked this question not rhetorically, but with curiosity.

"We're going to wait." She shifted, her body on his legs now, one hand flat on his chest, and they lay, staring at each other for some minutes. When he spoke, it was dryly.

"And what are we waiting for?"

"For my friend Peretz. He'll come to get you in about half an hour. He'll get us out of here."

"Yeah? And how will he do that?"

"Peretz was an antiterrorist commando in the Israeli army."

"And he'll risk his life for you?"

She looked at him appraisingly. "Dymitryck, what's that, a Russian name?"

"Montenegrin. I think it's a bastardization. My dad was fourteen when he came here, and they shortened it at immigration."

"Not Jewish though, right?"

"Right."

"Well, Dymitryck, you are a long way from home, you know that? Half my first-grade class spent high school in the JDL—the Jewish Defense League—and about half of those then joined the Israeli army after graduation: elite units, every one. You know who paid their way to Israel? Same guy who poured millions into every Jewish organization from Kahane Chai to the World Jewish Congress. These guys worship my father."

He answered slowly. "Kahane Chai. Your father supports the followers of Meir Kahane? How's that work?"

"Oh, you liberal. Guys like my father, they have two politics, one for Israel, one for the world."

"I understand that. It's all fucked up."

She smiled. "Oh. Well, that's not on this test."

He watched her for a moment. Then: "So now what? Peretz gonna blast our way out of here all alone?"

She laughed now. "I think he'll be able to scare up some friends. Just be still now."

He was, for a minute, lying with her hand on his chest, looking through the window and at the sky. Then he faced her.

"By the way, I told you before, I'm not a liberal."

"Yeah." She put a hand on his face. "God, that seems like a long time ago."

Lying, half pinned by her weight, her face inches from his in the dark, Nicky saw them suddenly as children, hidden in the living room, playing a game of secrets. A police car passed in the street, throwing a diffuse arc of flashing light across the ceiling. He spoke again in a whisper.

"So the Yiddish Rambo and his posse save me. Then what? I can kill Diamond's prosecution, but there's sure to be others. Stan can't be the only person you scammed."

"Yeah." She nodded, and watched him for a moment. "That's okay. Let Diamond go ahead."

He stumbled over his response. "Why?"

"Because I don't want to be saved."

"That means you want to be caught?"

"If you want. All I need is for it not to happen for two weeks. I need some time."

"You can't have it: the election's in a couple weeks and Eastbrook's ahead in the polls."

"Don't worry. I'm going to help you. Remember what you want from me. Stay focused."

He didn't answer for a moment. Then: "I don't want that anymore."

She looked at him now, expressionless, and spoke slowly.

"Don't be silly."

"Fuck you."

"Nicky, you're not listening. I don't want you to save me. If you want to help me, do what I say. I need more than just two weeks' delay. I need you to make sure Diamond proceeds in his prosecution."

"You're crazy."

"Maybe. I've thought about all this before, Nicky, and I don't need a test."

"Then don't make me ask all these questions."

A silence. Then, as if relenting, Nicky spoke again.

"There is no way I'm going to get Jay to wait till after the elections before Diamond goes ahead. That means Eastbrook will be senator-elect before Diamond even has you extradited to Massachusetts."

"I know. It's worth the wait."

"You don't know Jay."

"Stop saying that. Tell him you know how to prove Greg Eastbrook is impeachable for illegal arms sales to Iraq."

Nicky was silent now. Then he said, as if sadly: "You'll testify about the meeting between Eastbrook and your dad?"

She nodded her understanding. Then she shook her head. "No."

Nicky nodded, not surprised that she understood him. "Then you have the videotape?"

"Yes."

"How good is it?"

"As good as it gets. You get Eastbrook himself, acknowledging his role as U.S. government facilitator for Cardoen's exports to Iraq. The real approval, not that bullshit Teledyne and Cardoen trotted out to Highsmith. This is classified Israeli material. Eastbrook says in it, on tape, that Cardoen is under his personal protection."

"Acknowledging to whom?"

"My father."

Nicky thought. Then, shaking his head: "This'll launch an investigation of a U.S. senator, Alley."

"I know."

"You'll be front-page news from Washington to Madras."

"You too."

"And it'll flush your father's defense down the toilet."

"His problem."

"Let me see."

"No."

He looked at her without answering. Then: "And what do you want me to do?"

"Nothing. Until I say so. Then I want you to have Diamond file suit."

She was utterly composed, perfectly calm, and without any humor at all.

"This is as illegal a thing as has ever been proposed to me in my life."

"Yes."

"And as immoral."

"No." Now she was not whispering, she was hissing. "It's justice."

"Alley. I don't have the heart for it."

Then the phone rang.

She answered and spoke two more Hebrew words, first, *"Ken?"* Then, *"Beseder gamur."* She hung up and spoke to Nicky.

"Come. My friends are here."

"How do we get out?"

"Follow me."

They put on their coats and she led him down the stairs, moving quietly and without turning on the hallway lights. She took him down the staircase, pulling him behind her by his hand, and stopped at a small metal door, on which she pounded with an open palm. When it opened, she took him through the kitchen, behind the bar, and through a small door under the cash register.

Copying Allison's movements, he lowered himself backward into the door, feeling his way down a steep flight of stairs to a basement stockroom. Bobby was there, bent over under the low ceiling. He crossed the room and opened a padlock on a metal loading hatch.

They were all moving very quickly now. Allison climbed halfway up, peeked out, and then motioned for Nicky to follow, which he did, emerging into the evening on the sidewalk under the bar's big window on Eighth Avenue. Immediately, she pushed him toward the open door of a van, and he climbed in, a hand guiding him to a seat on the floor. Turning, he saw Allison looking into the van.

"Nicky, Peretz. Peretz, Nicky." The driver turned, and Nicky found himself looking into the bearded face of a man wearing a yarmulke. Then Allison was speaking.

"Peretz, here's the key to my zaideh's place. Nicky, go with Peretz. I'll meet you later."

"You come too."

"No. I've got to do something. Peretz'll take you somewhere safe, and I'll be there tonight. Go now."

She slid the door shut, and as the van drew away, Nicky was able to rise long enough to espy her watching them draw away, before a hand fell on his head and gently pushed him down again.

3.

Alone, Alley watched the van draw off with a sudden feeling of desolation. Slowly, she returned around the corner of the bar, and found herself face to face with the two men who'd been waiting outside her apartment. A jet of adrenaline tingled her scalp, but she had only the briefest glimpse of their faces as they passed her at a run, and as she turned after them, she saw them climbing into a small car and, engine roaring, taking off up Eighth Avenue after Peretz's van.

That didn't scare her as much as fill her with extreme anxiety. And it wasn't because she was afraid that Peretz and his practiced friends couldn't handle her father's hired assassins. It was because, she admitted to herself now, she had known what this evening was going to bring to those two men. She knew it, although she doubted that Nicky did. Yet. She wondered how long it would take him to figure it out.

In her apartment again, she found herself unable to focus. Everything she had done since meeting Dee Labor Day weekend had been directed toward this night, and now that it had come, her confidence in what she was doing had abandoned her. For a long time she sat in the darkened apartment, staring at nothing, feeling a sensation she could not identify.

Only when she arose did it occur to her, and she stood, unmoving, while a memory rushed through her head. The sensation was of a day on the island when she was six or seven. Her father had discovered, one morning, a litter of newborn dogs in the garage: a stray had found her way in during the night and died during the birth. All the pups were dead but one, and this one, a fat black beast no more than four inches big, they had spent the morning trying to feed with a dropper. Toward noon, her father had decided it was hopeless, the pup could not survive, and taken it out back to put it down. Unfortunately, he had decided to strangle it, which is a very bad way to kill even a baby dog, born with a thick sheath of muscle protecting its throat. It had taken a long time. Now Allison remembered, vividly, waiting on the porch, stomach clenched, wishing the evil thing, the necessary thing, to be over.

4.

Besides Peretz, driving, there were three other men in the car. From his seat on the floor, Nicky saw that they all four wore beards and yarmulkes, white shirts with the fringes of prayer shawls showing. Two wore leather coats, two wore sheepskin-lined jean jackets.

The van was moving through traffic, weaving, throwing Nicky back and forth against the sidewall, and for a time they drove in silence. Then the driver spoke, not in Hebrew this time, but in a language Nicky realized must be Yiddish, and one of the men in the back seat climbed to the back of the van and looked out the window. For a time they continued, the man looking out the back reporting from time to time, the van driving straight for a bit, then swerving abruptly, then driving straight for a bit. Finally, the driver—Peretz—spoke to Nicky in a Brooklyn accent.

"You might as well get comfortable. We're not gonna lose them."

Nicky sat up to find the van high up in the air, surrounded by the black of a starlit night. They were, he realized, on a bridge, crossing a river. He looked behind at the headlamps of thick traffic, and the man next to him said: "It's the blue Nova. Two men. That them?"

He couldn't see well enough to identify the men, but he had no real doubt. He answered: "I think so."

Peretz spoke now: "Well, they been following us since Alley's. And I can't lose them in this piece of Jap shit." He didn't sound worried.

"What are we going to do?"

Peretz turned and looked at him with a humorless smile. *"Ma she tagidlanu."* Nicky didn't respond, and with some surprise, Peretz asked, "You're not Jewish?"

"No."

"Really? Well, that was a language called Hebrew. It means, what you tell us. Essie said it's your party."

Nicky didn't answer; Peretz didn't seem inclined to expand. They crossed the bridge in silence, the old van rattling mercilessly, the four men now ignoring Nicky completely. The man in the passenger seat was talking softly into a small tape recorder, his eyes darting back and forth through the windows and out the rearview mirror, which was set, Nicky noticed, so that he could see behind from the passenger seat. Nicky could not hear, in the traffic, what he was saying. Then a bubble of unease popped in him.

They clearly could not escape the Nova. But if they actually were caught, and Peretz spoke to the men in the Nova, it wouldn't take ten seconds for them to discover they were all on the same side. Then what?

Would Peretz hand him over? For a time, Nicky considered this. And he could not avoid concluding: probably.

Nicky dead, Peretz alienated, what would happen to Alley's plan, whatever it was?

And what would happen to whatever evidence she was planning to give him?

For a time Nicky considered, anxiety and dread equally mounting in his belly. Finally, he asked Peretz:

"Do you know who those men are?"

"Mr. Rosenthal's enemies."

Nicky literally bit his tongue to stop himself from talking. Then he said, suddenly: "They've tried to kill me. Twice."

This was greeted with a raised-eyebrows glance between Peretz and the man in the passenger seat, who then turned to Nicky, showing a face that looked as if it had once, long ago, been beaten to a pulp.

"Give us the word, pal. We can't be doing this all night long."

And now a cold jet went through Nicky, a cold jet that

ran, in an instant, from his heart to his scalp and then clean through his blood.

He said: "For all I know, these people are on a government payroll."

Peretz, pursing his lips as if speaking to a child: "Don't be so scared of the government, pal. Just a bunch of thugs. Just like us."

That, to Nicky, was a convincing speech. He nodded, dry-mouthed: "All right."

Thinking, trying to think, of another way of keeping Rosenthal's two sets of employees from meeting.

The end of the bridge was at hand now, and Peretz, no longer driving fast, angled down an exit ramp, crossed a couple of populated blocks, then turned down a steep hill. He flipped on the radio to Chrissie Hynde's voice: *Come to me darling / With a message of love*; the man with the tape recorder said something in an angry tone and snapped the radio off again. At the bottom of the hill, Nicky saw the river, the great arc of the bridge they had just crossed rising up on massive stone arches, and recognized it as the Brooklyn Bridge. Then they passed into a series of deserted streets, lined with warehouses.

And here, in this dreamy urban landscape, as the van cruised bumpily from deserted street to deserted street, the atmosphere in the car changed. There was no more talk besides the voice of the man speaking into the tape recorder, in what Nicky could now hear to be Hebrew, in the silence of these deserted streets, and Nicky became slowly aware of the ammoniac smell of sweat. He spoke, as if awakening from a sleep.

"Peretz. Take me to the police."

The man answered calmly, without turning. "Essie Rosenthal said to take you elsewhere."

He leaned forward, raising his voice. "I do not want them murdered."

Peretz kept driving, his eyes darting from one side of

the street to the other, and answered in a conversational tone: "That so? Why not?"

"For every reason. You know why."

Now Peretz turned in his seat, slowing somewhat, to look directly at Nicky. "No, I don't."

"Those are dangerous people."

"Are they?" In quarter profile to Nicky, his face turning back to the windshield, the man smiled. "I think they're stupid people."

He looked at Nicky again, driving: "Be a big boy. I think you know we don't have a hell of a lot of options. What do you say?"

And now Nicky was very scared, more scared than he could remember ever being before in his life. Or perhaps *fear* was not the word, but *dread*. Fear, after all, may have driven him to do something. And yet he did not move, but sat feeling each second pass as a discrete moment of horror, slowly realizing that he was not even going to try to stop this thing, whatever it was. That he did not want to stop it. And with that realization came a horror even stronger. And then he heard himself talking.

"Okay."

5.

The decision made, the atmosphere in the van changed entirely. For a short time, however, they continued to drive, as if nothing were different. Finally, at the end of a long street running next to warehouses, Peretz accelerated sharply, distancing himself from the Nova, then turned a corner and, just as sharply, braked. As the van slowed, the man in the passenger seat turned back, opened the side door, and the two men in leather jackets slipped out of the moving car, pushing the door closed behind them. Nicky saw them entering the doorway of a warehouse, and then the Nova turned the corner behind them, flooding the street with light. Still driving slowly, as if to give the Nova time to catch up, Peretz continued down the street for a time, next to the warehouse, then turned through an open gate in a storm fence surrounding what appeared to be a factory parking lot.

Now, in front of the van, Nicky could see water and the lights of Manhattan across the harbor. As if rehearsed, the Nova drew in behind them, and the van stopped. For a moment, nothing happened; then the doors of the Nova opened in unison.

Nicky tensed, wanting suddenly to crouch on the floor, but none of the men moved, nor did the two occupants of the Nova appear, and slowly Nicky realized that they were crouching behind the open doors of their car. He knelt, straining his neck to look behind, while the windows of each open door rolled down, then two gunshots sounded and the back window of the van suddenly showed a ragged design of cracks around a small hole. Nicky ducked.

But when he looked up again, he saw that perhaps Peretz had been right about these men.

Perhaps they were stupid.

Because behind the Nova the two men in leather jackets were approaching from a doorway in the warehouse, each cradling something in his arms like a small baby.

And before Nicky had time to think again, there were two short bursts of gunfire and, one by one, the two men from the Nova fell sideways onto the ground next to their car.

He watched them, lying on the tarmac in a strange fetal position, his heart huge. Behind, standing straight now, Peretz's men were approaching the corpses, one each; and each, in a movement impossible not to recognize, placed a coup de grâce in the corpses' temples. Then, still moving calmly, they searched the Nova.

When they entered the van again, with the sliding

door open, Peretz drove in a wide curve next to the water, and each of the leather-jacketed men tossed their guns, wood-stocked shotguns with stumpy barrels, over the edge of the dock, then peeled off surgeon's gloves and tossed those too. Then, still driving slowly, they left the parking lot, pausing briefly for one man to descend and lock the gates behind them, and they drew off into the little streets.

Now the man in the passenger seat was talking again, into the little tape recorder, and as they pulled away from the factory parking lot, Nicky, his heart calming, could hear that his accented speech was in fact English. "Entering the Navy Yard, two cars, ATP116 and Hoodie 75. Adams Street, light on, fourth floor, number 205. Park Street, red light. Tillary Street, moving east from Court. Male black, six foot, green parka. Police at intersection, NY 12, Seventy-sixth Precinct. Jay Street, going south . . ."

Driving scrupulously, Peretz piloted the van south, then east, deep into, Nicky guessed, Brooklyn. Slowly, he realized that the one with the tape recorder was documenting possible witnesses. He wondered what that would be good for if they were caught.

Still, the tension in the car melted away, and the four men began to talk softly, in Yiddish. Apparently he, Nicky, was the subject of the conversation, for in time one of the big men who had performed the murders turned to him and said in a curious tone: "So you're a friend of Mr. Rosenthal?"

Nicky hesitated, lighting a cigarette. "Of Allison's." Surprised at how normal his voice sounded.

"Oh? Where from?"

Nicky paused. Then he said, "College."

"No kidding?" That seemed all the explanation the man needed, and disregarding Nicky, he made a comment in Yiddish, apparently a joke, because the others started laughing quietly. When they stopped, Nicky addressed a question to the big one.

"Where do you all know Allison from?"

For a moment Nicky thought he wasn't going to answer. Then he said, briefly: "The shtetl, before she turned goyish."

From the front seat, Peretz, still laughing, said: "Look who's talking. Menachem here has a Ph.D. from Stanford."

"That right?" Looking curiously at the man, Nicky asked, "In what?"

But Menachem apparently didn't care to discuss it. Briefly, he said: "Philosophy of religion." He turned away, lighting a cigarette himself, and then turned back with a strangely friendly smile.

"But my postdoc work was more important."

"Oh yeah? Where was that?"

"University of East Beirut. Shatila campus."

Nicky said nothing while the others laughed.

In time, Peretz began stopping the van, letting off two of his men, one after the other, at different locations. When only the three of them—Peretz, Menachem, and Nicky—were left, they stopped at last in front of an apartment block and went through the ornate and shabby lobby of the prewar building and into an apartment where, at a large dining room table in a room bordered by file cabinets, they sat. Only now did Nicky think to check his watch, and found it to be midnight. After perhaps a quarter hour, Nicky heard the elevator doors opening in the corridor, then footsteps, and then a key in the front-door lock. Calmly, Peretz withdrew a gun from his breast pocket and sat with it leveled at the door. It opened, and Allison came in.

There was a brief discussion among the three, a discussion that quickly grew heated. Alley left the two men talking to go down a hallway, then returned with a thick wad of money in her hand. They argued for a moment more, then, as quickly as the argument had flared up, it died. Ignoring the pile of bills, now sitting in the middle of the table, the men rose, Peretz heading immediately to the door, Menachem pausing to turn to Nicky and say, "*B'hatzlacha*, pal. Good luck. Whoever the fuck you are."

Then they were gone. Alley, still standing, turned her face to Nicky, and he saw for the first time the deep lines of fatigue on her cheeks. They regarded each other while outside, and far away, a siren passed. Then she moved to the light switch, turned off the lights, and, holding Nicky again by the hand, led him through a set of doors into another room.

Here, street lamps dimly illuminated what Nicky gradually saw to be a living room from another age: heavy furniture covered with sheets, an oak coffee table, bronze lamps with silk shades. Alley pulled the sheet from a couch and they sat, watching each other again. After a moment, Alley shifted, pulling her legs up on the couch, and lowering her head onto his chest. At the same time, she pulled the sheet up and around them both. He felt her shivering, and put his hands, gingerly, around her shoulders. For a long time, silence. When he spoke, he found himself whispering.

"Where are we?"

She answered, too, in a whisper. "My grandparents' apartment."

"What were you arguing about?"

"I wanted them to take some money and leave the country. They said they didn't need to."

"Who won?"

"They did."

A pause. Then she said, tonelessly and still whispering: "I knew they were going to do it."

Nicky answered immediately. "I know."

"Did you see?"

"Yes." He paused, and she shifted her head under his to look at his face. Now his palm was on her brow.

She nodded.

"Those guys thought they were helping your father."

She nodded again, and took his hand from her shoulder and held it, under the sheet, against her breast. "I know. Listen now. There's a plane to L.A. tomorrow morning at six. From Newark. I booked you."

"So what do we do?"

"We wait here. I'll take you to the airport in a few hours."

"And then?"

"Then you go home and get better. And when I tell you to, you have Diamond file suit."

It was as if they were an old married couple, returning to the frayed arena of an ever-repeating argument. With a sigh, he told her, "You'll be arrested immediately."

"I know that."

"What good will that do?"

"Don't think about that." There was exhaustion in her voice. "Just promise me, Nicky."

Instead of answering, he asked another question. "How did you know I was looking for the videotape?"

"Your interview in Paris with Peleg was taped. My father had a transcript in his safe."

"Did you read it?"

"No. Just a glance. That told me all I needed to know. Can I ask you something?"

"Yes."

"How did you find Peleg?"

Nicky paused, a long moment, before answering. Then:

"The same way I found Hourani, Alley. Your brother told me."

Eyes absolutely blank, she absorbed the news. "When?"

"First in the spring of '92, first time. In New Haven. Then he called me again, in early June. I . . ." He fell silent now, and watched her, as if seeking a clue from her expression for what he should say. When she gave him nothing, he went on. "Why didn't you read the transcript?"

She nearly spat the answer. "I don't care about that shit. I didn't need to."

"Well, Peleg told me he didn't have a copy of the tape. He told me what happened in it, but he couldn't be a witness. He was too disreputable, no one would believe him. He told me that you had witnessed, but that you wouldn't help. But he told me your brother might."

"Pauly wasn't there." Again, there was no tone in her voice, and no expression in his eyes.

"Peleg says he was. Off camera. He says your brother walked into the room through some maid's door from the kitchen."

This made her, literally, flinch as she absorbed it, like a blow to the body.

"Go on."

"Peleg said your brother would help me. I asked why, but he said I wouldn't understand, because I wasn't Jewish. So they recorded the whole damn conversation, did they?"

"Yes."

"I see." Nicky thought for a moment, his eyes abstracting. "I got Peleg killed, didn't I?"

"Yes. What happened next?"

"I went to Martha's Vineyard to find your brother. It was late June. And when I got there, I found out about his . . . suicide."

Nicky stopped talking, and they watched each other's eyes. And only after a long time of suspension did Alley say:

"Jesus, Nicky. You were on the island in 1992?"

"Yes."

She leaned toward him now and let her head rest on his chest. "Oh, God, I wish I'd known you then."

Time passed. When she sat up again, presenting him her face, she had been crying. She wiped her nose on her sleeve, and then spoke.

"Well. I have the tape. So you get what you want after all."

"Except I don't want it anymore."

That made her, nearly, smile. "Isn't that funny?"

"Let me see it."

"No way." She shook her head, once, sniffing. "Don't even ask. Not until Diamond files suit."

"And when does Diamond file suit?"

"When I tell you so."

"Then you give me the tape?"

"Yes."

"Original?"

"Yes."

Nicky thought, watching her. "And how do I tell a judge I got it?"

She watched him now through the darkness. Then she licked her lips, and took a deep breath, talking as she exhaled.

"It'll be mailed to you. FedEx. From Dee—David. Dennis. The prosecuting attorney."

6.

Nicky's mouth opened. "What, that guy? Why the fuck would he want to do that?"

She spoke automatically now, delivering the lie as she thought it. "He needs it leaked. It makes his case against my father."

He said nothing for a moment. Then: "Your father'll never set foot in this country again."

"Focus, Nicky. You'll force Eastbrook to resign before he's even inaugurated. For Christ sake, I am giving you the resignation of a U.S. senator, a fanatic rightist. What'd you call him? A 'radical enemy of democracy'— right? This is the sweetest thing to happen to the American Left since Watergate. You'll have fifty-year-olds in ponytails popping champagne from Woodstock to Berkeley. You are looking at a piece of American history."

"I don't give a fuck about Eastbrook. I care about you."

"Then do what I say."

She watched him carefully as he spoke. And to her surprise, he spoke in a sad voice.

"This is really what you want to do?"

And she, too, answered in a different tone than she meant. "It really is."

He looked up to the ceiling, and it occurred to her that throughout the conversation, his hand had stayed on her breast. She moved it now, lifting her shirt and placing it against her skin.

"And me? I go back to L.A.? And pretend I never met you?"

"We'll talk every day. When it's over . . . when it's over, you can tell me the story of your life or something. If . . . if you still want to."

"I don't understand. You're in jail, your father's stuck with a bigger crime than ever."

"But you get to off Eastbrook."

"Yeah? What did I do to deserve to be the sole beneficiary of this whole mess?"

She shrugged. "Nicky. Come on. At the end of the line, *someone* has to get what they want. This time, it's your turn."

She let him wonder what she was referring to: Eastbrook or her bed. Then she leaned forward over his chest.

"Nicky. Please."

"What are you up to, Alley?"

She answered quickly. "Can I ask you a question?"

"Sure."

"What do you think I'm up to?"

He thought now, for a long time. Then he said: "I don't know."

"Guess."

"I can't. I only know two things about it. Not enough."

"What are they?"

"It's illegal, and it's immoral."

"No. No." Hissing at him in the darkness: "It's something beautiful. It's justice."

Nicky paused, thinking. Then he spoke slowly. "And that's reason enough for how ugly it is?"

She answered immediately, in a surprised tone. "Yes. Yes, of course it is."

Not looking at her, he nodded, as if having just that moment decided. "Okay."

"That's not enough."

"Okay, I'm going to do what you tell me."

"And exactly what I tell you?"

"Yes."

And now she lowered her head completely—onto his chest, onto the chest of this small man lying on her grandparents' couch in their Borough Park apartment at two in the morning; she lowered her head to his chest and hid her face, blushing, with a sudden access of gratitude.

Of amazement.

They slept. Briefly, for the darkness left of the night. They woke, together, at four, and left the apartment for the street, cold in the last hour before dawn.

The highways to the airport were nearly deserted; Alley drove silently, with one hand, her other lightly in Nicky's palm.

At the airport, she saw him to his gate. They kissed, their eyes level, and she let her hands travel once up and down his back, under his leather jacket.

"Alley." His voice against her ear as she held him.

"Yes, Nicky."

"When I went to the Vineyard, in '92? The papers said your brother had committed suicide. Why did you say he was murdered?"

She lied before she could think about it. "I didn't mean that, Nicky. Not literally. My brother was a complicated person. He was very brilliant, and very beautiful. But he was gay. He had HIV, and his boyfriend had full-blown AIDS. That's why he killed himself. It had nothing to do with you."

"I'm so sorry."

"I know, I know."

"Alley, one more thing."

"Yes."

"What did Peleg mean, I wouldn't understand your brother because I wasn't Jewish?"

That made her laugh, humorlessly. "Did your father ever try to send you back to where he was from?"

"Montenegro? If I tried to go, he'd have disowned me. My middle name is Jefferson, for Christ sake. My father's the most American Yugoslavian known to man."

She laughed again. "Peleg was right. You wouldn't understand. Now go get your plane."

Then he was gone, and she was walking back through the terminal to her car, feeling more exhausted than she could remember ever feeling in her life.

But she could not let that stop her. There was just too much to do.

PART FOUR

Thus the Jews smote all their enemies with the stroke of the sword, and slaughter, and destruction, and did what they would unto those that hated them.

And in Shushan the palace the Jews slew and destroyed five hundred men.

And Parshandatha, and Dalphon, and Aspatha. And Poratha, and Adalia, and Aridatha, and Parmashta, and Arisai, and Aridai, and Vajezatha. . . .

ESTHER 9:5-9

CHAPTER 15

October 26, 1994.
New York, Los Angeles.

1.

From the airplane, Nicky called Jay to pick him up at the airport, then spent ten minutes being interrogated for details of his trip.

"Jay, would you take a chill pill? I'm on a cellular connection from thirty thousand feet in the air. The intercept area probably covers the entire continent."

"Goddamn it, Nicky. You be sure you're sober and rested when you land, you hear?"

But, in fact, Nicky was not listening: he had just found a thick envelope in his briefcase, an envelope he had never seen before, and it held all his attention. Heart quickening, he thought that Alley must have put it in while he was away with Peretz: she had brought his luggage along to Borough Park. Silencing Jay by pushing the phone into its cradle in the back of the seat, he opened the envelope to find a small pile of photographs, a single page of typescript, and a note, a single line on a postcard, reading: "This is why."

The loose photographs, which he laid out on his little

plastic table, were all taken at Ocean View. Powerful images, flooded in thick summer sun, rich with the colors of
the past. They showed Alley, as a baby, lying in her father's arms in a lawn chair, her father young, his bare
chest strong, his hair thick over his head. Alley and Pauly,
children, lying in a hammock, their pretty blond mother
in a summer dress swinging them. Paul as a teenager,
doing a handstand on the beach, the house visible between his legs. Alley, perhaps sixteen, in a black Speedo,
reading on a couch before the big windows that gave
onto the sea.

The typescript was the poem he had stolen from
Ocean View, together with the newspaper clipping about
Paul Rosenthal's suicide: she had taken them from the file
in his briefcase where he'd held them and put them with
the photographs. He opened it now, a single sheet of type
on Corrasable bond, and read:

> He, who once was my brother, is dead by his own
>   hand
> Even now, years later, I see his thin form lying on
>   the sand
> where the sheltered sea washes against those cliffs
> he chose to die from. Mother took me back there
>   every day for
> over a year and asked me, in her whining way, why
>   it had to happen
> over and over again—until I wanted
> never to hear of David anymore. How
> could I tell her of his dream about the gull beating
>   its wings
> effortlessly together until they drew blood?
> Would it explain anything, and how can I tell
> Anyone here about the great form and its beating
>   wings. How it
> swoops down and covers me, and the dark tension
>   leaves

me with blood on my mouth and thighs. But it was
  that dream,
you must know, that brought my tight, sullen little
brother to my room that night and pushed his
  whole taut body
right over mine until I yielded, and together we
  yielded to the dark tension.
Over a thousand passing years, I will never forget
  him, who was my brother, who is dead. Mother
  asked me why
every day for a year; and I told her justice. Justice is
reason enough for anything ugly. It balances the
  beauty in the world.

LAX. They landed at eight that morning, local time. Jay,
waiting at the gate, hustled him through the airport and
out to a waiting car: Stan's driver, who sped up and out of
the airport as if they were being followed. Only then did
Jay allow himself to comment.

"What the hell is going on, Nicky?"

He thought before answering, finally: "I don't know,
Jay."

"What is this girl trying to do?"

"To convict her father."

"What?"

"To convict her father."

An uncharacteristically slow response, for Jay; a
strangely long pause for thought. "You're crazy."

"Maybe. But that's what she's trying to do."

2.

New York. Outside the Federal Courthouse, walking
next to his father after the day's session, David Dennis
passed Allison Rosenthal walking with Bob Stein. For a
fraction of a second, their eyes met. Then the two pairs

of people moved on and were swallowed up by the milling crowd.

Dee was not sure why his father had come up for the night. Normally he would not be that curious: Ed Dennis often had reasons to be in New York. This time, however, appeared to be different, or so Dee thought, to judge by his father's degree of gravity, verging on the taciturn.

From the courthouse his father had led him, without explanation, past City Hall and, to his surprise, up the walkway of the Brooklyn Bridge. Only when they were up away from the street did his father stop. Then, reaching into an inside pocket, he withdrew two tiny blue pills.

"Take these, boy."

His father was more nervous than Dee could ever remember seeing him. Reaching for the pills, he raised his eyebrows in question. His father answered expressionlessly.

"Beta blockers. Harmless. Just take them, okay?" With a shrug, Dee swallowed the two pills. Then, without talking the father and son mounted the long curve of the bridge into the chill of autumn air. A low sun was out on the water, the tide on the flood, a nearly stationary barge trying to fight its way into the harbor. Finally, in the middle of the bridge Dee, squinting through the light at his father, spoke.

"Dad? You know, we have conference every day after court."

"Not today." Ed Dennis spoke without missing a step, and as they went on, in silence, Dee felt more like a child being taken in to punishment than he could remember ever feeling in his life. On the Brooklyn side of the bridge his father led him down Pierrepont Street toward the Promenade, then into an apartment building. As the elevator mounted to the penthouse, he spoke to his now very confused son.

"Deedee, I'm taking you in to see someone. Whatever he asks you, you answer to the very best of your ability. Do you understand?"

"Yes." Dee found himself feeling—under the effects of the drug—a strangely impersonal fright, one that carried no physical effects.

"Even if your answer implicates you in a crime, you answer. You hear me? If there's something you need to get off your chest, now's the time. It's as good as taking Five."

"Okay."

The penthouse apartment, impersonally furnished and carpeted in white, gave the impression of not really being anyone's home: this was, Dee understood instinctively, what was meant by a "safe house." The windows showed a panoramic view from the Statue of Liberty to the Empire State Building. The living room, in which they sat, was empty. Ed Dennis poured himself and his son a scotch from a liquor cabinet, and they sat in silence for perhaps five minutes until Dee heard the front door opening with a key and three men entered.

While his father watched, two of the men set up a machine next to Dee's chair, and the third, pouring a drink, sat opposite him. When Dee saw what the machine was—a polygraph—he understood what the pills had been for: many people in public life, he knew, used beta blockers to decrease the peripheral effects of anxiety, precisely the effects a polygraph measured. That his father thought he needed them for the polygraph surprised him and, curious, Dee looked over at him. As much as his father ever showed any emotion, he was showing it now: something that looked like sheepishness. Or guilt.

When he was connected, the man seated opposite, without any preamble, began to speak. First he asked a series of innocuous questions, meant, Dee realized, to establish a baseline for the lie detector. And only when one of the technicians had signaled his approval, did a real question come.

"Mr. Dennis, what is the source of your information about Ronald Rosenthal's business?"

Dee hesitated visibly. "I don't understand."

Now, for the first time, the man's bland expression altered. "What don't you understand? The question is simple."

"Well, sir, I thought it was obvious. Mike Levi, the State's witness under questioning, is my source."

"Yes. But what led you to your line of questioning?"

He hesitated again. "Common sense."

"No, Mr. Dennis. That won't do. You diverged from your planned course of questioning from the first day of the trial. Why?"

Dee turned to his father, as if for help, but Ed Dennis was standing now at the window, back to his son. Dee let a long pause go by.

So that was what this was about. Somewhere in the labyrinthine reaches of the so-called Intelligence Establishment, someone had grown suspicious of Dee's conduct of the Rosenthal prosecution. Dee could imagine what kind of person this was: the kind who needed neither White House approval nor a constitutional basis to set up an investigation. The kind whose efforts, under the umbrella justification of national security, were virtually free of legal constraints. In order to get him in a private place for a private questioning, this person had called on Edward Treat Dennis for help. And Edward Treat Dennis had said yes. For a last instant, Dee wondered why his father had thought he needed chemical help for this. To protect his son, or to protect himself?

As if deeply unwillingly, he answered.

"The *NAR*."

"Pardon me?"

"The *North American Review*. The magazine. It gave me all my leads about Rosenthal. Everything I asked Levi was suggested there."

In the periphery of his vision, Dee saw his father turn from the window. The interrogator, Dee noted with satisfaction, was actually silenced by the answer. "Asshole," he said, but only to himself. What kind of idiot did they think he was?

"And why did you turn to the *North American Review*?"

"Why?" Now Dee let loose into his voice the contempt he felt. "Because this journal's investigative reporter, who was responsible for my defendant's arrest, was murdered. That's why. I don't know whether you're from the semicompetent three-letter organization or the notoriously incompetent one, but in my branch of the government we are able to recognize and investigate a suspicious circumstance when it slaps us in the face. The second I heard that Dymitryck had been killed I understood that someone was covering up the real reason, and I went for the *NAR* as quick as ever I could. And I'll tell you this: if we had an intelligence operation that could do R and A as good as the *NAR*, we'd be in a damn sight different international landscape today."

For a long while there was silence in the room. Then, as if in exact reverse of their entrance, the polygraph was removed from Dee's fingers and chest, and the three men left the room without another word.

When they were gone Ed Dennis poured an enormous slug of scotch into his glass and downed it. Dee noticed his father's hand trembling. They left the apartment. Still without speaking, his father led him out to the Promenade, where, in the early dusk, they stood side by side over the water. And then his father reached an arm around him, the first time Dee could remember being touched by him since childhood, and squeezed his shoulders, hard enough to hurt.

"What is it, Dad? What's it about?"

When there was no answer, he went on.

"I just got spooked, right?"

No answer.

"It's okay now?"

"Is it okay now?" his father at last answered. "Does a frog have a watertight asshole? Yes, it is okay now. It is so okay now that I can't tell you without violating my security classification. Boy, the two of us just saved our careers."

It was as much emotion as Dee had ever seen his father express. When they returned to the street a black Lincoln was waiting for Edward Treat Dennis, White House counsel. Dee noted now, vaguely, that the walk across the bridge to Brooklyn must have been to allow the tranquilizers time to take effect—his father had been very, very worried indeed.

But as they cruised up through the streets of the north Heights, a flashing light on the car clearing traffic away, Dee wondered again for whom his father had been so scared.

Whom he had been trying to protect.

And for whom he was, now, so entirely, joyfully, relieved.

3.

Sometimes it seemed like the moment for which she had been waiting all day. Sometimes it seemed to be the most precious moment of her life. As the November 8 elections drew closer, each night after Dee fell asleep, Allison went out to a pay phone on Hudson Street and called Nicky in California. Long, low conversations. One night she called at moonrise in New York, and they spoke until it rose in L.A. Like that, their call encompassed the movement of the planet.

And each night, his voice was the most intimate physical experience, carrying through a late-night satellite connection every nuance of his lips' movement, centimeters from the receiver and a continent away.

He answered, each night, on the first ring, and she imagined him in bed in his father's sprawling Malibu house.

"How are you?"

Only to him could she tell the truth of how she felt, not because it was secret, but because it was so complex. "Scared. Lonely. When you're lonely, you know you're alive."

"And when you're scared."

"Yes." It was like watching a tightrope walker: again and again, expecting him to fall, and finding, again and again, that he understood.

"I wish you'd let me help you."

She said simply, gratefully: "You help every time you answer the phone."

"No I don't." There was real frustration in his voice. "You won't let me. You won't tell me anything."

"I can't, Nicky. Not yet."

"Then I can't help you."

"No one can."

"No one? No one's ever helped you?"

There was a long pause while she watched the lights of taxis running down Hudson Street. Then her voice came again. "I once thought someone had helped me."

"And?"

A pause. "It was a childhood friend. We met again as adults, and for a few minutes, I thought I was in love."

"What happened?"

Now there was a very long pause. Then she said, simply: "Then I met you."

"Yes." It was like acknowledging a legal fact, what had happened between them.

"Nicky."

"Yes."

"If I told you, you'd have to stop me."

"No." The word was like a confession. She laughed.

"Yes. You're too good. You're like a priest. You couldn't allow it."

He laughed too. "Alley. I'm a bolshie atheist. You're the one with a moral tradition."

"Yeah. Which tradition is that? The one where they bulldoze Arab family homes so Jews can return to their biblical birthright? Or the one where they arm dictators and train repressive regimes for profit?"

Her eyes clenched shut as she listened to him. "Stop being absolutist. Those are the fringes of your culture. Most Jews don't even know about the arms trade, and most dislike fundamentalism whether it's Jewish, Muslim, or Christian."

"Thanks. You're right. Sometimes I forget: my religion's a warm, fuzzy, normative humanism implicating universal nationalist liberation promoting an inclusive liberalism. Right?"

He paused, suspiciously. "More or less."

"Well, there you have the reason that it's becoming a religion of radicals, boy: it's hardly distinguishable from some kind of High Church Protestantism. Even I'm in love with a goy."

That voice, across the line. Each night as the electrons approached, it gained new tones. Deep tones, of affection, of fatalism, of irony: tones that he thought of as Jewish. Hard tones, the tones of her reasoning, her uncompromising cynicism. And another tone, one harder to name, that grew in pitch, he thought, as the nights progressed.

Lying on the floor, the phone pressed to his ear as if every ounce of pressure brought her closer, he absorbed the statement for a moment before he was able to answer. In the silence, he heard the far noises of a New York street in the early, early morning.

"That you and a goy are in love doesn't make you less Jewish."

"Maybe not. And my kids?"

Now his eyes were open. Carefully, he said: "I bet your goy would convert before you had kids."

"Oh yeah? Great, then I'd have company in this

ridiculous neurosis. I'm so sick of it, Nicky. I'm so sick of the whole damn thing."

"You're wrong. You're lucky, and you don't know it. The goy who—who loves you, he'd be delighted to have what you have."

"Which is?"

"A tradition."

"Maybe."

"Why?"

He heard her licking her lips. "Tradition involves a certain amount of hypocrisy."

"I suppose so. But . . ."

"Go on."

Now he spoke gently. "It's not an odious kind of hypocrisy."

"All hypocrisy is odious."

"Only to the guilty."

She paused, surprised. "What's that mean?"

"You see, only the guilty are so absolute about hypocrisy. You spend any time with criminals, you find that out."

Instead of an answer, from across the line, he heard her humming.

"What's that song?"

She sang, now, in a low voice. *"It's like I told you, only the guilty can play."*

"You mean the lonely."

"Yeah, yeah."

"Anyway, I don't agree with you."

"I know you don't."

4.

New York, five fifty-five in the morning. Alley, stretching in her nightdress, rose to look out the window. She had talked to Nicky until three, then worked at her desk until now. She could not remember when last she had slept a full night.

The thinnest of light showed in the sky over Jane Street, a great October moon hanging low over the city. At this angle, the street below was in its shadow, but its thick yellow light fell upon her face, upon the white of her nightdress. She waited, holding her arms up to the light, as if to bathe them, despite the cold air that penetrated the windowpanes. Then an alarm went off in her bedroom, and after a short pause, Dee emerged.

Naked, he crossed the room to cradle Alley from behind, briefly. Then he left her to step into the shower. By the time he had dressed, casually, for a Sunday morning meeting, poured coffee from her Krups, and returned to her, the moon was nearly gone in the rising gray of morning. Standing behind her again, his shirtsleeved arm holding the coffee around her neck. Now she put a hand behind her to rest on his hip.

"McCarthy said again she wants to call for a directed conviction."

"You going to do it?"

"I don't know."

She considered. "You got the burden of proof."

"I know. But I don't see Thomas going for it that quick."

"Maybe." She paused now, feeling her heart. Then:

"You want a directed conviction?"

"Of course I do."

"Then get Levi to tell you about a meeting between him, my father, and Greg Eastbrook in my father's house in 1985."

Nothing surprised Dee anymore. She felt him nod. "I introduce Eastbrook as?"

"NSC liaison in charge of facilitating Cardoen's supply route. Then ask if my father ever directly met with him. Don't stop till he tells you about a late-night meeting in my father's house."

"Okay. Alley."

"Yes?"

"I got to call Andy Speigel in San Francisco. I got to tell him yes or no."

With wonder, she realized how completely he had missed the significance of what she had just told him. Then she forced her attention to the other question. "You want the job?"

His answer was immediate. "I don't give a fuck. None of this has any meaning unless you come with me. There, or somewhere else. In two weeks I'm going to be able to pick my job. I don't care."

"Yes."

"Will you come with me?"

She turned in his arm now, and leaned her head up to face him squarely.

"Yes."

And as she lied, she felt entirely, intensely, alive. More alive than she could ever remember feeling before.

"It's weird not to know the future."

"Then everyone's weird."

"Nonsense. You know your future."

"Do I? What is it?"

"You go back to the *NAR*. You write a book. In twenty years Nicky Dymitryck'll sound like I. F. Stone."

"Right. And you?"

She laughed softly, cherishing his voice. "In twenty years, Allison Rosenthal'll sound like Robert Vesco."

He said nothing.

"I'm sorry. I don't mean to tease."

"When can I know?"

"Soon."

"When?"

She paused. "Don't ask me how I know this."

"Okay."

"The prosecution'll call for a directed conviction late this week."

"How do you know?"

5.

On Tuesday, the eighth of November, Oliver North was defeated in Virginia, and Gregory Eastbrook was elected in California. When the results were in, Jay called Nicky.

"He's in."

Nicky, in his living room, turned off the TV.

"I know."

"Sorry to hear you sounding so broke up."

"A few more days, Jay."

That afternoon, in New York, Allison Rosenthal called Martha Ohlinger at work from a pay phone in Columbus Circle. When the switchboard finally connected them, she said: "Martha."

"Hey, baby. What's going on?"

"Nothing. I need a favor."

"Anything."

"Can I come up and use a typewriter?"

"Sure, Alley. Come on up."

Upstairs, Martha took her into a busy office looking out over Sixty-fourth Street. A blond man who needed a haircut sat at a messy white desk, smoking and poring over a manuscript. After Martha introduced them he stepped out, as if by arrangement, and Alley sat down at his IBM. While Martha waited, she withdrew from her bag the FedEx slip with Dee's signature, and, reading from a scrap of paper, typed Nicky's address at the *NAR* into the correct boxes of the form.

6.

On November 9th, under direct examination by the prosecution, a surprised Michael Levi told the story of a late-night meeting in Ronald Rosenthal's house between Mr. Rosenthal and a member of the National Security Council staff called Colonel Eastbrook.

"Mr. Levi, what was the point of the meeting?"

"Ron told Eastbrook that the state of Israel would put even its relationship with the United States in jeopardy to stop Cardoen."

Stein, rising. "Your Honor, this is the fourth time Mr. Dennis has posed questions for which the witness is clearly unprepared. What is the source of his evidence?"

Dee: "Your honor, the witness has just given yet another example of the defendant's willingness to oppose U.S. government interests."

"Overruled, Mr. Stein, it's relevant."

"I wish particularly to enter an exception at this point, Your Honor."

"Noted, Mr. Stein."

Allison hurried home after court. Without removing her coat, she crossed her apartment, passing through the kitchen and into the little back bathroom, where she removed her package from under the pedestal sink. At her desk, standing, she unwrapped the material she had taken from her father's safe and packed it carefully into a FedEx box. Then she placed the FedEx slip, addressed to Nicholson Dymitryck in Los Angeles, preprinted with the U.S. attorney's return address, and holding Dee Dennis's signature in the lower right-hand corner, and put it into the FedEx box's plastic envelope. Then she ran to her bedroom to change. Emerging in bicycle tights and a sweater, she put the box into a saddlebag and shouldered her bicycle out the door. Outside, in the falling evening, she sprinted on her bicycle, right downtown to the

FedEx office at the World Trade Center, where she dropped the package addressed to Nicky at the *NAR* in the outside box.

Late that night, Dee asleep in her bed, she called Nicky from the phone on Hudson Street.

"Your FedEx left this morning. You'll get it tomorrow."

"What do I do?"

"Is Diamond's lawyer ready?"

"Yes. Her name's Gillian Morreale. She'll file for an interstate warrant at the same time. She has a friend in Giuliani's office. You should see the police tomorrow afternoon."

"Good. Tomorrow's Thursday. If you see my name in the paper Friday morning, then you can open the package. Otherwise, wait till you see it. Chances are, it'll be tomorrow though. Okay?"

"Okay."

A long silence. Then Nicky: "When will I speak to you again?"

Standing at the phone, watching the traffic stream south. She had hoped to avoid this. At last, she spoke slowly.

"I doubt you'll want to."

He answered immediately. "I'll want to."

"Nicky."

"Yes."

"I warn you to think the worst of me. Don't say I didn't."

"I won't. I won't say that. And I will want to see you."

"Nicky." The word, now, was like a breath, a long exhalation.

"Yes."

"If you change your mind, I'll understand."

When they hung up, Alley paused in thought for a long time. Then she went back home. She had to go through her apartment with a microscope, now, removing everything she didn't want the police to find. Such as the uncashed checks from her father. Then she had to go out to La Guardia Airport. She needed to know what the airport bar looked like. The plan was vague in her mind, but she knew it had to happen at La Guardia, and she knew that she'd need to call on Drew—Peretz—again for help.

Still, she didn't move. La Guardia, that trip was needed only to figure out how to escape. And suddenly, a vast exhaustion swept across her. Escape: the thought was nearly irrelevant.

CHAPTER 16

November 10, 1994.
Los Angeles.

1.

On November 10th, a Thursday evening at eight o'clock, Nicky Dymitryck stood smoking in his office, watching the fax print a page.

Outside, night had fallen, and against its black canvas Nicky showed in an attitude of concentration, a tableau in which it could be plainly seen that the material being faxed was from a newspaper, the small type smudgy and irregular.

Still, it was legible enough to recognize from the headline and dateline that what was being faxed to Nicky was an article from the front page of the *New York Times*, Friday morning edition, just back from the printers in New York and being faxed by a friend of Nicky's straight from the newsroom. When the first page dropped out of the roller, Nicky picked it up and read the headline from page B1, Metro Section.

DAUGHTER OF RONALD ROSENTHAL
ARRESTED FOR WIRE FRAUD

And underneath, the subhead:

Charge Is Fraudulent Rental of Father's Vacation Property

The article led with:

NEW YORK, Nov. 10—Esther Rosenthal, daughter of Ronald Rosenthal, the American representative for the Israeli arms dealer Falcon Corporation and a central figure in the Iran-contra hearings, was arrested in her Greenwich Village home this morning. The charge was interstate wire fraud, stemming from an investigation mounted by one of her alleged victims, Stanley Diamond, founder of Organic Communications. Ms. Rosenthal, who is known by the first name Allison, was served with an interstate warrant originating in the Massachusetts State Attorney's office at 8:30 this morning, and currently awaits ruling on the Massachusetts State Attorney's extradition request at the Manhattan Women's Detention Unit. The ruling is expected

Nicky pulled the second page from the fax, page B7, he noticed, and continued to read

to be handed down tomorrow morning.

Ms. Rosenthal is the only surviving child of Ronald Rosenthal, a figure who gained national attention when he was named as key supplier of arms to Iran as the Israeli liaison to Oliver North. Currently, Mr. Rosenthal is in the national eye due to his trial in absentia by the U.S. Attorney in New York for what Emily Harden, in the *New Yorker,* called "the most shameless practice of arms export violation since Edwin Wilson did business with Libya."

In Boston, the State Attorney for Massachusetts announced his intention to prosecute Ms. Rosenthal for "the fraudulent lease of her father's Martha's Vineyard property to an unknown number of tenants, in full awareness that the property was shortly to be held under federal escrow pending seizure." The exact number of the renters of the property is still unknown, although informed sources place it at "eighteen and counting."

At one o'clock this afternoon, in a press conference held at his office, Robert Stein of Stein, Goldman & Driscoll announced his intention to represent Ms. Rosenthal. Mr. Stein, who has represented Ronald Rosenthal for twenty years, both appeared with Mr. Rosenthal before the joint committee on Iran-contra, where he was credited for negotiating a blanket congressional immunity for his client, and currently represents Mr. Rosenthal's defense against federal charges. Esther Rosenthal, he announced, "would fight the extradition to Boston and, should that fail, would enter a not-guilty plea in Massachusetts court."

A source close to the State Attorney's office in Boston however, who spoke on the condition of anonymity, said that Mr. Stein's defense will need to be grounded in legal technicality, as the evidence presented by Gillian Morreale of Stockard, Dyson, a prominent Boston legal firm, is "rock solid."

Such an estimation is not unlikely: the resources behind Gillian Morreale are substantial. Ms. Morreale, who last year negotiated the surrender of Mimi Luria, the last Weatherman remaining at large, and for twenty years on the FBI's most-wanted list, told the *New York Times* that her investigation was undertaken in partnership with Jay Cohen, the editor of the *North American Review*. Mr. Cohen became suspicious that Mr. Diamond was being defrauded during a casual conversation and put the services of his office at Mr. Diamond's disposal for a preliminary investigation. When that investigation revealed evidence of fraud, Mr. Cohen said this afternoon by telephone, he put the matter before the attention of Ms. Morreale.

Finished, without a pause Nicky picked up the telephone and dialed.

"Max. I got it. Did you send Jay a copy at his home? Thanks."

Now he listened for a moment. Then: "All I can tell you is that what you want to do is get on the next plane for Los Angeles. Take the midnight plane. Be in Jay's office at ten tomorrow."

He hung up, and, rereading the article, waited for Jay to call.

That day, Nicky had taken the trouble to drive into Westwood and have his hair cut. When he woke on Friday morning, he showered, washing his hair twice and conditioning it, then blow-dried it and shaved, very carefully. He put on a thick swipe of deodorant under each arm, then walked in his underwear to his closet and dressed in a white shirt, a black English suit, a powder-blue tie. He drank coffee and smoked in the kitchen, reading the *Los Angeles Times*'s version of Alley's recent past. It, too, took the trouble to point out that her real name was Esther, as if it were significant that she did not use that name. Finished, he put on a black cashmere overcoat, and left the house.

He arrived at the *NAR* at nine-thirty to find his usual parking place taken by a white Lincoln Continental, in which waited a uniformed driver. Nicky parked behind a bar on the street, then walked back around the corner to the door and ran up the stairs. In the office, which someone had actually tidied, Jay sat behind his desk. Wooden chairs were arranged in front of him, and in them sat the two lawyers who represented the *NAR*; Max Holtz, just arrived from the *New York Times;* and two congressional aides, to Patty Murray and Carl Levin: the first on the Senate Ethics Committee, the second on Senate Intelligence. An aide from Torricelli's office was also present, although this was a courtesy, as Torricelli served in the House and Eastbrook would serve in the Senate. Finally, an FBI technician from the state office was there, sitting uncomfortably in the armchair beside Jay.

Jay performed introductions and, at a nod from Nicky, turned on a video camera on a tripod next to his desk. He lifted, next to the camera, a sealed FedEx box with a return address of the U.S. attorney's office in New York and the signature of David Treat Dennis. He handed it to the FBI investigator, who examined it carefully, then rose to photograph it, front and back. The three congressional aides performed their own examinations, then Jay's lawyers repeated the photographing. While this ceremony took place, Nicky removed his coat and took his seat by the window.

When they were done, the lawyers handed the box back to Jay, who in turn held it out to Nicky. Nicky stepped forward to the side of the desk and pulled the box's tab. Inside were a short stack of transcripts, some photographs, and a videocassette. He removed them by the edges and laid them on the desk to be photographed twice, front and back. He gathered them and, standing next to the desk, read through the transcripts. Then, expressionless, he handed them to Jay, responding to Jay's raised eyebrows with an affirmative nod. Jay read—or more properly, devoured—the pages, and then looked up, his eyes shining, his black beard split by a boundless smile.

"Gentlemen. We have high crimes, and we have misdemeanors."

Then he turned to Nicky and nearly lifted him off the ground with a hug.

When the papers had made their rounds, Nicky, accompanied by the aides, copied them on the office Xerox. Meanwhile the videocassette was duped on four VCR decks. Then the aides took the originals; one placed them in a locked briefcase with a slim gold handcuff closing the lock and wrapping around his wrist, hidden by the sleeve of his overcoat, and the three left the office. Nicky then handed out copies to interns, who collated them with cover letters and began to fax, from the five machines Jay had installed for the purpose, copies of Allison Rosenthal's transcripts and photographs to a list of ninety-five fax numbers Jay had compiled, ranging from President Clinton's office and that of the Senate leaders to the country's top newspapers and the state's top legislators.

While the faxes went off, Jay saw his other visitors out, then stood next to Nicky, wordless. Once, he reached his arm around Nicky's shoulders and squeezed his arm, hard.

That, Nicky thought, looking up at Jay, is pure joy.

The faxes took a couple of hours. Then it was time for Jay and Nicky to leave for Stan's offices, where, before the virtual entirety of the American news media, Nicky was to give a press conference to announce that he had received unimpeachable proofs, that morning, from the office of the U.S. attorney, Southern District of New York, currently engaged in the prosecution of Ronald Rosenthal, detailing the central participation of Senator-elect Gregory Eastbrook in the illegal sale of military equipment and technology to Saddam Hussein throughout the eighties, sales that resulted finally in the necessity for an American military engagement that cost the country some half-billion dollars a day. And, in the opinion of the *NAR*'s lawyers, the criminal action it detailed would, if taken seriously, require nothing less than the resignation of Senator-elect Eastbrook. Finally, Nicky Dymitryck would say, in his opinion, and the opinion of the four other people who had read the documents, that

there was no way on God's green earth that these documents would not be taken seriously, because they were
supported by memorialization in the form of photographic evidence.

Or, as Jay Cohen put it later that day, over a bottle of
champagne, poor Mr. Eastbrook was about to take the
ride of his fucking life.

2.

It was, however, a short celebration that took place in the
offices of the *NAR*. For one thing, the *NAR* was rushing
the transcripts to press that evening. But more important, in the steadily accelerating pattern of events that
now set themselves in motion, there was little time for
partying.

At nine o'clock that night, as Nicky and Jay proofed
the type of the *NAR*'s publication of Allison's transcripts,
the *New York Times* Saturday edition came over the fax.

This time, the story of Esther Rosenthal's arrest had a
large-point headline, but it was column two on the left.

Center of the page, the banner headline was devoted
to Nicky's press conference about the Eastbrook revelations.

Underneath this, a second article reported that the
U.S. attorney had moved for a directed conviction in the
Rosenthal prosecution.

But the right-hand column—the column reserved for
the most important news of the day—held the story of
the hour, and it was a story that, Nicky thought ruefully
even as realization flooded over him like a cold shower,
was absolutely impossible to predict.

For it detailed that during her extradition hearing in
state court, while discussing her diaries, introduced as evidence for the records they contained on her fraudulent
rentals of her father's vacation properties, Esther Rosen-

thal had addressed the provenance of the transcripts and photographs that Nicky had revealed that day.

Esther Rosenthal, who is known as Allison, stated that the Special Counsel to the U.S. Attorney David Treat Dennis had told her about the videotape last summer on Martha's Vineyard, where the families of both hold property. She did not know where Mr. Dennis had obtained the videotape, which implicates Senator-elect Gregory Eastbrook in the illegal sales of military equipment and technology, ranging from cluster bombs to nuclear know-how, to Iraq prior to the Gulf War. In so doing, they also undermine Ronald Rosenthal's defense against Arms Export Control Act violations, probably fatally.

Ms. Rosenthal, who was visibly upset, then went on to say that throughout the summer she had been coerced into providing Mr. Dennis with evidentiary material from her father's secret files, which Mr. Dennis then introduced in court in a series of surprise maneuvers that virtually assured the directed conviction of Mr. Rosenthal. Questioned as to the identity of the person who had coerced her, Ms. Rosenthal, pointedly ignoring her lawyer's attempt to intercede, informed the court that she had been coerced by Mr. Dennis himself. She then went on to say that Mr. Dennis and she had been involved sexually during the entire pretrial period, as well as during the trial. This relationship, Ms. Rosenthal said, dated from their childhoods, including a brief period of sexual involvement while Ms. Rosenthal was under age and Mr. Dennis was in college. Given their long-standing relationship, she had been shocked when Mr. Dennis had failed to recuse himself from her father's prosecution, and only later come to understand that he intended to use that relationship to further the prosecution's case. Finally, she added that Mr. Dennis had been moved to the U.S. Attorney's office due to the influence of his father, currently serving as White House Counsel, and that the case was expected to launch Mr. Dennis's political career. This, she thought, was surprising given Edward Dennis's long-standing enmity toward Mr. Rosenthal over Mr. Rosenthal's development of his Martha's Vineyard property, as well as the unethical, if not illegal, nature of the White House involvement in a criminal trial.

During the exchange, Ms. Rosenthal's lawyer, Robert Stein, who also represents Ronald Rosenthal in his current prosecution, listened, visibly in the same shock as the rest of the court. Ms. Rosenthal was then remanded into custody pending the organization of a separate hearing, which is presumed to be scheduled for tomorrow.

Ms. Rosenthal's Greenwich Village apartment was sealed this afternoon by the FBI, which has refused comment on the case. A source close to the investigation who spoke on the condition of anonymity revealed to the *Times* that a first investigation had found both evidence of Mr. Dennis's presence, ranging from fingerprints to court documents and clothes in the apartment, as well as Ms. Rosenthal's diary, in which Mr. Dennis figures heavily. According to this source, the diary documents Esther Rosenthal's daily provision of material from Ronald Rosenthal's private files to Mr. Dennis, as well as the pressure Mr. Dennis exerted to ensure that provision, including physical violence. This same source confirmed that Edward Treat Dennis had indeed used his influence to place his son in the U.S. Attorney's office, and that Mr. Dennis Senior is prominent in the Washington circles behind the prosecution of Ronald Rosenthal.

In a telephone interview, Mr. Stein was prepared only to comment that he had entered numerous objections to the prosecution's leading of a key witness, and that his exceptions to key elements of the prosecution's evidence were a matter of public record.

Following the article, Max Holtz, just returned to New York, had been considerate enough to fax the front page of the *New York Observer*, which had rushed to press an issue containing photographs of David Dennis and Allison Rosenthal in conversation at a dusty Little Italy bar.

One set of neural controls was sufficient to govern both Jay and Nicky as they read the story, so precisely did their eyes move in unison. When they reached the end, their eyes met.

"What the fucking hell is up with this?"

Nicky, wonderingly: "She is trying to disbar David Dennis."

He saw the realization dawn in Jay's eyes as he spoke the words. Jay turned to the editorial assistant who had brought the fax, then stayed to watch the reaction.

"Deb, call the press and tell them we're holding the issue for a few days. They give you trouble, tell me."

She left, unwillingly, and Jay and Nicky returned their attention to each other. Jay spoke first.

"You didn't tell me this girl was brilliant."

"Is she?"

Jay answered at once. "Oh, yes. She's not disbarring Dennis, Nicky. Fucking him was enough for that. She's scuttling the entire prosecution."

Nicky's voice rose. "She's going to scuttle a federal prosecution? She is going to have to *prove* everything she says. She is going to have to face David Dennis in open court."

"Never. Never in a million years. They're *never* going

to court over this." Jay was holding a hand to his forehead as he talked, tipping back in his chair. "Where the fuck did she learn how to do this?"

Nicky, flatly: "I don't get it."

And Jay, brought to himself by the question, turned to his associate editor, his face so full of wonder that he did not even bother noting Nicky's noncomprehension. "Nicky, this was supposed to be a nice, quiet little vendetta against a rich Jewish arms merchant. It was not meant to be a goddamn bloodbath. Christ, man, look at the body count: one senator-elect, a White House counsel, a deputy U.S. attorney. I'll give you dollars to dimes that before this is over the attorney general resigns, and if Sid Ohlinger weren't the oiliest bastard in the universe, I'd have said his ass is out of Washington too."

"Then why'd they start the damn trial?"

"Man, they started it in Clinton's first year. They needed it to keep NATO in the Bosnian peacekeeping force, and it seems they had a personal vendetta to boot. October surprise, I don't doubt. Back then, these guys were drunk with power anyway. Now it's midterm, their approval ratings are in the fucking garbage. This is not the kind of publicity they were looking for."

Jay shook his head, once, decisively. "I don't think they'll see Allison Rosenthal in court, I don't think there's any way in hell. I think, they get a chance at a mistrial, they'd drop the case. And you know what? I think Allison Esther Rosenthal, whatever the fuck her name is, understands all this and more."

The dawning wonder of understanding was overtaking Nicky now. "That's crazy."

"I don't think so."

A long silence, staring at each other. Then Nicky tried another angle. "That might be true, but an admission from David Dennis is still the only thing that could kill the prosecution."

"No. The evidence is still inadmissible. Dennis

dumped the case they'd prepared, based the whole case on new evidence, and now every bit of it is inadmissible."

"What evidence?"

"The evidence David Dennis coerced from her. You see? She gave him a line of prosecution that convicted her father, and he went for it. Now he's been shown to have coerced it from her. It's all inadmissible, and Rosenthal'll probably have double jeopardy on his side, too. That must be what she's doing. It's the only thing that makes sense."

"Dennis didn't coerce anything from her."

"No? That may be, but they still got his tighty-whities on her bedroom floor. And there's no way that tomorrow morning he won't stand accused of it."

Nicky blanched as he realized the truth of that. Still, he went on:

"That doesn't mean he coerced anything from her. Dennis'll fight it in court."

"And while he's doing so, everything he's introduced into evidence from the girl's information is inadmissible. She's made the truth—the fucking truth!—legally inadmissible. She sticks to her guns, they'll be months in court over this, and the fact remains, this guy was fucking that girl. Where's their prosecution during all this? Jesus Christ Almighty, by the time they get back to trial—if they get back to trial—Rosenthal'll have a Knesset seat, and you can't extradite a Knesset member even if you convict him in absentia."

But Nicky's stomach was plummeting, plummeting. Deep in his belly, he absorbed how profoundly, how utterly he had been betrayed. Then, with a real effort of mental will, he managed to say: "But she'll still face prosecution on Ocean View. Even paying back the money won't matter. Jail time for interstate wire fraud."

"Is that right? Are you sure? Do you know what she has in mind?"

There was something penetrating in Jay's question,

and Nicky registered the sureness of his instinct. He answered quickly, before Jay figured it out.

"No. But in any case I don't think she cares."

"No. I don't either. Maybe she'll serve some jail time. But she's scuttled a federal prosecution long enough to save her father. You know what this is? This is desperation. This is genius. It's a covert operation of the soul."

But still Nicky was not done. He thought, eyes direct on his boss, for another moment. Then, as if completing the description: "It's the most shocking abuse of the system. It's the most shocking betrayal."

Jay was unconcerned. "Bullshit. It's the way the law works."

"No. It's a shocking abuse. What is this—post-Iran-contra law? Does someone teach this shit somewhere?"

"Hey, Nicky. You teach this shit. You teach this shit every time you write a fucking article. You think your readers in D.C. share your outrage when you write about sleazy deals in the arms trade? Boy, they read you to find out how to do it. Come on, Nicky, you telling me you've never fucked some Paris air show hostess to get to a source? The law? The fucking law? I've seen you break the law on four continents."

"I broke bad laws for good reasons."

"Oh, come off it. Everybody's got a greater fucking good that lets them do what they want."

Nicky was nearly shouting. "I never did anything nearly this cynical!"

"Really?" Jay looked at him, suspiciously, and again, Nicky felt his boss on the edge of understanding his role in this. "You call it what you want. You ask her, she'll tell you her father's the Jew being scapegoated for a government vendetta. She has overturned an unjust prosecution of her father. If the law is subservient to the truth for you, then it is for her too. You can't have it both ways, pal. And in any case, fuck Rosenthal, and why? Because we get to indict a very bad man, a man who has only slightly less contempt for the Constitution than he has ignorance of it, a man you yourself called 'a radical enemy of democracy.' That's justice, and it's reason enough for anything else that happens."

So that, thought Nicky, watching Jay with open eyes, is justice.

And then he thought, with a sinking heart, how unfair it was that he should, right this minute, just after losing everything else, lose Jay too.

3.

In a conference room in the Manhattan County Minimum Security Detention Unit, Allison Rosenthal sat at a long table. Around her were a deputy U.S. attorney, his assistant, and Bob Stein, who, at her father's orders, was continuing to represent her. The U.S. attorney was deposing Alley gently in questions designed less to find out what she knew than how far she was prepared to go, as if aware of the power that a pretty woman, especially one in tears, brings to a courtroom.

"Did you start renting Ocean View before, or after, you met Mr. Dennis?"

She had looked away out the window, hiding her expression—or rather, her lack of expression.

"After. My dad was in jail. I had tuition due on my last year of law school. I was broke."

Bob listened without expression: her father's many checks to Allison had been issued out of his office. The deputy U.S. attorney made some notes, then looked up again, silently inviting her to go on.

"I thought . . . I thought that if I had enough money, I could get away from him. But . . ." She dropped her eyes now, and finished simply. "But I couldn't."

"Why?"

She answered simply. "He told me he could get Daddy

off. If I cooperated. I believed him. I don't know why, but I believed him. My brother died two years ago, it nearly destroyed my father. And Iran-contra, they nearly crucified him. And then the arrest, and losing our house. I was panicking."

"When did you start doubting him?"

"Oh, God. I guess in mid-September. The *Times* said that conviction was certain, and then he asked me to find out about Falcon's role in the Iraq thing. I knew my dad had done a lot to stop the arming of Iraq. And I suddenly realized he was looking to show that Falcon had acted against U.S. interests over Iraq, and I got suspicious. I mean, I'm in my third year of law school. So I refused to tell him and . . ."

She stopped, her chin trembling, and with horror the deputy U.S. attorney realized that she was very convincingly on the verge of tears. He wondered, briefly, if a jury would be able to see the contradiction between the trembling chin and the observant green eyes and decided, with regret, that they would not.

"Take your time, Alley." Bob speaking now, directing a look of calm challenge at the deputy U.S. attorney, accentuating the threat of tears.

"Okay." Wiping her nose. "Then he showed me the transcripts."

"Did he say where he got them?"

"No. He wouldn't say."

"And?"

"And he threatened to release them to the press if I didn't help him."

"Where did you go for information about the Israeli attempt to stop the Iraq trade?"

"My father has his files hidden in my grandfather's apartment out in Brooklyn. Dee knew that. I've known him since I was a kid."

"You went to your grandfather?"

"My grandfather is dead. I went to his apartment."

"Why didn't you get help?"

"I was afraid. I've known Dee for years. He is an extremely violent man. Ask anyone: he got suspended from Exeter for fighting. He was on probation at Cornell twice for fag-bashing. He just nearly got kicked out of the bar by my house for threatening a guy half his size."

"And what made you keep the diary?"

At this, she had looked straight across the table at him, then slowly at each of the men at the table.

"I was hoping this day would come."

There was a silence in the room. Then, clearing his throat, the attorney spoke dryly. "You seem to know the system well enough to know how to go about getting help from blackmail, Ms. Rosenthal."

She looked away. And then she looked back and spoke in an even, controlled voice. "We were having a sexual relationship, counselor. I first slept with Dee Dennis when I was fifteen years old and he was eighteen, which I now understand is statutory rape. What agency should I have gone to for recourse for that?"

And Bob Stein watched with an emotion that, if it weren't so completely bedazzled by the performance he was witnessing, might well have been called pride, as the other two men showed just how appalled they were.

That was Saturday morning. Saturday afternoon, something even more astounding took place, something that would keep the story in the right-hand column of *The New York Times* and give it a large-point headline too.

In the World Trade Center offices of the U.S. attorney.

When Dee Dennis announced his intention to enter a plea of nolo contendere to Allison Rosenthal's charges.

4.

Edward Treat Dennis, White House counsel, slammed shut the door of the U.S. attorney's office's conference room with a force that sent two secretaries scurrying after papers swept from the table by the draft. Present were the attorney who had deposed Allison Rosenthal, Daniel Edelson, Beth Callahan, and Shauna McCarthy, as well as Wayne Barlowe, the deputy attorney general just arrived from Washington, several paralegals, numerous secretaries. And Dee himself.

Then Edward Treat Dennis paused, and seated himself somewhat more quietly, as if he had expected to enter a war zone and found instead an armistice council. What his father was experiencing, noting the tension in the room, was evident to Dee, and for a brief, intense moment, it hurt his heart with a physical pain. The meeting had been going on already for fifteen minutes.

Shauna McCarthy spoke, from the head of the table. "Now, Ed, we all understand your concern. Let me start by assuring you that there is not a soul in this room who does not know these allegations to be entirely without substance. And I have just informed the attorney general of my intention to defend David in court."

"I'll serve as associate counsel."

Wayne Barlowe cleared his throat and spoke, somewhat apologetically. "Ed, the decision of whether or not to fight will be taken in Washington. You don't need me to explain the dice game there."

Shauna: "Wayne, I myself will offer my resignation unless this case is fought."

Silence. Then Edward Treat Dennis, as if flipping a switch on his anger, spoke in a placating voice that reminded his son that his father was a lobbyist.

"Wayne, Shauna. Maybe we're ahead of ourselves here. Let's start at the beginning, okay? Where are we at with this girl? What's she want?"

Boy, Dee thought to himself with some admiration as he watched his father cover his bases. That was fast.

Shauna nodded to the attorney who had deposed Alley, and he spoke with evident hesitation. "Mr. Dennis, I have to tell you from the outset: we'll need support in Washington. This girl is very, very smart, and she has presented a very, very sophisticated challenge. There's not a lawyer in the world wants her on a witness stand, either: she's beautiful, and she's ready to cry on demand. That girl crying in front of a jury is a lock, and Stein knows it. That's the bad news.

"The good news is that she's lying. It's an ugly case to defend—we'll have to subpoena Sidney Ohlinger's daughter—but it can be done. Let me start with the allegations, and then we can look a little further into the extenuations and then at the burden of proof . . ."

Dee wondered, sitting with his back to the window, how his father had managed to make himself the focus of this meeting. He turned now, and let his gaze wander out over the harbor and to the sky of November gray over Jersey. Perhaps the first time he had paused for thought in the past two days.

Or two nights.

For the first time his mind shifted, at long last, into synthesis rather than apprehension, as he listened vaguely to the lawyer outlining Alley's claims. To Dee Dennis, each one was less an allegation than an explanation. A piece of a puzzle.

Perhaps love, thought Dee, was always a puzzle, and perhaps there were always pieces missing.

This intimate puzzle, every piece was in place.

He saw it now, so clearly. Each step in their intimacy had been a step in Alley's reasoning, each exposure of himself through trust another piece of evidence, and he, he had been blind.

And yet, could he honestly say that he had been innocent? This love affair that also happened to save his career? Had his original intentions been innocent?

Only the losers in any game, Dee knew, can say for sure that they were not willing to cheat.

It was as if she had played his own subconscious like a hand of cards.

Blame?

Dee pronounced the word to himself.

It was like a foreign language.

All he felt was wonder.

Faster than Jay Cohen, certainly faster than Nicky, Dee Dennis had seen the entire complexity of Alley's genius the moment he'd learned, from the *New York Times* reporter who'd called him for comment, what she had done. One fact, and everything had fallen into place, everything. From the FedEx slip to her careful guidance of his prosecution, and across all the moments of nakedness between them. Each detail of doubt he remembered immediately. How he had blinded himself to them.

And he understood more than the facts. He understood the motivation. He understood the calculation and he understood the need. He understood with his analytic capacity; he understood with his sensual knowledge. This woman. He understood her, in her passion, in her skill, and in her courage.

And in that understanding, for Dee Dennis, in that understanding not only of her person but of her past, of her family, of the entire shared world of rarefied compromise and cynical ambivalence in which they had together grown up, for the first time the wall of the past came down and a continuum stretched, unbroken, from the slim, small-breasted girl with the light on her skin on Hancock Beach to the woman by whom he stood now accused.

He understood, in short, with the empathy of real love.

∽

The attorney who had deposed Allison had finished and Dee's father, still the de facto chair of the meeting, was speaking in his "Getting to Yes" voice again.

"Okay. Ladies, gentlemen, let's not bullshit each other, okay? Shauna, Wayne knows, and I know, you're with us. We also know that you're coming from the Beltway Disneyland, and that you deal with Mickey Mouse there, not people. So let's not bullshit each other. Who can we count on?"

Dee watched with attention as Wayne, then Shauna, each in turn, hedged. So, she didn't want to name names. Dee understood that: if there wasn't any support for this prosecution in the White House, who wanted to be allied with his father on his defense? And as Shauna unwillingly put her cards on the table, Dee saw that the odds against him were very long indeed: as he had suspected, this whole prosecution had lost its original support in the two years since, early in the Clinton administration, it was launched at his father's urging. The odds were long: so long that it would take real principle, and real courage, to oppose them. And suddenly Dee wondered what side his father would fall on.

That doubt, unlike his thoughts of Alley, gave him real pain.

Perhaps, he thought—his thoughts again taking leave of the meeting—that was because the choice before his father was a radical test, whereas nothing Alley had done contradicted her profession of love. Perhaps, he thought, the love of another is always just a reflection of the love for self. But the stuff of self, Dee thought, the stuff of self is always the reflection of a parent's love, and when the parent's love is dishonest the self is so crippled. Yes, he thought, with a strange detachment. We can leave a lover behind and survive, but these people, these terrible people, are with us for all of our lives. And Alley knows that. Nothing else matters. Alley knows that.

He turned, and looked around the table of his superiors, trying to face facts. How silly. There was only one thing to do. He had been doomed from the very first day he had seen Alley on the porch of the Up Island General Store. All her other allegations, all the mad fiction she had built out of him, it didn't matter: his conviction was assured in the first moment. He had slept with the enemy. He had slept with her that night on Hancock Beach, and he had left her bed hours before she was arrested on an interstate warrant.

And he had been caught.

How was Edward Treat Dennis's son to react? Gazing around the table at these self-satisfied people, the kind of people who had surrounded him all his life, calmly analyzing the ins and outs of Washington politics, he experienced the same excited feeling, suddenly, as he had felt when he'd dropped his first bombshell in court.

There was only one conclusion to the question. Sooner or later, they would get there. But if he spoke now, if he spoke now and said it for them, then he would not have to see which side his father would take, and he would not have to live forever with whatever he saw.

"Just a moment." His voice broke the conversation at the table in an instant.

"I think I can save us all some time."

5.

NO CONTEST. The words in the *New York Times* headline, the Sunday edition, emerging sideways from the fax, appeared to Nicky's wide eyes letter after letter. Then the next headline, a two-line head, came out: first EAST-BROOK on top of the word EXPECTED, then CALLS over TO, then PRESS, over ANNOUNCE, then CONFERENCE over RESIGNATION. He removed the page and read it again, then again. First: DAVID DENNIS ENTERS PLEA OF NO

CONTEST; then: EASTBROOK CALLS PRESS CONFERENCE, EXPECTED TO ANNOUNCE RESIGNATION.

Holding the fax, Nicky Dymitryck sat heavily in his chair.

What was in Nicky Dymitryck's mind as he sat? Something that defied description.

As if the one fact about Alley he did not know, the fact that she and Dee Dennis were in love—the one irreducible ambiguity in the story he had for so long followed—had at last cast his mind out of the analytic and into the mystical.

For *mystical* is the closest word to describe Nicky Dymitryck's experience, that Saturday night in his office: a synchronic state in which all the meanings of his present appeared in perfect equivalence, the death, the loss, the depth of love he had felt, the enormity of betrayal, the completeness of his solitude, the thoroughness of the state change of his life, as if it had turned from water into gas, and it were floating, floating away.

Really, even better than *mystical*, the word to describe what happened to Nicky that moment was *epistemological*, a change in his very definition of all he knew, of the truth, and of himself.

A strange way, an abrupt and very tragic way, to have one's heart broken.

6.

On Monday morning, November the 14th, Bob Stein successfully argued for Allison Rosenthal's release on bond, relying heavily on the extenuating circumstances of her position and David Dennis's plea of no contest.

Bail was set at fifty thousand dollars, and Stein immediately dispatched an assistant for the bond. Allison waited in a holding room for the hour it took to get that.

While she waited, a subpoena was served on her to appear in state court, Boston, the following morning. At 11:45 she was released into the cold of a gray November day. She wore the clothes in which she had been arrested: jeans, black leather loafers, a black jersey, and a long black cashmere overcoat.

Stein was waiting with a limousine, and helped her shoulder her way through the reporters and into the car. It drove off with difficulty. But it did not go far. On North Moore and Varick, clear of the reporters, it stopped. Alley got out, spoke to Stein for a moment through the window, and hailed a cab. Inside, she asked for La Guardia Airport. As the cab pulled out, she noted through the back window, a white Taurus driven by a single man pulled out after her.

She rode to La Guardia silently in the cab, followed by the white Taurus, her eyes out the window on the grim landscape between the airport and the city. A familiar landscape and one, she knew, she would not soon see again. At La Guardia she made her way to the Delta Shuttle, noticing that the driver of the white Taurus had parked illegally and was walking after her. He wore a London Fog raincoat. She purchased an open ticket to Boston, and then sat at a table in the little restaurant off the rotunda of the terminal, watching the man from the white Taurus take a seat at the bar.

In time, three men entered the restaurant, all bearded and in business suits and hats. Two stood at the door while one, carrying an oddly feminine suitcase, crossed to her table, sat, and spoke briefly with Allison in a foreign language. Then he looked over at the other two and motioned with a tip of his head. Following the direction of his movement, they crossed the restaurant and sat at the bar, on either side of the man from the white Taurus. A brief discussion ensued, during which the man from the white Taurus withdrew and displayed to his companions an FBI badge. The discussion seemed to grow heated, until one of the men settled whatever was at issue with a gesture under his suit jacket. Whatever he was concealing there seemed to convince the man from the Taurus, for he paled, and then allowed the other two to escort him out of the restaurant.

Now, at her table, Allison accepted from her childhood friend Peretz the suitcase, the keys to a car, a passport, and a small bundle of currency. With a nod, she rose and walked out of the restaurant and out of the terminal.

As for Peretz, he rose a moment later and followed her at a distance. He watched her cross the street to the parking lot, then open and board the rented Buick in which he, Menachem, and Ben Gordon had arrived. He watched as she threw the bag in the back and drew out of the lot toward the airport exit, not acknowledging him as she passed.

Only then did he turn and, eyes thoughtfully to the ground, walk slowly back to the terminal.

That evening, at eleven o'clock, a woman in a rented Buick parked in the lot of a truck stop near LaFargeville, New York.

She entered and settled at a table. Then she rose again, and crossed the restaurant to a pay phone.

With a credit card, she placed a telephone call.

Her hands, it could be observed, were shaking as she dialed.

What was the expression on her face as she waited for an answer?

There was hope, a tremulous expression in the lift of her eyebrows, the tip of her tongue showing between her teeth.

There was dread, a heavy set of her lips, a stiffness of her cheeks.

And there was courage, a slow green burn in her eyes,

as if she had come to this phone, in this restaurant, ready to face the truth.

The conversation with Nicky lasted perhaps one minute.
  "It's me."
  Silence while she listened. Then, a single word:
  "Please."
  Another silence. And then, with a small smile.
  "I told you you wouldn't want to hear from me again."
  With that she hung up and stood by the phone, leaning against the wall, as if too weak to walk. And only after a long moment did she manage to cross back to her table, her face, now, devoid of any expression whatsoever except the saddest of the three, which was courage.

Alone at a table, she drank coffee, then just sat, staring out the window, for three hours. For those three hours, she sat still, with the exception of a short period in which she read, several times, the title page of a small, thin, blue booklet, the size of a passport. Then she returned her gaze out the window, her lips moving slightly, as if she were memorizing something, or reciting a mantra.

  At two in the morning she rose, paid, and left the restaurant. She started her car, drew out of the truck stop north on Highway 81. Forty-five minutes later, Tziporah Rosen showed a small, blue Israeli passport with a valid Canadian visa to the customs inspector at the border, submitted to a brief search of her car, and then drove into Canada.

  Had someone been following—no one was—they would have followed her from here to Montréal International Airport, where a ticket was held in her name for a direct flight, later that morning, to Paris.

CHAPTER 17

December 15, 1994.
Paris.

1.

December 15; rue de la Paix.

In front of the Hermès picture window, Allison stood, gazing at the Christmas display.

Or so it seemed. In fact, it was her reflection she watched: her face pale and lips red in the damp Paris winter, dark pools of fatigue under her eyes. Peering at her face, mercilessly, she wondered if it would ever come back to itself.

But what was itself? She corrected herself: to what it had been. Her eyes met her eyes and an expression crossed her face, of annoyance, of disgust. Three o'clock. Her father had arrived that morning in Paris, resuming his duties for the Falcon Corporation. She was due to meet him at his hotel at four.

She had been walking already for hours, and a bone-deep weariness was in her, the accumulated exhaustion of the month past, of the months past. As if all the nights she sat up at her desk on Jane Street, falsifying her diary, working with the court transcripts and her father's private papers, making love to Dee and talking to Nicky, as if all those nights had caught up with her and were taking their toll now. She had been very sick when she'd arrived in Paris, first strep throat, and then pneumonia, for which she had been hospitalized in Neuilly for a week. She should have accepted her father's offer of a ticket, via Bob Stein, to Martinique. Instead, she moved into Chevejon's apartment on the rue de Fleurus, and recuperated slowly in the European winter.

Now, in front of the window at Hermès, thinking of all the sleep she had missed that fall, she pictured her desk in the apartment on Jane Street, the window next to it illuminated by the streetlights at the intersection of Eighth Avenue and Jane.

Then she saw the beach at Ocean View, a slanting snow darting like commas into the wash of the waves.

Hypnagogic memory. Quick, involuntary hallucinations, precisely detailed, of past locales. She had experienced them a lot since she'd been sick: her fatigue, which weighed on her mind as much as her body, seemed to encourage it.

She sighed now, watching her breath mist the window, then turned in the direction of Angelina's on the rue de Rivoli, thinking joylessly of the thick hot chocolates she and Pauly had so loved there, a little Jewish boy and girl, immaculately dressed, visiting Paris with their mother.

She could wait there for an hour with the paper, she thought, or a book from W. H. Smith, right down the street, then head up to the Ritz to meet her father.

The vision of Ocean View still fresh in her mind, she wondered how Dee had spent the month. He had written to her after Bob Stein had withdrawn her charges against him, a short, factual letter in which he told her that he would be moving to San Francisco, and that he did not blame her for what she had done. It was, she suspected, something of a liberation for him. Perhaps he realized the aspirations she had forced him to sacrifice were too factitious to have any real meaning. When she tried to feel anything deeper about him, however, she felt blankness. She was sorry for what she had done to him, she supposed. But she could not help but feel that somehow, somewhere in this, Dee had been happy to let her go. Perhaps she knew, now, that ultimately, no matter where Dee might venture, he would return to his conventionality. It was, she admitted now, not only for him but for nearly everyone she had ever known in that little trapezoidal world between the Vineyard, Boston, New York, and Washington, too powerful a force.

And Martha. She had not heard from Martha even once since she'd gone, as if finally Martha had understood the difference between the worlds of their fathers. Martha's encounter with this willingness so blatantly to use illegality without government protection would have scared her. Faced with the possibility of moving entirely out of Beltway logic, entirely out of conventionality, she knew, Martha too would never really take the step. Marty. She could not imagine life without her, and yet that was what faced her.

Nicky Dymitryck she could not think about. It was funny that the one person as fundamentally maverick as herself was the one who had so cleanly rejected her. Of all the things that had happened to her, that hurt the most. It had hurt when it happened, and it hurt now, throbbing in her chest with the regularity of the thin Paris rain pissing down onto her. It would, she thought, throb like that for a great while.

And now she was in front of W. H. Smith, under the covered sidewalk on the rue de Rivoli, thick holiday crowds moving around her like the slowly shifting roll of a wave, and she wasn't sure how she had gotten there.

2.

W. H. Smith. The warmth, the dry warmth of a store full
of English-language books on her face now. Hands still in
her coat pockets, she shouldered her way through the
lines at the cash registers and to the back of the store, the
poetry section. Gazed blankly up at the shelf of paper-
backs, her eyes resting on names and editions she knew:
Clark, Coleman, Malanga, Reznikoff, Wakoski. She
stopped at this last name and, after a hesitation, took the
book, *Emerald Ice*, and moved back to the cash register.
Outside again, clutching the book under an arm, she
made her way to Angelina's, took a table, and ordered a
chocolat.

Earlier that morning, Bob Stein had called her at the
rue de Fleurus. Three in the morning, New York time; he
must have woken especially for it. Her father was on his
way to Paris. He did not yet understand what had happened. Bob thought that it might be some time before
her father understood the full extent of what she had
done. So far, he had refused to discuss it.

As for her, the deal was almost cut: if she honored the
Ocean View leases, all concerned were willing to drop
charges. Except for Stan Diamond, who would settle only
if he could have Ocean View farmhouse itself. That
meant that Alley would lose the summer on the island—
the first season of her life she'd miss there. He spoke as if
she would be in the States for the season, as if she would
have the luxury of deciding where she would summer. In
the living room of the apartment, she had listened impassively, her eyes watching the rain drip, dropping down
the outside of the big French doors looking out over all
Paris; her eyes seeing soft snow drifting on the streets far
below the window of Bob's office in downtown New
York.

"So my view is, stay put till after New Year's. Your
dad's thinking of Corsica. Go with him. Get a tan."

She didn't answer, and as if, on the other end of the line, Bob had understood her, he went on. "You come back here early January, they'll arrest you at the airport, I'll have you out the next day, tops. We'll cut a parole deal the next day."

"Parole for how long?"

"Maybe a year, honey."

"Where? Massachusetts?"

"No, you could stay in New York."

"No. I'm not coming. I'll honor the leases, and Diamond can have his season. But I'm not serving a parole sentence, and I'm not coming back without an order of extradition."

"No, I don't think there's gonna be an extradition order. Justice has had about enough of you."

That, she thought, at least gave her the quarter million. She no longer considered Ocean View her father's property—he had, in his willingness to lose it, sacrificed his ownership of that magical place. And then, she had a job—of sorts, one that promised to be very lucrative.

3.

Now, waiting for her hot chocolate at a table at Angelina's, she thought ruefully how immediately Stein would have understood her new job.

When she'd arrived in Paris and taken a room she could not pay for at La Louisiane on the rue du Seine, she'd immediately called Mr. Chevejon to find out where her money was. He was not in, but his answer arrived the next afternoon by messenger.

Florence
Dear Ms. Rosenthal,
    Your money is in an account with Crédit Suisse, numbered per the enclosed. It is immediately avail-

able by wire through their Paris office. I have withdrawn from it my expenses, per the enclosed re-
ceipts.

More importantly, I would like to extend to you
my offer of help, whether providing you a quiet place
to stay or, forgive me, extending whatever financial
help you may need, as I would guess that the sum
you deposited in Switzerland may be subject to some
pressure for return.

The letter had shown two addresses, but one, on the
rue St. Honoré in Paris, was crossed out, leaving one on
the Piazza Santo Spirito in Florence.

Then she had fallen very ill, and been hospitalized in
Neuilly, and for some days had been unable to do anything. When she could write again, from her hospital
bed, she had sent him a letter:

Dear Mr. Chevejon,

I wonder if I can draw on your goodness once
again. It would be of great use to me to have a quiet
place to stay for some time in the New Year, preferably in Paris. Would you know of an agent who can
arrange such a thing? I can pay up to $3,000 U.S. per
month.

She had received a brief answer, Chevejon's voice
withdrawn again to formality, as if to mask the generos-
ity of his offer:

Dear Ms. Rosenthal,

It happens that my business partner has at his disposal an empty apartment in the sixth. We'd both be
delighted if you would make yourself at home in it.
If you'd like to contact me when you are ready to
leave the hospital, I'll let the concierge know you're

coming. The address is 6, rue de Fleurus, sixth floor left.

The rue de Fleurus, she knew, was near the Luxembourg Gardens. This seemed to her perfect, and in the end she had found herself arriving in a luxurious apartment, protected by massive Fichet locks and a computerized burglar alarm, with windows giving out over all Paris, the wintry lead roofs, the bare trees, and the always steely gray sky. There were sparse furnishings: a living room with empty shelves, an empty office. But the minimal furniture was enough: a couch in the living room, a bed with linens; the kitchen was equipped, and the entire place had clearly been very recently cleaned. This, evidently, had been overseen by Chevejon, whom she called that evening in Florence.

"Mr. Chevejon. I don't know how to thank you."

"Not at all, Ms. Rosenthal. I'm sorry I couldn't be there to greet you. Do you need anything?"

"Thank you, no. Thank you very much, Mr. Chevejon."

"I see." He answered somewhat obliquely, and then after a pause, continued.

"Tell me, Ms. Rosenthal: what do you plan to do in Paris?"

She was silent a moment. And then, suddenly: "Whatever I have to, Mr. Chevejon."

"I see." A pause, and she imagined him smiling. "You have finished law school?"

"No. Nearly so."

"I see."

She hesitated, but only for a moment. "Mr. Chevejon? I know how to paper a sale—any kind of sale—in any state of the U.S. and also in Israel. I know accounting practice and I know both a network of very savvy people in New York and some of the wealthiest people on the

East Coast, as well as most of the major players in Israeli arms. I don't have a law degree, granted. But I think I have a lot to offer."

His answer was unequivocal. "Precisely what I think, Ms. Rosenthal." He paused. "You do understand that none of the work I have to offer is, strictly speaking, legal?"

She considered, suddenly tense. "You mean, in the sense of drawing on my law school education?"

He laughed. "No, Ms. Rosenthal. That is extremely useful to me. I mean in the sense of being sanctioned by law."

She relaxed. "Yes, Mr. Chevejon. I understand that."

"When might you like to come to Florence?"

Her heart skipped, so unambiguous was his job offer. "My father is in Paris. He leaves in a day or two, so perhaps next week."

"Splendid, Ms. Rosenthal. And, Ms. Rosenthal? Why not stay put in the rue de Fleurus for the time being. Does that suit you?"

At that she practically smiled.

4.

At her table at Angelina's now, the crowds on the rue de Rivoli, where a thin snow had started to fall, passing outside the window, the warmth of the crowded restaurant slowly permeating her skin, the swirl of conversation around her slowly drawing her out of her thoughts. A voice beside her said *"N'en fait pas, cheri, ça va aller."* Then again: *"Eh, du calme, eh? Où en es-tu avec ton chocolat? J'en commande un autre, ou ben non?"* She looked over, and saw a man with two children at the next table of the crowded salon, a girl in a chair and a baby in his lap. The girl, sitting with her chin at the table and kicking her legs, was looking at her.

She looked away. The oddest part was, now that it was over, she knew how big a role chance had played. The whole thing couldn't have stood up to a spirited defense from Dee. What if Martha Ohlinger had been subpoenaed, would she have perjured herself for Alley? That was a hard question to answer: Martha was deeply loyal, but she was also sincere in the ethics that guided her politics. But then, Martha would not be so anxious to show that she had let her job, for which she had fought tooth and nail, be used in a criminal agenda. Martha, Alley thought, might be feeling just a little bit guilty herself right now.

And Nicky? Again, the wound of his cold rejection throbbed in her. It was fed, she knew, by his disgust with himself, with his complicity in her crime. But in the end, the positive good of indicting Eastbrook had overridden his concern with himself, and he had said nothing. Still, she doubted that he would be going for the moral high ground again soon.

And yet luck was involved. Nothing, after all, was perfect: luck was always involved. Really, she thought, not for the first time, she owed it to Dee, to Dee refusing to say a word, in public or in private, in his defense.

Sometimes she wondered about that. But she knew that Dee could not think that she had planned this, had used a pretense with them to carry it out. She knew that he would understand that there had been no plan, there had just been an objective. The emotions that had lived between them were not pretenses, they had all been true. It was just that they had all had double meanings. But what doesn't? What doesn't mean two things; what doesn't carry a fundamental ambivalence, tenderness and violence, hope and regret? All that divided her from Dee was her willingness to read, and to use the shadow meaning that always tails behind what we think of as the truth.

Alley found herself staring at the little girl at the neighboring table, and made a last effort to focus on the book in front of her.

And could not. A cup of hot chocolate, untasted, sat before her, next to the book of poetry, unopened. She knew nearly every piece in it by heart, anyway: it was more a talisman, a fetish. But it was also a bridge to another time, not a time of happiness but a time when she had suffered only a simple shame.

Because now she knew guilt. Pure, unambiguous, convicted guilt. Crime. The kind her father knew. Now she knew justice, that implacable reality, where two wrongs clash and one outmuscles the other. Once she had known mourning, a pain that never ends but renews itself each day, a gift of endless resource, and she had thought it to be guilt. How foolish she had been. The guilt she knew now, she would live with it forever, no longer a child but a felon, and it would never be absolved, and never go away.

She knew betrayal. With these two men, she had spent a moment of perfect trust and not once, but twice, she had betrayed each lover. The weight of that guilt lay now in her womb, and she knew that never, ever would it either pass from her body nor would it cease to struggle to be born.

All those people her father had killed. Laos, Cambodia, Guatemala, Iran, Angola. Not just soldiers but citizens: retirees, journalists, masons, nuns, accountants, schoolchildren—the assorted victims of cluster bombs and land mines, of napalm and heat-seeking missiles. There was a randomness about the variety of people who died that in itself was frightening. Chileans, Colombians, Africans, Christians, Muslims. There were even some Jews.

And did he feel guilt? Did he feel this black heart at the center of his being, this thing that ached? She felt now, for a long time, for the answer to this question, and perhaps she would have found it. But in the event, her attention suddenly went, totally out of her control, to someone who, she found, was standing next to her, bumping against her leg.

It was the little girl from the next table, standing with one hand on Allison's knee. She was perhaps three, dressed in jeans and a red sweater, and she stared up at Allison with a grave face, her big cheeks around a red rosebud mouth, her nut-brown hair, which had probably never been cut, swept back in a ponytail. One cheek held a perfectly placed beauty mark; her eyes were serious, unblinking, showing massive brown irises in the middle of long, very long lashes.

"Je peux avoir un gout de votre chocolat?"

Stock still, as if a wrong movement would break the spell, Allison answered. *"Oui. Vas-y."*

The girl stood on tiptoe to reach her mouth to the cup, tipped it with a pink hand on which, hyperaware, Allison noticed a small red birthmark and a gold bracelet, then stood back again, a mustache of thick chocolate on her upper lip.

At a loss, Alley asked: *"Il est bon?"*

"Oui, il est très bon."

Allison could not remember ever speaking to a child this age. For a moment the girl and she regarded each other, the girl gravely through her clear brown eyes, Allison curiously.

Then, from the next table the father called: *"Leila. Qu'est-ce que tu fais là?"*

The girl heard, and wended her circuitous way through the chairs over to the man, a man not much older than Nicky, with thinning hair and a black beard, a strange, harsh look halfway between a rabbi and a spy, who sat feeding a bottle to a very small boy in his lap. He was, Allison registered, Jewish. Ashkenazi, which wasn't often the case in Paris. When the girl was close enough, the man spoke absently.

"Eh, toi. Je fais bouffer à Jacob, puis que veux-tu qu'on fasse?"

"Aller aux Tuileries." She answered matter-of-factly, a hand on her brother's stomach.

"Bon, ça y est."

The girl agreed, then, with a hand on his shoulder, stood on tiptoes to speak in his ear. He listened, then started to laugh. Then he met Allison's eyes and stopped.

"Désolé, madame. Je vais vous en commander un autre."

She answered with a shake of her head, without really raising her voice. *"Vous en faites pas. J'étais sur le point de m'en aller."*

But she did not go, not yet. Now the girl was sitting up on her chair, her legs dangling above the floor, ending in pink galoshes. The man had returned his attention to her brother, who, his wet lip round on the nipple of the bottle, a fuzz of blond hair over the crown of his head, gazed up at his father with shining eyes. The two looked ridiculously alike. The father made a face and the boy's lips stretched in open-faced delight.

And the father, balding with his black beard and Jewish nose, smiled back. His eyes behind his glasses crinkling with another kind of delight, a delight tempered by the age of his face, yes, but more by the worry of love, the worry that was love. The girl climbed off her chair and moved to his side; he curled his arm around the baby's neck to hold the bottle and with his other arm free, now, turned the girl's face to his, wiped off her chocolate mustache, and bent down to kiss her.

As for the lady with the hot chocolate, she had ceased to exist for them.

But she sat, transfixed. Feeling pity, fear, regret.

Pity for that balding man with his love corrupted by mortal fear.

Fear for those children, stuck with a devotion they had never asked for and could never lose.

And a searing regret that passed through and through her and left her, yet again, on the verge of tears.

Rising, leaving money on the table, leaving.

That girl with her father. What did they know about love?

5.

Four-fifteen, the Hotel Ritz. In the living room of her father's suite. A uniformed waiter had opened the door for her, but for once, she seemed to be expected: she did not need to explain who she was, and her father, in shirt-sleeves and suit pants, was at the window of the living room, watching out. For a moment he did not notice that she had arrived. Then, when she spoke, he turned and she was in his arms, smelling aftershave and cigarettes mixed with the wet-wool smell of her coat.

Busily, he took her coat, put her into a chair, directed the waiter's tea service in his lousy French, all the while talking to her. The government had returned his files to him, so much for Mike Levi, that damn liar. He'd be back stateside in a few weeks. *Le Monde* was coming to interview him at five.

She seemed to see him more than hear him as he spoke. Even the crime she had committed did not seem to breach the limits of his paternalism. She wished she could offer him the same lack of condition. But her affection no longer seemed adequate to her response to this man. Nor, however, like a curse on her, would it abandon him, and as she watched him talking, pouring tea, lighting a cigarette, talking, she ached with desire for him to kiss her as that man, this afternoon, had kissed his daughter.

His monologue slowed at last, and a silence fell between them. Finishing his tea and lighting a cigarette, he rose and stood by the big windows that gave out onto the Place Vendôme. Turning in her armchair, she watched him in profile: a strong, rather squat man with the embonpoint of a life of wealth and power, a weathered face, a piercing green eye. At last, not looking at her, he spoke in a quiet voice she had not, she realized, heard for years.

"Now, Essie, I'm not going to ask about what happened. I know neither Stein nor the papers got the truth. I don't believe I need to have it either. Is there anything else you want to tell me?"

"Yes."

"Go ahead."

She was quiet for a moment. Then she answered.

"I want you to give Ocean View to the Trustees of Reservations. I want a guaranteed stewardship for me and my heirs. If I have no children, then it reverts to reservation land. The rental houses I want demolished. At your expense."

Her father nodded, as if he had been expecting this. "Agreed."

"There's more. I want you to stop sending me checks. I'm not going back to law school, and I no longer want to be supported."

That, at last, made him blanch, as if she had dealt him a physical injury. She softened her tone, but she went on, as if administering a just and implacable punishment. "And I want you to know that whatever I might one day inherit from you, I will not accept. The half that should have been Pauly's, I want you to give to Yale. The half that should have been mine, I want given to nonpolitical charities."

This time, he countered, as if he had already prepared his response. "Agreed. On two conditions."

Suspiciously, she waited.

"Firstly, when I sold Abba's store to Metrotech I put the money in trust for you and Pauly. I want you to take that."

Through her head passed a quote from Balzac: *Tout se transige.* "Everything is negotiable." It was a lawyer who'd said it, too.

"I'll take my half. Pauly's goes to charity."

Her father nodded. "Secondly, I think you should have someone to talk to."

She rose now and walked to the room's left-hand window, her arms crossed tight around her breasts. For a brief second, she felt regret. And then it was over, her moment of control gone, and she listened, a girl being spoken to by her father. "By talk to, you are meaning . . ."

"Psychiatric help. Psychoanalytic, I think, but it's up to you." He was talking fluently now, fully in charge.

"Essie, it used to be, I worried about you, I'd make you go to law school, or something." He looked now, across the bay between the two windows, at her, and smiled a smile that strangely resembled, she thought, her own. "But you seem to have grown up now."

"So your solution to this rite of passage is to send me to a psychoanalyst." She noticed she was childishly accentuating the educated in her diction, in counterpoint to Rosenthal's emphasis of the Brooklyn in his.

"Yeah, I think that's appropriate." He was watching out the window now, and she listened carefully. "Essie, you know the score. It scares me not to be able to take care of you. But then I think, well, maybe it's time for Essie to take care of herself, anyway. She sure seems to want to."

Now it was her turn to look out the window. It occurred to her suddenly that she had thought only of herself as having lost everything when Pauly died. Suddenly she felt his . . . his asphyxiation by life, his panic at being forced to interrupt the idyll not of his, but of *her* privileged life with the reality of its buried roots. It was like a curse. She looked back, a twenty-seven-year-old woman, in a cashmere sweater and jeans, the only surviving member of what once had been a family sprawled throughout the Lithuanian shtetl, all gone now, all gone but her.

"Okay."

He looked at her, pensive, then shook his head, once. "I need a lot better answer than that."

"I mean yes. I want to. I want to take care of myself." And, when she saw how worried he looked, she said in a different tone: "It's no big deal. I have a job. I'll be living in Paris from now on."

"And you'll find yourself a shrink?"

A shrink. A shrink. Suddenly she wanted to scream. What right had he to try to help her? Even to have had her? What right had he to put an ideal, intellectualized and ridden with corruption, above his children? She wanted to pull from the darkest point in her the things no child should ever say to their father and coldly, harshly destroy the man she had sacrificed everything to save, as she knew she could.

When she spoke, she said: "Yes, Daddy. I'll find myself a shrink."

And then his breath of tobacco and his warm skin were against hers and then she was outside, standing on the rue de Rivoli again, not knowing how she had gotten there.

Night. She lay on the bed in Mr. Chevejon's apartment, the room dark but for the light of the street lamps coming in from the high, dry, wintry European night that had moved in over the rue de Fleurus.

After she had left her father, she'd walked across the river and stopped, on her way home, for an omelette at La Palette: since she'd been sick, she found, she was nearly always ravenously hungry. She knew the owner there, and had sat at the bar in his warm presence for maybe an hour, as if putting off the inevitable. It had been toward seven when she'd gone up to her rooms then undressed and gone to bed without turning on the lights.

She slept, immediately, mercifully.

Then, just after midnight, the telephone had rung:

short, scary bursts from the living room, and she had woken, eyes wide, fear expanding like a spill of water across ice.

But only the innocent, she knew, wake unafraid, and she had risen to sit next to the phone until it stopped.

Now, back in her bed, before her eyes were the father, his daughter, and her brother, that afternoon.

And now it was night.

She hadn't even liked Pauly when they were children. An annoying, active little child, always into everything, always taking her mother's attention. Now, in her memory, it seemed that it was only when her mother had left, when they'd been at St. Ann's that she'd started noticing him. By then he was a thin, graceful boy, blond as she, pretty as she with their father's green eyes, but brash where she was retiring, rebellious where she was obedient, angry at everything. When their mother had gone he was fourteen, she sixteen. He took it very hard, her leaving, and from the moment he heard, he blamed his father. Nights in their suddenly empty brownstone on Grace Court, nights when her father was out, or away, and the maid was long asleep, he'd arrive at her bedroom door in tears of rage.

That's when she got to know her brother, really: that's when he stopped being an annoying sibling and became, suddenly, a person. That year in Grace Court had been, perhaps, a lonely one for her, too: Dee was gone after the summer; by bad luck Martha's father was teaching at Oxford, and had taken his family with him. And so she had the occasion to come to know the complex, smart person her little brother, in his loss, in his misery, had so precociously become. And so she had had the occasion for her little brother to become, in the solitude that year, her friend.

Or so she thought.

It shocked her, she remembered, when she had under-

stood one day how utterly different he was from a friend.
Martha was a friend. Pauly, for all he could smoke pot
with her, joke with her, walk down the street with her in
his jeans jacket and swinging blond hair, was fundamentally different. He was family.

It was an early evening. Her father was out, they had
gotten stoned together on the back porch, and under the
sway of a towering ailanthus and the—suddenly so astounding—shiver of its leaves she had watched him
standing, shirtless, watching the sky.

What makes friends, she suddenly saw, is their *difference*. But Pauly was not different from her. For the first
time she saw, in the fall of his thick blond hair, in the
sway of his back, in the tone of his skin, how *same* they
were, this boy and her, how equally one genetic dose of
matter had been shared between them. No one would
ever be the same to her as he, she thought, the lock and
key of their creations had been taken apart, by divorce, by
menopause, and now the meioses that defined the molds
of their beings were unrepeatable historic events. And
now they were, each, the key to the other. And as she
thought that, Allison Rosenthal, at sixteen, standing
under a bowing ailanthus at night on the porch of her
Brooklyn house, had her first experience of adult love.

Now, years later, that night stood in her mind as myth,
so powerful, so seminal, that sometimes it seemed to her
that this central event of her life could not have been simply a revelation, a vision, but must have been something
more. And when she wrote about it, years later in a poem,
she had found coming to her pen images of brute sym-
bolism: a swan with beating wings, red blood on the
white of a sheet. He himself she could feel, in that poem,
in all his familiarity, his smell, his touch. And as time
passed, it was as if the poem had replaced the memory, or
rather as if memory had become confused with its own
mythicality, and really, she no longer knew what had happened.

Except that time passed. And she'd left for New Haven. Leaving Pauly alone to return to a new house, her father's new apartment on Park Avenue.

She'd left him, alone, to her father.

Only her mother had understood. Her father, with his endless stories about growing up in the streets of Borough Park. Of the gang fights, the Jews against the Micks; the refugee life on the streets of New York; the jobs and petty crime. Of how at seventeen, the day of his graduation from yeshiva, her father had run away to Israel and enlisted in the army. How he'd returned to Brooklyn College, then against all odds gotten into Yale Law School, and how he'd worked his way through both. Only her mother had understood the indoctrination in righteousness, entitlement, and reparation to which Allison had abandoned her brother.

The year she went to college Pauly had entered Dalton. Now, in his senior year, her father started in earnest. He wanted Pauly to go, as he had gone, straight out of school to Israel. The army was a great experience, for a boy, for a Jew, and as he had done his service, so should his son. He owed it to Israel, he owed it to his grandparents.

Pauly hadn't wanted to join the army. He wanted to join his sister at Yale. Pauly didn't want to have anything to do with Israel, and as that year went on their arguments subsumed any other part of their relationship. Pauly had always been too young to understand the pathos of Zionism, to him his father was all kitsch, all rationalization, all bogus stories of a heroism that no longer meant anything in a world where Israelis were an occupying force and the Holocaust a subject for Hollywood films. And as the year went on he dug deeper and deeper into his father's affairs to hold him in accusation, so deep that his father had grown, in the end, scared that Pauly was going actually to do something crazy. So scared that finally her father had agreed to let him go to college before the army.

Pauly at Yale. Lying in a bed in a foreign city, a stranger's apartment, she saw his beautiful, brilliant, boyish face, filled with strength and grace, eager to make everyone his friend. Every night he'd be at her dorm room, to study with her, to sit with her, to sleep curled on the floor.

And then he'd met Johnny. When she first saw them together, toward Christmas of his freshman year, at a Lambda party, Pauly had looked momentarily afraid of her. Which was funny, because she hadn't given it a second thought, so natural had he looked in that crowd of hip, handsome young men. Then, after seeing his expression, understanding had come in a flash and she'd stepped over to him without hesitation, to hug him, kiss him, to meet Johnny and talk to his friends. His expression—grateful to her, proud of her—had never long left her mind.

Perhaps there had been something else in his expression. Perhaps he had seen her relief, and it had broken his heart.

God, he'd blossomed that year. Nothing stopped him: the Writing Program, squash team, those endless coked-up parties, he had time for everything, and in everything he'd done well. He was a junior when she, having finally made her deal with her father, had gone, reprieved from law school, to Paris. And a senior when, on the phone from New Haven to Paris, he'd broken to her the unbelievable news that her father had started again on him to make plans for Israel after graduation.

At first, the summer after he graduated, she'd thought that after all, it was going to be okay. Pauly was holding his own, determined to resist his father. He thought, in fact, that the old man was weakening: Pauly had come out to him, and was confident the shame of having a gay son would make his father want to keep him home, under wraps.

At first. She stayed in Paris, the summer following his graduation, dawdling in the European summer, delaying returning for the late summer in Ocean View, having too much fun to want to end her precious time away. Anyway, she had agreed to give her father some time to be alone with Pauly. She thought Pauly would hold firm, she thought it would be all right.

Then it had all started to go wrong, and when Pauly had called, in early June, she had understood quickly that it was not all right. Her father was entirely unconvinced by Pauly, more than ever determined to have his son follow in his footsteps, and was planning on leaning heavily. Allison knew what it was like when her father leaned. Pauly tried to sound cheerful on the phone, but the strain had come through. And when she heard his voice she'd known that she had to come straight home, right away, Charles de Gaulle to Kennedy to Logan to the little island airport in two days, abandoning her life and her possessions in Paris.

At Ocean View, you could cut the atmosphere with a knife. Having a daughter had turned her father into a feminist. Now he was a gay-rights activist, too. Pauly silent, her father fuming quietly for days until bursting out, "I don't give a fuck what you are. It's all the more reason to do what you have to. Hitler killed gays, too."

And Pauly, in turn, grew more and more militant, less and less circumspect. He was drinking heavily that summer, drinking and doing coke and partying the nights away in the scene of young, hip gay men on the island. And one night at a party in Ocean View, where many Israelis in their shirtsleeves milled with their wives around the room, holding drinks and talking to counterparts from defense businesses on the mainland—Electric Boat, Bath Iron Works—and government figures from Washington and Jerusalem—Greg Eastbrook, Amiram Nir, Al Schwimmer, Robert Earl—she saw Pauly approach her father unsteadily.

Worried, she excused herself from a conversation and came close enough to hear him say: "So this is what I'm going to defend, Dad?"

She took his arm, but he was raising his voice: "So this is the pioneers of Israel protecting the interests of the Jewish people, is it, Dad? This is what you want me to go give three years of my fucking life for, is it?"

She tried to pull him away, while her father was saying in Hebrew—as if to keep it in the family of Israelis in the room: "Pauly, you are to leave the room this instant." And Pauly, as she pulled him, answered in Hebrew also.

"*Lama ze, Abba?* What are you ashamed of? This is Zionism. Assassinating Gerald Bull was Zionism. Trying to buy Carlos Cardoen was Zionism. Training SAVAK and arming Mobutu was Zionism. Threatening Greg Eastbrook was Zionism, and now serving him drinks in your fucking living room, it's all for the good of the goddamn Jews, Dad."

And as she pulled him, forcibly now, out of the room, Alley saw pass between Greg Eastbrook and Amiram Nir a look that sent ice into her blood.

She'd begged him to stop. She'd pleaded for him to stop.

Now she knew, because Nicky had told her, that it was already too late.

Now she knew, because Nicky had told her, that Pauly had already contacted Nicky twice, once to send him to Munich, and then again to send him to Paris.

And in Paris Peleg had told Nicky to come back to Pauly for proof, proof not of her father's guilt, as Pauly wanted, but of Eastbrook's. And the whole thing, the whole thing, had been taped.

And now, years later in a Paris apartment, for the first

time, she understood what that look between Eastbrook and Nir had said.

And then it was that late-June morning when they'd planned to sail to Cuttyhunk, and she'd woken before dawn and gone to wake Pauly for an early start, and his bed had been empty, and she had known, deep in her, that something was terribly wrong.

She'd taken her bike—not the Canondale but the Mongoose mountain bike with its big sand tires—and ridden along the hard sand by the water's edge, right up past Black Rock Beach, Hancock Beach, Lucy Vincent, Philben, all the way up to the clay cliffs of Gay Head, because she knew he and Johnny camped there sometimes on the gay beach up around the point. And when she saw him, lying clothed on the sand, facedown on the low-tide sand, she'd thought he must have fallen asleep drunk, only when she knelt to wake him, she found him wet, and cold, and when she turned him and saw his beautiful face, his beautiful face, streaked with the red of the cliff's red clay, like an Indian warrior, and the black of his eyes and the blue of his swollen lips, and in his chest, the middle of his T-shirt, a black burnt hole in the middle of an aureole of blood drilling through to his heart.

For a time she sat, moans like an animal coming from deep in her throat, his head in her lap, while the waves lapped up at them. For a time she sat on the endless, empty beach in the crepuscular dark. Nicky had explained to her how, but even then, even then, she'd known why. And because she knew why she stood, gingerly moving his limp neck to lay his head in the soft sand.

Later she realized that the whole way back to Ocean View she had ridden slowly, carefully, as if knowing that one bad fall, one blown tire, and everything was lost.

Later she realized that in the madness of her grief she had still known that Pauly was gone, and nothing would ever make that better, but that if her father knew what had happened he would be gone too, and nothing would be left her, nothing. Tens of thousands of fathers had given their sons to Israeli wars. Her father must never know he had given his son to Israeli *industry*, he could not stand it, and she, she who had now lost everything, would lose him too.

What she had to do, had to do, was make this be the death of Pauly alone, one death, Pauly's death.

At Ocean View her father slept heavily in the rising dawn while she gingerly opened his bedside drawer and withdrew the nickel-plated handgun he kept there.

And then she was riding again, up the empty beach, the apocalyptic pink sun lighting the sea a weird, ghostly green, too early on a Sunday morning even for fishers, and then running again. And in the silence of the empty beach where her brother lay she pointed the gun to the sea and fired once, a thin sound that the enormous landscape of sand and sea and sky swallowed up nearly before it happened. And then, kneeling, she'd wiped the gun clean against her T-shirt and, lovingly, lifted Pauly's limp hand and placed the gun in it.

Or had she? For now, kneeling by her brother, the minutes past seemed to be clouding into the mythological past, just like the night with Pauly under the ailanthus, just like when she had started to betray Dee and Nicky, and it was as if she did not know whether she had done what she'd done or just thought of doing it, a plausible deniability of the soul. Had she done it? Remembering, now, it seemed to her she had just arrived on the beach, just come around the point and found her brother, and turned him from where he lay facedown in the lapping waves and seen the black of his eyes and the blue of his swollen lips, and in his chest, the middle of his T-shirt, a black burnt hole in an aureole of blood, and in his hand the gun he had stolen from his father to kill himself, and then all at once, on the empty beach at dawn, begun to scream.

There was never a question asked. When the police arrived, from nowhere in her mind came the next step, as if then, like now, her plan had been made somewhere in the covert reaches of the soul. She told them that Pauly had been HIV-positive. That satisfied them, as she knew it would: the fag had killed himself, and there was no autopsy and no question. Pauly had killed himself because he was gay, nice and neat, and his body had been taken and buried without ever a soul asking to match a bullet to the gun or checking the thumbprint on the trigger with the impossible angle at which he would have had to fire. It satisfied her father, too: Pauly had killed himself because he was gay, and he was sick, and that was why he had said all those crazy things also.

But Pauly never would have killed himself. Pauly, handsome and brilliant, so alive, would never have killed himself, not if he'd had HIV, not if he had been forced to go into the army. He'd have died with grace had he been sick; he'd have excelled—as strong, skillful, and intelligent as the best Israeli soldier—in the army.

Besides Allison, only her mother, come from California for the funeral, had understood. Without knowing any of the details, she had still understood what Allison was determined to keep her father ever from knowing. Only her mother had understood who had killed her son, and why, and after the funeral Allison had driven her, day after day, to the cliffs at Gay Head to stand on the place where he'd shot himself and dropped into the sea while her mother, her rich, elegant, glamorous mother wept and wept into her diamond-ringed fingers.

And as for Allison, those days, standing next to her sobbing mother, slowly she felt the gray mist of memory rise and surround what she had done, pulling it into that mythological place where we tell stories about the things we cannot explain, where we come from, why we die. So much so that when she came to write about Pauly in a poem she described the incest that she thought had happened and a symbolic suicide that she knew had not and turned what she had done into a poetic myth just as her father turned what he had done into a political one. And that, too, she stored in the place where we half forget the stories we cannot bear to remember and hide what we cannot bear to know, the promises we have broken, the creatures we have killed, the people we have betrayed and, for some of us, the way we make our money. For Alley, the place where she kept the things she did for that man she had never wanted to love and could not bear to lose.

Now she saw it again, Pauly facedown on the empty beach, a sky of smoky clouds, the red clay cliffs.

She saw Ocean View, a lone house against the snow-swept beach, the green Atlantic raging beyond it.

She saw the face of the girl at Angelina's with her father.

And suddenly, in the same visual detail, she saw, at last, the dead.

Bodies subjected to the force of cluster bombs, land mines, bullets. Bodies broken in mud, severed limbs, gaping holes in T-shirted chests, faces resting, cheek down, on pillows of blood and dirt. She saw bodies sprawled like Pauly on the beach, covering the surface of the earth with their unnegotiable departures: every jungle, every desert, every corner of the vast breadbasket and marketplace into which people like her father divided the world for their use and their profit, the millions of dead that traced the track of her father's career.

Killed people, ruined people, wasted people. Children with ponytails and rosebud mouths, perfect beauty marks on their cheeks. Fathers with balding heads and graying beards, staring the worry of love at their babies; babies with lips wet around the nipple of a bottle of milk.

And at last, the huge shame finished the gestation that had so long measured her growth, finished its gestation and burst out in her chest, like an incubus, like a monster. And she cried not for Pauly, not for her father, but at last for herself, deep sobs that shook her body on the bed, weeping, whispering into the dark of the room: "Daddy. Daddy. How could we do that? How could we do that to him?"

EPILOGUE

What did I know, what did I know
Of love's lonely and austere offices?

ROBERT HAYDEN
"Those Winter Sundays"

EPILOGUE

January 1995.
Fiesole.

1.

Throughout the night she had held me in the focus of those green eyes, as if more than anything that had happened, it mattered that I understand her.

Now, for the first time, that gaze fell away onto the carpet, and her face, which had been bathed in a pool of lamplight all night, fell into shadow.

I watched her for a long time, as if unwilling to accept that she was done. My heart was skipping beats on the waves of nicotine I had pumped into my blood during the night, and I rose and opened the window to find some fresh air for my aching lungs. Outside, some of those odd winter birds were trying to sing in the glacial still of the air. A thin light was up on my winter-parched lawn.

I never much knew my father, a sad man, I gather, who died under the blacklist when I was very small. My mother, I believe, is dead, and as for my only sibling, a sister, when, during the night, Rosenthal's daughter mentioned her incidentally, and without knowing what she had said—you who like mysteries, I will let you figure it out—it was the second time I had thought of her in many years. I knew them all too little to understand this strange, nonnegotiable love that people seem to feel for even the worst families; and that of which I have no experience, I do not like to judge. I will say this, though: in that distasteful choice between abandoning moral principle for love and abandoning love for principle, I tend to find the former slightly less bizarre.

I knew I could not indulge my thoughts too long, and so when my heart had slowed, I turned and crossed back to the girl, still staring down at the carpet. I crouched before her and turned out the lamp, which let me see her face. She did not turn away, although I was very close. That may have been because she did not notice me, so lost was her expression, so desolate; it may also have been because she was past caring.

I said many things to her, then, crouching before her absent gaze, my face inches from hers. I told her that most people go through their entire lives without living an eighth as much as she had, at twenty-seven. I told her that most people never come close to knowing what she knew, about love, about people, about themselves. I told her that life is horrible, not just for her, but for everyone—rich or poor, beautiful or ugly—life is horrible, and the more thoroughly, the more honestly we live it, the more horrible it is. The real aristocracy, I told her, is not the rich or the famous, but those who are brave enough to live life openly, honestly, in all its unspeakable horror. These, whether they are criminals or saints, are the only ones who have a chance of being free. I told her that she was an extraordinary person, of singular courage and amazing originality, and that for all she had suffered, one day she would find that it had made her into that rare thing, an adult. And I told her that here, in my little world, she may always be in danger, but she would always be among peers, and she would always be free.

She was, apparently, listening. For when I had finished

she nodded, and drew a huge breath into her chest. Then, again, she focused her green eyes on me and said simply, "If you still want me to, I'd like to work for you, Chevejon."

It was a strange job interview.

Still, I did not think her story quite done.

2.

Over the next few months Rosenthal's daughter shuttled between the epicenters of our little operation. Working mostly with Natalie—they quickly established a friendship that I thought must resemble that between Rosenthal's daughter and her friend Martha—she set up her corporations and offices, not where I had requested but in Paris, Vienna, Zurich, and Prague, anticipating thereby an eastern European source for our product, which in the event turned out to be quite right.

My business partner, meanwhile, working with his younger brother, arranged transportation. As always, container ship was his method of choice, but he had of late purchased several sailing yachts, and they had proven surprisingly useful for smaller, very valuable cargoes, several of which we would be handling for this project. Finally, there has been a lot of press lately about the availability of post-Soviet submarines on the black market. Most attempts to sell them had ended up in sting operations revealing incompetent—even risible—Russian thugs as the sellers. Not so ours, which, of course, had not made the press.

That left one problem to solve, purchasing. And although it was a large one, I believed I had found rather a neat solution.

Besides, I could not have Rosenthal's daughter wandering around like a little Natalie Rostov, pining for her Prince Andrei.

And so it was that Allison's story did not end with that winter night in Fiesole, but some months later, in a Los Angeles spring.

3.

In early April, Nicky Dymitryck was sitting in his father's living room, doing more or less nothing.

This was not an unusual activity for him, not since the furor over the Eastbrook resignation had died down. For some time he had been just about the most sought-after person in the media, as from *Nightline* to the *New Yorker* journalists sought to uncover the strange and circuitous roots of what had, by then, come to be universally known as "Ronaldgate." So intense had grown the fever pitch of the media event—especially after first a U.S. attorney, then the White House counsel, and finally the attorney general himself all resigned—that after a few days of refusing all calls, Nicky had simply left, flying to Stan Diamond's house in Aspen for the remainder of the winter.

And in the face of resolute silence from all of the principals, leading to the impossibility, for the media, of anything other than speculation, the furor slowly, finally, died down.

One more thing connected with Ronaldgate happened to Nicky.

When he returned from Aspen by commercial flight, early in January, he changed planes in San Francisco and, waiting for his connection in an airport café, found himself looking at a tall blond man, just off the red-eye from New York, drinking coffee thirstily. Slowly, Nicky recognized Dee Dennis, and Dee, apparently, Nicky, for they watched each other for several poisonous moments. Then, slowly, Dee rose, leaving money on the table for his unfinished coffee, and left the café. Nicky, in turn, after a moment in which he bitterly acknowledged that nothing had healed, left the café too.

And now it was April and still nothing had healed for Nicky Dymitryck, which was why he had not yet been back to work at the *NAR* and why, this day, he was sitting doing nothing in his father's living room when the telephone rang.

It was a woman, speaking with a light German accent.

"Mr. Dymitryck? Good evening, sir. My name is Natalie Benami. You don't know me, sir."

He answered absently. "Yes, Ms. Benami."

"Sir, I am in Los Angeles with some colleagues. We have a proposition we would like to discuss with you. Might you be free to join us here at your convenience?"

"What is the proposition, Ms. Benami?"

"May we tell you in person? We have no doubt whatsoever that it is something that will very much interest you to discuss."

"I see. Well, Ms. Benami, I'm rather on hiatus from my work just now. So I'll pass, if you don't mind."

The woman spoke hurriedly, before he could hang up. "Mr. Dymitryck, please don't say that. I believe we have a great deal to discuss. We have friends in common."

"Do we? Who?"

"I can only tell you in person, Mr. Dymitryck."

At this, Nicky paused. Then, at last. "Where?"

"The Beverly Wilshire, sir. Please ask for me."

"Two o'clock tomorrow afternoon."

"Shall I send a car?"

"No thank you. I'll be there at two."

"Thank you very much, Mr. Dymitryck. I wish you a very good day."

4.

Nicky arrived at the hotel just before two, and was directed to a twelfth-floor suite by the concierge. The door was opened by a very large man in a very good suit, who looked at Nicky, then stood aside, but not before Nicky had noticed the bulge of a firearm under his suit jacket.

Inside, another huge man was standing respectfully at a distance, and seated on a sofa was a rather lanky man of perhaps forty, impeccably suited in black, with a gaunt face and widely set eyes, also black, under thick black hair. Standing was a blond woman in her mid-thirties, in well-pressed jeans, Gucci sandals, and a silk blouse that revealed, under its neck, what was clearly some very expensive jewelry. It was she who spoke, in a German accent, extending a hand.

"Mr. Dymitryck, it is an honor to meet you. May I present my husband? Luke, Nicholson Dymitryck. And my colleagues, Pietro and Gianlucca."

The black-haired man rose slowly to shake Nicky's hand under a piercing gaze. The other two men, clearly bodyguards, stood back and nodded respectfully. The woman kept talking, and as she talked she turned to open a closed door.

"Please come with me. Just so, *gut.*" They were in a bedroom now, in which the bed had been removed and replaced with a table. And at the table, next to the curtained window, sat yet another enormous man, this one in a beige cotton suit, with a suntanned face and an air of great authority. The woman was approaching now, holding in her hands a plain bottle with a white label on which Nicky saw a penciled number.

"A present from my employer. We're told you appreciate whiskey. And here, Mr. Dymitryck, is the man we'd like you to meet."

It was, he had to admit, a very skillfully orchestrated seduction.

5.

The woman was speaking.

"May I present to you Commandante Tierce of the United Guatemalan Resistance? For your own protection, I will not name him further. Will you hear him out?"

At Nicky's nod, the man began speaking in fluent, educated English.

"Señor Dymitryck, I have fought for two decades on behalf of the people of my country against the government your country installed in 1954, I do not need to tell you that. And I do not need to tell you that since— the Cold War over—your country has withdrawn its endless support for that government, we have been successful in forcing it to the negotiating table. A national reconciliation on the order of Argentina and South Africa is about to take place in my country: we are due to sit down in six months to begin the process of peace. You know all that."

Nicky nodded. "I understand the military situation in Guatemala, Commandante."

"Then you understand my position. The CIA has negotiated interdictions of my major lines of supply to put pressure on the upcoming negotiations with the government. It is the last American move of support for their longtime clients: to leave them in a strong position when the talks start. We have therefore no suppliers at the state level; my munitions are critically low, and without them I cannot go as an equal to the table. They are engineering a castration of my negotiating position, and if they succeed, my country will lose the reconciliation for which we have been fighting for years."

The massive man stood, and as he did so, Nicky asked, instinctively, a reporter's question.

"Where is the front?"

He hesitated only briefly. "The front lines have moved

in to the city, señor. Our leaders are at preliminary negotiations."

"Will you be at the table, Commandante?"

"No sir. I am a doctor. Guaranteeing the negotiating
position of the Guatemalan people will be the last act of
my military career."

Standing, he awaited another question. But Nicky was
silent, and at last, he concluded.

"Thank you for giving me a hearing."

Then he was gone, followed by the bodyguards, and
Nicky was alone with the couple.

In the small silence that followed, Nicky reached for the
bottle of scotch, opened it, and drank from its neck. The
man said something to the woman in German; she
agreed. Then, at Nicky's questioning glance, the woman
explained.

"He said that our employer would not be happy to see
his single-malt drunk that way. He is a great amateur of
scotch."

Nicky shrugged the comment off. "What is it you
want from me?"

And now the woman leaned forward, talking earnestly.
"Mr. Dymitryck, we intend to supply Tierce with what
he needs to conduct his negotiations. We can undertake
to paper anything through a corporate structure my colleague in Paris has developed. We do not believe there is
the will to prosecute this in the States. In any case, we
have a great deal of experience evading customs law. As
for a covert CIA interdiction, forgive me, that is not a
threat we take seriously."

At her gesture, Nicky turned to see the man opening
a suitcase. Inside he recognized night-vision glasses, a
small submachine gun, a Czech antipersonnel mine,
rounds of ammunition, and a handgun.

Nicky turned away. "For a profit."

Undisturbed, the woman nodded. "We are businessmen, certainly. But I assure you, we choose our clientele wisely. We would not insult you with any other proposition. And, sir, I assure you, our expertise is unequaled."

. She was, Nicky found, hard to disbelieve. "Go on."

"We know that money is not a consideration for you. But we ask you to consider whether or not it is time to put your knowledge, and your skill, in the service of what you cannot fail to recognize as the good fight."

"I see." Nicky rose now, and walked to the case of armaments, picking up the small plastic mine and holding it in the palm of his hand. It was no doubt from a post-Soviet stockpile, long common on the black market. This, the night-vision glasses, the assault weapon: he could buy them with a telephone call. As for the rest of what they would probably need—mortars, surface-to-air missiles, shoulder-launched antitank missiles—a few weeks in Europe would be a generous estimate. He turned back to the woman.

"Tell me, Ms. Benami. Who are your sources?"

She answered with a direct look. "Tziporah Rosen is our colleague in Europe, Mr. Dymitryck. She is the architect of our corporate framework, and handles any licensing issues. You know her as Allison Rosenthal."

And Nicky, to what he realized was the satisfaction of the quiet man watching, felt shock.

6.

But the woman was talking again.

"Mr. Dymitryck, please do not make your decision now. Here are some documents that our employer has taken the liberty to prepare for you. You'll find here a passport and some other identification. They're under the name of Benjamin Black, and I assure you, they are impeccable. I have also a ticket to Rome leaving tomorrow night, and then Florence. You'll note it's round-trip.

Accept these and go to Florence, just to discuss this with our colleagues. They are formidable persons. You will be glad to have met them."

There was a different tone in her voice at these last words, and Nicky looked at her absently, without curiosity. Then, without a word, he rose and turned to leave the room.

But the man was blocking him at the door.

"Mr. Dymitryck. Refuse what we ask, that is your choice. But please, just take the documentation with you. If you don't use it, destroy it. Whether you do that, or even if you simply go to Florence to see Allison and then return, I give you my word. You'll never hear from us again."

Now Nicky paused, looking up into the man's oddly spaced black eyes. With a nod he turned and took from the woman the package of documents, and the whisky bottle from the table.

"Thank you for your time."

And Nicky left the room.

7.

For a time, after he returned to his car, he was all right. But only for a time. Then, without thinking, he opened the bottle, and, in an open car on the highway, took a drink.

He drank steadily all the way up Highway 1, disregarding the fact that he was in a convertible on an open road. Once at home, carrying the bottle into the house, he continued to drink by the living room window, overlooking the sea, in the silent house. The sun sank over the cliffs, the garden around the swimming pool stepped into shades of green, the sea blackened, and Nicky, standing, drank.

Until at last, mercifully, it was night.

When he woke it was light again. Outside the window children were squabbling in the yard next door, and Nicky was undressed in his bed, with no memory of getting there. Wincing, he stood and managed to get to the sink before vomiting.

For a time he rested on the linoleum of the bathroom floor. When he could, he negotiated the hallway to the kitchen. Clumsily, he put together a cup of coffee, then drank it with a shot of bourbon. That made him gag, but it also stopped the pounding in his head. Only then did he try to piece together the events of the previous day.

Panic flowering in him, he managed to rise and get to the bedroom. There, he saw that it all had really happened. The bottle of scotch, nearly empty, was on his bedside table, next to the neat little folder with the airline tickets. Nicky sank to sit on the floor against the bed.

For a long time he sat like that, listening to the children fighting next door. He rose once, to get more coffee, then he sat down again. After a time, he shifted, but just enough to reach his cigarettes from his jacket where it lay on the floor.

The dim sound of a dog barking far away.

The children fighting in the garden next door.

He continued to sit.

It was so bitter to him. She had allowed him to get rid of Eastbrook simply because it served her purposes: had it not, she would not have cared. And in what she did, so much damage had been done to so many important things: cruel and ugly damage, to people, to the law. Not for years would a government attempt a prosecution like this again; not for years would the outrage of selling death for profit be brought again into national debate, what he had struggled for his whole working life. Governments would continue to seek their own short-term interest, profits would always carry the day, and only the innocent, only the innocent would ever care about the dead.

And against that? Justice, she would say, was reason enough, even for something this ugly. Her father *had* been guilty, only not of what he had been charged with, and the justice of saving him was an absolute.

Justice is reason enough for anything ugly. It balances the beauty in the world. Those last lines of her poem had never long left his mind, and never for a moment had he felt he understood them. Now, suddenly, in the quiescence of his hangover, it occurred to him that perhaps he had never understood because beauty did not exist in a world devoid of guilt. And perhaps, therefore, it was not something that people like him, the righteous, could ever really see.

Rising slowly to protect his pounding head, he admitted to himself that helping Commandante Tierce was not the problem. What frightened him—and it frightened him badly—was that after all the terrible things he had witnessed, and all the terrible places he had been, it should in the end be a criminal—the gun runner's daughter—who would finally show him something beautiful.

Pulling his much-used briefcase from the closet, packing for another night flight across continents, as always when traveling toward danger, Nicky Dymitryck felt something like hope.

October 1997, Nassau Street

NOTES ON SOURCES

Any faults, inaccuracies, and mistakes of this novel are my own. Whatever political acuity and documentary accuracy it contains, however, are predicated upon the sources below.

For interviews, I am grateful to Joost Hilterman and Stephen Goose of the Human Rights Watch Arms Project, David Isenberg of the Center for Defense Information, Lora Lumpe of the Federation of American Scientists, Caleb Rossiter of Demilitarization for Democracy, Mr. Adam Yarmolinsky, and Dr. Dov Zakheim of Systems Planning International. I am particularly grateful to Professor Daniel Nelson for his insights into military supply in Bosnia, and to the journalist and writer Frank Smyth.

Published sources from which I drew include Noam Chomsky, *The Fateful Triangle: The United States, Israel and the Palestinians* (South End Press); Leslie Cockburn, *Out of Control: The Story of the Reagan Administration's Secret War in Nicaragua* (Atlantic Monthly Press); Andrew and Leslie Cockburn, *Dangerous Liaison: The Inside Story of the U.S.-Israeli Covert Relationship* (HarperCollins); David Corn, *Blond Ghost: Ted Shackley and the CIA's Crusades* (Simon & Schuster); William D. Hartung, *And*

Weapons for All (HarperCollins); Seymour M. Hersch, *The Samson Option: Israel's Nuclear Arsenal and American Foreign Policy* (Random House); Herbert Krosney, *Deadly Business: Legal Deals and Outlaw Weapons: The Arming of Iran and Iraq, 1975 to Present* (Four Walls Eight Windows); Gary Sick, *October Surprise: America's Hostages in Iran and the Election of Ronald Reagan* (Random House); Warner Smith, *Covert Warrior: Fighting the CIA's Secret War in Southeast Asia and China, 1965-1967* (Presidio); M. Wesley Swearingen, *FBI Secrets: An Agent's Exposé* (South End Press); Jack Terrell with Ron Marz, *Disposable Patriot: Revelations of a Soldier in America's Secret Wars* (National Book Press).

Ronald Rosenthal is an entirely fictional character, with no real-life counterpart. His profession, however, is a real one, and in imagining Rosenthal's professional activities I have been inspired by several real life events. I am particularly indebted to Ari Ben Menashe's *Profits of War: Inside the Secret U.S.-Israeli Arms Network* (Sheridan Square), whose historical account of his years of work for Israel's clandestine agencies led me to create several fictional scenes: Ronald Rosenthal's videotaped argument with Greg Eastbrook, Ronald Rosenthal's trip to Chile to negotiate with Carlos Cardoen, and the Israeli intelligence complicity in the murder of the supergun inventor Gerald Bull. I have also, in my research, drawn heavily on Theodore Draper's *A Very Thin Line* (Hill and Wang) and Lawrence Walsh's account of his work as special prosecutor for Iran-contra matters, *Firewall: The Iran-Contra Conspiracy and Cover-Up* (Norton). Finally, I am grateful to Kai Bird for his monumental work *The Chairman: John J. McCloy and the Making of the American Establishment* (Simon & Schuster).

Video sources include *America's Arms Monitor*, produced by the Center for Defense Information, generously made available to me by Mark Sugg; *School of Assassins*, produced by Robert Richter/Maryknoll World

Productions; and *Coverup*, produced by the Empowerment Project. Internet sources include, in addition to those named earlier, the indispensable Nambase database published on www.blythe.org and www.pir.org, and the Octopus and Patriot archives, on www.tezcat.com.

Readers familiar with Diane Wakoski will recognize this novel's constant dialogue with and homage to her essay "Creating a Personal Mythology."

Throughout this book I have attempted to ground all reference to the arms trade, covert or governmentally licensed, in historical reality, with one notable exception: I know of no source, written or unacknowledged, that implicates any Israeli company, government organ, or private entity in the supply of the Bosnian Muslim Militias, an arms transaction wholly invented—to my knowledge—by me for the purposes of this novel.

picador.com

blog
videos
interviews
extracts